D0489178

Joanna Courtney's first literary acco~~~ prize at primary school and from that point on she wanted to be a novelist. She was always reading as a child and often made up stories for her brother and sister on long car journeys, but it was when she took a degree in English literature at Cambridge, specialising in medieval literature, that she discovered a passion for ancient history that would define her writing.

Joanna began writing professionally in the sparse hours available between raising two stepchildren and two more of her own, primarily writing shorter fiction for the women's magazines. As the children grew and obligingly went to school, however, her time expanded and she started writing novels. Her first series, *The Queens of the Conquest,* is about the women married to the men fighting to be King of England in 1066 and while researching that period, she came across King Macbeth and, more importantly, his wife. She was intrigued to learn that they had been real rulers who ruled Scotland wisely and well for about fifteen years. These were not the cruel, frantic, half-mad characters of Shakespeare's wonderful play and she had to know more.

Further research unveiled other great Shakespearean women lurking in the wings (where women in the 'dark ages' are so often consigned): Hamlet was a real Danish king in around 600 AD, with Ofelia as his consort and shield-maiden; Lear was a Midland's war leader around 450 BC and his daughter Cordelia a Boudicca-style warrior princess. Joanna knew then that, dearly as she loves Shakespeare, these three amazing women had to be freed from the shackles of his brilliant but restrictive narratives and allowed into the world as they truly were. The *Shakespeare's Queens* series is here to do just that.

Get in touch with Joanna on Facebook: @joannacourtneyauthor, twitter: @joannacourtney1 or via her website: joannacourtney.com.

Blood Queen

Joanna Courtney

piatkus

PIATKUS

First published in Great Britain in 2018 by Piatkus

1 3 5 7 9 10 8 6 4 2

Copyright © 2018 by Joanna Barnden

The moral right of the author has been asserted.

All characters and events in this publication, other than those
clearly in the public domain, are fictitious and any resemblance
to real persons, living or dead, is purely coincidental.

All rights reserved.
No part of this publication may be reproduced, stored in a
retrieval system, or transmitted, in any form or by any means, without
the prior permission in writing of the publisher, nor be otherwise circulated
in any form of binding or cover other than that in which it is published
and without a similar condition including this condition
being imposed on the subsequent purchaser.

A CIP catalogue record for this book
is available from the British Library.

ISBN 978-0-349-41950-3

Typeset in Baskerville by M Rules
Printed and bound in Great Britain by
Clays Ltd, Elcograf S.p.A.

Papers used by Piatkus are from well-managed forests
and other responsible sources.

Piatkus
An imprint of
Little, Brown Book Group
Carmelite House
50 Victoria Embankment
London EC4Y 0DZ

An Hachette UK Company
www.hachette.co.uk

www.littlebrown.co.uk

For Emily and George
May your marriage contain as much love as Cora and
Macbeth's (and considerably fewer battles)

ALBAN ROYAL LINES

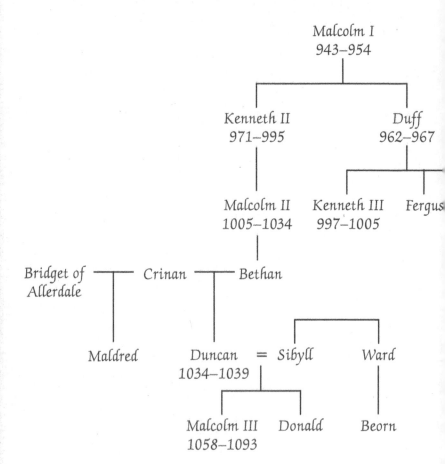

LINE OF
CONSTANTINE

Malcolm I
943–954

Kenneth II
971–995

Duff
962–967

Malcolm II
1005–1034

Kenneth III
997–1005

Fergus

Bridget of
Allerdale ——— Crinan ——— Bethan

Maldred

Duncan = Sibyll
1034–1039

Ward

Malcolm III
1058–1093

Donald

Beorn

(Dates given are dates of reign as King of Alba.)

LINE OF AED

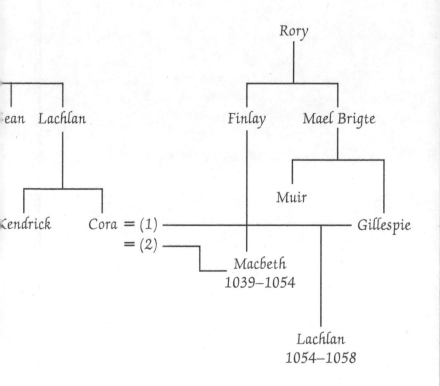

```
                                            Rory
                                              |
 ean  Lachlan                   Finlay      Mael Brigte
        |                          |            |
        |                                  Muir
Kendrick      Cora = (1) ——————————————————————— Gillespie
              = (2) ——┐
                      └__ Macbeth
                          1039–1054

                                        Lachlan
                                        1054–1058
```

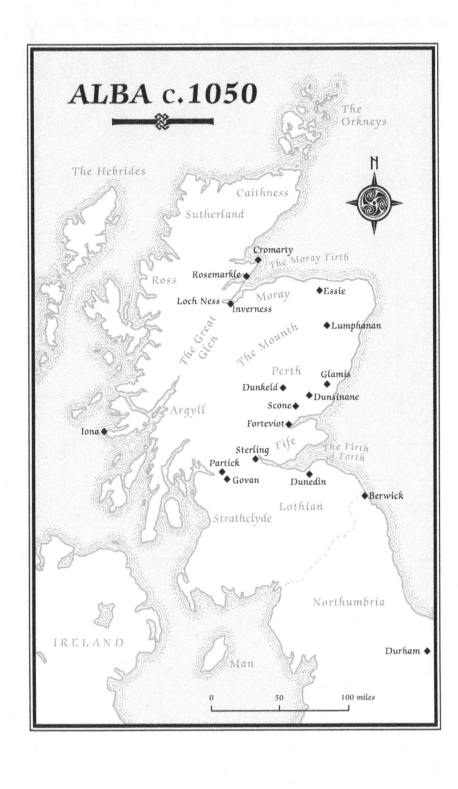

ALBA c.1050

The Orkneys

The Hebrides

Caithness

Sutherland

N

Cromarty

The Moray Firth

Rosemarkle

Ross

Essie

Loch Ness

Moray

Inverness

Lumphanan

The Great Glen

The Mounth

Perth

Glamis

Dunkeld

Scone

Dunsinane

Forteviot

Argyll

Iona

Fife

Sterling

The Firth of Forth

Partick

Govan

Dunedin

Berwick

Lothian

Strathclyde

Northumbria

IRELAND

Durham

Man

0   50   100 miles

Prologue

I did not ask to be queen. I did not look for gowns and crowns and the weight of a country upon my shoulders. I wanted only to join my hand to that of the man I loved and be Lady Macbeth. I wanted only to be a wife and mother and to build a contented home upon the welcoming shores of the Moray Firth.

Or did I? I fear maybe my heart was not forged so simply. Yes, I wanted love – what girl does not? – but I wanted more too. I wanted position, pride, achievement. My blood is royal and royal blood is a prickly fluid. It does not run as freely as that of normal men and women. With such blood in your veins you are a receptacle not just for your own life but for so many others, past and present, whose hopes and duties and privileges you perpetuate. I did not ask to be queen but I did look for the *right* to be so and the way the times turned around me, it amounted to the same thing.

Did God intend me for the throne? It would be comforting to say so but I'm not sure God thinks that highly of me, or of any of us. Alba's kings and queens are inaugurated on the Stone of Destiny but they have to seize that stone first – they have to *make* that destiny for themselves. They have to climb the Hill of Belief to sit upon that stone and it is not so named for nothing. I did not ask to be queen but I believed I could be.

And she, the other one – Lady Duncan – did she believe so too? She had no royal blood, nor Alban blood neither, but she took to our country as if she had been waiting for such a gift all her life. She had her own destiny to chase and it was perhaps just an accident of fate that she was chasing it in the same time and space as I. The threads of our lives, in the end, crossed in so many places that they became almost a single chain – a chain to hang around Alba's neck and decorate her history.

My heart was not forged simply but it was forged strong and it beat out a rhythm I can never regret. I did not ask to be queen but neither did I refuse. I made my destiny and I followed it all the way across Alba to its throne and its tomb. I was Lady Macbeth and I was Queen and I can only hope that in some small way Alba was richer for it.

Chapter One

Cora

Inverness, August 1025

Cora MacDuff stared contentedly up at the soft Moray sky. The patch of vivid blue directly above her was framed all around by waving bulrushes and marked by a single small cloud which, if she half-closed her eyes, looked very like a beating heart. A smile fluttered at the corners of her mouth but then, ashamed of her foolish fancy, she exhaled and the bulrushes surrounding her sighed in protest.

'What are you sighing about, Cora? Not me, I hope.'

Macbeth raised himself up on one elbow to look down at her and, despite herself, she smiled.

'No, not you, Macbeth.'

How could she sigh over him? With his mop of blond hair and dark brown eyes, he was a fair sight for any lass and somehow he'd turned that fine gaze of his on her. He made her ridiculously happy and *that* was the problem. She didn't want to be happy; she wasn't *meant* to be happy. She was meant to be angry and resentful and full of hate, not mooning around in bulrushes cuddled up to handsome young Mormaer's sons as if all was right with the world. For it was not; it was not at all.

Cora had arrived in the northerly province of Moray a few months ago after a desperate flight from the vicious enmity of

King Malcolm's men. The king was their father's first cousin but had seen their shared blood as a threat not a tie. She grasped at one of the bulrushes, welcoming the sting of its sharp-edged leaf against her skin as she forced herself to picture the desecrated body of her father, Mormaer Lachlan, cut down in his cornfields and then hacked apart like an animal. They hadn't needed to do that. He'd been dead at the first stroke, or so she prayed. The rest had been the king's cruelty.

Not that King Malcolm had killed his cousin himself, nothing so crude, but what king did his own dirty work? She'd known it was a royal edict the minute she'd looked up from her father's rich Fife farmhouse and seen the armed men crashing towards it through the corn. It hadn't taken Lachlan's hoarse cry of 'Run!' to tell her the mortal danger they were all in, for she had seen it written in the line of raised swords.

She and Kendrick had run for the woods beyond their estate, trusting to their knowledge of the paths to help them evade their father's murderers. But it had been clear as they'd huddled deep in their favourite cave that they couldn't go back. For them the comforts of home had been curtailed as surely as their father's life and that very night, in just the clothes they stood up in, they'd turned north.

Cora released the bulrush and lifted her hand to stare at the thin line of blood it had left across her palm. Macbeth flinched away and for a moment she felt sorry for shocking him but he should know what he was getting into. She was no forlorn exile who needed soothing and looking after. She was a woman with a purpose and it was best that he realised that and turned his damned kisses elsewhere. Though they were such lovely kisses . . .

'Cora?' His voice was soft – too soft.

He was always so wonderfully gentle but she couldn't let him soothe her too far. Her hurt had to stay raw to keep her purpose alive. She sat up, pulling away from him.

'Why do you bother with me, Macbeth?'

'Why?' He looked surprised but gave the question careful thought before he replied. 'You intrigue me, Cora MacDuff. You're different.'

'Different? That's it?'

Amusement sparked in his chestnut-coloured eyes.

'Wrong answer, my sweet? Then I'll try again. How about the fact that I love your dawn-red hair and your sun-freckled skin and your wishing-pool eyes?'

'Wishing-pool eyes? Really, Macbeth?'

She looked towards the pond they were lying by, which was indeed as pure green as her eyes. Local legend had it that in the morning mists you might catch a glimpse of the faeries bathing here, but right now the sun had chased the mist away and the pool was good only for cooling their bare toes. Cora pulled hers back, hugging her knees against her chest.

'I'm not looking for empty compliments, Macbeth.'

'They're not . . .'

'Keep them for your Moray girls. I'm sure pretty words will please them well enough.'

'True. See – you're different.'

She rolled her eyes.

'Of course I'm different. I'm from Fife. We have villages of more than three crofts and roads you can actually drive a cart on and we can attend court whenever we wish. We don't just wander about herding sheep and watching dolphins dance.'

Macbeth grinned.

'You love the dolphins.'

Frustratingly, that much was true. Cora had been astonished the first time she'd seen the great fish leap from the waters of the Moray Firth, twisting and turning for the pure joy of it. But life wasn't about joy, or at least hers wasn't. Not anymore.

'I won't stay long.'

'Fair enough. It must be nearly dinner-time anyway.'

5

'Not at the pool, Macbeth. I mean here, in Moray. I won't stay long.'

At this, at least, he looked hurt.

'You don't like it?'

'It's very nice, very pretty. It's just so far away.'

He frowned.

'No, it isn't. It's right here. See.'

He reached out and flicked pond water into the air. It danced in sparkling droplets between them but Cora turned her head from the pretty sight.

'Not far away from *us*; far away from important things.'

'Like?'

'Like the throne.'

'Ah. And is that more important, then, than us?'

'Well, of course it is.' He nodded back at her. So calm, so thoughtful – so irritating. Cora leaped to her feet. 'You don't understand, Macbeth.'

She turned to walk away but he was up too, remarkably quickly for such a big man, and clasping her against him. Cora felt her blood pulse and struggled to fight its petty impulses.

'I don't,' he agreed, 'but I'd like to. I like *you*. To me, you resemble a piece of iron – whenever you get near the slightest heat, you spark like crazy and that fascinates me.'

His face had dipped closer to hers. His brown eyes were fixed on her 'wishing-pool' eyes and somehow, just like that, he seemed to suck all the hatred out of her and make her long to reach up and press her lips to his and lose herself in his dolphin-like joy in her. But what use would that be?

'Iron?' she choked out and he pulled back a little. 'You're right – I am iron. I must be iron. I must make of myself a sword to avenge the wrong done to my father by his own blood.'

Macbeth took her hands, rubbing them gently between his fingers.

'I know that, Cora. I know what King Malcolm did to your father and I swear I will help you find vengeance. All Moray will help you.'

'When, Macbeth?'

'When the time is right.'

She smiled at him bitterly.

'It is kind of you to say so but the time will *never* be right, not for your father's men, and why should it be? This is my problem; mine and Kendrick's. We are grateful that you have sheltered us, truly, but this is not a fight for Moray.'

She felt Macbeth release her. He turned away and she longed to go after him but she mustn't. He wanted to heal her with gentleness and love but it couldn't work that way. Could it?

'Macbeth . . .'

He turned back.

'Marry me, Cora.'

'What?'

The soft meadowland seemed to shift beneath her feet.

'Marry me. Be my wife. I love you, Cora. I love your passion and your determination and your damned ferocity. I want your fight to be my fight and I want to help you win it. Marry me, please.'

She stared at him. There was a word fighting its way up her throat and biting against her tongue to be let out. 'Yes,' she wanted to shout. 'Yes, yes, yes.' Macbeth was like no one she'd ever known. He was so easy in his skin, so at one with the world. He took her every raw argument and considered it with a care and logic that reduced it to something so much easier to cope with. He made her feel comfortable and safe and, yes, happy. But she wasn't meant to be happy. She was meant to be angry and resentful and full of hate.

He came closer again, a new, more serious light in his eyes.

'I have a claim too, Cora.'

'A claim to what?'

'To the throne. My father spoke of it with me last night. My family are the last of the line of Aed.'

Cora's eyes widened. He spoke true. There were two royal

lines in Alba – descending from Aed and Constantin, sons of the first king, Kenneth MacAlpin – and under the rules of alternate inheritance the lines were meant to take turns upon the throne. King Malcolm was a Constantin, as was she, and he had plans to put his grandson, Duncan, on the throne after him. The Aed line in the south had died out, leaving him unchallenged, but up here in Moray there was a second line, a line that dwelt quietly beyond the sheltering crags of the Mounth – the fearsome mountain strip cutting Alba in two – or who had done so far.

'You have a claim too,' Cora repeated hoarsely.

'And if we married and were lucky enough to have a child, he would combine the two royal lines for the first time ever. He'd be Constantin and Aed: the ultimate heir.'

Cora stared up at him. He'd thought hard about this – of course he had – and he was right.

'With such an heir we could challenge King Malcolm. Or at least Prince Duncan.'

'Yes!'

'And then you would have your vengeance.'

Cora shifted her feet. It sounded so cruel.

'Restitution,' she corrected. 'I want restitution for the injustice done to my father by his own vicious brother.'

'And would his grandson being crowned not be a fine way to achieve it?'

She nodded slowly.

'It would take time though, Macbeth.'

'So impatient, my sweet? We *have* time. We are young. You and Kendrick can grow strong here in Moray and gather support. And meanwhile I'm sure we can find something to do to while away the hours ... '

He ran a finger lightly up her arm and across her neck, sending shivers of wanton delight through her body and drawing her irresistibly towards him.

'What did you have in mind?' she murmured.

In response, he kissed her long and deep and all his gentle strength seemed to surge into her with his embrace. She'd come to Moray lost and hurt and torn apart and somehow God had blessed her with the love of this man. How could she refuse it?

'So, Cora MacDuff,' he said when they finally pulled apart. 'Will you marry me?'

'Yes,' she gasped. 'Oh, Macbeth, yes.'

And then he was kissing her again and she was clinging to him and praying he was right and that restitution could be found, not just with the piercing immediacy of hatred, but with a care and deliberation that might build her and Kendrick and all of Alba a better future than the one afforded it by murderous King Malcolm.

Chapter Two

Sibyll

York, October 1025

'Try a little, my lady. 'Tis a fine drink.'

Sibyll eyed the tumbler suspiciously. It looked pretty, certainly, for it was made of glass and etched with a pattern that seemed to fold light into the liquid within it. And the liquid itself was a glorious colour – a deep, dark gold, like late honey or a lazy summer sunset or the amber stones the traders brought from Baltic lands. Her brother's intriguing guest, an abbot from way up in Alba, held it out to her, swirling the liquid so that it winked and rolled in the flickering light from the candles as if drawing the flames into itself. Sibyll was mesmerised.

'Sibyll! Take the drink Abbot Crinan is offering you so kindly.'

She blinked up at her brother. The normally genial Earl Ward sounded unusually tetchy.

'Goodness, I'm so sorry. It just looks so beautiful, does it not? Almost magical.'

'We don't believe in magic, do we, Sibyll?'

Ward shot a nervous glance at the abbot but Crinan threw her a smile that transformed his austere face.

'I find it mesmerising too, my lady,' he said, 'and even more so once I've had a few sips, for the taste is very . . . involving.'

'Involving?'

'Oh, aye. Usquebauch asks questions of you. It teases your tongue and shifts in your throat. You think you have the taste of it but then it surprises you with another, subtler flavour hiding beneath. It is a truly fascinating drink if made well.'

Sibyll took the tumbler and lifted it to look more closely at the contents and now the scent hit her – smoke and peat and heather, as if someone had poured a moorland evening into the liquid. She breathed it in slowly.

'Try it, Sibyll,' Ward urged. A man who had risen in life by his sword, he was rarely at ease in social situations and looked nervously towards their guest, but Crinan silenced him with an easy wave.

'There is no rush. Usquebauch is to be savoured.'

'Usquebauch?'

'It is Gaelic, my lady. It means "water of life".'

Sibyll smiled.

'A good name. Usquebauch.' She tried it on her tongue, enjoying the soft sounds.

'Or uiskie for short.'

'Uiskie. I see.'

Ward was watching her anxiously so Sibyll raised the tumbler to her lips and . . .

'Only take care, my lady, for it is quite fiery.'

Too late. Already she had taken a deep sip and, Lord, but fiery was not the word! It was a veritable inferno in her mouth and already the flames were searing her nose, her eyes, nay, her very mind. All the peaty smoke seemed to be engulfing her and she fought to swallow, knowing she would be sending the hellfire into her stomach. Sure enough, there it was, burning down her throat and flaring in her gut and she closed her eyes against the stabbing heat.

She could hear Ward protesting, thinking their guest had poisoned her with this uiskie. But it was no poison, for the flame was settling and now only the smoke remained, curling seductively around her innards. And the abbot was right, for new flavours were unfolding themselves: the honey the colour had promised and something like grass fresh from the scythe. She opened her eyes, blinked back the tears, and looked straight at Abbot Crinan.

'That,' she said, 'is a glorious drink, though I might, in future, take a slightly smaller sip.'

Abbot Crinan roared with laughter and Ward, with a sigh of relief, patted her fondly on the back.

'You like this Alban lifewater, sister?'

'I do. Very much. Where is it from, Abbot?'

Crinan plucked at the embroidered cuffs of his voluminous sleeves.

'It is from my own abbey at Dunkeld, my lady. My assistant, Brother Cullen, is in charge of its production. He is very talented, is he not?'

He nudged forward a young monk and Sibyll looked at him in some surprise. Brother Cullen was but a lad, his body lanky and awkward and his skin shiny and marked with a dusting of pimples.

'You made this?' she questioned him. 'But you are so young.'

'Just turned seventeen, my lady,' he said in halting English.

'As am I and I have produced nothing so accomplished.'

'I'm sure that's not true,' Abbot Crinan said.

'Oh, but it is. My tutors despair of my handiwork, for my stitching is messy and my weaving uneven. But then, the end product could never be so fine as Brother Cullen's uiskie.'

Brother Cullen blushed a dark red that had at least the merit of covering his blemishes.

'You're too good, my lady,' he mumbled, bowing low into his skinny chest.

Sibyll took another cautious sip of her drink. Much better. Now the flavours blossomed on her tongue without blazing a path of destruction across it and made her head mist in a very pleasant way, which was fortunate as Ward was saying some strange things about her.

12

'She jests of course, Abbot. Sibyll is a most accomplished young lady. I have seen to it myself that she has had the finest of educations and her tutors are very pleased with her, despite her coy modesty.'

Coy? Sibyll looked suspiciously up at her brother. She was Danish-born and although she had been in Northern England a long time, her height and almost moon-blonde hair still marked her out as a Viking and they were never 'coy'. Besides, she'd been brought up by Ward to stand up for herself and know her own worth – it had been the only way to survive.

Born to the leaders of a fishing community in Denmark, they had lost both parents in a terrible attack by the fearsome Wend tribe when Ward had been sixteen and she eight. Even now, ten years later, Sibyll sometimes woke in the night gasping for breath as if she were still hidden beneath a smoking beam, not daring to crawl away from its looming danger for fear of stepping into the path of the murderous marauders running roughshod over what had once been her village.

Pushing her into the smoky hole had been her mother's last act. The poor woman had died in the street, hunched around the spear thrust into her gut, but she'd kept her pain-filled eyes fixed on Sibyll, begging her to stay hidden and save herself. Hours she'd crouched there after her mother had gone to God and hours more after the Wends had finally ridden away. The beam had shed so much ash upon Sibyll that she had turned as ghost-white as her mother's corpse and might easily have slipped into oblivion after her if it hadn't been for Ward.

He'd been in the hills with the sheep when the Wends had struck, helpless to do anything other than watch the slaughter. But later he'd come down to search for survivors, found her and coaxed her out and onto his horse. From then on it had been just the two of them, fighting their way back out of the ashes. And fight they had – all the way to England with Cnut's army where Ward had gained promotion from foot-soldier, to guard, to elite royal housecarl, and finally, last year, he'd became Earl of South Northumbria.

Sibyll looked at Crinan again, trying to dredge her uiskie-fuddled mind for all Ward had told her of him. If she remembered correctly this was no ordinary cleric but a nobleman in his own right. He owned his abbey at Dunkeld by hereditary title and was as much a prince as a priest. Plus he was married and to a daughter of the Alban King Malcolm too. A powerful man then. And, of course, a father.

Sibyll felt her gut clench as tightly as it had when the uiskie had hit it. This sharp-eyed abbot was surely here looking for a wife for his son and she, Sibyll, was an earl's sister. Her brother had brought them this far; was it now her turn to elevate their family further? Nervously, she sipped at her drink, which seemed, despite her caution, to have all but gone.

'Is dinner ready yet, Ward?' she asked, glancing hopefully around the hall but sadly there was no sign of the servers.

'Not quite yet. Though we can sit if you are tired, Abbot?'

Ward gestured to the top table and the row of fine carved seats behind it, each one a gift from a thegn on his overlord's appointment as earl. Crinan eyed them appreciatively but shook his head.

'I am content to stand, though the lady may not be?'

'I am, thank you,' Sibyll said quickly.

She had a hatred of simpering girls who demanded to be coddled and looked after. Ever since she had ridden here from Denmark, she had been determined not to be a burden. That journey, made in an autumn that had turned all too swiftly to a biting winter, had been long and hard. She'd been a child but the only way for their group to survive had been for her to grit her teeth, sit astride her horse, and deal with the cold winds, flooded rivers and bitter, hungry nights like the others did. She had slept rolled up in fur with her big brother but in every other respect had quickly learned to stand on her own two feet. It was not a lesson she could ever unlearn.

'Sibyll is a very resilient young woman,' Ward announced.

'You are being very free with your praise today, brother,' she protested.

'Well deserved, Sibyll dear.'

She looked over at Crinan and saw him smile again.

'You are no fool, I see, Lady Sibyll,' he said.

'I hope not, Abbot.'

'So you must know why your brother sings your praises to me?'

'I would not presume to guess.'

'You mean, you would not presume to speak your guess out loud?'

Sibyll nodded, charmed. She took a chance.

'So why then, Abbot, do *you* believe my brother praises me?'

He met her gaze, held it.

'I believe it is because he knows I seek a wife for my son Duncan.'

'And Duncan is a prize worth winning?'

The abbot's eyes narrowed a little and she cursed the treacherous uiskie for making her too bold, but when Crinan spoke it was without rancour.

'Duncan is my eldest son by my second wife, Princess Bethan – daughter of King Malcolm of Alba. He is, therefore, in direct royal descent and is also the eldest male in Malcolm's line as the king never fathered a son of his own. He has, Lady Sibyll, been named as Malcolm's Tanaise.'

'Tanaise?'

'Successor. He is destined to be the next King of Alba and his wife would, therefore, be the next queen.'

Sibyll glanced at the tumbler in her hand. She felt as giddy as if she had swallowed another large draught of the uiskie. Queen of Alba? She could see now why Ward had been courting the abbot so assiduously and wished he'd thought to explain as much instead of leaving her to splutter on fire-breathing lifewater and ask impertinent questions.

15

'That would be a great honour for the chosen lady,' she managed.

'It would but it is no easy role, so I seek a "resilient" woman to cope with it.'

His eyes twinkled but it was not his praise of her that caught her attention. She'd learned from an early age that all advancement had to be fought for; learned, too, that it paid to know what you might face in the fight.

'Why would it not be easy?' she queried.

Crinan took a step forward.

'Alba is a land of clans – fierce family groups carving out their own advancement and fighting to maintain their status.'

'England is very similar.'

'Perhaps, but in Alba the clans dwell in the valleys between our great mountain ranges, isolated from each other. Such a situation is not conducive to any attempt at unity. For every claimant to the kingship there is at least one rival and Alban kings rule, on average, for less than ten years.'

'They are killed by their own sons?'

'Ah ... no. And therein lies the major difficulty, my lady. In Alba we practise alternate succession.'

'Alternate?'

'All Alban kings descend from the lines of the two sons of the first high king – Constantin and Aed. One line is succeeded by the other, turn and turn about. This, in theory, means no family gains too great a share of power and that there is always a strong, healthy young male to lead the country.'

'There is a certain sense to that.'

'The theory is good, aye. The practice, however, is more ... bloody.'

'The next king does not wish to wait for the current one to die before he has his turn?'

'Exactly. Earl Ward, your sister is both resilient and intelligent.'

16

Sibyll flushed as Ward puffed out his huge chest so far he almost knocked her backwards. Behind them she could see the servers bringing out great earthen tureens of soup and knew they would soon be called to table. There was no time for niceties now.

'So your son is of the same line as the current king?'

'The line of Constantin, aye.'

'And he has been named as Tan . . . '

'Tanaise.'

'And accepted the honour?'

'Aye, and while Malcolm is alive that will always be so, for he is a strong king. It is when he dies that any rivals will seek to assert themselves. Malcolm believes Alba should move to the modern way of establishing a single royal line, as do our neighbours here in England and on the continent, but the line of Aed, up in the wldnorth of Moray, will not take the overturning of centuries of tradition lightly.'

'I see,' Sibyll said carefully and now Crinan fixed her in the full light of his penetrating gaze.

'I cannot lie to you, my lady – Duncan's reign, when it comes, will be drenched in bloodshed. If the blood is that of his rivals he will emerge as the figurehead of a new system that will favour his own sons by his wife and queen. If it is *his* blood that is spilled, however, his reign may last no more than months and his queen could be a widow before ever a son is born to her.'

Sibyll stared. She had wanted to know what she might face but now she did it felt horribly harsh.

'I am sure the good abbot's son is a valiant man,' Ward said a little desperately.

'I am sure he is,' Sibyll agreed, recovering herself. Nothing worth winning was ever easy. 'But the abbot honours us with his honesty. Many men would prefer to paint a false picture.'

Crinan grinned.

'You do me too much credit, my lady. I would paint a false picture if I thought it would benefit me, but it does not. Duncan is young and Malcolm is hale. My son's inheritance should be years away, but Alba is a volatile country. The testing time may come much sooner than we think and when it does Duncan will need a woman at his side who can help him forge the new system I believe Alba needs. If this disturbs you, Lady Sibyll, say now and we will enjoy our delicious dinner in peace and friendship and say no more of it.'

'And if it does not?'

'Then I believe that, with your brother's agreement, you should travel to Dunkeld next spring and become my daughter-in-law. And I offer you this in token of your betrothal.'

He drew something from the pocket at his belt and held it up. It was a beautiful amulet of pure amber that glinted in the light as if it were the abbot's own usquebauch made into a jewel. Sibyll stared at it, captivated, then looked at Ward.

'That is a beautiful jewel, Abbot,' he said carefully.

'For a beautiful lady. One who, I am sure, appreciates both the artistic and economic value of such easily transported treasures.'

Sibyll swallowed. Of course she did. It was only her mother's jewel-box, snatched from the ruins of their house, that had kept her and Ward in funds in those first hard years and it seemed Alba's queen too might have need of similar portable security. Did she want that for herself? And yet how, after so many years of fighting to secure a comfortable existence, could she refuse this chance? Queen? Ward being made an earl had been an unlooked for honour but this was yet another step higher and she owed it to both her brother and herself to take it.

Crinan's intelligent eyes were still fixed upon her, awaiting her decision with patience and, she thought, hope. He wanted her for his son and for Alba. He wanted her to help him hold the throne against the wild northerners and keep his country stable. She could not turn down such a noble role.

With sudden decisiveness, Sibyll dropped into a curtsey before him and bowed her head. Crinan leaned forward and hung the beautiful amulet around it and, just like that, in the normally light-hearted hour before dinner, the path of her life turned inexorably north.

'More uiskie?' Crinan suggested, waving Cullen forward, and gratefully Sibyll accepted.

Chapter Three

Inverness, October 1025

The fortress breathed louder at night. The oak pillars seemed to relax into the ground with comfortable creakings, the huge fire to hunker down gently into its own silken ashes, and the mossy thatch of the great sloping roof to come quietly alive with mice and moths and the whisper of spiders spinning their webs. Cora had noticed it many times before as she'd lain behind the thick woollen drapes of her bed at the far end of Inverness' huge hall, but never in such vibrant detail as now – her wedding eve.

Tonight her skin seemed to pulse with the sounds of Moray: the snores of Mormaer Finlay's guards on their pallets, the uneasy shuffling of those on duty at the big door and the giggles and gasps of the luckier members of the noble household who were warming themselves with more than just blankets and furs. Tomorrow Cora would be one of them. She wrapped her arms around herself, trying to imagine they were Macbeth's, and moaned in anticipation. At her side her friend Eilidh shifted sleepily.

'Shhh, Cora, for heaven's sake. It's late.'

'I'm getting married tomorrow.'

'I know it. I'm worn out carting all those damned flowers into the hall just to make you into Lady Macbeth. The whole place stinks so sweet people will think we're in frigging Lothian.'

'Eilidh, hush! They're pretty.'

She could feel that her friend was smiling, even in the darkness behind their curtains.

'Nearly as pretty as you, my wee bride.'

Cora shoved her.

'I'm not pretty. I'm all scrawny and pointy.'

'Pointy all right,' Eilidh agreed, rubbing her ribs, 'but you scrub up well and your groom seems taken enough with you.'

'Macbeth is just doing as his father has decreed. As am I.'

'Right, and I'm a child o' the white witch of the moor, Cora MacDuff.'

'You're the child of the devil, Eilidh. Now hush up. It's late.'

This elicited an indignant squeal and only a gruff command to 'whisht' from Mormaer Finlay in the next bed cabin shut them up. Eilidh gathered the blanket close and settled back to snoring but Cora couldn't sleep. It was all too exciting. Finlay had welcomed the idea of their betrothal when Macbeth had gone to him with it two months back and had moved fast to arrange the ceremony. All of Moray was here to see them wed and tomorrow night it would be Macbeth not Eilidh at her side. Cora flushed at the thought.

'Go on, Cora,' Macbeth had begged her earlier when they'd been back up by the wishing pool, lying amongst the tall rushes with their clothes more than a little askew. 'Why not? You have my heart. Nay, you *are* my heart and we'll be married this time tomorrow.'

'And we can do it then,' she'd said firmly.

'What difference does it make? It'll be much nicer out here with the sun on our backs than in a fusty bed in the hall with half the court listening in through the drapes.'

He'd had a point.

'Well, we'll come up here then. It's a full moon tomorrow so it'll be light enough to see the way and even prettier than it is now.'

'It's not the view I'll be looking at, my sweet one.'

He'd hoisted himself up on his burly arms so that he was suspended over her, his whole body just a finger's length from hers at every point. Slowly he'd lowered himself to drop a lingering kiss on her lips before he'd pulled back and said: 'Don't you want to?'

And, oh, she had, but self-denial had been part of her quest to keep herself hardened. Several times since her betrothal she'd nearly yielded to him but she'd held firm and this afternoon hadn't seen the point of capitulating with one more day to go. Not that she'd told Macbeth that – better for him to think he wasn't *that* tempting. And soon enough she would be his Lady Macbeth.

Cora shifted again, wishing the night would be on its way. Her mattress was goose down and usually very soft but tonight it was as if she could feel the individual quill of every damned feather sticking into her skin, trying to embed itself in her flesh. She squirmed around, listening to the low voices of the last men around the dying fire and wondering if Macbeth was amongst them, or Kendrick, and if she could go and join them. It wouldn't be decorous, she knew, but so what? Macbeth said he liked her 'wild', whatever that meant. And Kendrick treated her like a boy anyway, had done ever since they'd run around the beaches and woodlands of Fife together as motherless children.

She half rose, reaching for the heavy woollen shawl on a hook at her bedside, but paused as the voices rose a little. She caught the accent of Lord Muir, Finlay's cousin, a nasty, narrow-eyed man who was perpetually followed around by Gillespie, his oaf of a brother. If they were amongst the men at the fire then joining them was a far less tempting prospect. She hovered, listening intently, but then caught a shuffle of uncoordinated feet and a ripple of slurred goodnights and realised she was too late. The thud of peat sods on the embers confirmed that the night was at an end. Feeling disgruntled, she threw herself back down on the scratchy mattress and fiddled with the ends of her fire-coloured plaits.

Maybe she should have danced more but so many of the visiting nobles had wanted to talk to her there'd barely been a chance. Gillespie had been particularly keen to press his company on her. A wide, cumbersome young man with a belly that already hung ponderously over his kilt, a beard that looked to be growing its own fungi, and livid boils, he'd seemed to harbour some unfortunate delusions about his attractiveness, not to mention the level of his intellect. He'd done his best to monopolise her and Cora had been hugely relieved when Macbeth had rescued her. She squirmed pleasurably at the memory of his hand resting on her waist until Eilidh kicked out indignantly.

'Cora, please get to sleep or you'll be no use to your groom tomorrow.'

Cora groaned.

'You're right, El, but I'm just not sleepy. Maybe it's the pollen from all your bloody flowers.'

'*Your* bloody flowers.'

'Girls, whisht!'

Finlay's voice was ferocious and Cora subsided immediately.

'Sorry, Finlay, I'm just, you know ... '

'Annoying,' the Mormaer filled in, but with at least half a smile in his gruff voice.

'Night,' she said.

'Night, daughter – or nearly so. Too nearly actually, so not a peep out of you or anyone else until dawn!'

'Aye, Lord.'

'Good.'

Cora clamped her lips determinedly shut, wondering if Macbeth, sleeping with Kendrick in the bed cabin the other side of Finlay, had heard and was laughing at her. Probably. Ah, well, tomorrow night she'd be able to shut him up herself, and every night after that until they grew so old that his fine muscles

23

shrivelled and her fire-red curls turned to ash. She shut her eyes but within moments they'd sprung open again.

She stared at the drapes around her bed. The rich golden wool was embroidered with red lions rampant, the symbol of the line of Aed, and they were catching in a breeze so that they seemed almost to dance in the dull light of the remains of the fire. She looked up to the thatch but it was not shifting as it did if the winds were rising up over the Black Isle so why the movement?

Finlay's hall was a fine structure, solidly built and carefully maintained. The gaps in the wood were regularly plugged with the thickest of mosses and the plaster on the inside had been renewed so recently that the acrid scent of the lime still lingered even over the heady scent of her bridal flowers. Besides, the myriad shields weren't rattling on their hooks as they did if an autumn storm was rising. No, there was only one reason why the drapes would shake – the door was open. Not the much-used little back one to the privies but the big front door, and it was never opened at night, not unless important guests arrived in a hurry. Either that, or . . .

The yell, when it came, was so laced through with furious intent that it seemed to reach right down into Cora's throat and clamp around her heart. Attack! In an instant, images of her father spattered across her mind like his blood across the corn and she was running again, running through thick woods and across endless moors and over the saw-toothed peaks of the Mounth with enemy breath forever in her ears.

They'd come. Malcolm's murderers had come to get her and Kendrick and tear them apart before they could challenge his bloody throne and her heart almost burst through her chest with the fear of it. But moments later came another, wilder cry from the next bed – surprise cut through with fear and then a ragged roar of pain.

'Finlay?' Eilidh cried and the word cut through some of Cora's terror.

She fought to breathe, to think. How had the murderers got in? There were always two guards just inside the great door and it was always secured at night with a huge oak bar. No one could have entered unless someone inside let them. And then she heard yet another cry: 'Treason!'

Of course. This was not the vengeful Malcolm come to wreak terror on his Fife relatives. Whoever had attacked Finlay had already been inside his hall when the latch was dropped, which meant that out there it was friend against friend. Or, worse, cousin against cousin – blood tie severed by ambition. There had been so much talk of the Aed line taking the throne recently that it must have sparked hopes in more than just Mormaer Finlay. And all because of her. Cora was up in an instant and reaching for the drapes but Eilidh caught at the hem of her shift and yanked her back.

'You can't go out there,' she hissed.

'I can't stay here and wait for them to come for me.'

Cora pulled back the drape a fraction and looked out, horrified – hell itself seemed to have come to quiet Inverness. Everywhere men were fighting in twos and threes, slashing furiously at each other. Howls of pain mingled with the clash of steel as Finlay's many wedding guests were yanked out of their contented stupors and grabbed for their swords, arms quicker to react than ale-fuddled brains. Women ran for cover, children clutched close, and those that were lucky enough to make it through the melee without being cut down in a cross-swipe huddled against the wall, weeping. It was all Cora's worst fears and more brought to life. She should have known. She'd let the softness in, let herself be seduced by gentle Moray, and now she would pay the price.

Desperately she scanned the hall for escape routes and shuddered as she spotted Kendrick, in nothing more than a short shift, wielding sword and shield against a fierce opponent. She looked past him for Macbeth. Her groom-to-be was just a few paces away, positioned in front of his father's desecrated body and wielding his sword with desperate ferocity as he defended the poor corpse. His mother lay across Finlay, clawing at his chest as if she could somehow snatch back his life, but already his blood was soaking into her shift like a crimson tide and she turned her face almost gladly to the downward thrust of an enemy sword. Cora flinched away and grabbed for Eilidh.

'We have to go. Out in the open we stand a chance of slipping between the men and reaching the door.'

'And then what?'

'I don't know, El, but at least we'll be alive.'

Eilidh looked up at her, her eyes white with fear.

'I can't, Cora. Listen, it's a battlefield.'

'All the more reason to get out. Come on, the privy door is no more than ten steps away and they'll be too busy fighting even to notice a pair of girls.' She yanked her friend to her feet on the mattress. 'You have to be brave, El. Brave and quick. Ready?'

'No,' Eilidh whimpered, but Cora wasn't listening.

She grabbed the drapes and, on a deep breath, yanked them back – only to find her way blocked by a huge, blubbery figure, his face so close to hers that she could see the pus in the heart of his biggest boil.

'Going somewhere, wee bride?'

Gillespie leered in at her and, glad of the additional height conferred by the sleeping platform, Cora drew herself taller.

'This doesn't seem the best place for a lady,' she told him.

'I agree.'

With that, he thrust one beefy paw around her waist and lifted her up against him, jerking her away from Eilidh.

'Get off!'

Cora battered at his thick back.

'I'm keeping you safe.'

'I can keep myself safe.'

'You probably can but, you see, I'm keeping you safe *for me.*'

'What?' Cora struggled against his grip but his arms, though

fat, were strong and he held her as easily as if she were a newborn.
'Get off, Gillespie! I'm spoken for.'

'By Macbeth? Not anymore, I think you'll find.'

He gestured across the hall to where Macbeth was fighting with
someone she recognised – Muir. The man's single brow bristled
in fierce concentration as he thrust at Macbeth and though her
young groom was defending himself valiantly, Muir clearly had
the upper hand.

'Macbeth!'

He glanced over, saw Gillespie holding her and redoubled his
efforts. At his side, Kendrick dispatched his own opponent and
ran to help his friend, but his arm was bleeding profusely and
Muir easily backhanded him to the floor where he landed, dazed.

'*You* are the traitors?' Cora demanded of Gillespie.

'Not traitors, no. We are true to our own cause and that of the
Aed line. If anyone is going to challenge for Alba's throne it will
be us. But Moray first. Muir will take it as his own and you, wee
bride, with it.'

'Muir is married.'

She had seen his wife, a timid-looking woman, pale and bulging with his child.

Gillespie chuckled.

'Aye, he is.' One of his hands felt for her bottom, squeezed.
'But I'm not.'

Cora fought harder and now Eilidh threw herself at Gillespie
too, scratching at his hands to try and break his hold. He
spat on her.

'Get off me, cat.'

Eilidh raked her nails across his skin, drawing blood. He
gasped but didn't let go of Cora. She could see bodies littering
the floor, blood flowing as freely now as the wine had earlier, and
Macbeth, poor dear Macbeth, still fighting desperately for his life.

He looked over at her then and she saw his eyes were rimmed
red with pain and exhaustion. She had brought this horror to

27

Moray. She had brought it as surely as if she had carried it from Fife wrapped up in all her own anger and hatred and need for vengeance. It was *her* hurt, *her* purpose and it could not swallow Macbeth. She could not bear that.

'Flee!' she screamed at him.

'Never.'

'Please, Macbeth, for me.'

'How touching,' Gillespie said and now he was wrenching her shift up around her waist, exposing her to all. 'Fancy a look at what you'll be missing out on, Son of Finlay?'

'Stop it!' Eilidh shrieked and flung herself once more at Gillespie. But the big man, his grip painfully tight on Cora's bare thigh, simply drew a dagger from his belt and, in one emotionless thrust, drove it deep into Eilidh's slim back. The girl gave a tiny cry and went limp, sliding down to land in a broken heap at his feet.

'No!'

Cora struggled harder and Gillespie hit her across the cheekbone with the handle of his dagger.

'Shut up,' he growled, 'or Muir will let every one of our valiant soldiers take you before I do. Twice.'

He kicked Eilidh's body out of the way and advanced on Macbeth, pinned against one of Finlay's bedposts by Muir's sword.

'Flee!' Cora screamed at him again.

But Macbeth could do nothing now. Muir's soldiers stood in a semi-circle behind him, blocking any hope of escape. Cora's eyes sought his. If he had to die, let him at least do so in the light of her love, however much it hurt her to see it. But at that moment Kendrick reared up with a ferocious shout, catching Muir's ankle and toppling him so that he stumbled into several of his own men, knocking them down like skittles. Grabbing Macbeth, Kendrick yanked him away, skipping through the clumsy gap in the death-circle and springing down the corpse-strewn hall for the door. A guard leaped forward but Kendrick swiped him with his sword, sending two fingers flying, and the man cowered back, then they were gone.

'After them!' Muir screamed, purple with fury, and Cora found herself flung onto Finlay's desecrated bed as Gillespie leaped to obey.

She scrambled up but Muir stalked over and looked down at her through his narrow eyes.

'Stay there, wee bride. Rest. You have the ultimate heir to make, remember?' She squirmed as he pressed his sword-blade lightly into her neck. 'You have spirit. That is good. Fret not, for Gillespie will plough you far better than soft-hearted Macbeth. And then – then we will challenge for Alba! You wanted some-one with the balls to stand up to King Malcolm and his damned grandson and here we are.'

Her heart twisted as surely as if he had pierced it with his sword.

'You call murdering innocents in their beds at night having balls?'

Muir's hand twitched but he controlled himself.

'I call it effective. Now, as I said – rest. It's your wedding day tomorrow and you wouldn't want to spoil it, would you? See how pretty the hall looks for you. Lovely flowers.'

With a cruel grin he gestured around the hall where Cora's bridal flowers, so lovingly gathered by poor, dead Eilidh, lay shredded and scattered over the bodies of her guests, their heady scent lost in the stench of foul murder. Bar a few other whim-pering women and children, she was, it seemed, the only one left alive and she wished she were not for this would be a bitter wedding now.

Chapter Four

Dunkeld, April 1026

Sibyll looked at the abbey that was to be her home in astonished relief. It was beautiful. After a long ride over rough hills and moors in squalling rain and winds fit to blow the ponies over, she had feared Alba was a country that had not been introduced to the idea of spring. They had stopped for a night in an impressive place called Dunedin, a Lothian stronghold dominated by a rising crag topped with a fearsome fortress. It had seemed to loom in on her as they'd been led up the steep road to its gates and she'd half feared she might never leave this place again.

Her hosts had done little to allay her fear. This area of Lothian had only truly been given over to Alba five years ago and Mormaer Artair had taken great delight in taunting them with this fact. Ward had calmly pointed out that both he and Sibyll were Danish, which had diverted their ribaldry a little, but she had still been greatly relieved to escape the dark crag the next morning. Every time she'd looked back it had seemed still to be there and she'd feared Alba was a land jammed with such watchful mountains, but now at last she was in Dunkeld and it was pretty beyond her fondest imaginings.

The scenery had changed promisingly a while back, the road dipping down from the sparse purple moors into a vibrantly green valley, bordered to either side by pines bright with new growth and apple and cherry trees in radiant blossom. Even the sun had come out, winking at her as if saying: 'Fooled you there, didn't I?' And it had but no more – the Alba before her was a place of which she could truly be proud to be queen.

The abbey was pretty too, newer than the great church at York but every bit as elegant. It sat easily in the countryside, looking south over a wide river and surrounded by myriad workshops, stables and domestic buildings. Animals grazed all around and she could hear hammers and bellows and the busy chatter of working men. On the south side, well-tended vegetable and herb gardens made the most of the water and the sun, and on the north side rich meadowlands stretched to meet the soft cornfields before these rolled on to the gentle, protective hills beyond.

'Home,' she tried; it sounded good. As a warrior's sister she had rarely stayed long in any one place and was eager finally to settle, albeit it without Ward.

'You like it here, sister?' he asked now.

'I do.'

'There's no sea, I'm afraid.'

Sibyll smiled. Her brother loved the waves and she sometimes thought he'd have been happier fishing like their father than landlocked as an earl. Indeed, when earlier this year his wife had birthed him a fine son, Beorn, but sadly lost her own life to the fever, he had put out to sea for two weeks. They had feared they would never see him back but he had returned, proclaiming his grief cleansed by the water and thrown himself into caring for his son with such diligence that Sibyll counted herself honoured he had been prepared to leave the child long enough to see her safe to Dunkeld. She was grateful in so many ways. For years he had built a life for them both; it would be her pleasure to do a little for him in return by making this match.

'No sea, Ward, no, but a goodly river and I expect there are ships upon it at times.'

'Boats maybe,' he said gruffly, but then remembered he was meant to be filling her with enthusiasm for her new home and forced an awkward chuckle.

Sibyll didn't care. She already loved Dunkeld. Eagerly, she kicked her horse forward towards the abbey.

'No fencing,' Ward mumbled behind her as they approached the abbey buildings.

'The church is stone,' Sibyll pointed out over her shoulder. 'If there was ever trouble the monks could shut themselves within its walls and be safe.'

Ward grunted, unconvinced, but Sibyll was charmed that you could ride all the way up to the great church door without a guard stopping you. Guards were, in her experience, surly creatures with ideas way above themselves. She was frequently stopped even in Ward's own compound at York by upstarts using the rain or the low cloud or the dazzling sunlight as a reason to hold her while they deliberated the use of their petty power of admittance. Dunkeld by comparison felt inviting and she leaped down from her horse as the big abbey doors burst open and Abbot Crinan himself stepped out.

'Lady Sibyll my dear, how wonderful to have you with us in our humble home at last. Welcome. This is my wife, Princess Bethan.'

A woman came out of the abbey behind him and stepped up to Sibyll, silently offering her hand. Sibyll took it and, bowing low, kissed it. She was unsure if that was what was expected of her but Bethan seemed pleased.

'Welcome, Lady Sibyll. It will be good to have another woman at Dunkeld.'

It was a kind thing to say but her tone was stiff and her smile even stiffer. She was a stocky lady with broad, almost muscular shoulders and a proud bearing. Her gown was elegant but plain, its only ornamentation a magnificent golden link-belt at her waist. The effect was impressive.

'It will be an honour to be housed with you, my lady,' Sibyll managed.

The smile loosened a little but Bethan offered nothing in exchange and it was with relief that Sibyll turned back to Crinan.

'I'm afraid Dunkeld must look rather small to you after the grandeur of York,' he said, 'but I hope you will grow to like it.'

Sibyll looked up into his smiling eyes.

'Come, Abbot, such false humility does not become you.'

The men filing out behind Crinan looked stunned but Bethan laughed, as did the abbot.

'You speak true, but proud as I may be of Dunkeld, my lady, I do not know if it is to your taste?'

'Then let me assure you it is very much so. I find it a beautiful and peaceful place. It is also, in my experience so far, the only sunny spot in Alba.'

Now several of the onlookers laughed too and one man stepped forward.

'We like to think, my lady, that God shines his light on Dunkeld more often than elsewhere.'

Sibyll looked to the speaker and had to bite back a gasp of astonishment. My, but he was handsome! Not perhaps in a conventional way for he was only a little taller than her, his hair was muddy brown and his features somewhat crooked, but they fitted together so well when he smiled, as he was doing now, that it made him seem twice the sum of his parts. Crinan patted his back.

'Lady Sibyll, meet my son.'

This was Duncan? Sibyll wondered what she had done for God to bless her so kindly. Maybe the Good Lord had been watching as she'd borne those horrible years after her parents' death and here was her reward. She had been excited at the chance to be queen but suddenly the thought of being this man's wife seemed even more enticing.

33

'Pleased to meet you ... er ... '

She hesitated. How did she address Duncan? Son of an abbot, grandson of a king – what was his title and why on earth had she not thought to ask before?

'Maldred,' he said with an easy bow.

Maldred? She combed her mind for this term but could find nothing. All winter she had been learning Gaelic with a kindly monk Crinan had left behind to tutor her. She liked languages and it had come easily but she did not remember this word. Mormaer, yes – an Alban word for an earl – but Maldred?

Crinan stepped quickly between them.

'Lord Maldred is my eldest son by my first wife, Bridget of Allerdale.'

Sibyll blinked stupidly. Of course, Maldred was his name, no more, but that meant ...

'And here is my second son, the eldest by my dear Bethan.' He nodded almost deferentially to his royal wife. 'Your betrothed husband, Prince Duncan.'

'Prince,' Sibyll's brain registered but it made little impression as she took in the youth now stepping past Maldred.

Duncan was a big man and still carrying some adolescent flesh, which made him look young, though she knew him to be two years her senior. He bowed low and when he raised his head his eyes shifted sideways so that he looked more at her headdress than her face. Sibyll glanced towards Crinan and saw that he was, for the first time, looking unsettled. Swiftly she held out her hand to Duncan and after only a moment's hesitation he took it. His grasp was stronger than she'd expected and his hand warm and dry and now he did meet her eye and smiled shyly.

'I am honoured, Lady Sibyll, to have someone as beautiful as you for my wife.'

She felt herself blush like a fool. Duncan had clearly practised the words before she arrived but they were delivered sincerely.

'The honour is all mine, Prince.'

'Call me Duncan, please. Prince is so . . . so formal.'

He'd been going to say something else, she was sure of it, but now was not the time to press him. Crinan was watching them intently, as if he could will them to like each other and she didn't want to disappoint him. She fought not to look over to where Maldred stood; she was here for Duncan and he should not be made to feel that was anything other than welcomed by her.

'Dunkeld is very pretty,' she told him.

Duncan's eyes lit up and she noticed how unusually blue they were and what a sharp contrast they made to his dark hair.

'I'm so glad you like it.'

'The landscape reminds me a little of my own childhood home in Denmark.'

'Denmark . . . ? Of course, you are a Viking.'

'Not really. I left there when I was nine.'

It was such a simple sentence on the surface, but so fraught with hurt beneath and she struggled momentarily to keep her composure. Duncan did not seem to notice.

'I see it in your fine colouring and your strong bearing.'

'You do?' Sibyll twitched at her blonde hair. 'Is that . . . ? That is, does it please you?'

'Oh, yes,' he said instantly and she felt herself relax a little. 'We have many Vikings around Alba's shores. They are a menace if they stand against you but a wonder as an ally. Now, shall I show you round?'

He offered his arm and she took it, feeling Crinan, Bethan and Ward drop in behind them as they moved forward. She wished they'd keep back, for it was strange enough meeting the man who would be her husband without the others listening in to their every word, but it was hardly her place to complain.

'So you were raised here, Duncan?' she asked.

'In my early years, aye, but then I went to my grandfather's court to learn to be king.'

35

He said it as simply as another man might say 'to learn to ride' and seemed to take little joy in it.

'Do you want to be king?'

'Want?'

He looked startled.

'Not all men would.'

'Not all men *can*. It is my God-given destiny, Lady Sibyll. My grandfather, King Malcolm, is most clear about that and no man can deny God's will, can he?'

'No. No, of course not.'

He looked at her curiously.

'I suppose it is not the same for you. You did not know you were God's chosen until last year.'

Sibyll was not sure she had been 'chosen', except perhaps by Abbot Crinan. In her experience life was what you made it but clearly it had not been the same for Duncan.

'I'm sure you will help me to understand,' she said demurely, ducking aside as three small children came staggering past carrying a sack of flour, presumably from the mill she could see a little way down the river. 'Tell me about how Dunkeld was when *you* were small, Duncan.'

'Gladly, for I was very happy here. I confess I don't remember carrying flour, but I helped in the fields at harvest and in the blacksmith's forge whenever I was allowed and Maldred and I would often fish together. Is that not right, Maldred?'

He beckoned his half-brother forward and Sibyll felt her face bloom with heat as Maldred stepped gracefully up on her other side.

'Fish? Oh, aye. Duncan was always more skilful at it than I, though. He has patience, you see. I was forever fidgeting – even when I hooked something, I would be way too eager to reel it in and so lose it back to the depths.'

'That's not true,' Duncan protested. 'Well, not fully. And besides, Maldred was better than me at everything else.'

It was said, to Sibyll's surprise, without rancour but Maldred's reply was sharper.

'But my blood is not so fine as yours, brother.'

There was an awkward silence at that. Sibyll sought desperately for something to say.

'You have a distillery here, I believe?' she managed eventually. 'You make *usque . . . usque . . .*'

'Usquebauch,' Duncan supplied. 'Aye. Brother Cullen is a very clever man. He came to Father as an abandoned orphan, you know, but has grown into one of his greatest assets. Have you tried his spirit?'

'Your father brought some to York. It was delicious, like several layers of taste in one drink.'

'Exactly right,' Maldred agreed eagerly. 'That is all created by the process of making it. There are several other places in Alba that produce such a drink but theirs are vastly inferior to ours. I have told Brother Cullen he should take his expertise travelling so that all can enjoy the subtle drink he creates, but he is reluctant.'

'I'm not surprised,' Sibyll said. 'I think I would protect it too.'

'But then . . .'

'Shall we go and see where it is made?' Duncan interrupted.

Sibyll nodded and he turned her to the north side of the church. The sudden change of direction nudged her into Maldred and as she stumbled he put out a hand to catch her.

'Thank you.'

'My pleasure.'

They stood together while Duncan strode on. The warm air seemed to shimmer between them and for a moment they both struggled to speak. Maldred recovered first.

'I apologise, my lady, if I sounded bitter before. I am not usually jealous of my half-brother for he is very good to me and I do not begrudge him his good fortune. Today, though . . .' He looked down. 'I'm sorry. I think I must . . .' He swung suddenly away. 'I shall go and check the meat for dinner, Lady Mother.

We do not wish the venison to be tough for our honoured guests, do we?'

Bethan looked at him in something like amusement but Duncan turned back, puzzled.

'The cooks will have it in hand, I'm sure. Come, Maldred, you love the distillery.' He came back to speak to Sibyll. 'As I told you, Maldred is better than me at most things but especially when it comes to uiskie for I confess I have no taste for it.'

'Oh, but it is . . . ' Sibyll caught herself and turned away from staring after Maldred's retreating figure. 'I'm sure that's very wise for I fear it fuddles the mind.'

'Aye,' Duncan agreed easily, 'and mine needs no further fuddling. This way.'

The distillery was to Sibyll a place of magic. The building was large and circular, like an ancient roundhouse, but there was nothing ancient about the interior. At the centre sat the still – a large copper vessel as tall as a man with a wide, bowl-shaped base tapering off into a long fluting pipe. It looked like something new-thinking faeries might create, though when Sibyll said so Brother Cullen's brow creased.

'There is no magic to uiskie, my lady. It is all science.'

'Of course. Silly me. Do tell me more.'

And he did, in exhaustive detail. He took her to the low trapdoor where the barley grains came in to be malted then showed her where they were steeped in water in a trough, dried upon a raised bed and finally baked in a large clay container set over a low peat-fuelled fire. This filled the room with sweet-smelling smoke that swirled up to the small, high windows and added to its almost mystical air, not that Sibyll said as much. Instead she let herself be led on to two large vats, one apparently for 'mashing', the next for 'fermenting', though she lost track of the differences between the two and knew only that the smell from both was musky and rough and nowhere near the refined scent of the drink she had enjoyed back in York.

She could sense Duncan watching her as she battled to understand Cullen's earnest and very full explanations of the whole process and was grateful when he finally secured her release for dinner. She took his arm as he led her outside. It felt solid and reassuring and she leaned gratefully into it.

'Why did you ask me if I wanted to be king?' he asked, as they stepped out into the blessedly fresh air once more.

She looked up at him in surprise.

'Why? Curiosity, that is all. You are the first Tanaise I have met.'

'I suppose so. Your Gaelic is very good, Sibyll.'

'Not as good as your English.'

'My grandfather insists it is spoken at court so that ambassadors can understand us. No one else speaks Gaelic.'

'So it is special.'

'Special? I like that. King Malcolm says that it is a dead language.'

Sibyll blinked.

'He sounds a little harsh.'

'He has to be. He is king.'

'And kings must be harsh?'

'Sometimes. I will have to be, you know, for the men of Aed will surely attack.'

'The opposing line?'

'That's right. My grandfather tried to wipe them all out but some survive over the Mounth. Look there.' He pointed to the tower of the main abbey buildings from which flew a banner as blue as the sky and slashed with a vivid white cross. 'That is the cross of St Andrew, the mark of the Constantin line, and King Malcolm wishes it to fly over Alba forever more. But the men of Aed march beneath a red lion rampant and it is a greedy beast. To keep our own colours flying, I will have to be harsh and decisive and . . . and inspirational.' He grimaced. 'I am working on that one.'

Sibyll laughed.

'You are very honest, Duncan.'

'Simple, do you mean?'

'No!' She stopped dead, just outside the abbey doors. 'Why would you think that?'

'Father says I am simple and he's right, you know, for I am useless at dissembling.'

'That, surely, could be a strength?'

'And at telling when others are dissembling.'

'Ah.' She thought for a moment. 'But, Duncan, you have me now. Maybe I can help you with that?'

He looked at her, truly looked for the first time.

'Maybe you can.' He grinned suddenly and his pasty face took on new animation. 'You know, Sibyll, when I told you that you were beautiful, I did not know for sure if it was true . . . not even when you were standing in front of me looking so radiant. But it is.' He grabbed her hands. 'Truly, I find you beautiful, and clever too, so you will surely help me hold Alba. God has chosen well.'

'You don't think perhaps your father had something to do with it?'

'Oh, aye, of course. But he is an abbot so closer to God than most.'

'Not as close as an anointed king.'

'I suppose not.' Her husband-to-be gave a little laugh, almost a giggle. 'I will be above him.'

'Surely, as Tanaise, you already are?'

'I had not thought of it that way.' Duncan's chest swelled slightly and already he looked more manly. 'I shall go and speak to him now, I think, and tell him that four weeks is too long to wait for our wedding. You are ready, Sibyll, to marry me?'

Her thoughts flashed to Maldred but she pushed them back into the dark where they belonged. She was here for the honour of her family and to secure her future; she must not compromise either for petty emotion. She set her shoulders and smiled back at him.

'I am ready, Duncan.'

Chapter Five

Inverness, May 1026

'You're useless, Gillespie, absolutely bloody useless! One job you had, one single job, and not even a tough one either. She's comely enough. Bit skinny and with a hell of a mouth on her but that can soon be stoppered by a real man. I'll show you, shall I?'

Muir leaped up from his stool nearest the fire and in two strides stood over Cora. He thrust his fingers into her red curls, yanking on them to pull her face against his groin, and his group of his cronies gave a lewd cheer. For once Cora was glad of Gillespie at her side, for he leaped up too and faced down his brother.

'Let go of my wife!'

'I will if you'll bloody well do your job and get your seed planted in her.'

Muir pulled on Cora's hair so hard she was forced to her feet then suddenly let go so that she crashed down, knocking her stool into the fire and jarring her hip against an uneven floorboard. None of Muir's thuggish men moved to help and it was left to Aila, Eilidh's younger sister, to scamper forward and pick her up. The young noblewoman had cleaved to Cora since the wedding-eve attack and Cora scrambled gratefully away with her as Muir and Gillespie squared up to one another.

'There's an ocean of seed gone into her,' Gillespie snapped. 'It just doesn't grow. She's set her womb against me, I swear it.'

All heads turned suspiciously Cora's way. She heard the word 'witch' and longed to run but where would she go? Beyond the Mormaer's fortress of Inverness there was nothing more than a handful of crofters and she could hardly throw herself on their mercy with Muir and his hounds on the hunt. It wouldn't be fair.

'Maybe your seed isn't strong enough for my womb,' she threw back defiantly.

He reached her in two strides and yanked her towards him.

'You'll regret that, wife. I'll show you how strong my seed is right now.'

'Right *now*?'

She stared him down, and as something clicked into place in his slow brain, he shifted. He had an almost morbid fear of her bleeds. The first time he'd seen it he had reared back with a horror that had almost made her laugh. Cora had not been slow to exploit it and now, as far as Gillespie knew, she bled every two weeks. Aila, whose grandmother had been a midwife, had taught her which days in her own moon-turn were most likely to produce a child and with a little help from the butcher she 'bled' at that time as well as the usual one. She was confident Gillespie would never find out for it was hardly a topic for male banter and so far, praise God, it had served to keep his child from her womb.

'I will prove it with my belt if you don't whisht.'

'Aye, husband. Sorry, husband.'

No one was fooled by her show of subservience but it was all a game anyway. In truth, Gillespie offered her a rough sort of kindness when they were alone, but in front of his brother he always felt the need to play the man. Muir and Gillespie's household was an uneasy one, regularly flaring into fights and arguments. No one trusted anyone and, despite all the supposedly grand plans to conquer Alba, all were too busy watching their own backs to make the rough-edged Moray court into a powerful one.

Cora felt the familiar stab of grief as she thought of what could have been. Her wedding day had been dark and terrifying. Finlay's servants, commanded by a sword-wielding Muir, had been up at dawn clearing the bodies of their previous lords into a rough pit of a grave behind the fortress. No one, though, had been able to clean the floorboards of blood or to pick Cora's shredded flowers from the cracks and she had been manhandled across them by her new husband, to preside over a grisly meal that had been more victory celebration than wedding feast – with her as the spoils. Not Lady Macbeth as she had expected to be, but Lady Gillespie.

Her only consolation had been that so far Macbeth and Kendrick had not been tracked down, but it had been hard to hold onto that thought when Gillespie, urged to it by his brother, had thrown her onto the same bed where he'd coldly stabbed Eilidh the night before and taken her with the Aed lions on the drapes dancing manically and his men cheering him on. Cora had wept throughout the humiliation and when Gillespie had finished, with a cry like a huntsman spearing a deer, had curled into the tightest ball she could and prayed for mercy. So far it had not come.

Gillespie paid her little attention beyond rutting with her. At times she saw flashes of humour in her gruff husband but he was too afraid of Muir to do anything other than his bidding – and that mainly involved getting her with child. At first her new groom had forced her legs apart in the mornings, at night and, more often than not, the daytime too. The more she'd protested, the more he'd insisted, until she'd learned to submit and pray for it soon to be over. And then she'd bled and, thank the Lord, it had repulsed him enough to earn her a respite and a way of undermining him and his damned seed.

Now he flung her aside and she shrank thankfully back against

Aila, drawing warmth from her friend as the men hunkered around the fire. More ale was produced alongside a jar of usquebauch that someone had brought back from the tiny monastery at Rosemarkie. There was loud grumbling about the quality of the spirit but they drank it anyway, their voices rising with each turn of the jug.

'I hear they make a uiskie down south that tastes so good you'd think God had pissed it out Himself,' someone grunted.

Cora eyed her bed at the far end of the hall but did not wish to draw attention to herself by moving.

'Where in the south?' Muir asked.

'Dunkeld. Abbot there's got some lad with a magic touch.'

'That'd be right,' Gillespie spat. 'Damned Abbot Crinan is the devil's assistant! He's got King Malcolm under his holy thumb and has had his own son officially named Tanaise too. It's not right. The line of Aed should be next and *we* are the line of Aed.'

'We are,' Muir agreed, his voice icy. 'And if you'd put a babe in that Constantin bitch's womb we'd have the ultimate heir – son of both lines. We'd be unstoppable.'

Cora winced. 'Ultimate heir' had been Macbeth's words on the sweet day of their betrothal. Back then it had seemed a wonderful thing to produce a child to unite Alba but Gillespie and Muir could never unite themselves let alone a whole country and she feared for any child in their clutches.

'Tell that to *her*,' Gillespie threw at his brother, pointing a vicious finger at Cora.

'I might do more than that one of these days,' Muir retorted.

'What d'you mean?' Gillespie was on his feet again. 'What do you mean by that, brother?'

'My wife has three children and another ripening. My Aed seed is proven and, after all, what difference does it really make which of us ploughs her?'

'She's my wife, Muir.'

'Then do your duty and get us a son on her and soon – or I will.'

*

44

Three days later news came in that King Malcolm was sick and the court wolves were poised to inaugurate Duncan and overturn the ancient order of Alba. That night Muir ordered Gillespie out along the Moray Firth with the tax gatherers, saying the crofters were proving rebellious and needed a firm hand from a powerful man. Gillespie, foolishly pleased, strapped on his sword, donned his cloak and rode forth at dawn. Cora, however, had seen the flint-spark in Muir's eye and taken Aila and several of the young lads out peat-gathering, staying in the hills until the sun had dipped into the firth below and it was too dangerous to linger any longer.

Even once they were back, she stayed in the stables with her pony, Balgedie – named for her father's lands in central Fife – praying Muir was at ale with his cronies. Lovingly she rubbed the horse down to ease his back after the load of heavy sods he'd carried home and for a moment, lost in his contented whickers, she felt as close to content as it was possible to be since she'd been forced to marry the wrong man. But then her thoughts were drawn to Macbeth and sadness engulfed her once more.

She'd heard from him only once, via a young man either brave or poor enough to risk all to bring her the missive. Macbeth and Kendrick had apparently fled to Ireland, seeking the protection of the Norse King of Dublin who welcomed all sorts of malcontents and exiles to his court. They were alive and well save for their raw grief for all they had lost – Cora most of all. Macbeth had written:

I will return, my Cora, my sweet one. I think of you every moment and beg you to stay strong and well until I can release you. It will take time. We are poor men here and must earn our way to favour but we will do so, I swear it. With my dear father dead, I hurt too, my heart, and understand your anger a little better, though I wish it were not so. I will have my retribution and then you will have yours. Stay strong in my love,
    Macbeth

She'd had to burn the letter after reading it but the words had stayed in her heart and every day she scanned the horizon in the hope of seeing his blond head against the sky. So far there had been no sight of him and sometimes it felt as if her betrothal been an illusion, like a faerie in the mist. But there was little use in giving in to self-pity; she was alone and must manage alone.

Determinedly she ran the brush down Balgedie's tired back, working it into the knots in his powerful little shoulders, and considered, not for the first time, saddling him up and pointing him down the Great Glen to Ireland. If Macbeth and Kendrick could not come to her, why should she not go to them? One day she would.

'One day soon,' she whispered in the pony's ear and moved to hang up the brush.

Balgedie snorted an answer and kicked up his back legs as if keen to go. Cora laughed but now she saw that his ears were back, his teeth bared and the whites of his eyes as wide as moons in the low torchlight. Slowly she turned and there, framed in the doorway, stood Muir.

'Clever,' he said. 'I wondered where you'd got to and all along you were out here waiting for me.'

'I wasn't waiting for you, Muir.'

'No? Ah, well, I'm here now. And I tell you, Cora MacDuff, I've been waiting for *you* a long time.'

He came forward, his broad frame blocking her access to the door beyond. Cora pressed back against the wall of Balgedie's stall.

'Then you can wait longer,' she flung at him.

He shook his head, pretended sadness.

'No, Cora. No, I can't. I've stayed away out of respect for my brother.' She snorted disbelievingly but he grinned back. 'That respect has gone now. You want a child, Cora.'

'No.'

'You need a child. *I* need a child. We must unite the lines of Constantin and Aed. You and me, Cora – it has to be.' He was close enough now for her to see a stark madness in him. He meant what he said. 'Strip.'

'No.'

He drew his sword.

'Strip, Cora.'

'You can't kill me – you need me.'

'True, but I don't need your stupid pony.' He swung his arm suddenly and with a crazed laugh sliced the top off Balgedie's ear. The poor creature bucked in pain and Cora had to press herself deep into the straw to avoid his flailing hooves. 'Strip!' Muir roared.

Shaking, Cora fumbled at the big brooch clasping her over-tunic across her chest. Finally the pin came loose and the thick plaid dropped to her waist.

'Good,' Muir purred. 'And the rest.'

She scrabbled at the plaited leather belt and pulled it loose. Her tunic fell to the floor leaving her exposed in just her undershift. She glanced hopefully towards Balgedie but he was pressing himself against the far wall so as to avoid Muir and would be no defence. Still Muir waited, an icy calm in the straight set of his shoulders and his sword glinting in the flame of the torch set into the sconce above his head. She glanced at it.

'Shall I come to you?'

He grinned.

'That's more like it.' She sidled out of the stall and stood beneath the sconce. He lifted the hem of her shift with his sword. 'Now this. I want to see what poor wee Macbeth is missing out on.'

The dear name shot courage through her veins.

'No!' she yelled, making a dart for the sconce and wrenching the torch free.

For a moment she thought she'd succeeded in her attack but then his big hand clasped over hers and he twisted her wrist so that she screamed in pain and the flame turned her way. She tried to drop it but his hand was gripped too tightly over hers and now he was pushing it up under her chin. She felt the heat bite at her skin and then, finding an easier fuel, flare across her shift, firing her all over. Muir let go of her and shoved the torch back into the sconce as she flailed before him, heat searing across her chest.

'Look,' he cackled. 'You are on fire for me, Cora MacDuff. I knew it.'

The pain was too great for her to care about his insults but then he was upon her, shoving her to the ground and rolling her against the rough earth, forcing the flames out, though they scorched on deep inside her skin. And now he was yanking away the charred remains of her shift and pulling her onto her knees to drive himself into her and she knew not which was the greater pain – the burn across her chest or the one deep inside.

'No one defies Muir,' he gasped, 'least of all a southern bitch with ideas above herself. You're here to give us a babe to challenge bloody Duncan, Cora MacDuff, and you will do so if it kills you. Understand?' The world was swimming before her, pain like liquid fire through every part of her, and her throat so raw she could not even cry. 'Understand?' Muir screamed, pounding harder.

'I understand,' she gasped in desperation and the last thing she heard before everything went black was his cry of triumphant release.

Chapter Six

Forteviot, May 1026

It was the way his face lit up when he saw her that made Sibyll feel she could in some way love this man. It would not be a helpless, skin-tingling passion, but Duncan was good and kind and earnest. He would care for her and that was worth having. She took the last three steps up to the grand church at Forteviot with her head held high and heard cheers ring around the royal compound as her bridegroom seized her hand.

'I'm so glad you're here with me in front of all these people, Sibyll.'

He gestured with a twitch of his fingers to the vast crowd, rolling his eyes as if they were a mob waiting to see him hung rather than Alba's noblest families gathered to bless the wedding.

'You do not like crowds?'

'Not when they're all looking at me.'

Sibyll's heart sank a little.

'But you are to be king, Duncan.'

He gave a funny grimace.

'I know, and I did not say I could not do it, simply that I do not like to. And that I like it more with you at my side, for who will notice me when you are so beautiful?'

Her heart swelled. She was dressed in the richest gown she had ever worn. It was of a forest green that set off her fairness and the matching headdress was trimmed with so much gold that she seemed almost to sparkle. Long loops of gold chains – a gift from her soon-to-be husband – hung from her jewel-studded shoulder-brooches and even her shoes were trimmed with the glorious metal, as if the fairies had sprinkled her all over in dream-dust. She had felt shyly pleased with her reflection in the copper mirror in her bedchamber but was glad Duncan too admired the effect.

'You look very fine as well,' she told him.

It was true. Duncan wore a dark red tunic with a richly embroidered sash and a matching cloak clasped at the neck with a magnificently carved brooch. He was standing straight for once and thus, thankfully, was taller than her. On his dark head was a simple diadem studded with rubies to match his clothing and the wearing of it forced his chin up. Sibyll could swear he'd lost some of the spare flesh around his jowls in the few weeks since she'd arrived but perhaps it was eased away by his broad smile.

He had not, in the end, talked his father into bringing their wedding forward. Indeed, the interval had been extended when an order had come from King Malcolm that he wished to hold the ceremony at his own royal palace in Forteviot. Ward had looked haunted by the idea of being away from little Beorn for a further two weeks but the chance to consort with the King of Alba was too good to miss for he would be a valuable ally in Ward's fight to take Northern Northumbria.

Crinan too had been delighted by the elevated status of the wedding.

'The king wishes everyone to see you both,' he had told Duncan and Sibyll proudly when he'd sat them down to explain that their wedding was to be a state affair.

'Will we process through the streets at Forteviot?' Sibyll had asked.

'Streets?' Duncan had queried and Crinan had laughed.

'You will find, my dear, that Alba does not have "streets", for she does not have towns.'

'None?'

'Not as you would think of them, no. We are an agricultural nation. An Albaman measures his good fortune in cattle and space to the horizon. We care little for being crammed in with others. And besides, in my brief experience of them, towns are noisy, cramped and unsanitary.'

'That's true,' Sibyll had conceded, 'but they are also vibrant and exciting and full of novelty.'

'Novelty?' Crinan had rolled the word around his tongue like a plum stone. 'Novelty does not hold much value here.'

'And yet Malcolm would change the succession laws – is that not a great novelty?'

Crinan had conceded defeat with a wry tip of his head and later, over dinner, Duncan had pressed Sibyll for information about towns, begging her to describe York, though when she did he could scarce believe her.

'Hundreds of dwellings all nudged up together? But why? Do men not want their own land?'

'They do, but they sacrifice space for the chance to be near the markets and churches and public buildings inside the walls.'

'Walls?'

She had given up then. Maybe Duncan would see Ward's city for himself one day but in the meantime they had the prospect of the royal estate of Forteviot, which was as busy as any town. King Malcolm had sent messengers out all over Alba and nobles had been flocking in to see the Tanaise and his new bride. There had to be two hundred people here and King Malcolm, unlike his grandson, was revelling in the attention. He wore finery twice as rich as Duncan's and his golden armlets and magnificent crown sparkled in the capricious light from two huge braziers burning either side of the church doors while his sharp eyes fixed on the crowd like a vulture's.

He was just turned seventy-four, a startling age though not one you would guess from his upright bearing and well-muscled arms. Sibyll had been introduced to him last night and found him a fierce, intense man, almost manically intent upon controlling his fractious country and its boisterous lords.

'Lady Sibyll,' he had said to her, 'Crinan assures me that in you he has found a worthy queen for Alba. I trust this is true?'

'Abbot Crinan seems a wise man,' she had responded and he'd surprised her with a sharp bark of laughter in return.

'A fair answer, lady. What make you of Alba?'

'It seems a very fertile place.'

'Wet, you mean?'

'Well-watered.'

'Hmm. I hope you will prove as fertile as your new country, my lady?'

'I hope so too. It would be an honour to bear Alba an heir.'

'It would.' He'd grasped her arm then, pulling her close to him. 'A *direct* heir. You know, Lady Sibyll, that I am breaking our custom by passing Duncan the kingship?'

'I have been told so, yes.'

'Is he up to the job?'

It had struck Sibyll as a curious, almost vicious question and she had felt instantly defensive of her soon-to-be husband.

'Surely he must be, Sire, for did you not train him yourself?'

King Malcolm's fingers had tightened on her arm.

'And I will train him further yet. You should know that I am a long way from the grave.'

'I am glad of it.'

'I doubt it. Not many are. I was ill a few months back and my nobles were scampering around like mice in a barn, but much to everyone's distress I recovered. I have been king twenty years and that is far longer than we are used to here in Alba. The men are bored by all this stability and yearn to scrap again – idiots!' Sibyll had not known what to say to this but eventually, to her relief, he'd released her. 'You will do,' he'd said with a curt nod and then, thank the Lord, he'd been gone.

'Grandfather likes you,' Duncan had told her, rushing to her side.

Sibyll had forced a smile but all she'd been able to think was: God help anyone, then, whom he likes not. And today she must share a dais with him.

Despite the springtime it was a grey day but Malcolm had ordered his own suns to be lit in great iron baskets and the clouds could not compete. They hung sulkily over everyone's heads as if they longed to quench the defiant fires but didn't quite dare. Sibyll was glad of it, though the heat down her left side was so great that she could feel her face growing foolishly red along the line of her nose and pulled her gown in close against her legs for fear of it catching fire.

Luckily the Abbot of Forteviot was twitching nervously at his own fine robes and hastened the ceremony on. Within a handful of Latin sentences he was lifting their clasped hands high and proclaiming them Lord and Lady Duncan. The crowds, surrounded by Malcolm's guards, cheered obligingly and Sibyll felt herself fill up with pride and joy and excitement at this new future.

She pictured herself cowering beneath smouldering beams the dread day when the murderous Wends had ridden in and cut her life out from under her. She pictured her mother's death-filled eyes begging her to save herself and wished she could see her now, risen to Princess of Alba. Crinan had gifted her several beautiful brooches, Duncan her gold chains and King Malcolm himself five huge stones, to set however she chose. She was rich now and, above that, she was valued. Her mother would have been so proud of her and that knowledge was worth more to Sibyll than any jewel.

She bowed her head as the abbot lifted up a beautiful diadem of plaited silver with Cairngorm-stones of all colours winking from every link. She felt it come to rest on her brow and lifted her chin once more. Let them all see her. She might not yet wear a crown but this was a symbol of intent and of belonging and wearing it, she felt blessed indeed.

It was a fine feast. The hall at Forteviot was huge, big enough for four runs of trestles and a dais at the end. King Malcolm sat himself at the centre of the high table, Sibyll to his left with Crinan on her other side and Duncan to his right with Bethan beyond. Sibyll worried what she would say to the formidable old king but Bethan chattered to him across her son with rare animation, leaving her thankfully free to turn to her new father-in-law. They conversed easily until the sweetmeats were served and several of the local lords claimed the Abbot's attention.

Sibyll sat back gratefully then, surveying the scene as the court rose from the benches to chat among themselves. This hall was similar to the one at Dunkeld, a little larger but decorated with the same elegant, curling plaits and crosses that Sibyll was swiftly learning characterised Celtic art. The basic structure of the building was identical to a Viking or Northumbrian one but the intricacy of the decorations was new to her and she liked it. She spent some time happily lost in contemplation of a pattern painted on the wall to her left before Crinan spotted her isolation.

'Maldred! Maldred, come here and talk to Lady Duncan for she is abandoned.'

'No,' Sibyll said hastily. 'No, truly, I am quite content, I ...'

But Crinan was pushing his eldest son towards her and there was no further chance to protest. Sibyll looked at Maldred as he sank into his father's vacated chair and smiled shyly.

'You are enjoying your day?' he asked.

'I am, though I might have preferred the ceremony to be held in Dunkeld.'

'You like our abbey then?'

'It's very beautiful and it fascinates me. It's much bigger than English abbeys and so much more connected to the community. In England monks don't usually mix with normal people.'

Maldred laughed.

'How strange. What would Christ make of that, do you think? He loved to talk with "normal people".'

Sibyll flushed.

'I know not, my lord. I am no philosopher.'

'I've offended you, I'm sorry.'

He made an apologetic grab for her hand and then, as their fingers touched and heat seemed to flare between them, he swiftly dropped it. Both of them looked away.

'Do you know the rest of Alba well?' Sibyll managed to say eventually.

'Not really. I was brought up in Dunkeld for most of my childhood but Father took me travelling a few times once Duncan had gone to the royal court to learn to be king.'

His eyes strayed towards his half-brother.

'Travelling where?'

They returned to her.

'Mainly to Strathclyde in the west – my mother's land. My birth mother that is, not Princess Bethan. My uncle is Mormaer of Strathclyde and when he dies that title will fall to me.'

'I see. And will you, then, have to go and live there?'

'I will. In Partick.'

He sounded rather gloomy at the thought.

'Is it not a welcoming place?'

'Oh, it is, very, and powerful too for it has strong links with the Britons of Rheged, Wales and Man, as well as the Norse rulers over the sea in Ireland.'

It was an impressive claim but still he looked despondent.

'And have you . . . have you a betrothed in Strathclyde?'

He fixed her suddenly with the light of his hazel eyes.

'No betrothed, no. No doubt Father will find me one as he has for Duncan, though my brother gets all that is best and wives, it seems, are no exception.'

He was looking intently into her eyes and it spiked a restless longing inside her that felt horribly uneasy. All her life since fleeing Denmark she had worked to try and find stability and security and here, just when she should be celebrating her success, was a threat – and from inside her own heart. Confused, she fumbled for her new diadem as if it might steady her.

'We all have our paths to follow,' she said woodenly.

Maldred kept looking at her for an unsettlingly long time and then gave a stiff little bow.

'We do and I must to mine. This is not my place.'

'Maldred, please. Stay.'

He hesitated then shook his head.

'I cannot.'

And then he was gone and Sibyll was left feeling somewhat foolish until she felt a soft touch on her back and a quiet voice said, 'Would you care to dance, wife?' She turned gratefully to see Duncan at her shoulder.

'I would love to,' she agreed and placed her hand in his, noting again how warm and dry it felt.

'All eyes are on us again,' he said ruefully as people parted hastily before them.

'Let them look,' she said, 'for they will like what they see. You will be a good king, Duncan.'

'I will?'

'Better than your grandfather.'

'Sibyll, hush!'

She laughed.

'Malcolm cannot hear me, Duncan.'

'Don't you believe it. He has many ears, Sibyll, for he rules over all.'

'Only by fear.'

'It is the best way.'

'A man cannot rule by trust and kindness?'

'Not in Alba. I will need to learn ferocity.' He looked nervously around the packed hall then shook himself free from the thought and turned back to her. 'But not tonight.'

Her thoughts flew to the bedchamber that awaited them.

'I hope not,' she agreed.

He took her in his arms.

'I will be gentle.'

And as even more people turned to watch him guide her formally and carefully onto the dance floor, she knew that he spoke true and that she should be – nay she *was* – grateful for it.

Chapter Seven

Rosemarkie, June 1026

Cora blinked slowly, giddily, awake. Her eyelids felt as heavy as if someone had tied sling-stones to them and her body as fragile as winter ice. She shifted carefully and felt a shiver not so much of pain as dark discomfort. Then suddenly, piercing through the ache, shot a barbed arrow of memory: Muir.

She heard herself whimper and sensed movement at her side. Terrified, she flicked her eyes towards it, wondering what fresh horror awaited. It was not, thank God, Muir, but it was not much better.

'Gillespie?'

His craggy face was creased with what looked almost like concern.

'Cora? Oh, Cora, thank the Lord! The monks said you had seemed more coherent this last day and and now you are back with me.'

Confused by his tentative tone, Cora shifted again, feeling the soft sheets laid over her. She raised her head and saw she was in a small room, warmed by a roaring brazier and scented with fresh herbs. The walls were plain and the one window opening was sealed over with nailed-in leather and offered no clue as to her surroundings.

'Where am I?'

'Rosemarkie. At the monastery. I brought you here after … after I found you.'

Again the memory: fire and earth and Muir like a merciless dagger inside her. She closed her eyes, seeking to create enough darkness to obscure the pictures in her mind.

'I should have stood up to Muir,' Gillespie went on gruffly. 'You are my wife and he had no right to attack you. I will take steps to … to make amends.'

His words were stiff and awkward but, it seemed, truly meant. She felt his fingers tentatively brush hers and, giddy at the kind touch, let him take her hand.

'How?' she demanded. Speaking was an effort but it felt important.

'I am taking you away from him. I am building a hall of my own – *our* own. It will be here at Rosemarkie. My men are already digging foundations. I am expanding the monastery too, Cora, and building my own church and will set up a distillery and invite men from the south to create a fine spirit, which I will brew in my own name. I am not going to live under my brother's thumb any longer and he will not touch my wife again, not ever.'

It was roughly spoken but well thought out and Cora clutched his hand, praying he spoke true. If she wanted to climb out of the hell-hole Muir had plunged her into, she had to believe that he did.

'How long have I been here?'

'A week. I brought you to the monks the moment I found you.'

'Thank you.'

'It is not me you must thank but Aila. It was she who found you when no one else went looking, she who cooled your burns with poultices and stayed with you in that damned stable for two whole days until I returned from along the firthside and found you there. I do not think she had even eaten for she was as pale as you were ... were red.'

He stumbled to a halt and Cora felt a new grief assail her. She pulled her fingers from his and felt for her face. Her neck was covered in bandages and as her fingers fluttered nervously down she found strips of linen wrapped across her chest as well.

'Am I very scarred?'

'They tell me it's too early to be sure. Your skin is raw but not destroyed so maybe not, but ... I'm so sorry, Cora.'

It was the first apology she'd ever heard from his lips but she barely noticed as she put her fingers back to her face. The bandage, at least, did not touch her mouth which felt whole, nor her nose or eyes. Oh, but ...

'My hair!'

Her curls were gone. All she could feel was stubble, like hayfields after the reaping. She rubbed frantically at it.

'It was all singed away on one side,' Gillespie said, trying to stop her. 'The monks cut the charred ends off and Aila instructed them to go all the way around for it looked peculiar lop-sided.'

Cora felt something like a smile tug at her lips and seized on this. She would not let Muir's cruelty break her.

'What do you know about it, Gillespie?'

'I know that Muir attacked you and burned you and left you for dead.'

'And that he raped me?'

The word pulsed in the fire-warm air between them, as ugly a scar as any on her body.

'When?' her husband growled. 'Before the fire?'

'After.' He stared at her. Cora fought to keep breath coming, the words with it. He had to know. 'He shoved me in the dirt and ripped off what was left of my shift and then he, he ...'

The tears came then, leaking out of her eyes and coursing down her cheeks to soak into the bandages on her chin. Still Gillespie stared, then suddenly he leaped to his feet.

'I'll kill him.'

'No!'

'I will. Now. I should have done it sooner. He has always patronised me and this is the final straw. I will ride to the bastard's stolen hall and make him fight me.'

'Gillespie, no, please.'

'I must avenge the wrong he has done me, Cora.'

'Done *you*?' she asked weakly, but he was heading for the door and did not heed her. She struggled up on her pillows. 'Gillespie, stop! Please. Muir is surrounded by his men. The odds would be desperately against you.'

He looked furiously back at her but did at least pause.

'I cannot let this pass.'

'And you will not. But there will be a better time.'

He came slowly back towards her.

'You are right. But, Lord, Cora, it boils my blood.'

She grabbed for his hand.

'Promise me you won't put us at risk in that way. Please, Gillespie, promise.'

He sighed.

'I promise – for now. But, Cora, what if . . . '

'If I have a child?'

'Yes. What if Muir's seed is truly stronger than mine?'

'It is not. It is simply that I have been avoiding conception.'

'What?' His brow clouded with anger but he visibly restrained himself. 'How did you manage it?'

'It matters not. I won't do it again.'

'But Muir . . . '

She nodded, shifted beneath the sheets. The skin on her chest felt as dry and cracked as summer mud but it did not hurt, not really. Muir's fury had, at least, put out the flames before they could sear too deep. Her legs moved freely, as did her arms. She was not whole but she would mend. All her of would mend, for plenty of women did.

61

This was a timely lesson that she had let herself grown soft. She had come to Moray steeled with anger and resentment and hatred but had let herself be lured into believing that she might be able to find a way forward in love instead. Even after the wedding-eve attack she had hidden away, relying on Macbeth to come and save her, and it would not do.

Muir had forced home to her in the most violent possible way that she was alone now. She had to find her own path to restitution and a child of her body was the best possible tool. What matter the father – a son would be hers and hers alone and somehow, some day, she would make him king. Drawing on all her strength, she lifted the sheet and looked at Gillespie. He looked back, puzzled.

'Bed me, Gillespie.'

'No! Not now, not with you like . . . that.'

'I repulse you?'

'No! But you are burned – sore.'

'Maybe, but you *must* bed me, then if there is a child we can at least hope it is yours and not, not . . . '

'His.'

'Aye. Please.'

'It feels wrong.'

He looked uncomfortably about the room as if someone might be watching, trying to catch him out.

'I will not recover from this by hiding away, Gillespie, for if I do so it will always be out there waiting to catch me. Please.'

He stood slowly.

'You will say if you want me to stop?'

'I will.'

He moved to drop the bar on the door and then began to undress, his ever-ready arousal clear. Her thoughts slid, as always, to Macbeth but she slammed a door shut on them. That time was gone and its glorious innocence with it. If only she had given in to him by the loch that afternoon before what should have been their wedding, she might have known sweetness in bedding. But she had not and life could only move forwards.

'Come, Gillespie.'

He slid in next to her.

'You will say if you want to stop?'

'Truly I will.' She felt his manhood prod at her thigh but still he hesitated. 'Now, Gillespie, please.'

It had to be fast, before she quailed and pushed him away for if she did that she might never manage this again. She tugged at him and he raised himself over her, holding himself away from her damaged chest on his powerful arms, and suddenly, clumsily, he was thrusting into her. She bit at her lip and, with an effort, he halted his movement.

'Shall I stop?'

'No.'

She lifted her head to bury it in his beard. It did not hurt. Muir had not harmed her inside and, save for the fire, the actual act had been something she had endured plenty of times before. Gillespie was now moving more carefully than he ever had in the past and that, at least, was a blessing in the darkness. She put her arms around his neck and tipped her hips up, felt him move faster and then, thank the Lord, conclude. When she pulled back a little he flung himself sideways on the bed and looked at her.

'You are sure I cannot kill him?'

'I am, Gillespie. You are sure there was seed?'

'Sure.'

'Good. I think, perhaps, I should rest now.'

'Aye. Aye, of course.' He leaped from the bed and began yanking on his clothes. 'I will call Aila. She will be so glad to see you alert. And I will go and see how the men do with the foundations of our new hall. You would like to live here at Rosemarkie, Cora, wouldn't you? It is very pretty down by the sea and warmer, they say, with the Black Isle hills behind. And we are nearer to the dolphins.'

'I like the dolphins.'

'Good. That is good. You can watch them from here, once you are better of course, and . . .'

'Gillespie . . .'

'Aye?'

'Hush now.'

'Of course. Right. Yes. I'll go.' He darted back and kissed her awkwardly on the forehead. 'Rest well, wife.'

'I will.'

She meant it. She would rather not have to heal but heal she would and if her new skin was harder than her old, so much the better.

Chapter Eight

Dunkeld, November 1026

Sibyll woke to a soft, rhythmic noise that seemed to call to her from straight out of her childhood – not, for once, the shriek of Wends bringing terror but a sweeter reminder of an earlier, happier time. She shifted and Duncan murmured and laid a gentle arm around her waist. It weighed against her stomach, which had seemed strangely unsettled recently, but it felt warm and secure all the same. Her husband was protective of her even in his sleep and she blessed him for it, but now the noise was niggling at her. What was it?

She sat up and edged aside the leather curtain across the window above the bed. White winter sun shot into the chamber and with it a cry of: 'Man the ropes!' Of course – the sound was that of oars in water and her whole body quivered with an echo of joy, for as a child it had always meant her father was home. Now she could hear men hallooing a welcome and scurrying to help draw the boat into the landing stages. They sounded pleased to see this craft, whatever it was, and Sibyll felt a pleasurable stir of curiosity. What riches might it bring to quiet Dunkeld this morning?

She nudged her husband awake.

'There's a boat arrived, Duncan.'

'Huh?'

He squinted up at her as she scrabbled onto the bed to peer out of the window. Again her stomach turned but she cared little for there, on the sun-dappled river, was a glorious sight.

'*Two* boats!' she squealed. 'Big ones.'

Duncan laughed.

'It will be the trading craft. They always come around this time of year on their way home to Denmark for the winter.'

'Denmark?'

Sibyll eyed the boats with new joy, noting the fine carved dragons on the elegant figureheads and imagining them sailing proudly into her childhood home. But now men were leaping out and unloading crates and chests with practised ease and Alba seemed a fine enough place to be.

''Tis a market!' she cried and Duncan laughed again and pulled her down on top of him.

'It is indeed and if you are lucky, wife, I will buy you a bauble.'

'A bauble, Duncan? Is that all I'm worth?'

He pretended to consider then sobered and took her face gently between his big hands.

'Nay, Sibyll, you are worth all the jewels in Alba to me but I fear we will not find them for sale here.'

She kissed him quiet, guiltily aware of the weight of his devotion. He had been so good to her, so kind, and she had given him little in return, or little that she truly meant. She was a far worse person than he.

'But perhaps,' he was continuing, 'there will be a silversmith from whom we could buy settings for the jewels Grandfather gave you at our wedding. Would you like that, my love?'

Sibyll nodded. She would like that very much indeed and rang instantly for Elspeth, her maid, to dress her with all possible speed. They were not the only ones hurrying to rise, however, and by the time they reached the impromptu market at the water's edge most of the inhabitants of Crinan's monastery were already there, exclaiming over tools and cloth and trinkets. There were no coins in Alba yet but all had hacksilver and Dunkeld had rich goods of its own so there was plenty with which to trade.

Sibyll saw their cook in lively debate over a herd of small goats that had come dancing out of the rear boat, and the smith stroking a fine pair of bellows being displayed by a dark-skinned leatherworker. One man sold honey, another wine and a third a variety of nuts. Beside the stalls their wives had set a fire and were mulling the wine and toasting the smallest nuts in honey for a sweet treat that had the children flocking. The air was alive with chatter and Sibyll smiled to hear it, though the rich smells were churning her poor stomach.

'Honey nuts?' Duncan suggested.

She shook her head.

'It's a little early for me.'

Her husband looked at her askance but she had spotted a silversmith and pulled him eagerly in that direction. Detecting a lordly customer, the man leaped to his feet to greet them and was soon displaying all his finest wares. Sibyll's stomach settled and, at Duncan's urging, they chose a pair of fine shoulder-brooches in which to set King Malcolm's jewels.

'He will be delighted to see you display his gift so well,' Duncan said and Sibyll realised with a twinge that this expedition to the smith was as much to please the king as to please her. Then she reminded herself that did not mean it had to please her any the less and accepted the brooches graciously.

'Careful – careful, please.' A voice behind them sounded a little panicked and Sibyll looked round to see Brother Cullen fretting over two sacks being unloaded from the first boat, wringing his thin hands and darting about to supervise the process. 'A cart,' he snapped at a young novice at his side. 'And quick, before the sacks tear. Very poor quality hemp, very poor.'

The lad looked around in a panic of his own but then a tall, slim lady with the darkest hair Sibyll had ever seen placed a hand on his shoulder and said, 'Here, use mine.'

The boy snatched at the offer and as the sacks were laid into the trolley Cullen sighed in audible relief and turned to his saviour.

'Thank you, my lady. There is barley within and had the hemp split all would have been lost.'

Sibyll saw the lady suppress a smile.

'Do we not have barley at Dunkeld, Cullen?' she asked.

So she knew him then. Sibyll looked at the woman more closely for she was sure she had never seen her here before. She was older than she had seemed at first glance but very beautiful with fine cheekbones and eyes as bewitchingly dark as her hair.

'We do,' Cullen was agreeing, 'but this is from the coast. I have had it brought in specially to breathe new flavour into my latest usquebauch.'

'Ah. A worthy cause then.'

Abbot Crinan came hurrying over.

'It is indeed,' he agreed, an undeniable bounce in his step. Maybe he, like Sibyll, was pleased by this break from routine. 'Brother Cullen's uiskie grows famous, you know. I have had men send asking for some from Dunedin and Partick and even England.'

Cullen flushed violently and fussed at his sacks.

'And further yet,' he said, though more to the barley than the abbot.

'What's that?' Crinan demanded.

Cullen coughed.

'Further yet, Abbot, for I had a letter the other day from . . . from Moray.'

'Moray?' Crinan's eyes narrowed. 'What did *they* want?'

'My expertise.'

'The cheek!'

'A man called Gillespie is starting up a distillery at a place called Rosemarkie and has asked for my help. He's offered to pay handsomely and apparently this Rosemarkie is right on the sea so, so ...' He trailed off as he saw Crinan's dark expression. 'I will say no, of course. Will I?'

'You will,' Crinan thundered. 'This Gillespie is married to the MacDuff girl and could be a threat to us all.'

Cullen cowered and Sibyll felt sorry for him but then a curious thing happened. The dark-haired lady put a hand on Crinan's arm and he stilled and looked to her.

'It might not be such a bad idea to send him, Crinan,' she said, her voice soft and sweet. 'He could find out exactly what is going on up there above the Mounth without anyone suspecting a thing.'

Sibyll looked towards Duncan.

'Who is this?' she whispered, but now Crinan was spluttering and nodding and agreeing.

'That's true enough. And you'd like that, wouldn't you, Cullen, a trip? New barleys, new waters, new peats?'

He looked delighted.

'I would, Abbot, truly – if you think I can be of use.'

'I believe you can. It's a fine idea – a uiskie-spy! I should have thought of it sooner. Come, let us discuss this further.'

He strode for the abbey, beckoning Cullen to follow, but the monk looked stricken.

'Oh, but, my lady, we have taken your cart. What about your own goods?'

'They will only be light. I can manage with a basket, truly. What I look for is too costly to buy much of anyway.'

Sibyll was intrigued for the woman was standing by a herb-seller who could surely have little luxurious to offer. She edged forward and the lady, noting it, gave her a ready smile.

'You wish to know which herbs could be so fine?' Sibyll blushed but nodded. 'See here.' She indicated a tiny copper tub, which the seller lifted reverently. 'This is chilli, all the way from Byzantium. It is very good for agues and it smells of fire.'

The seller lifted the lid and Sibyll's new acquaintance nodded her forward so she leaned in and sniffed. A musky, dry scent curled up her nostrils and prickled at her eyes. Her unsteady stomach recoiled instantly and she clapped a hand over her mouth.

'I'm sorry, I . . . '

She was going to be sick. She could feel it rising in her gorge and stumbled away. There seemed to be people everywhere and she dashed desperately for the bushes further up the slope but, to her shame, did not make it in time. Her stomach was, at least, too empty to produce more than a little bile but everyone was staring and she felt mortified. Then a cool hand was on her forehead and someone was murmuring soothingly in her ear and she looked into dark eyes and felt strangely reassured.

'Who are you?' she asked.

'I am Morag, my lady. Are you well?'

''Tis my stomach. It rebels, especially in the mornings.'

Morag nodded.

'It will.'

'Why?'

'Because it looks to me as if you are with child. Is that possible?'

'I have wondered,' Sibyll admitted, 'but I had no way of being sure.'

'I think you can be sure now.' Morag turned and relinquished Sibyll into a hovering Duncan's solid care. 'Congratulations, my lord Prince,' she said and then, with a wink, she was gone.

'Congratulations?' he asked, his eyes wide with hope.

'I believe that I may be carrying your child,' Sibyll admitted.

'Lord be praised! Truly?' She nodded. 'Why, you, my beautiful, beautiful wife, are a marvel.'

And with that he picked her up and spun her round so that

70

her poor stomach churned once more but she cared not. Now, it seemed, she had truly given Duncan something of value and she was endlessly glad of it. The sun was shining on Dunkeld, Brother Cullen was poised to check on their enemies and she held Alba's next heir in her belly. The trading ship had truly brought riches to her life this morning.

Chapter Nine

Rosemarkie, February 1027

'Right,' Gillespie said, rubbing his hands and trying to be jovial –
a look that did not suit him. 'Uiskie.'

The thin monk looked him up and down.

'Uiskie,' he agreed non-committally.

Gillespie shuffled and with a sigh Cora hefted herself out of
her chair to join the two men by the fire. Her babe was due any
day and she had to tuck her hands beneath the great swell of her
belly to waddle (there was no kinder word for it) forward, but
she carried her burden with pride for, however hard it had been
gained, it was her future. And now Brother Cullen was come from
Dunkeld to discuss uiskies and they must make sure his great
knowledge was used to their advantage – both in producing their
new spirit and in their quest for the throne.

'I hear tell,' Cora said to the young man, 'that you have a great
gift for flavours. God, it seems, has blessed your tongue with more
sensitivity than others.'

The monk flushed a dark red and Cora saw pock-marks where
he must once have suffered from pimples.

'You are too kind, my lady, but I am sure I am no more blessed
than all God's people.'

More so than me, Cora thought bitterly, but this man had access to King Malcolm and she kept her smile fixed brightly upon him.

'Every man and woman has something special to bring to God's service, Brother, but it honours Him that you are working hard to make the most of your particular talent.'

'You think so?'

'Of course. You blend malt with peat in perfect harmony, or so I am told.' She saw his pride at that in the way he held himself straighter. Gillespie was watching the exchange carefully but thankfully was leaving it to her. 'You must come and see our own little distillery, Brother. My husband has equipped it well, I think, though we would greatly value your opinion as we have not the expertise to make it shine as it should. We are blessed indeed that God has seen fit to send you to us.'

The young man looked thoroughly overcome at this compliment and let Cora lead him, docile as a lamb, to the distillery at the back of the monastery. He was almost certainly here as a spy for Abbot Crinan but if he came with the skill to make good uiskie then Gillespie had decided it was worth the risk. Anything to get one up on Muir.

'What, really, is there to see here save the dolphins?' he'd told Cora. 'And perhaps we can learn things from him too.'

Now Brother Cullen rushed into the big room, exclaiming over the mash tun and the drying kiln and caressing the big copper still as other men might a beautiful woman.

'It will do?' Gillespie asked after too long in silence for his impatient spirit.

'Oh, it will do very well,' Brother Cullen agreed eagerly, 'and your water is excellent.' He plunged his hands into a pailful brought in earlier. 'See the colour.' He lifted his hands to let it run through them and Cora peered at the dull, brown liquid Cullen was lifting to his lips as if it were manna. 'Such peat! With this you should be able to make a finer uiskie than any I can achieve at Dunkeld. And you have the sea too!'

'The sea helps?' Gillespie asked.

'Oh, aye!' Cullen agreed. 'It breathes depths into the process.'

'Depth?' Gillespie echoed faintly.

'How?' Cora asked.

Cullen waved his hand airily.

'That is for God to know and us to enjoy.'

'Of course, of course. How clever you are. And how blessed our monks are to have you here.'

Gillespie nodded two keen young novices forward, bobbing and singing Brother Cullen's praises. Cora saw the visitor flush again beneath their enthusiastic adulation and knew they had him.

'Those two are sharp?' she asked Gillespie quietly.

'The abbot says they are the finest minds in the monastery.'

'Good. They will learn fast then.'

'They will. Thank you, Cora, but I can take it from here. Should you not be resting?'

'Resting?' She wrinkled her nose. 'Resting does not suit me. The babe will come when it is ready.'

'The babe will surely come when *God* is ready?' Brother Cullen suggested, looking up momentarily from the buckets of barley malting in the corner.

'That too,' Cora agreed obediently.

And it seemed God was readier than she'd realised for that very night at dinner she felt the first twinges low down in her belly and could not suppress a cry.

'Cora, are you well?'

Gillespie leaned across Brother Cullen, dining in the seat of honour between them.

'Quite well,' she agreed.

The cooks were bringing out roast capercaillie and as she'd had a particular yearning for its rich, resinous meat these last weeks she did not wish to miss out. Another twinge came, a clearer cramp this time, but she was ready for it and bit back a gasp as her bird was served.

'Your time must be close,' Gillespie said, still watching her.

She could only nod and jab at her meat to distract herself from the jolts of pain.

'The Lady Duncan is also with child,' Brother Cullen said, out of nowhere.

Gillespie turned his eyes instantly to his guest.

'Prince Duncan's new wife?'

'The same. King Malcolm is delighted. He has consulted the best midwives in Alba and all say it will be a son.'

'Of course they do,' Cora said

'My lady?'

'Would you tell the king that his heir is going to be a mere girl?'

'Not his heir,' Cullen pointed out primly, 'but his heir's heir.'

'And yet,' Cora said thickly as another cramp hit, 'does our country not practise alternate succession?'

'She *did*.'

This time Cora couldn't disguise a cry. Cullen leaped up in alarm, Gillespie just a step behind.

'It is coming, is it not? *My* heir is coming?'

Cora nodded dumbly.

'Praise God,' Cullen managed weakly.

'Praise God you don't have to bear it,' Cora snapped at him and he looked startled.

'As you said earlier, my lady, we all have our own talents. Mine is making uiskie. Yours, I hope, is bearing children for your lord.'

Cora wanted to contradict him in so many ways but a new pain robbed her of breath and in the space of it Gillespie, with uncharacteristic wisdom, had Aila whisk her away to their chamber.

The labouring seemed to go on forever. As night unfolded into day and crawled desperately back into night again Cora felt as if her body was trying to turn itself inside out. For hour after hour she paced the room, clawing at the walls until her fingers bled with scratching away the plaster. Her red hair, grown back now to shoulder-length, clouded around her head like flames until Aila bound it back with linen.

The poor girl followed Cora, encouraging her to lean against her and use her strength, but they were both tiring. A midwife came from somewhere in the hills bringing herbal potions and unguents to rub on Cora's pulsing belly but they did little save make her sick. She felt locked in an endless agony so intense that she prayed merely to be burning again.

'You must rest, my lady,' the midwife all but begged as they stumbled exhausted into the second dawn of her labouring.

'Rest!' Cora screamed at her. 'How can I rest?'

'Between the cramps. You are making it worse.'

'I am?'

Cora forced herself to stand still, to breathe.

'You are,' Aila agreed gently. 'The babe will come when it is ready as you have always said. You must surrender to that.'

Cora pressed her forehead against the bedpost. Another cramp was coming.

'I have never been very good at surrendering,' she said wryly and then there it was again, tearing her up inside so that she thought she might never rest again.

'Lie down, please,' the midwife urged when the pains had passed and Cora was panting.

'It hurts my back.'

'I know but just for a moment. Let me see where the child is.'

Cora nodded, clambered onto the bed and rolled reluctantly onto her back. Her spine felt as if it must surely be sticking out of her skin it was so raw but, if so, no one said anything. The midwife disappeared between her legs and Cora wrapped her hands deep into the furs as another pain came towards her like a horse at full gallop. She fought not to kick the poor woman but knew not if she succeeded.

'My lady,' she heard eventually, 'I can see the child.'

'God be praised!' Cora opened her eyes and looked down at the midwife. 'It is on the way then?'

'Sort of.'

'What do you mean?'

'I'm afraid, my lady, that I can see the feet. That is why your back hurts so. The baby is the wrong way round.'

Aila ran to Cora, clasping her so tightly that Cora knew this must be bad news. She stared up at her.

'What does that mean, Aila?'

'It means it will be hard.'

Cora almost laughed.

'It is hard already.'

'Harder,' the midwife said grimly. 'But I'm going to help. Lady Aila, run to your master for goose fat, quick now. Tell him I will see this child safe.'

'And the mother?' Cora whispered.

'*And* the mother,' the midwife said determinedly. 'Now, when the next pain comes, you push.'

Afterwards, Gillespie told Cora that her screams had been so loud the monks had feared the apocalypse and all been on their knees, praying for God's mercy.

'They'd have been better praying for my health,' Cora grumbled.

Somehow, with the aid of the foul-smelling goose fat and a strong arm, the midwife had eased her baby into the world with them both whole or, at least, like to be so again one day. Cora could barely move, cried when she had to go to the latrine, and needed down cushions to sit upon, but truly she cared not for she held her child in her arms.

'A boy,' Gillespie breathed, when he saw him. 'An ultimate heir.'

Cora clutched her baby close. An ultimate heir was what Macbeth had promised her but Macbeth was long gone. She had not heard from him again and no longer looked for his return. This babe was hers. He had had to struggle as hard as her, God bless him, for he had come out blue and dark-lipped, but at the midwife's insistent slaps had coughed and spluttered and then lustily wailed into life. Cora had never heard a sweeter sound. Her son was a fighter, thank the Lord; *her* fighter.

'What shall we call him?' Gillespie asked now.

They looked at each other. The answer should of course be Gillespie but Cora cared not.

'He is called Lachlan, after my father.'

'But . . . '

'He is called Lachlan, for it is his destiny to avenge his grand-father's murder and when he is King of Alba all will know so.'

'King of Alba?'

'Exactly and with you – his father – at his side, set above all other men.'

Gillespie squared his shoulders, almost as if he stood behind the coveted throne already.

'Lachlan,' he said, rolling it over his thick tongue. 'It is a fine name.'

'Lachlan Gillespie,' she allowed and at that he smiled.

'It sounds well. May I?'

He held out his arms and she had to force herself to relinquish her son. Somehow all the pain of both his conception and his birthing had turned themselves as inside out as her poor body and emerged as pure, fierce, urgent love and she was grateful when Lachlan cried and Gillespie handed him hastily back. She drew aside her shift to let him feed. The scars from the burning torch laced across her breast and pulled the skin unnaturally tight but the nipple was soft and the baby's tiny mouth found it and latched on keenly. Cora felt her milk start to flow and smiled but then came a knock at the door. They all froze. It came again, soft but certain, and Gillespie moved over and opened it a crack.

'You!'

'I hear it is a boy, Gillespie. I hear you have a boy.'

Cora had not heard that dread voice since it had roared at her above the fiery pain and she shrank back against her pillows, pulling Aila onto the bed so that she could serve as shield for the still feeding baby.

'Go away, Muir,' Gillespie said.

'Can I see him?'

'No.'

'Please. He is the ultimate heir, brother. He is Alba's destiny. You have done so well and Lady Cora too.'

'Cora is exhausted.'

'Of course. I won't be long. I wish to . . . to make amends. We have great work to do now. With this child we can challenge King Malcolm. We can knock Duncan aside and take the throne of Alba for Moray.'

Gillespie looked nervously back at Cora, who forced herself to sit up a little.

'He is right, Gillespie. Let him come in.'

'Really?'

She looked down at Lachlan, his lips budding around her nipple and his tiny hand resting contentedly against her scarred skin. How could this helpless child carry such hopes? And yet she knew already that he did – and not just Muir's but her own. She and Kendrick had sworn at their father's death that one day they would have vengeance on King Malcolm and this new Lachlan *was* that vengeance.

'Really. Let him come in.'

She drew Lachlan off her breast and pulled her shift back into place. The baby gave a mew of protest and his lips worked at the air but then, with a soft snort, he fell asleep. Cora smiled down at him, drawing strength. Lachlan was why she was still here. He was the reason she'd survived this and she fixed her eyes firmly on the doorway as Muir stepped through it.

'My best wishes to you, Lady Gillespie.' She raised an eyebrow. 'Truly. And to your son.'

'Thank you. My husband and I consider ourselves very blessed.'

'Aye. Aye, of course. You have Alba's future in your charge.'

'We know it.'

'And I will assist in seeing the boy one day to his rightful place.'

'Thank you.' It was what she so badly wanted to hear though looking at her rapist was almost too much for her to bear. 'I am tired now.'

'Aye. Aye, of course.' Muir looked very out of place in this feminine chamber but he was determined to make his point. 'We can forget the past now?'

Cora put up a hand.

'Not forget it, no. But we can put it behind us.'

'Good.' Muir looked to Gillespie. 'I hear Duncan's wife is whelping too. We should attack.'

'Attack where?'

'Dunkeld. It is an easy target. We will whip their damned cross from the church and let our lion rampage as it should. And we must kill Duncan for Malcolm can hardly pass the throne to a dead man, can he? It is time, Gillespie – time to show Alba that Moray is a force to be reckoned with. We are the line of Aed and we have the ultimate heir.'

He gestured to Lachlan and Cora tightened her grasp on him. She had never thought to look to Muir as an ally but it seemed that in this at least his aims met her own and she must steel herself, for now, to use him as her sword.

'You have my blessing on this honourable plan,' she said stiffly.

Muir looked surprised but seized on her compliance.

'Thank you, my lady. Brother – a drink to wet the baby's head? And then we make plans.'

Gillespie hesitated but Cora nodded him away and with clear reluctance he went. She could only pray they would not fall to quarrelling for, much as she disliked it, she needed these rough men for her own aims now. Even so, as the door closed on them she let out a long breath she hadn't even known she was holding and clutched Lachlan close, breathing in strength with his soft baby scent. He was so wee, so helpless, but, without even knowing it yet, he was so very, very powerful. It was both a torment and a source of joy.

Chapter Ten

Dunkeld, June 1027

Sibyll started awake, the taste of ash on her tongue and the sound of screams echoing around her head. Instinctively she clutched her knees to her chest, but as they met the bulge of her ripe belly sense began to penetrate her muddled dreams and she fought her way out of her dark past. She was in Dunkeld with Duncan and Crinan and all their monks and soldiers. She was safe.

She shook her head at her own foolishness. Maybe it was the babe snatching at her mind as well as her body. It seemed to want not just her womb but her shaky legs and her sickly stomach and her poor bladder. Especially her bladder. Feeling an all-too-familiar press of need, she rolled herself out of bed with a groan. Even during summer in Alba the nights were chill and she winced as her bare feet hit the cold boards. Kneeling with some difficulty, she felt under the bed for the pot, unwilling to wake Elspeth though the swell of her belly made it nigh on impossible to bend low enough to reach.

Her fingers felt the earthen handle and gratefully she pulled it out. Her eyes had adjusted to the darkness and there was enough moonlight coming through the wooden shutters for her to see her maid snoring contentedly on her pallet-bed. The sight made her smile and, thank the Lord, banished the last of the nightmare and she hefted her shift up and tried to hover over the pot. Damn, but it was difficult without losing hold of the fabric or toppling backwards. What she needed was a taller, stronger pot that she could actually sit on as she relieved herself. She made a note to talk to someone about it tomorrow, though perhaps not Duncan. He'd been very nervy since Brother Cullen had returned from the north and was forever holed up with Crinan or leading drills.

A little of Sibyll's unease returned. The men seemed to be always at sword-play these days and it disturbed her. She should find comfort that Dunkeld's defences were so well-prepared but the sense of danger which the men's noisy training brought to her home made her sick with childish fear. She had asked both Duncan and Crinan why they felt the need to train so keenly but they had ducked straight answers as cleverly as they ducked sword-tips in the yard.

'Routine training,' Crinan had told her airily.

'We must keep the men fit,' Duncan had agreed, but she knew they were hiding something. Perhaps it was this and not just the babe that had brought back her nightmare.

She stored the pot away and felt gratefully for her covers, wishing Duncan were here to keep the bed warm. He was a comforting presence for he slept soundly and, if half-roused by her return to bed, would draw her in against him and settle back to sleep so easily that she would find herself doing so too. With her birthing due very soon, however, Crinan had decreed that he should sleep in the next-door chamber, to give her space. She'd been furious until she'd discovered the abbot's first wife had died birthing Maldred and protested no more – though worried no less.

Now she pulled the fur-lined blanket tight around her, trying to mimic Duncan's warmth, and prayed for sleep. It did not come. She heard the monks shuffling from their beds for Lauds then their voices rising pure into the night and she lay stroking her belly while the babe, restless too, turned within. And that was when she heard it: hooves on the meadows. At first she thought it was just her mind playing tricks again but as the sound grew in volume she knew this was no nightmare and was up and pulling on her cloak instantly. Hooves in the night meant only one thing – trouble.

'Wake up!' she shouted at Elspeth.

The girl sat up, startled, but Sibyll was already yanking open her door. Duncan's chamber was empty but Bethan was coming to the door of the one beyond, her eyes wild.

'Sibyll. Oh, lord, Sibyll, they've come.'

It was the first time she'd ever seen the hard-faced lady of the house flustered.

'Who've come?'

'The Moray men. Just as he said they would.'

'Who said?' Sibyll ran forward to shake her mother-by-marriage. 'Who said that, Bethan?'

'I did.' Sibyll spun back and there in the doorway stood Brother Cullen, wearing an incongruous leather jerkin over his monk's robes and clutching a small axe. 'We must leave.'

'Leave? Why? Can we not hide in the church?'

For reply, Cullen tugged her to the main door, his usual formality abandoned in the charged mood of the night. Peering into the half-light, Sibyll saw men arranged in a semi-circle before the church door and realised that her worst fears had come to pass and her dear new home was now a battlefield. Above them St Andrew's cross snapped in the wind, as if waving the invaders furiously away, but they were paying no attention and their dark force drew closer by the minute.

'Where can we go?' she gasped.

'To Morag,' Cullen said. Bethan spat with fury but Cullen, for once, stood up to her. 'It's the Abbot's orders.'

'Morag?' Sibyll asked, recalling the dark-haired lady who had first spotted her pregnancy and whom she had not seen since. 'Where does she live?'

No one answered. Sibyll heard the rumble of a war chant growing louder as the enemy closed in on them. How many men had ridden in from Moray and how many did Crinan have to keep them back? He kept a goodly army for an abbey but it could not be more than fifty. If these invaders had come in their hundreds, they would be helpless before them.

'What will they do with us?' she whimpered.

'What do you think they will do?' Bethan snapped, eyes fiery and looking suddenly very like her royal father. 'They are fierce over the Mounth. Half-Viking, they say, and only just Christian.'

'That's not true,' Cullen protested, but Bethan silenced him with a glare.

'Those men out there attacked the previous Mormaer's hall at night, as they attack us now. They killed Mormaer Finlay and his wife and all his men. And they took his son's bride for themselves on the very night of her wedding.'

Sibyll shook.

'But we are both married, Bethan.'

'At the moment,' she said grimly. 'Let's go.'

'Where?' Sibyll gasped and again came the mysterious reference to Morag but there was no time now to ask more. She grabbed her jewel-casket and hurried after. She would not be trapped again; she could not bear it.

They slid from the bower and ran, heads low, round the back of the farm buildings. The animals were squealing in fear and the labourers were grabbing hoes and scythes to join the warriors in the fray. Behind them Sibyll could hear the clash of swords as the attack began and shuddered to think of Crinan and Duncan and Maldred fighting for their lives – and hers – so few paces away.

'How are they so prepared?' she gasped as they ducked along the line of piggeries.

'Because I warned them they must be,' Cullen said over his shoulder.

'That is why there have been more drills recently?'

'And more swords sharpened and more arrows made and men urged to sleep apart from their wives – aye.'

'But how did you know?'

'I was in Moray, remember, teaching the monks at Rosemarkie the art of decent uiskie. And it *will* be decent, I tell you, with the conditions up there.' He paused. 'Do you know they have . . . '

'Cullen, the attack!'

'Of course, sorry.' He started moving again, heading for the far end of the compound. 'I happened to be there when Lady Gillespie, King Malcolm's own niece, birthed a boy-child, Lachlan, and I heard the men saying that he gave them sound reason to attack Duncan.'

'Why?'

'He is, so they say, the ultimate Alban heir.'

Sibyll's hands went to her belly as if she might cover the ears of the babe within. Her breath was coming hard and fast now and she was grateful when they paused in the shadow of the distillery.

'*I* carry Alba's heir,' she panted.

'You carry *an* heir, aye – a Constantin heir.'

'So?'

'It is a fine thing, my lady, but theirs mingles the blood of Constantin through the MacDuff line with the blood of Aed through the Moray line. It is a powerful combination.'

'But Duncan is Tanaise.'

'Which is why, my lady, they attack him. Can you go on?'

'Where?'

'To Morag,' Bethan snarled, striding into the trees.

'You know who she is then?'

'Everyone knows who she is,' she threw over her shoulder. 'Now hurry up.'

Cullen was plucking nervously at her gown and Sibyll saw that she was queen-in-waiting no more but just a body to be moved before she brought danger to them all. Wrapping her hands beneath her belly as if she might take hold of her courage with her unborn child, she pushed her bag of jewels to her back, picked up her feet and ran after the others.

Her heart was pounding with exertion and fear and the sickening awareness that she had been lured by pretty Dunkeld and her state wedding into thinking Alba civilised, sophisticated, safe. Now she remembered the wild moors of Fife and the fearsome men of Dunedin and the uncompromising control exerted by King Malcolm and saw that she'd been wrong. This was the land where kings rarely held their throne more than ten years, where bloodshed was an intrinsic part of inheritance, and where men ruled by the sword. Crinan had warned her of this. He'd even warned her that she might be a widow before she bore a son and tonight that could come to pass. Indeed, tonight she might be lucky to birth a son at all.

They broke through the trees and took a rough herder's path round the bottom of a sloping hill to the north-east of the abbey. The cries of men and clash of swords grew fainter as they pushed on but they did not stop until they were a long way round the protective line of the hill and Sibyll begged for rest. Bethan tutted and Elspeth squirmed but Cullen came over and put a gentle arm around Sibyll's shoulders. She leaned gratefully against him, gulping breath into her seared lungs and heard him give a strange, low sigh.

'You did well to get us away, Cullen, thank you.'

'We are not safe yet.'

'Where is Morag?'

'The Loch of Lowes, just around the curve of the hill.'

Sibyll nodded, remembering. She had ridden out to the loch with Duncan before she had grown too fat with his child for such pursuits.

'Why there?'

87

'You'll see. You can go on?'

'If you'll help me?'

'Of course. Take my arm.'

So she did. Finding it thin but strong, she leaned gratefully upon it and they set off again. The sun was coming up, casting pretty kisses of light across the grasslands and any other day it would be beautiful but today they all walked with their heads down, ears strained for sounds of pursuit.

'Just around this bend,' Cullen assured them and sure enough as the path unwound Cora suddenly saw the Loch of Lowes stretching out beneath the pink sun. She looked hopefully along the shingle but saw no dwellings.

'Morag?'

'She's at the end of the beach. Can you make it?'

Sibyll crept out on to the shingle, painfully aware of it crunching loudly beneath her feet. They were too far away to hear the battle now but she was tensed for the sounds of pursuit and felt desperately exposed with the early sun casting its cheery light upon their bedraggled group. To her surprise Bethan hung back and it was left to Elspeth to lead them.

'Run ahead,' Cullen urged her. 'Run ahead and ring the bell.'

'Bell?'

Sibyll looked fearfully at Cullen. Morag had seemed kind, calm and reassuring when she had briefly met her at the trading craft but there had, nonetheless, been something unsettlingly ethereal about her.

'It is quite safe,' Cullen assured her kindly. 'See.'

He gestured to where Elspeth was tugging on a rope in a tree. A bell jangled out and then another and another and looking up, Sibyll saw the tree was full of them.

'She lives up there?'

'No!' Cullen almost laughed. 'Out there.'

Sibyll followed his pointing finger and past the bend in the loch she saw a round building crowned with neat thatch that rose in a pretty curve over an arched door. To its left stood a strange wooden tower, higher than the tip of the roof and, most peculiarly of all, the whole thing sat out in the water, perched upon wooden posts with their feet in the loch some twenty paces from the shore. Sibyll cast around for a boat but there was none.

'Watch,' Cullen said softly and Sibyll obeyed as the woman she had met just once before appeared, ducking out of the doorway and straightening up like a vision from a legend. She looked out across the water and raised both hands palm outwards.

'They have come then?' she called, her voice soft and sad.

'They have come,' Cullen confirmed.

'One moment.'

Morag moved to the side of the little house and Sibyll watched, unable to believe her eyes, as she turned a handle and the odd tower began to lower, revealing itself to be not a tower at all but a bridge. It came slowly down and Sibyll glanced back up the beach, terrified this crazy escape might come to nothing at the last minute, but they were still alone at the lochside. The bridge clicked into place and then Elspeth was upon it, running towards Morag. Sibyll looked to Bethan to go next but Crinan's wife shook her head.

'You go.'

'You will follow?'

'I think not.'

Cullen put out a hand to her.

'She is not, you know, his, his . . . '

'I know, but she beguiles him all the same. I shall take my chances on the lochside, thank you, for I know it better than any damned Moray men.'

Cullen looked panicked but Bethan was gone, slipping into the trees like a sprite, and he turned back to Sibyll.

'You will come?'

'Of course.'

Morag's little house, or crannog as she called it in her musical voice, was every bit as charming inside as it was out and for a moment Sibyll forgot there was war at Dunkeld, forgot her aching feet and her tight belly, and looked around, enchanted. At the centre of the circular room was a fire enclosed within an iron box that glowed with comfortingly steady heat. On top sat a pan of porridge and a wide pipe led up to the apex of the roof and out into the air so that there was no smoke to clog either vision or lungs.

Two semi-circular benches stood either side of the fire, high-backed and padded with sheepskins dyed in soft yellows and greens. To one side stood a low, wood-framed bed topped with an embroidered blanket in the same pastel shades as the seat cushions and on the other a long table was covered with bowls of all sizes. Knives were housed in a neat holder at one end and all manner of herbs and powders stood in pots along the front. Behind, more herbs hung from the walls to dry, casting a fresh, fragrant scent around the whole room.

'What a beautiful home,' she breathed.

'Thank you,' Morag said. 'Come, sit. You must be hungry and sore.' She ushered Sibyll solicitously onto one of the benches by the fire-box. 'Your time must be near?'

'Very.'

'You did well to get this far on foot.'

In a rush the troubling memories came back to her.

'What do you think is happening at Dunkeld?' she asked fearfully.

'Crinan is winning.'

'You can see that?'

Morag laughed.

'No! I am no magician, my lady. But nor do I see the point in tormenting ourselves with negative possibilities.'

'Oh.' Sibyll stared at the flames contained within the fire-box and, despite her fear, her eyelids started to droop.

'Perhaps you would like to lie on the bed?' Mora suggested.

'Oh, no. I . . . ' Sibyll felt a twinge low down in her belly. 'Maybe just for a minute,' she conceded and let herself be led across.

She sank into the mattress, every part of her sighing in relief at its softness – every part save her belly, which twinged again. Cramped even. She put a hand to it.

'It could just be an early warning,' Morag said.

Sibyll looked up at her.

'I pray so.'

But she saw in Morag's eyes that she did not think it likely and with a stronger twinge coming Sibyll had to agree.

'Early warning of what?' Cullen asked squeakily. 'Not the babe? Please not the royal babe. Not now.'

But it was. Sibyll, it seemed, would have her child tonight and could only pray between birth pains that his father would survive to see him.

'Victory! Victory for Dunkeld!'

The cry came up from the beach and Sibyll felt tears spring to her eyes as they had not done even when her son had been placed in her arms. Victory, praise God! This was not like the last time. She was not to be left cowering from the world and that knowledge felt like a rich blessing on both herself and her baby. She clutched him close against her as Elspeth and Morag ran to the door to welcome the messenger.

The birthing had been hard but fast and, if nothing else, a welcome distraction from war. Morag had been a marvel, giving Sibyll a herbal drink that had seemed to dull the edges of the pains and encouraging her to walk and to push with the cramps and to birth the baby while standing, with Elspeth poised to catch it. Cullen had hovered outside the door throughout, praying to God for mercy, though whether for Sibyll, the baby or himself it had been hard to tell. Sibyll had remembered at one low point that he had lost his mother in his own birthing but had pushed the thought swiftly away. Whatever the cause, it had been Cullen who had cried when, in the late afternoon, the baby had been born.

'You did it,' he kept saying. 'You made a baby – another human.' It had seemed churlish to say that she had been making it for the last nine months and anyway his awe had been too touching to spoil with denials until he'd said: 'You did it better than the other one.'

'Other one?'

'The Moray woman. Lady . . . '

But that was when they heard the cries from the beach and instantly far-off babies had been forgotten.

''Tis the abbot himself,' Elspeth called from the door now. 'He is riding high up in his stirrups, my lady, his bloody sword held aloft and a St Andrew's cross flying high above him. Oh, and Morag has run to him and Crinan is swinging her up on his horse before him like a dragon-slayer of old.'

Elspeth giggled with glee and Sibyll smiled and waited in her childbed, half expecting the pair to ride into the crannog at full gallop. In the end, though, Crinan crept in, helmet beneath his arm and brushing sweat apologetically from his high brow with his white and blue banner.

'You are victorious, Abbot,' Sibyll said.

'As are you, daughter. May I see him? May I see Alba's heir?' Smiling, Sibyll beckoned him forward and presented her son. 'I knew I'd made the right choice in you,' Crinan said reverently. 'I shall see you showered in jewels.'

'You are too kind, Abbot, for 'tis God's hand in this. And Duncan's seed. He is well?' Crinan nodded keenly. 'And the others? Your captains and, er, Maldred?'

'All well. Weary, aye, but victory eases a man's bones like nothing else. Many *are* dead though and Dunkeld is much scarred. It might be best, if Morag is willing, if you stay here a day or two.'

'Duncan will come?'

'Of course. He wanted to ride with me now but I asked him to stay and command the troops.'

'I see,' Sibyll said, though she saw Crinan's eyes slide towards Morag and suspected there were other reasons for him taking this mission from his son. 'Bethan stayed on the lochside,' she added, though he had not asked.

'She would,' Crinan said. 'I will find her – if, that is, she isn't back at Dunkeld already.'

'How did you win?'

He blinked.

'What do you know of war, my dear?'

'Plenty, Abbot. I was with my brother throughout his training as a housecarl when we first came to England and he told me much of a warrior's ways.'

'I see. Of course. Well, I wish I could dazzle you with our military tactics but I am an honest man and in truth I am not sure how it happened. Indeed, I thought at one point that we might be doomed for there were so many of them and they seemed to be all over us. We were backed against the church wall and I honestly thought we might all die right there but then ... ' He frowned. 'Then their leader, Mormaer Muir, a murderous creature with a jet-dark brow, fell from his horse. It was a spear between the shoulderblades. Must have been one of our men who'd crept in round the back of them, though no one is claiming the glory. Perhaps the poor man died in his turn but if so he will surely go to heaven for that turned the tide for us.

'Muir's men were shocked and Duncan, seeing it, led the charge and led it well. The next thing we knew they'd turned tail and run for the northern road. We have left their dead beneath a white flag but I doubt they'll be back for them. We'll have to dig a pit. Or maybe make a mound – a victory cairn to mark the glorious day of this wee one's blessed arrival.'

Sibyll's heart quailed at the thought of a pile of bones marking her precious baby's birth but better enemy bones, she supposed, than their own.

'What shall we call him, Abbot?'

He looked at her and gently shook his head.

'Surely you know that?'

'Duncan?' she suggested hopefully but he shook his head again.

'Malcolm. The baby must be Malcolm and one day he will rule all Alba as Malcolm III. I chose you, Lady Duncan, for your strength and this is why. The very manner of wee Malcolm's birth tells you of the world he must one day fight to rule over and that he cannot do it alone.'

'He has his father.'

'He does but you must see by now, my lady, that Duncan is not so assured a prince as he might be. I apologise if I brought you here under any false apprehensions but it was done for a good reason – it was done for this.'

He put out a hand to baby Malcolm who clasped his tiny fingers around Crinan's bloody one. Sibyll looked from her son to his grandfather. Part of her wanted to crawl under Morag's deliciously soft covers and ignore the abbot and his huge expectations, but if there was one thing life had taught her already it was that you couldn't just hide or you would end up ghosted with the ash of others' victory. You had to step out and move on.

She looked down at the child in her arms – her son, her Malcolm. She never wanted him to be tainted by the fear that had torn her own childhood apart. His rise must be as secure and easy and well managed as she could possibly make it and she must draw on his royalty – and her own – to be certain of that. Slowly she reached out and took the banner from her father-by-marriage. It was a little torn but clean and as bright as a springtime sky. Carefully she wrapped it around her baby. He squirmed, but then dropped Crinan's finger to grasp at the pretty fabric and Sibyll smiled.

'I will see Malcolm to his throne,' she said. 'Whatever it takes, Father, I will see him there.'

Chapter Eleven

Rosemarkie, February 1030

'A feast, I think,' Gillespie said, throwing open the shutters so that the freezing morning mist seemed to rush inside as if keen to get into bed and hide from its own misery.

Cora shivered and dug lower under the covers, peering in disbelief at Gillespie who stood naked at the window.

'Are you not cold?'

'It is good Moray air, Cora.'

'It is *cold* Moray air.'

'You're too thin.'

'You're not.'

Gillespie's brow furrowed but then he chose to slap his big belly proudly.

'No, and I'm not cold either. A feast, Cora, to celebrate Lachlan's third birthday. It has been a hard winter and my men deserve a treat and what better occasion for it?'

'It would please him,' Cora conceded.

'Good. I will order him a special chair made – a lordly one like mine with an Aed lion carved into the back for he will one day be Mormaer in my place.'

'He will,' Cora agreed, noting that there was no further mention of kingship.

That had been Muir's obsession and Muir was gone, even his body left behind in the frenzied retreat from Dunkeld. Cora had asked Gillespie how his brother had died but he had been very hazy on details.

'I was in another part of the field, Cora, so did not see. He took a spear in the back, I'm told. One of theirs must have crept round our lines. It was a difficult battlefield, you see, in and out of the abbey buildings. It was hard to keep order.'

He'd avoided her eye, though, and spent an unusual amount of time in church for a man normally efficient in his worship, and Cora had wondered at this unseen enemy so conveniently placed. It had cost them the victory over Malcolm's Tanaise but had won Gillespie Moray and that, she suspected, had been all the victory he'd desired.

'You are surely not grieved that Muir is dead?' he'd demanded.

'I am not,' she'd told him firmly. 'It's strange to be suddenly in control, though.'

'You are Lady of Moray now, as you should be.'

'Aye,' she'd agreed, but without knowing it he'd put his finger on the precise nature of her unease.

When Muir had been Mormaer her life had still felt transitional, temporary, wrong. She'd spent her days looking for rescue from Macbeth but now, with Gillespie in charge and Lachlan to absorb her, life had become more defined – more real. It unsettled and even disappointed her that this was now her world. It was as if her royal blood was being diluted with every day that passed. She could almost prefer the fear of the early years for at least then there had been something to fight for.

She shook herself. This was foolish thinking. Macbeth had been gone almost five years, Kendrick too. Their names were never spoken in Gillespie's hall but occasionally she caught snippets of traders' gossip and learned they were still alive in Ireland.

It hurt more than she would ever admit and she had tutored herself to forget them as best she could. She had to bide her time for a few years until Lachlan was more of a man and then she could strike. It was the only thought that kept her going.

Reluctantly she sat up, drawing the blankets with her. For all his bluster Gillespie's slack skin was going blue, making it even less attractive than usual. Then again, maybe Macbeth had got fat in Dublin. She hoped so.

'I shall talk to the cooks,' she said.

'And I shall arrange a hunt. The snows are all but gone.'

'I might come.'

He frowned.

'I suppose you may as well.'

He turned away, finally reaching for his trews, and Cora closed her eyes against both the sight of him and his bitterness. No further child had been conceived despite his best efforts and she knew it increased his suspicions that Lachlan was Muir's son.

'You tell Lachlan of the plans,' she suggested, forcing herself out of bed. 'He'd like that.'

Gillespie fastened his belt.

'Aye,' he agreed thoughtfully. 'Aye, I will. But first ...' He pulled his buckle loose again. Damnation, why had she not stayed beneath the blankets? He grabbed for her, his cold hands roaming all over her and his lips pressing down on hers. 'I will get you with child, Cora,' he said and then he was picking her up and laying her back on the bed and entering her, not cruelly as he had back at the start of their forced marriage, but still with more determination than care.

Cora, fearful that it was her own indifference that kept her womb empty, tried to enjoy it but she was cold and his belly wobbled as he thrust and his face turned an odd purple with his own excitement and she was grateful when it was over.

'Stay and rest,' he suggested benevolently, happier now. 'I'll take Lachlan riding to check out the forests for game.'

So she did but it was less rest than avoidance and in the end she got up and got on. It was the best way.

The hall was not full for Lachlan's birthday feast the next week but those within it were lively and as the ale barrels emptied the sound rose. Cora looked to Lachlan, clamped proudly into his grand new seat, a half-scale replica of the Mormaer's own. The boy's green eyes were bruised with tiredness but he was determined to make the most of the promise that for this, his birthday, he could stay up as late as he wished. Even so, Cora saw him flinch as one of the men rose to demonstrate a new jig to roars of encouragement from his fellows. Most nobles had sent their excuses so the only women present were those brought in by the Mormaer as a treat for his lonely soldiers. Already they were being pulled onto laps and openly fondled. She leaned over and put her hand on her son's arm.

'Shall we go and have a wee party of our own, Lachy?' she suggested.

He looked at her suspiciously.

'Where?'

'In my chamber.'

When they'd moved back to Inverness she'd had a new, more private sleeping apartment built behind the hall and she would be glad to escape there.

'Not *my* chamber?'

'Oh no. Unless you want to go to bed?'

'No!'

'Well then, mine. Perhaps Aila will come too and bring some of her honey-cakes?'

Lachlan's eyes lit up and Aila came quickly forward, holding out her hand. His, however, were still clamped to his chair.

'Can I take this?'

'It's very heavy, Lachy.'

'I'm strong.'

'You are but the Mormaer's chair should really stay in the great hall as a symbol of his authority even when he is not seated upon it.'

'Oh.' He considered this. 'Can I sit on it again tomorrow?'

'Of course. To break your fast if you wish.'

'Really? Very well then.' He stood up gracefully, already every inch a miniature lord, and looked around the hall. 'Let's go. It's getting very noisy and, Mama, what are they doing to that poor lady?'

Cora turned him hastily aside.

'Just a funny game I think. Come.'

'But Father . . .'

Cora looked for Gillespie and saw his thick-set back amongst those cheering on the 'game'. She felt a prickle of anger that he could so easily forget Lachlan and then a burst of relief that he might slake his eternal appetite on someone else tonight.

'Father is controlling his men,' she lied easily. 'I'm sure he will come and kiss you later.'

Lachlan accepted this readily for he was drooping now and Cora had to half-carry him out of the back door of the hall. The family sleeping apartment was only a few paces away but it was a dark night and after the glare of the myriad candles she paused a moment to let her eyes adjust.

'It's cold, Mama,' Lachlan protested.

'I know, my love. A minute more and we'll be warm and safe.'

'Cakes,' he managed but was almost asleep.

With a smile Cora looked for Aila in the darkness but as she made out her friend's outline she saw a large hand go over her mouth and her eyes widen in fear. Now hands were upon Cora too, cutting off her screams and leaving them trapped in her throat. She scrabbled for Lachlan but he was yanked away and borne off as she was lifted unceremoniously off her feet and marched in his wake. She kicked out hard and heard a satisfying grunt of pain as she connected with a kneecap but her captor did not let go. She fought for purchase on one of the fingers over her mouth but whoever it was held her lips cleverly shut and she only bit her own tongue.

She jerked furiously and a voice hissed in her ear: 'Cora, whisht, will you?' She froze. 'Better,' the voice said and even in that whisper she caught a familiar cadence.

She twisted round, trying to see her captor's face, but the clouds hung low over the moon and even this close it was too dark to see more than a hint of blond hair. Suddenly her body was disorientatingly alive but she dared not believe it was him. She tried to protest further but he did not release his grip until they were some two hundred paces from the hall and into the line of low pines where finally he set her on her feet and peeled his fingers away.

'What on earth . . . ?' she gasped.

He put them back.

'Cora, shhh. It's me. It's Macbeth.'

Could it really be? Her blood spiked and she tried desperately to make out the lines of him in the darkness as he unpeeled one finger.

'You took your time.'

He clamped his hand down.

'Be quiet, please. It's taken years to put this plan into place.' She wriggled in angry agreement. 'And I don't want you spoiling it now. Will you be quiet?'

She nodded and kept her word until his hand was free of her mouth.

'Five years,' she hissed. 'You've been gone five years, Macbeth. I thought you'd forgotten me.'

'Forgotten you? Oh, Cora, never. You are so deep in my heart it would not beat without you.'

She blinked angrily.

'You sent no word.'

'I did. Many times.'

'Nonsense.'

'I did and you returned messages that I would be best to stay away. You said it was too dangerous and my cousins were too well supported to make an attack feasible.'

Cora groaned.

'It seems Gillespie is cleverer than I thought. I sent no such messages, Macbeth, believe me. If I'd caught one word from you I would have sent a letter in my own blood saying, "Come. Come now." Instead I have had to set myself to managing alone.'

She felt his fingers tighten on her arms and heard his breath come raggedly.

'I'm sorry,' he said. 'I had no support. I had to win it man by man. Kendrick too.'

'Kendrick is here?'

'He has your maid.'

'And Lachlan? Where's Lachlan?'

'The boy?'

'*My* boy.'

'He's safe. Davey has him.'

'Who's Davey?'

'Does it matter?'

'It does if he has my son.'

'Of course. Sorry. I'd forgotten how fierce you are, Cora.'

'Lucky you. But I'm afraid I am fiercer than ever for I am a mother now.'

'So I see. I wish . . . ' His voice cracked but he recovered himself. 'What has gone surely does not matter for we are together now.'

She drew in a spiky breath. Her head was in a spin, her body too. He *was* here. Macbeth was here and his presence was sending long-suppressed feelings coursing through her in a way that hurt almost as much as birthing Lachlan. She longed to grab him and crush him against her as if he might make her whole again but she had vowed to be whole without him and she must not weaken this time. She fought to compose herself.

'I thank you for it, Macbeth, but if you truly wish to help, please tell me who Davey is and please get me Lachlan.' Macbeth sighed but gave a low whistle and Cora felt her son pushed at her. She bent gratefully and clasped him close, smoothing back his sweaty hair and kissing away his tears. 'Hush, baby, hush. Mama's here.'

'What's happening?' he whimpered. 'Where are we? Where's Da?'

Cora looked up at Macbeth, or at where she thought he might be. He bent down and his blond hair brushed her cheek as he reached out his hand to Lachlan. His body pressed against hers and she felt every part of it. He had not, it seemed, grown fat in Dublin and her throat went dry with longing, but he was talking to her son and she had to listen.

'I will be your da now, Lachlan,' he was saying, at which her son burst into tears.

'What do you mean?' Cora gasped. 'Macbeth, what . . . '

But now she heard a crackle on the air, a familiar hearth sound amplified ten times over. She straightened herself slowly and looked down the hill and suddenly the darkness was gone, lit up in a fast-moving line of fire along the foot of the great hall of Moray.

'No!' She stumbled forward, dragging Lachlan with her. 'Macbeth, no, you can't! You mustn't . . . Not like this.'

But Macbeth swung round, placed a fierce kiss on her protesting lips and was gone. She started to run after him but Davey, whoever the hell he was, grabbed Lachlan again and she could not leave her son. She pressed her fingers to her lips. How dared Macbeth kiss her? How dared he turn up here, all sword and flame, and expect her to be grateful? She was her own sword now and did not need his interference. She looked angrily around and jumped as a new figure leaped out in front of her.

'Don't you want to watch, sister?'

Cora's head spun faster.

'Kendrick? Oh, Lord, Kendrick, it's truly you too?'

'Of course it's me. Did you doubt it?' He threw his arms wide, beaming broadly as if he had just been off on a morning's ride.

He was lit up by the roaring flames below, eyes as fiery as the hall, and she could see that he'd grown taller and broader and more bearded; more of a man. 'We are come bringing retribution. We will retake our rights – first Moray, then Fife, then all of Alba. It is as we swore, sister.'

'As we swore six long years ago.'

'So? An oath never dies.'

'But the ways of fulfilling it can change.'

'What?' He frowned. 'You are talking in riddles and I haven't time for it. Stay here and stay safe.'

And then he was gone, whipping his sword from its scabbard and running, whooping, down the hill in execution of some plan Cora had been no party to and must simply stand and watch. It fired her blood as hot as the burning hall.

She looked furiously around once more and saw that the man called Davey was holding his hand over Lachlan's eyes and talking softly to him, for which she supposed she must be grateful. She felt Aila come up beside her and together they stood transfixed as the flames reached the thatched roof of the hall and danced wildly across the straw. She could feel the heat on her face even this far up the hill and could imagine the panic in the hall – *her* hall. There were men surrounding it, dark shapes against the orange inferno, swords at the ready, and as the big doors burst open and men came tumbling out, they stepped up to dispatch them with brutal efficiency.

'Vengeance,' Davey breathed behind her. Cora heard the soft lilt of Moray in his voice and realised this must be one of the few of Finlay's men who had escaped Muir and Gillespie's ambush. 'Vengeance for Finlay. And vengeance for you, Cora MacDuff.'

Cora sucked in her breath. He spoke true, she supposed, but this vengeance had not been of her choosing and she did not like the shape of it. Gillespie was not the man he had been at the start – though by now he was surely not a man at all anymore. She prayed he had died swiftly at the sword and was not burning up beneath the hellish beams of his own hall. A peculiar wave of sadness swept over her as she pictured him proudly unveiling Lachlan's special seat earlier. They had admired the carved Aed lion together before Gillespie had lifted the boy onto it and told him to look out over the men who would one day be his – the men who were now burning to death in that same hall where they'd drunk their young lord's health.

'Why?' she whispered to Aila. 'Why this way?'

'It is for honour, Cora.'

'Honour?' She gestured down the slope to the pile of flailing, screaming men. 'Does that look like honour to you?'

'It does, aye.' Cora sighed and Aila grabbed at her. 'Remember Eilidh, my lady. Remember how Gillespie stabbed her as if she were nothing but a beast. Remember how he forced you to the altar and took your virginity with his men cheering him on like it was sport. And remember Muir flaming you and then and then . . .' She stopped, forced Cora's hand to the puckered skin of her chin. 'Just remember, Cora.'

She sucked in a deep breath; she had never before seen kindly Aila so enraged.

'I remember,' she said softly, 'but I did not think Macbeth the same.'

'Then you are too soft.'

'Too soft? That's not true. That's not it.'

But what *was* it? Cora felt giddily for a trunk to rest her back against as she looked down at the hell below. The roof had caved in now and she could see straight into the mangle of fire and wood and bodies. It was quieter now, the only noise the whinnying of the ponies in the stables as Macbeth's men fetched and soothed them, their soft voices filling the evening air with the haunting sound of the Shepherd's Psalm. She looked anxiously for Balgedie and saw him at the front of the line, his half-ear silhouetted against the dark light of the remaining flames as if even her pony was reminding her why these men had needed to die.

And now Macbeth was coming back up the hill, Kendrick at his side and a clutch of soldiers behind. He held himself more tightly than the loose-limbed youth she had loved with such helpless passion but it was him all the same and every fibre of her seemed to contract as eagerly at his approach as if he had never been away. And yet he had – and for so long. However much it hurt her to admit it, things were not the same anymore. She drew herself up tall as he swaggered towards her and bowed dramatically.

'You are saved, my lady.'

'Saved from one murderous attacker by another?'

He looked taken aback.

'But we are in the right. We are exacting vengeance and justice and rescuing you, my bride.'

'Your bride? Macbeth, I have been five years a wife.'

'I know it. It has eaten me up inside.'

'And I.' Cora ran a hand down her neck, feeling the raised lines of Muir's cruelty still criss-crossing her flesh. 'It's too late, Macbeth. I am too much changed. Look.'

She yanked back the neck of her shift, exposing the ugly fretwork of her suffering by the glow of flames from the hall. Macbeth gasped.

'What happened?'

She shook her head.

'Much happened, Macbeth. Too much.'

'No! I can make it right. Years I've waited for this – for you.'

His words bit deep. She saw Gillespie flinging her down on her enforced wedding day, taking her like a beast while his men cheered him on. She saw Muir crushing the burning torch against her and grinding her into the dust and she saw a thousand bruising encounters since. She reached blindly for Macbeth but her hand met a muscled arm and her very flesh recoiled. She stepped away.

'That's very noble, Macbeth, very romantic. If only I had been able to do the same.'

'Cora ...'

'No, I'm sorry. I told you – I am too much changed. I have vowed to make my way alone with my son and it is best I do so. You are welcome to your Mormaership and I am glad of it, for your father whom I loved and for yourself whom I loved once too. But our time has gone.'

She reached for Lachlan. Davey looked to his lord but Macbeth, slack-jawed, nodded for the boy's release and he tumbled into Cora's arms.

'Aila?' she said and the girl scrambled reluctantly to her side.

'Where are you going?' Macbeth asked.

'To Rosemarkie. To the abbey. To pray. Good night, my lords. Help yourself to ale, won't you?'

It was all she could manage. Tears were welling and she would not cry. Over these last years she had toughened both her flesh and heart and she must keep them that way to survive. She pushed past Macbeth and headed away from what was left of Inverness, steering a wide berth around the smouldering remains of the once great hall and going only close enough to let the fierce heat of it dry the tears that, despite her resolve, fell from her stinging eyes.

Chapter Twelve

Dunkeld, March 1030

Sibyll shifted her feet on the hard ground and wriggled her toes gratefully in the lamb's wool boot linings Morag had given her as a Yule gift that she was in no hurry to relinquish however often Crinan insisted it was spring. She looked up the slope to where some twenty men were labouring and tried to believe her father-by-marriage knew what he was doing, but it seemed a fool's scheme to her and she wasn't the only one.

'A vineyard in Dunkeld?' Bethan had yelped at her husband when he'd proudly shown them what was in the large wagon that had rumbled up to the abbey last autumn.

'Why not?' he'd said. 'We already make the finest uiskie in Alba and now we will make the finest wine too.'

'The *only* wine,' Bethan had corrected him dryly. 'And that's if these peculiar things actually grow.'

She'd put a hand into the wagon and pulled out a funny-looking plant, brown and wizened and not fit to feed cattle let alone to produce fruit.

'They are in their winter state, Bethan,' Crinan had said, snatching the root off her. 'You wait. In the spring we will put them in the ground and they will flourish.'

'You've looked into this, Abbot?' Cullen had asked nervously.

'I have. And so has Morag.'

'Oh, well, if Morag has looked into it I'm sure we'll be serving wine from fountains by next Yule,' Bethan had scoffed.

Then she'd flounced off and uttered never another word on Crinan's mysterious plants until today when he'd forced her out with the rest of the court to see them planted on the slope behind the abbey.

'Will they grow, Morag?' Sibyll had asked earlier.

Her friend had been tempted into a rare visit to the abbey to help with the final preparations for the grand planting ceremony and Sibyll had been delighted to see her.

'We'll not know until we try. The sun is not as hot here as it is in Italy or Francia but they will be well watered at least.'

'You have told Crinan it will work?'

'No! Lord, no. I've told him a thousand times that it won't but there's a chance and Crinan is a man who likes to take a chance.'

'He took one on me.'

'Oh no. With you, the probability of success was assured. He told me that he knew within moments of meeting you that you were the woman to bring him a King of Alba.'

'Duncan?' Sibyll had asked and when Morag hadn't replied her temper had risen in a rare display. 'Crinan underestimates Duncan. The king does too. He is a good man.'

'That,' Morag had said quietly, 'is his problem.'

'So I must bring my son up to be cruel and harsh and ruthless like his namesake, must I?'

Sibyll would not usually dare talk that way of the king but Morag did not judge like others did.

'No,' she'd said, 'but you must bring him up to be clever and brave and good at reading men before they have even read them-selves, for if a king sees things before others then he does not need to cut them down to get there.'

Remembering the wise words, Sibyll looked for her son and found him seated gleefully upon his royal great-grandfather's shoulders. His neat three-year-old's bottom was square upon the ermine fur of the king's ceremonial cloak, his feet were kicking at Malcolm's golden armlets and, to Sibyll's horror, the great crown of Alba was firmly clasped in her son's pudgy hands.

'Malky, no,' she hissed but the boy looked back at her, grinned and plucked the crown right off the king's head.

Malcolm's brow furrowed furiously but then, as the boy chuckled above him, he looked up and, to Sibyll's astonishment, chuckled back.

'See – he's after my crown already,' he told the court, fanned out in shivering lines behind him.

He lifted Malky down, the crown still grasped in the child's hands. Sibyll prayed he wouldn't drop it onto the frosty ground but he held tight.

'Mine,' he said, his voice high and clear on the spring air.

'No, Malky,' Sibyll said firmly, but the king put up a hand to stop her.

'Let's try it for size, lad,' he said and bent down before his great-grandson.

Malky let him take the crown and lifted his chin high as the old man lowered it gently onto his dark curls. Sibyll thought it might drop right over his head and land on his shoulders like a spiked collar but it stayed on, sitting at a jaunty slant over one little ear.

'It's a bit big yet, young Malcolm,' the king said.

'It fits,' Malky insisted. 'See.'

He took a few steps, neck rigid. Everyone held their breath.

'Not yet,' the king said firmly, 'but one day it will.'

'One day soon?'

'If you grow fast enough.'

Malky looked around him and his eyes fell on the vine plants still waiting to be placed in the last of the two hundred holes that had been painfully dug into the hard Alban ground. In a moment he was across and squirming his feet into the nearest hole, the crown of Alba still on his head.

'Plant me here with Granda's vines. He says they will be full-grown by summer.'

Now the whole crowd laughed, courtiers and workfolk alike. Sibyll looked to Duncan to share the joke with him but his eyes were fixed on his son with an expression alarmingly like hatred.

'Duncan?' He blinked and the look was gone. Either that or she'd misread it. Surely so, for he loved Malky dearly. 'I think he might be getting a bit above himself,' she whispered.

'Ahead of himself, certainly,' Duncan replied, striding across to address his son. 'You must give Great-grandfather back the crown now.'

'Why?'

'Because he is the king.' Malky looked mutinous. 'And because it is time to bless the vines and we cannot do that if you are planted in their place.'

'The men can dig another hole.'

'You wish to stay here?'

'Aye.'

'Out on the slopes with rainwater to drink and only worms to eat?' Malky wavered. 'And wolves nibbling at your toes in the night?'

Malky lip wobbled but then his hand went to the crown and he recovered.

'No wolf would eat a king,' he said confidently.

King Malcolm cheered.

'Quite right, lad. You tell him. But even so, you will grow just as well in your own bed and be far more comfortable besides. Kings, you know, should be comfortable.'

With that he brushed past Duncan and lifted Malky from the ground to take him back into the bosom of the clapping court and Duncan was left standing there looking as if he had never been less comfortable in his life.

'Vines!' Crinan said hastily and his men rushed forward to pick up the last few precious roots, giving Duncan the opportunity to step back into line.

'Your grandfather spoils the boy,' Sibyll whispered.

She tried to take his arm but he pulled stiffly away.

'My grandfather adores him. Now, are we going to get these stupid Italian plants into the soil before we all freeze?'

Luckily Crinan was back in command. He ushered the monks into a white-robed semi-circle and as one they broke into the sweetest of psalms while the labourers dropped the last of the plants into the holes and hastily filled them in.

Crinan raised his hands high to God's heavens, obscured, as they so often were, by heavy cloud, and spoke: 'May the Holy Lord bless these vines, fruit of his soil, and grant them renewed life here in Alba. May they rise out of the winter soils as Christ Himself rose from the dead and may they bear fruit with which to celebrate His glorious passion.'

His voice rang off the abbey walls behind and shivered through the straight lines of his new crop. The common folk watched, rapt, as the courtiers bowed their heads and joined in the solemn Amens.

'God bless this venture,' Sibyll said quietly, for something about the stern, solid little plants appealed to her. They, like her, had been brought to Alba and had to put down roots in this new soil and she truly prayed that they would bear fruit, as she had. She put a hand to her belly and Duncan, noticing, leaned down to her.

'You are well, Sibyll?'

'Very well.' She looked at him. 'I believe I may be carrying a new child for us.'

Duncan's eyes sparkled and then, with a glance to Malky, he said, 'Pray God it is a girl.'

'A girl, Duncan?'

He recovered himself.

'Like her mother, for she is very dear to me.'

He kissed her and she tucked an arm under his as the court turned gratefully back inside, but now someone was coming up to join them and a treacherous feather-tickle in her heart told her exactly who it was.

'Malky will get himself in trouble one of these days,' Maldred said.

'The king is too free with him,' Sibyll agreed softly.

'The king wishes to see my son to the door of kingship before he bows out of it,' Duncan growled.

'Oh, Duncan, no. *You* are the next king.'

'Only if he gets on and dies soon.'

'Duncan!'

Sibyll looked around, horrified; this was treasonous talk.

'My apologies.'

Duncan bowed exaggeratedly low, then detached himself from her grip and slipped away. Sibyll turned awkwardly to Maldred.

'King Malcolm does not treat Duncan half as well as he does Malky.'

'Malky's a child. He's easy to indulge.'

'Maybe but Duncan feels it keenly.'

'He always has. He worries too much what others think of him.'

'And you do not?'

'Only *some* others.' He was looking at her intently and she felt her attraction to him swelling inside her like a spring flood. 'Sibyll, there's something I need to tell you.'

'There is?' She looked round but everyone was flocking past them into the great hall and there was no one to save her from the rising waters of her own foolish passion. She yearned to hear what Maldred had to say but must not allow it; whatever was between them should never be spoken out loud. 'Maldred, please. Is this the place? Should you . . . '

'I may be going away.'

'Away? Where? Why?'

'It is Father's idea. Well, his and Brother Cullen's.'

'Cullen? He doesn't have ideas beyond new uiskie blends.'

Maldred looked at her curiously.

'You think that's all he cares for?'

'Well, God, of course, and his master the abbot.'

'Nothing else?'

'Should he? What are you talking about, Maldred? And why would you go away? Oh – has your Strathclyde uncle died?'

He drew in a slow breath.

'Not yet but he is unwell and wishes me at his side to ease his burden. Also I . . . I am to marry.'

It was like a punch, low down in her gut where even now Duncan's second baby was forming.

'Marry?' she stammered like a fool.

'Is it such a crazy idea?'

'No. No, of course not. I mean, you should marry, of course you should. It's just . . . No. No, nothing. Who is she, then, the lucky lady?'

'Ask Brother Cullen.'

'Cullen? Honestly, Maldred, what has Cullen to do with it?'

'He brought her back for me with his peat and his barley and the silken threads of Crinan's networks.'

Sibyll frowned.

'Maldred, you are speaking in riddles.'

'I apologise. I am . . . It is . . . difficult.'

'Yes.' There was no need to say more. He was standing just a pace away. One single step and she would be up against him. 'So who is she?'

'Edyth of Northumbria.'

'The sister of Earl Eldred?'

'You know them?'

'Of course.' Sibyll's life in England seemed years away now but she could not forget Eldred, Earl of the great Northern city of Durham and Ward's deadliest rival for control of the northern kingdom. 'Why would you marry *her*?'

He shrugged bitterly.

'For power, what else? My Brittonic cousins will keep us secure in the west but this new alliance will link us into the east too. Father says it is the best match I can make.'

'And you always do what he says, do you?'

She turned away but Maldred grabbed for her arm and pulled her back.

'You know how it is. We cannot marry where we choose.' He was so close, so achingly close. She closed her eyes. 'Crinan says that an alliance with the Earl of Durham will secure Alban borders and he is right.'

'But *I* am the alliance that secures Alban borders.'

'Only against *South* Northumbria. My father likes to have eggs in all baskets.'

'And we are both his eggs?'

He sighed, spread his hands wide. There was little point denying it. Sibyll looked at his hand, still holding her arm, and quietly placed her own over it. 'But why must you go away, Maldred? Strathclyde is so far. I . . . I will never see you.'

He looked at her sadly.

'That might be for the best – for us both.'

He was right. Maldred, or to be more accurate her own treacherous feelings for Maldred, threatened all the security and stability she had worked so hard to create here in Dunkeld. He was a danger to her and she could not risk danger however much her foolish body seemed to ache for it.

'Shall we go inside?' she suggested stiffly.

Maldred sighed.

'Very well.' Still he held her arm. 'But you should know this – I do not love her and I *will not* love her.'

'You must try, Maldred, for her sake and for your own.'

'But how?'

She looked past him and up the hill to where the new vines were poking bravely out of the iron earth like so many dead sticks.

'I'm not sure,' she said, 'but the seasons turn and love may bud as the grapes will.'

'As the grapes *might*,' Maldred said. 'I fear Alba is no place for Italian fruit.'

'Nor for passion either,' Sibyll said, but Maldred, with a last fierce kiss planted on her hand, had gone.

Chapter Thirteen

Rosemarkie, March 1030

'Please, my lady, in God's name and for the good of our souls, let us in.'

Cora hid behind the outer door of Rosemarkie Abbey and groaned. So this was Macbeth's new tactic. Ever since he had reclaimed Moray he had been seeking an audience with her but she had resisted. It had been easy in the iron-grey cold of February but now spring was raising its head over the Moray Firth and the promise of light and life was sparking painfully sweet longings inside her. She drew in a breath.

'What of the souls of the fifty men who burned?' she called.

'We will pray for them too.'

It was a fair answer.

'You should be glad Gillespie is gone,' Aila told her daily. 'He was a tyrant and you are free at last.'

It was true, Cora supposed, but if she was finally free why would she shackle herself to another? She tried to devote herself to Lachlan but as a boisterous three year old, he wanted more than hearth-games and often chose to ride out with Aila, who'd become mysteriously diligent in her outdoor duties.

Cora was almost certain she was slipping down the Black Isle to Inverness to see Macbeth's men – or one of them. Aila had taken to asking her all about her childhood and Cora suspected the girl had a soft spot for Kendrick. Well, good. Let them marry. Aila had lands that Kendrick could settle on and their union might heal the breach without Cora being dragged into it.

'Please, Cora,' the voice said again, soft and so familiar. ''Tis Shrivetide and we are in need of a priest to cleanse our souls for Lent.'

He had a point. All men should attend Confession on this last day before the Holy Season and the only priests on the firth were here with her. She put her hand to the latch.

'In God's name,' she said piously and opened the door.

No one entered. Surprised, she looked around the edge of it and there was Macbeth, on his knees on the rough stone step, holding out a bunch of meadow flowers. They were very pretty and he must have walked some distance to find such a goodly bunch, for flowers were still sparse at this time of year even in clement Moray. She stepped hesitantly out over the threshold and he thrust them towards her.

'A peace offering.'

'Have you put flowers on Gillespie too?'

His eyes hardened.

'No. I care nothing for Gillespie. He killed my father.'

Cora bowed her head. He was right. She was not the only one with hurts here and perhaps, with Lent, it was time to put that behind them and move forward in a purer spirit. She took the flowers from him.

'I loved Finlay too.'

'I know it. He would be pleased to see us together again today.'

'We are not together.'

'We are in the same place.'

'But not together.'

'Clearly. You should put those in water.'

Flustered, Cora looked around for Aila and saw her standing close beside Kendrick. She coughed loudly and her maid flew to her side.

'I'll take care of those.'

'Thank you. And these men need a priest. Fetch Father Alasdair.'

'Of course.'

Aila's cheeks were flushed and her eyes alight. Cora felt a rush of jealousy at such clear joy in life but she herself must not succumb. She had done that once before and it had only caused more hurt. She advanced towards her brother.

'You are not too lonely up here, Kendrick?' she asked.

'I have God and my fellow soldiers for company, sister.'

'Really? I had not thought you so readily amused by male companionship.'

He shifted, blushed a little.

'There are women in Moray.'

'I know it, though precious few at Rosemarkie especially as my main companion is forever slipping away – I cannot think where to.'

Kendrick came a little closer.

'You should not be so careless with your attendants. A good job you have me to keep watch over them.'

He offered her a tentative smile and after a moment she allowed herself to return it, then, remembering her maid's fury on the night of the fire, leaned in and added, 'Just see you take care of her.'

Kendrick caught her mood and dropped his smile.

'I will if I get the chance. I like her well, Cora – almost as well as Macbeth likes you.'

Cora's skin prickled.

'Macbeth likes a previous me. I am not that woman anymore and he should accept that as I have had to accept it.'

Macbeth came up behind her.

'He does accept it,' he said, touching his fingers to her shoulders so that she yearned to lean back into him. 'He does accept it and he ...'

She forced herself to pull away, though it felt as if she were peeling resin from her skin.

'Do you not have shriving to attend to?'

'Aye, but ...'

'God bless you then, all of you. I will leave you in peace.'

'God bless the Mother Church.'

Cora was standing behind the abbey door plucking nervously at her hair. He was here. She'd known he would come, for he came every Sunday but he was later than usual and she'd started to worry. Well, not worry, but wonder. More for Aila's sake, really, for she'd been fidgeting and getting ready since daybreak and her nervousness was infecting Cora. She was letting herself get drawn into love-games, just as she had once before, and she must stop.

'You're late,' she said through the wood.

'We've been busy, my lady.'

'Too busy for God?'

'Not at all. Our work is to God's glory.'

Of course it was. Reluctantly, Cora raised the latch and sidled outside. It was a glorious morning. The new sun was catching on a line of low cloud, driving all its golden light down across the water of the firth. It sparkled on the waves kicking up their heels in the soft spring breeze and ran up the beach to her very feet. The rough sea-grass before the abbey was thick with a dew that threw up a thousand miniature suns and there, somehow, someone had lime-washed every stalk into the shape of a dolphin. Either God had sent Rosemarkie a mid-Lent miracle or the men had truly been busy this morning.

Cora went closer, tracing the outline of the pretty creature. Had Macbeth, then, seen her sitting watching the dolphins throwing themselves into God's skies for the pure joy of it? Every time she saw them she was snared between envy and contempt for their simple pleasure in life. It was fine for dolphins, she supposed, for they had nothing as itchy as royal blood to keep them tied to reality – or maybe leaping in the waves *was* reality for them? Oh, it was all so tiresomely tangled.

'It's beautiful,' she said eventually and Macbeth beamed.

'It's for you.'

'Not God?'

'God would be pleased if you were.'

'You credit me, Macbeth, with far too much influence on the Almighty.'

'I credit you, Cora, with far too much influence on *me*. I miss you.'

Cora opened her mouth to echo his sentiment but stopped just in time. Everything seemed to be rushing around her so fast. Blossom was budding on the trees and the birds were singing in heady joy, making the air so thick with scent and song that her head spun and her senses seemed to rule her. It was almost if she were back amongst the bulrushes, a sixteen-year-old maid once more, but that was definitely not reality and the turn of her fancy made her giddier yet.

'You will stay to eat after the service?' she managed.

It sounded ridiculously prim but Macbeth agreed graciously and at dinner, a less lean affair than in most of Lent to mark this middle Sunday and honour Mother Church, he was very attentive.

'It is so good to be home,' he told her. 'I felt lost in Ireland.'

'I hear Diarmait keeps a wild court.'

'A little, though his men are far from stupid. I talked a great deal with two who had just returned from a pilgrimage to Rome.'

'Rome?' Cora gaped. 'How long did it take them?'

'Almost half a year but they were full of the wonders they had seen. I was invited to join another party but . . . '

'But?'

'But I had work to do. I had to come back for you, Cora.'

Her heart turned over.

'Yes, well, that was very kind and obviously I appreciate it but you could have gone to Rome, you know, if you so wanted.'

'Maybe one day I will. Maybe you will come with me?'

She snorted.

'I'm too old for such adventures. Look – I found a grey hair last week and I have bags under my eyes as big as belt-pockets. You should find someone less wizened to take on your fancy travels, Macbeth.'

She glowered at him but to her shock he just chuckled.

'My, but you are a wee grumpling today, Cora MacDuff.'

Lachlan, on her other side, screamed with laughter.

'Grumpling! It sounds like a creature from the woods, Mama – one that lives in the caves behind the waterfalls and is covered in hair and . . . '

'And hunts princelings at night?'

He did not even flinch.

'Aye! Will you eat me tonight, Mama Grumpling? You won't, you know, for I have a sword now.'

Cora ground her teeth. Lachlan had a sword because Macbeth had brought it for him and had been cunning enough to present it direct so she'd had no chance to object to the gift. He wore it strapped to his belt at all times save in bed – and only then because she forbade it – and already it had replaced his wept-for chair in his affections.

'Who needs a chair anyway, Mama?' he'd said to her the other day. 'Chairs are boring. You can't kill things with chairs.'

'Neither should you with swords unless you must,' she'd retorted, but he'd laughed in her face and her heart had quailed at the wild child she was raising. Maybe he did need a father – or an uncle at least.

'Kendrick,' she called down the table. 'Will you take your nephew riding?'

Macbeth sat up and looked intently at Kendrick who, after an odd pause, said with exaggerated sorrow, 'Sadly, my dearest sister, I cannot. I am a poor rider.' Cora stared. Kendrick had been riding ponies bareback since he could totter over to them. 'Too wild,' he went on as if he could see where her thoughts had galloped. 'I would teach the lad bad habits. You need someone steadier.'

Suddenly Cora saw where this was going.

'And who would you recommend, Brother?'

'Macbeth.'

'Aye!' Lachlan agreed eagerly before she could speak. 'Aye, Mama, let it be Macbeth. His horse is the finest of them all.'

'That's because he's the Mormaer.'

'As I will be one day.'

Cora looked down at him. He looked so proud, so certain. But if Macbeth were to marry someone else and have a son, Lachlan would be displaced. She swallowed. She was twisting logic to fit her unsteady emotions and must resist such girlish weakness.

'If you are good,' was all she could manage.

She could sense Macbeth staring at her and his gaze heated her all over as if Gillespie's hall were burning before her again. She hardened her heart once more. Where would Macbeth find another wife in Moray anyway?

'I bring a guest to worship with us on the blessed Palm Sunday.'

'A guest?'

Cora flung up the latch and looked out into the low light of a squally morning. The wind had been raging all night and the sea was in a temper and flinging spray at Macbeth and his men, not to mention his 'guest'. Cora gaped.

'It is cold out here,' Macbeth prompted and she recovered herself.

'Of course. Sorry. Come in, come in. And you are . . . ?'

'Lady Lena of Caithness.'

'Caithness? You are a long way south, my lady.'

'My father is taking me to King Malcolm's court,' the young woman said, her voice as soft and pretty as her face.

'To find her a husband,' Macbeth put in. 'He seeks an influential man to help protect her from the Orkney Vikings.'

'I see.'

'I'm sure he will succeed, are you not? A lady this lovely deserves a good husband.'

'A Mormaer even?' Cora challenged, trying to catch his eye but he side-stepped her.

'Perhaps. Shall I escort you to the church, Lady Lena? It is small but pretty and the monks sing very well. And maybe, afterwards, they will let you taste their usquebauch. It is a fine drink these days.'

Cora slid quickly between them, offering Lena her arm.

'It is. I brought the expertise to Moray, you know, some years back when my husband was Mormaer. Do you like uiskie?'

Lena looked forlornly towards Macbeth but Cora had her tight now. 'You don't know? You must try it. I will get you a good big goblet full.'

Later, Kendrick told her she'd been cruel but, really, she hadn't said Lena was to take such a big swallow, not exactly. She'd only mentioned that she'd heard Dunkeld Abbey was cultivating wines as well as uiskie now. She hadn't actually said the two drinks were similar so was it her fault if Lena had made that assumption? Even so, she'd been sorry to see the girl struggling to breathe and to see that pretty dress all spat upon; even more so to see Macbeth solicitously helping her back to Inverness.

Cora spent the evening on her knees in the church, ostensibly musing on Christ's humble entry into Jerusalem though her thoughts struggled to stay on the Redeemer. Instead, she wondered if Lena was staying at Macbeth's partially rebuilt hall and if it had impressed her father. Caithness was on Moray's northern borders and the girl was pretty enough to grace any man's bed and Cora was uncomfortably aware that if she wanted Macbeth as husband she had to say so. And soon.

All logic was twisting her towards him. How, she argued to herself in the dark of the chapel, would she ever get Lachlan to the throne of Alba alone? She had the will, maybe, but not the might. This was not the Dark Ages; women did not lead men into battle any more. Even if she did not wish to succumb to loving Macbeth, he would be useful to her, would he not? And yet she knew that the moment she let him close her heart would betray her by giving in to love, and once she had lost her heart would she not lose her strength too? Again the logic twisted and it was a long night for her at Rosemarkie's lonely altar.

'Arise! Arise and sing glory to God who is risen before you.'

Cora scrambled out of bed and ran to the window. He was so early to Rosemarkie this Easter Sunday that the light was just a strip of heather-pink across the bottom of the sky. She flung open the window curtain.

'Macbeth?'

'Greetings, my lady. Happy Eastertide.'

'And to you.' Cora felt as pink as the sky. She reached out of the window and made a grab for Macbeth's tunic as he came over and bowed before her. 'You are very early.'

'It is an important day, is it not?'

'It is.'

'And I bring news.'

Cora froze.

'News?'

'Can I come in?'

She glanced back at Aila, still asleep on her pallet, and Lachlan curled up tight on his.

'I'll come out. Wait here.'

'No.'

'No?'

'I can't wait. Come this way.'

Then his hands were on her waist and lifting her clean out of the window opening. He set her on her feet but did not let go and she stood very still in case he remembered himself and did so.

'News?' she prompted nervously.

Surely he would not hold her so close if it were . . .

'I am to marry.'

Moray spun. The line of the light seemed to wobble and tear, the sea to bubble up, the solid Black Isle to crack.

'Marry?'

'It is time, I think. I am Mormaer after all and Moray needs an heir.'

'But Lachlan . . .'

'Stands now, aye, but . . . I did offer to be his father, you recall.'

'While you were burning his real one.'

'Or was I?'

'Macbeth?'

'I've been looking into it, Cora. The men of Moray tell me that Gillespie might not . . .'

The sound of the slap she dealt him rang around the firth. He put a hand to his cheek and she felt its absence from her waist instantly but she could not stand for this.

'You think what, Macbeth? That I was whoring myself between the pair of them? You think I was sporting in the beds of the men who murdered Finlay, my protector, who stabbed Eilidh, my friend, and who drove away you – my betrothed husband and my own dear love?'

She was waving her hands furiously and he caught them and yanked her against him.

'Of course not, Cora. Hush, I'm sorry. I can only guess at what you suffered and I so wish you'd tell me.'

'It would ruin you for your wife.'

'Nay, Cora, it would help me understand her.'

'Sorry?'

'You said I was your "one dear love".'

She flushed.

'Well you were – then. But that time is past.'

'And better is to come.'

'Not if you marry, not for me. I will have to go away. She won't want me here. She won't want my son here, whoever his damned father.'

'*I* am his father now.'

'Oh, Macbeth, stop it. You are making no sense. You have told me your good news so now go and pray.'

'No. You are not listening to me, Cora.'

'On the contrary, I have listened well. You have found a wife.'

His grip tightened.

'I found her years ago and like a fool I lost her. But I will not lose her again. I am to marry *you*, Cora MacDuff.'

'Says who?' she demanded, flustered.

'Says your blush when I lifted you out of the window and your fury at my news and the way you treated poor Lady Lena last week.'

'You arrogant . . . '

'And says this . . . '

Then his lips were upon hers, stopping her arguments and it was as if she was lost in the taste of Moray, spiced with her own hot blood and fiery with too many years lost, and she felt she could kiss him forever.

'You tricked me,' she accused when finally she came up for air.

'It was worth it,' he said and kissed her once more. 'But listen, Cora – I know you've had to battle alone and I know you worry that if you surrender yourself to my care it will not be as strong as your own.'

'No, Macbeth, I . . . '

'Listen, please. It is important. I hope that by marrying me you will *gain* in strength, not lose it. Truly, Cora, I will not try to control you or change you or steer you from your purpose.'

'Restitution?' she whispered.

'Exactly. It may take time, my love, as my return to you took time, but I will not lose sight of it and we will achieve it together. We will put Lachlan on the throne together.'

'Truly?'

He *did* know her, he *did* understand and her eyes filled with tears at the joy of it.

'Cora?' He tipped her chin up and she looked steadily into his eyes. 'Know this one thing – I do not want a wife to stand at my back but one to stand at my side. Can you do that?'

'Yes! Oh, Lord, yes, Macbeth.'

He smiled and gave her a soft kiss.

'Thank heavens. Now get back in your chamber and pretty yourself up for we have an Easter wedding to celebrate.'

'Today?'

'Today. Do you have any objections?'

But God help her, she had run out of objections and it was all she could do not to run to get ready. It was almost as if she, like the good Christ, was risen from the dead this Easter Sunday and at last her life – her real life – could begin.

Chapter Fourteen

Dunkeld, September 1030

'Grapes,' Crinan said proudly.

He lifted the dark little bunch and Sibyll watched King Malcolm closely as he considered the fruit. The court had come to Dunkeld to celebrate the harvest and the church was filled with produce: sheaves of fat barley and oats; bunches of leeks, cleaned to shining; and baskets of cherries, blackberries and apples. Crinan's offering was definitely the smallest but also the rarest of them all.

'From your soil, Abbot?'

'From *our* soil, Sire, good Alban soil.'

He gestured pointedly out of the church doors towards his new vineyard and, nodding approval, Malcolm took the bunch and turned it over in his big hands. It fitted snugly in one palm.

'Is this the size they are meant to be? I cannot believe that even the strongest labourer could squeeze much wine from these.'

Malcolm looked to Bethan, who gave a mocking little grimace that made Sibyll, to her surprise, feel pity for Crinan. He angled himself away from his wife and stroked his precious fruit protectively.

'They are a wee bit small, Sire, but that is usual for a first crop.'

'You are an expert now?'

'Brother Cullen is.'

'You are blessed in him.'

'I am.'

Sibyll looked over to Cullen, standing at Crinan's shoulder. His face was flaming darker than his lord's precious grapes and when Malcolm clapped a hand on his slender shoulder he almost visibly shook.

'I trust, Brother, that we can enjoy some of your famed Dunkeld usquebauch this evening?'

'I have saved my finest for you, Sire. It has been maturing for ten years and is, I think, very pleasingly flavoured.'

'It improves with age?'

'It does, Sire.'

'Like us all!'

Malcolm, now in his seventy-eighth year, clapped Cullen on the back again and beamed expectantly at him. Cullen's mouth worked but no sound came out and Sibyll stepped hastily forward.

'You are more majestic with every year that passes, Sire, but I trust, unlike uiskie, no more peaty?'

Malcolm laughed.

'I trust not too, Lady Duncan. I am not ready to be in the soil yet. For a start, I wish to see your son to manhood.'

Sibyll glanced awkwardly towards Duncan but luckily her husband was talking intently to a new arrival and did not hear his grandfather.

'Maybe both my sons,' she said, placing a light hand on her swollen belly.

'Maybe so. I am glad Duncan has proved himself able at something.'

Malcolm's eyes were narrowed, daring her to rise to the jibe. She touched her fingers to her jewelled diadem for confidence and looked him straight in the eye.

'Oh, Duncan is very talented. I can only assume he takes after you.'

Malcolm gave her a slow smile then a quick nod and turned to talk to the next person. Sibyll moved over to Duncan and tucked an arm under his. He looked around and pulled her close.

'Look who's at court, Sibyll,' he said warmly and, with a start, she saw that the new arrival with him was Maldred.

'You're here,' she stuttered. Duncan looked sideways at her and she fought to pull herself together. 'It's good to see you. Duncan misses you, do you not, husband?'

'Very much. Maldred has been telling me all about Strathclyde. It sounds a most interesting place. He lives in a grand palace at Partick on one bank of the River Clyde and his cathedral church is at Govan on the other side, with a great bridge between the two. There is nowhere else like it in all Alba.'

'It sounds fascinating. You like it there, Maldred?'

'It is very pretty.' There was an awkward pause. 'That is a beautiful amulet, Sibyll.'

Her hands went to the chain. After the success of her shoulder-brooches, she'd had the largest of the jewels Malcolm had given her set into the centre of a silver Celtic cross and had worn it today to show him her gratitude. The king had not noticed but now Maldred had it instantly meant more to her.

'I am very fond of Alba's silverwork,' she said foolishly.

'My wife is too.'

'Lady Maldred is with you?'

It hurt to speak the woman's married name and, hearing it, Maldred's eyes sought hers. They both looked swiftly away.

'She is. There.'

She followed where he pointed and saw his wife, an elfin, slender young woman, save for one notable swelling.

'She is with child?'

Sibyll felt a flare of unreasonable jealousy.

'She is, though not as far gone as you, my lady.'

'No.' Sibyll patted herself awkwardly. 'I am a lump.'

'Nonsense. You look beautiful.' Briefly, again, their eyes met then he added quickly, 'Does she not, Duncan?'

'Like an angel,' he agreed easily. 'Oh, it is so good to see you, Maldred. Come, we must all sit together at dinner.'

Sibyll's innards squeezed. She should talk with Lady Edyth, she knew, for she would be in touch with Earl Eldred and might let slip valuable information about Northern Northumbria that Sibyll could send on to Ward. Her brother still sought to take the land around Durham for himself and his son, now four years old, but the city was nigh on impregnable. He would appreciate anything she could do on his behalf but spending time with Maldred's wife felt impossibly hard. Sibyll set her jaw and hoped Bethan had not planned too many courses to hold them at the table.

She hoped in vain. It was a harvest supper, after all, and as it had been a fine year the barns were bulging. Fresh oyster-bread followed mackerel in wild garlic, followed goat cooked in its own milk, all of it delicious and all of it spoiled for Sibyll by the bitter taste of envy. And still the food came until at last there was whortleberry pie with honey cream and courtly stomachs were pronounced full.

Sibyll excused herself from the top table to 'circulate' with the court. The moment she escaped the dais, however, she made for the doors, seeking the solace of the stars. Tumbling out into the night air, she pressed her back against the hall wall and looked out to the beautiful abbey, so serene against the dark sky.

'Lord give me strength,' she murmured for her heart was shaking as if it might burst apart.

'He will,' said a quiet voice. 'And you have plenty of your own besides.' Sibyll jumped, horrified, but it was Morag who'd addressed her, lured to Dunkeld by the beauty of the harvest service. She could think of no response but her friend spoke again. 'It hurts, doesn't it, to love where you should not?'

Sibyll looked guiltily around but they were alone together beneath the stars.

'Crinan?' she asked. Morag nodded sadly. 'You were lovers?'

'We were,' she agreed softly. 'You and . . . '

'No.' Sibyll shook her head. 'No, Morag. We could not.'

'You are a better woman than I then, though I was young. Very young.'

'Can you tell me?'

Morag looked at her.

'I have told no one before.'

'But can you tell *me*?'

She nodded slowly.

'I think perhaps I must.' Sibyll took her hand and waited and suddenly words were tumbling out of Morag. 'It was the summer my mother died. She and I had been everything to each other for the long years since my father's death and I was stricken. Crinan found me weeping by the lochside one day. He kissed my tears away and the next moment we were tumbling into the heather. We stayed there all that summer, or so it sometimes seemed. I was sixteen, he nearly twenty, but it felt as if we were intended for each other forever.'

She tipped shimmering eyes towards the skies as if her memories were written in the stars.

'What stopped it?' Sibyll asked.

'His father did. He walked in on us in the crannog as the first leaves were falling and said summer was done. Crinan leaped up and told him he wanted to marry me but his damned father just laughed. I remember that sound still – like a north wind blowing between us. Crinan went away defiant still but the next time he came to me it was to say that he would be wed the following week to a Strathclyde lady called Bridget. She was at the abbey, he said, brought in with all her family, and he could not shame her by refusing.'

'That's so sad.'

Morag shrugged.

'It would have been sadder never to have had each other at all. And it was a long time ago now. He will soon be twenty-five.'

'Who will?'

Morag looked at her, seemingly confused, then said, 'Maldred, of course. He was born barely nine months later. Ironic, is it not?'

Sibyll's throat constricted and she squeezed Morag's hand tight.

'I understand,' she whispered.

Morag squeezed back.

'I know it.'

'It is easy when he is not here to believe myself content. And I *am* content, Morag. Duncan is a good husband and I am a lucky woman. But with Maldred here I am too aware of how much happiness there could truly be in the world and contentment no longer seems enough.'

Morag leaned over and pressed her cheek to Sibyll's and they stood there, drawing comfort from each other, until the rasp of a fiddle through the wall signalled dancing and the spell was broken.

'I should go inside,' Sibyll said. 'There is little to be gained by hiding.'

Morag smiled sadly.

'You think so? I find hiding very effective.'

Sibyll considered. Morag's crannog was a beautiful place but she could see now that it had been crafted that way to be Morag's shell, protecting her from the world.

'Do you truly?' she asked. 'I'm not so sure. I hid once, when the Wends attacked my village, and it kept me safe for a time but it would not have kept me alive. Hiding has its limits, Morag – in the end you have to come out into the open.'

Morag shook her head.

'I'm sure you're right, Sibyll, for you are a better woman than I. But, then, I am not the one who will be queen.'

Queen! The word shivered through Sibyll and she seized on it gladly, using it to steel herself. Morag dropped a kiss on her cheek and melted away into the trees, heading back for her lonely crannog, but as Sibyll watched she felt more sorrow for her friend than envy. She turned determinedly to the door of the hall. Old King Malcolm could not live forever and once he was gone and she was indeed Queen of Alba, she would surely be too busy to seek happiness where she should not.

Chapter Fifteen

Inverness, October 1030

'Now is the time.'

Kendrick strode up and down in front of Cora and Macbeth, pounding one fist into the palm of the opposite hand. The late sun fell on him through the many cracks in Macbeth's roughly rebuilt hall, making him seem to flash angrily before Cora's eyes.

'Why now, Kendrick?' Macbeth asked calmly.

'Why? Why not? You're married now.'

'It's only been a summertime.'

'It's enough.' Fury seemed to crackle around him, making Cora wince. He had been his usual happy self all summer but since the nights had been drawing in had become as jumpy as a hare-kitten and seemed to want everyone else to be so too. 'You have Lachlan already so we need to get on with it. Are you happy to let Malcolm's damned cross fly over the royal residences forever more?'

'You know I'm not, Kendrick, but ... '

'Is your lion not so rampant anymore? Is he too sleepy after rutting his new woman to ... '

'Kendrick, enough!'

Cora leaped furiously to her feet, glaring at her brother who had the grace to look ashamed.

'I'm sorry, Cora, but this is important to me and I thought it was to you too.'

'It is. Oh, Lord, Kendrick you know it is. I was there with you. I saw Father cut down just as you did. I ran with you and I hid with you and I swore vengeance with you and it has shaped my life ever since, but we can't rush. We can't . . . '

'Rush? You call this rushing? We have waited too many years already.'

His words bit at Cora's conscience. Was he right? Had she let herself get soft again? Or was she just applying sense, patience even? It wasn't a quality she'd ever been known for but Macbeth was teaching her its virtues and now she looked uncertainly to him for help. He approached Kendrick.

'I could not have got this far without you, friend, and I am grateful, but I am newly Mormaer of Moray and must gain the men's trust before I can lead them to war.'

Kendrick wheeled away and kicked at the wall. It wobbled alarmingly and several of the men sitting further down the hall shuffled their benches inwards.

'See, we have not even built a stable home yet. You must be patient a wee while longer.'

'So you can coo over your new bride and feather your cosy wee nest?'

'Coo?' Cora spluttered. 'Hardly. We are working every daylight hour to stabilise Moray.'

'And every night-time one to make her a new heir.'

Cora flushed. That much was true. After the roughness of her time with Gillespie, she'd been unable to believe the joy that could be found in the marriage bed. Macbeth had come to her so gently and with such delight, cradling her and exploring her, kissing her all over, even across her scarred neck and chest until she had begged for him to enter her.

Even then he had taken his time, had looked into her eyes as if she were not just a release but a completion. It had astonished and aroused her and though it was true that she worked tirelessly in Moray, her thoughts often strayed longingly to the coming sweetness of the dark hours ahead. And so what? She was owed a little pleasure, surely, and it would be an insult to God not to take it when finally he had blessed her with a loving husband.

'You could find yourself similar joy, Kendrick,' she said, looking pointedly over to Aila. 'You could take a wife.'

'I will. That is, I would like to, but I cannot saddle a landed lady with a husband who has not yet proved himself a true man.'

'You do not think that burning a hall full of traitors proved you "man" enough, Kendrick?'

'That was Macbeth's doing.'

'I seem to recall you at the heart of the fray.'

'I was and I am proud to have helped my dear friend but now he should help me. *Us.*'

'And he will, Kendrick, when the time is right.'

'Now is the time.'

And there they were – back full circle.

'Please, Kendrick,' she begged, 'just a wee bit more patience. Lachlan is only three.'

'But if we wait for him to grow we will be too late. Why not Macbeth, Cora? He has a claim too. Indeed, he has a better claim than bloody Duncan for he is of the line of Aed and it is their turn next. If we let Duncan take the throne, his Constantins will have their feet firmly under the table and it will be harder to put Lachlan forward. You know it will.'

Cora swallowed. Could Macbeth be king? Kendrick pounced.

'You *do* know it. Come, sister.' He ran over and grabbed her hands, pulling her up from her seat. 'Remember how it was after Father was murdered – murdered by his own brother! We swore we would avenge him, did we not? We swore it as we ran north for our lives and we swore it again when we found safety here in

Moray. Are we to forget that? Are we to put our comfort before our duty and languish in our marriage beds instead of striking out in our father's memory?'

He was shaking her with his passion and Cora felt tears spring to her eyes – tears of pain and of guilt. Kendrick was right; they *had* sworn so. She looked to Macbeth, painfully aware of his hearth-troops watching intently from further down the hall. He stepped closer and reached out to slide an arm around her waist but then, with a look to Kendrick, thought better of it.

'Next Eastertide,' he said.

Kendrick turned to him.

'What do you mean?'

'Give me until next Eastertide to establish myself in Moray. It is nearing winter now and no time to attack.'

'On the contrary, it is the perfect time to attack. Malcolm will not expect it. We can catch him unawares and you can be on the throne by Yule.'

'We could not muster the troops required that fast. I need to travel around to see all my people and claim their allegiance. And I need to build a worthy home.'

'A home?' Kendrick sneered.

'A home, aye, and a strong base besides. It is important.'

'You will improve this hall then?' Cora asked, looking around the hated hall at Inverness in distaste.

'No.' Macbeth's arm snuck round her waist as if it could not help itself. 'I thought Cromarty, at the tip of the Black Isle. It is fine land, commands an excellent view over the firth and is easily defensible should the need arise.'

'Cromarty?' Cora asked, delighted. 'What a wonderful idea. It is so pretty up there and it will be a fresh start to our rule.'

'That's what I thought. We can start very soon while the weather is still fine and . . . '

'No!' Kendrick's roar cut through them both.

'No?'

'Look at you, Cora – look at you talking about halls and homes and pretty views. Feathering your nest.'

'It has need of feathers,' she retorted, stung again.

'It has no such need. It is pathetic. If this is what marriage does to a person's sense of purpose then I will forsake the pleasure. Building a damned hall is not action.'

'A campaign needs a solid base, Kendrick,' Macbeth said, still calm in the face of his friend's frenzy. 'We cannot just ride forth with swords and trust to chance.'

'Not to chance,' Kendrick howled, 'but to right, to courage, to justice!'

He leaped down from the makeshift dais and strode between the men to the door.

'Kendrick,' Cora called, 'where are you going?'

'To vengeance,' came back the cry, loud and defiant, 'as should you.'

And then he was gone, slamming out into the dusk on a whirl of anger. Cora made to follow but Macbeth held her back.

'Let him cool down. We can talk again tomorrow.'

Cora hesitated. Kendrick was being too hasty but she knew why and she felt the rawness of his anger chafe against her skin like a knife-edge.

'I have to make him understand, Macbeth. I have to make him see that we need time.'

'And you will, but not tonight. He is hearing nothing tonight save the pulse of his own fury.'

Cora sighed at the truth of it. Let her brother and his wild accusations stew a little; he would see things more clearly in the morning when both the ale and his temper had drained from him.

But by the morning, Kendrick had gone.

Chapter Sixteen

Scone, Christ's Mass 1030

Sibyll looked around the hall of King Malcolm's palace at Scone and smiled to see the exuberance of the Yule decorations. There were so many firs and ivies strung around the walls that it looked more like midsummer than midwinter. Only the rich smells of wassail, spiced pastries and crisp boarskin told her that it was Christ's Mass and she was glad to be up to see it.

She had birthed her second son some weeks back but the labour had been hard and she had recovered slowly. Fearful Duncan had wanted a girl, she had kept the baby close in her chamber but her husband, thank the Lord, had fallen hard for little Donald and in the end they had spent long hours in there together. It had been a peaceful time but they could not hide from the world forever and she had dragged herself up to travel to Scone for Yule. Now she was glad she had for the happiness at court was infectious – if tiring.

'You do not dance, my lady?'

Sibyll looked up from the padded stool on which she was watching the entertainments to see Brother Cullen at her side.

'I am not yet ready for such exertions,' she said with a smile. 'I will leave it to Bethan for now.'

She indicated her mother-by-marriage who was at the centre of the dance floor with King Malcolm, laughing and turning and sparkling like a true royal princess as she did not in the quiet of Dunkeld.

'Remember last time you gave birth?' Cullen asked quietly.

Sibyll shivered.

'After you'd had to drag me to Morag to escape the Moray men's attack? I must have been a fearful burden.'

'On the contrary, you were very brave. Very strong.'

She looked at him, touched.

'That's kind of you, Cullen, but thank the Lord we are not so endangered this time round. Please, do not let me stop you enjoying yourself.'

She waved to the dancers but Cullen shook his head.

'I am quite content, thank you. It is not seemly for a monk to dance.'

'Crinan has no such scruples.'

They both looked over to where the abbot was whirling a young woman around the dance floor.

'Crinan is part monk, part prince. And the prince is, I think, the larger part.'

Sibyll smiled.

'They are saying on the continent that priests should not marry.'

'Why?'

'So they can better devote themselves to God.'

Cullen considered this carefully.

'Women are a distraction,' he said eventually, sounding so solemn that Sibyll dared not laugh.

Looking away to hide her mirth, she saw the doors open and a new figure step inside. The man paused on the threshold, lit up by the torches flaming on the ancient Hill of Belief beyond. He was richly dressed, save for some travel-splatter on his fine cloak, and held himself proudly. Guests were always welcome at court, especially on feast-days, but Sibyll had thought that after six years in Alba she knew all the lords and her ever-ready sense for danger sparked.

'Who's that?' she asked Cullen.

He squinted through the smoky air of the hall.

'God have mercy, 'tis Lord Kendrick MacDuff. I thought he was safe over the Mounth in Moray. He must be insane – this court is not a safe place for the king's disowned nephew.'

Sibyll tried to remember where she'd heard that name before. Of course – Cora MacDuff, mother of Alba's other possible heir and now reportedly Lady Macbeth. She shivered and watched the man as he threaded his way through the crowds towards them. He looked dangerously focused and no one else seemed to care so it was up to her to defend her home. With a deep breath, she rose and stepped determinedly into his path. Lord Kendrick started.

'Beg pardon, my lady, but I must speak with the king.'

'You must wait, I'm afraid – the king is dancing.'

She gestured to where Malcolm was whirling Bethan around with all the vigour of a man half his age, his golden armlets catching the candlelight so that the pair of them looked to be circled in it as they turned.

'How nice for him.'

There was something charged about this man, like the sky before a storm. Sibyll placed a calming hand on his arm.

'He will be finished soon. Why not have a drink? Some food perhaps? You have travelled far?'

Lord Kendrick fidgeted at a line of mud on his cloak.

'Far, aye, but I am almost done.'

His eyes followed Malcolm's progress, his whole body rigid.

'Please,' Sibyll said, 'let us find you a seat. You look weary.'

It was not true; the man was, rather, extra awake. She had seen that look before in her brother's men when they returned from war, as if they had found something other than sleep to sustain them. It had scared her then and it scared her now.

'I am not hungry. Thank you.' Lord Kendrick twitched impatiently at his cloak. 'When will the dance end?'

'Soon,' Sibyll soothed. 'The music is faster now.'

It was true – the jig was picking up pace, sending the dancers into a final frenzy. Across the spin of bodies Sibyll caught Duncan's eye. He looked from her to the visitor and back again then began fighting his way through the crowd towards them. Sibyll's heart beat faster. Malcolm was in the centre of the jig, spinning Bethan so fast her feet had lifted clear from the floor. Others had moved back to make space and Lord Kendrick pushed through them, his movements jerky. Sibyll followed close behind.

'My lord, please, you must wait until . . . '

But now the musicians were slowing their pace and King Malcolm with them. He set Bethan on her feet and bowed to his clapping court but Sibyll's eyes were only on Lord Kendrick. As he threw back his cloak, she saw a flash of steel.

'No!' she screamed as Kendrick lifted a long, thin knife and dived for the king, crying, 'Vengeance!'

She grabbed desperately for his arm but he flung her off so that she staggered back. A sharp pain lanced through her and she fell. Someone caught her but she barely noticed, so intent was she on King Malcolm as realisation of his own mortality shadowed his face.

And then suddenly Kendrick was flying sideways, crashing to the ground as a man dived at his ankles. The knife flew from his hand and went screeching across the floor between myriad feet as his head bounced against the wooden boards. He flailed furiously but his assailant had a firm grasp of his legs and the would-be assassin was helpless in the centre of Alba's horrified lords.

'Duncan!' Malcolm cried, looking down in clear astonishment. 'Thank you.'

'Thank Sibyll,' he said from the floor. 'She alerted me to the danger and slowed the traitor enough to give me time to get to him.'

All eyes turned Sibyll's way. She was still caught in the grip of her own saviour and looked backward to see Brother Cullen holding her fast. Sheepishly, he steadied her and let go. Sibyll took a hasty step forward.

'That's not true. I did little of any use. If not for Duncan, Sire, you would be dead now.'

The court fell silent as the truth of this registered. Bethan buried her head against Crinan's shoulder. Duncan bowed. Malcolm looked round at them all.

'I owe you a great debt of gratitude, Prince Duncan,' he announced.

'It is an honour to serve my king,' Duncan replied.

Sibyll sneaked a look at Malcolm and saw him regarding her husband with real respect for possibly the first time. Then his eyes moved to the prisoner and narrowed to dark slits. He stepped over Lord Kendrick, pinned to the floor by every struggling limb.

'You made an attempt on my life, Lord Kendrick – a foiled one, perhaps, but an attempt all the same. You are a traitor.'

'And yet *you* murdered my father, your own cousin, and are called king.'

The court gasped delightedly at this defiance. Malcolm growled low in his throat.

'I did not murder your father, as well you know. I was nowhere near Fife when he died.'

'The royal reach is long,' Kendrick spat back, 'and determined.'

'It is now,' was all Malcolm replied. He looked up to the decorated rafters, then back to his guards. 'String him up.'

The men looked at each other.

'Now?' one of them dared to ask.

'Now!' Malcolm roared. 'This man came into my hall on this blessed day of Christ's birth intending my death. It is only fit that, instead, he should secure his own.'

The court was pushing backwards, shuffling towards the very edges of the floor as its purpose shifted from dancing to executioner's stage. Malcolm stood alone in the centre, pointing up to one of the fir-strewn cross-beams that held the old hall together. Someone ran for rope as the guards hefted Kendrick to his feet. He was still kicking defiantly but his eyes had clouded and he looked suddenly more boy than man.

'Did he truly think he would get out of here alive?' Sibyll whispered to Duncan.

'I think he hoped to take my grandfather to the grave with him.'

'*Did* Malcolm kill his own brother?'

'Hush, Sibyll,' Duncan said, but then leaned in close and added quietly, 'almost certainly.'

'Why?'

'A king cannot have rivals.'

She grabbed at his arm.

'And you? When you are king, will you have to kill rivals too?'

He did not answer but she felt him shudder and remembered Crinan's words back when he had come proxy woo-ing: *I cannot lie to you, my lady – Duncan's reign, when it comes, will be drenched in bloodshed.* Today she had seen for herself how close to the surface rivalries and hatreds ran in this Alban court and now they would mean death. One of the guards was tossing a rope over a beam and looping a noose at the end. Lord Kendrick screamed out, high-pitched and desperate, but another guard clapped a hand over his mouth and the sound was muffled to a terrified murmur.

'Must we watch?' Sibyll gasped, but one look at Malcolm's set face told her the answer: they had all been witness to the attempt on his life and must now be witness to his retribution for it.

The guards dragged Kendrick forward and shoved his head through the loop. They had to release his mouth to tighten the rope and the scream issued forth again, mad with fear, but the young lord begged for no mercy until they pulled tight and his feet were yanked from the ground. Then, as the noose tightened, cutting off his life's breath, he looked straight at Sibyll, his green eyes piercing as he choked out one brief final sentence: 'Tell Cora I'm sorry.' Then he was pulled up high above them, his hands clawing at his neck and his legs kicking out against his fate until, at last, he was still.

His body dangled from the Yule decorations, quiet now, its shadow dark across them all as the flames from the hearth threw it into stark relief. No one spoke. Sibyll felt sickness well up inside and clutched at her aching belly. The danger had been averted, thank the Lord, but the reminder of ever-present enemies sickened her. She longed only to be back in her chamber with her sons and husband but they were a part of this fractured court and could not easily escape. The happy peace of Christ's Mass was shattered for her and she feared she would see Lord Kendrick's deathly shadow across Malcolm's rule for a long time to come.

Chapter Seventeen

Forres, January 1031

'There it is – the Moray Stone.'

Macbeth pointed and, peering into the frozen pre-dawn gloom, Cora could just make out a great column piercing the lightening sky ahead. It was the height of at least three men and its pointed summit seemed to stab arrogantly at the heavy Alban clouds as if demanding they part and let the spring sun through. If so, the clouds weren't listening for they clung on tenaciously and it was only out over the distant sea that a watery pink light, like blood washed from battle-robes, shone across this grey eastern coast of Moray.

Cora approached the stone cautiously. Close up it seemed even bigger, towering above her as if it might at any minute fall and crush her into the stony ground. It was of dark red sandstone, intricately carved with a vivid battle scene and, lower down, a depiction of a number of men having their heads hacked off.

'Is it not magnificent? Macbeth said, his hand tracing the myriad fighting figures. 'I am told there are many stones like this in Rome.'

'Your Irish friends said so?'

'They did. Do you know, Cora, there is a monument called Trajan's Column that is twice this height and covered all over with carvings – all carried out by one man.'

'It must have taken him a long time.'

'Five years. Imagine! I should like to see it – would you not?'

'In Rome?'

'I doubt I will ever have the power to have it shipped to Alba, my sweet.'

'Nor the security to leave her long enough to travel all that distance.'

Macbeth looked away.

'You may be right,' he agreed dully and Cora felt mean for scotching his dream but she could not contemplate fancy pilgrimages in this stark Alban dawn.

'I don't see why we have to come all the way out here,' she grumbled.

'You do, Cora,' he said patiently. 'King Malcolm's envoy asked to meet us here at dawn.'

'But why here? Why not in your hall where we can offer hospitality? Why on this frozen hillside with nothing and no one for miles around?'

'I know not, Cora, but it's been a meeting point for many years. Perhaps it is simply that they know the way.'

Cora nodded reluctantly and scanned the snow-nipped hillside again but could see no one coming up the track from the south.

'What if it's a trick?'

'To what end?'

'To kill us, Macbeth.'

'But why?'

'Because we are a threat to the king, as my father was a threat.'

He was at her side in an instant, wrapping his big arms around her. His embrace was warm and strong and loving but it brought her little comfort right now. There was no reason to trust Malcolm and Macbeth was a fool if he did so. She knew that,

Kendrick did too, but Kendrick was gone. Macbeth's soldiers said he'd returned to Ireland to find 'real men' with whom to enact his retribution and Cora felt guilty every day that he had not felt able to turn to her.

'What is the purpose of the damned stone, then?' she asked crossly, pulling away from the embrace.

Macbeth moved away to consider the carvings.

'It commemorates the coming of the line of Aed to Moray and our defeat of the Picts.'

'They are Picts then?' she asked, pointing to the poor headless men at the base of the stone.

'They are.'

'It looks to be a brutal attack.'

'It had to be. Moray was too great a prize to let go.'

He looked fondly around the bleak moor and, despite her unease at this strange morning meeting, Cora had to smile.

'Fife is very pretty too, you know.'

'Tell me of it.'

'Now?'

'Why not? We have time to kill and I have never been there. I would like to know more of your homeland.'

'Right.' Cora glanced to the horizon but still no one was in sight. 'It is a lovely place, Macbeth. My family held their lands right in the centre at Balgedie but I was often at my uncles' houses out on the coast.'

'Uncles?'

'My father's brothers. Fergus held St Andrew's and Sean Kirkcaldy but I have heard nothing of them since Kendrick and I fled. I assume Malcolm had them killed too.'

'I'm sorry.'

'As am I. One day I would like to restore my family to their lands, if there are any of them left.'

Macbeth took a sudden step closer.

'I'd like that too, Cora.' His eyes glowed with intent. 'I've been thinking a lot about what Kendrick said before he left. I was planning only on making Lachlan king and had not thought of myself.'

Cora looked around, nervous again, but the guards stood at a distance with the horses and she and Macbeth were alone together beneath the stone.

'You wish to challenge on your own account?' she whispered.

'Maybe. I told Kendrick I would be ready at Easter and I meant it. Our hall is nearly finished and men are swearing allegiance everywhere I go. It is for love of my father, I believe.'

'And of yourself, Macbeth.'

'Perhaps. I hope so. I am not yet sure that I could be king, Cora, but our first step should be to kill Duncan and once the Tanaise is removed we shall see where God takes us. When the snows thaw I will send men to Ireland to find your brother and we can make plans to attack. Proper plans.'

Restitution at last. Cora shivered again, unsure if she felt excitement at the prospect or something more like fear. She was going soft and had to focus.

'That's good, Macbeth,' she said firmly, but his eyes were fixed on a point over her shoulder.

She turned and spotted a band of riders on the southerly horizon – a small group, apparently led by a bare-headed monk.

'I think we are safe enough,' Macbeth murmured though something in the band's clear intent chilled Cora's blood.

'For now perhaps,' she said darkly, leaning back against the stone that suddenly seemed as much guardian as threat.

The king's men were drawing closer, their collective breaths a frozen mist above them, and she could see that the rear horses were drawing something. A litter perhaps – or a bier. To her left Balgedie whickered uneasily and a guard grabbed for his reins. Cora drew her cloak tighter around her.

'This doesn't feel right, Macbeth.'

He didn't contradict her, but pulled her tight against him, his back to his ancestor's great memorial and his face set rigid as he watched the visitors draw nearer. Cora recognised Brother Cullen, the young monk who had come to Rosemarkie to teach them of usquebauch and felt a brief surge of relief, but now the men were close enough for her to see what the horses were pulling.

''Tis a body,' she whispered.

She felt a shudder run through Macbeth and heard his guard step up behind them but her eyes were still fixed on the bier. The corpse was wrapped in plain linen, its only ornamentation a wooden cross. Above it the St Andrew's cross of the Constantins snapped and grumbled in the sharp wind but there was no personal standard marking the dead man, if man this was.

But she already knew. As surely as God sat above Alba's dark clouds, she knew who this sombre-faced monk had brought to Moray and felt her breath sucked out of her so that she sagged against Macbeth. His grip tightened.

'Be brave, my heart,' he whispered.

So he knew too.

'He didn't go to Ireland, then?'

'I fear not.'

Cora tipped back her head, looked up the endless length of the Moray Stone and wished she were anywhere but here. She thought with desperate longing of the soft beaches of her Fife childhood, she and her brother the only ones along their great expanse. She thought of them climbing trees together like squirrels and swimming like seals. She thought of their father's butchering and of their flight up over the damned Mounth – seemingly alone in the world but together, at least together. She had not treasured that enough.

'Greetings, Mormaer Macbeth, Lady Macbeth.'

She felt Macbeth's fingers digging into her waist and slowly lowered her gaze to meet the monk's.

'Good morning, Brother Cullen.'

'You remember me?' He looked almost childishly pleased at that but Cora had no time for politeness. She stared past him to the bier and, seeing it, his gaze slid uncomfortably after hers. 'I bring you a body, Mormaer.'

'So I see,' Macbeth said stiffly.

'A traitor's body.'

'No!'

Macbeth's grip on her was tight but not tight enough. Cora jerked herself free and ran to the bier. She dropped to her knees on the icy ground and scrabbled at the join in the linen, desperate to be proved wrong. The king's guards looked awkwardly at one another but did not stop her. The monk put out a hand but he did not stop her either and now the linen was loose and she pulled it away to reveal the poor, dear face within.

'Kendrick. Oh, God, Kendrick. What have you done to him?'

She glared at the monk, her hands fluttering over her brother's neck, which was scarred across with an ugly line of bruising. His face was bloated like a bull-frog's, his closed eyes bulging unnaturally and his poor mouth frozen in a grimace of horror. She ran her hands desperately through his hair as if she might soothe this terrible hurt from him and Brother Cullen coughed and shifted his feet.

'He was hanged, my lady. I am sorry. It was at least swift.'

'Hanged? Like a common man?'

'Like a common criminal. He tried to kill the king.'

Over the icy air Cora heard Kendrick berating her and Macbeth again for wanting to 'feather their nest'. They'd put his raging down to temper, to ale. They'd let him go uncomforted and the next day, when he'd been nowhere to find, had done nothing. They'd taken the men at their word and had not sent so much as one messenger to Ireland to be sure he was safe. Only Aila had truly fretted for him and Cora had paid her too little attention. It was unforgivable.

'Let him cool down,' Macbeth had said and she'd given in.

She'd given in because it had been easier that way. She was the one who'd understood the raw pain of their father's murder. She was the one who had sworn vengeance with her brother – and in the end she had let him go to it alone. She'd been blind. Worse, she'd *chosen* to be blind and now Kendrick, poor dear Kendrick, who had ever protected her and followed Macbeth, was dead. Her husband came quietly up beside her and she turned to fling some of these dark thoughts at him but saw in his eyes that he felt them already.

'We failed him,' he murmured, his voice breaking.

It was a stark, unavoidable truth. The king's guards were unfastening the rough bier, laying it on the ground before them and backing away.

'Thank you for returning his body, Brother,' Macbeth choked out.

'It was not so much a charity as a warning,' Cullen said. 'King Malcolm bade me tell you there will be no leniency for traitors. Alba needs a united people and he will not tolerate anyone who threatens that unity. It is, he says, too dangerous for us all. I'm sure you agree.'

He delivered the message in a firm voice but Cora saw his hands fidgeting at the ends of his monk's sleeves and felt a desperate need to know more.

'Would you like a cup of ale?' she asked. Surprise flickered in Cullen's eyes and he looked back to his guard. 'It is no trick. This is not your doing, Brother.'

'Indeed,' he said, voice suddenly eager. 'I tried to stop your brother. I saw him arrive, saw he seemed ... unsettled. Lady Duncan saw it too. We spoke to him but he ... he had a plan. He had a knife and a plan and he nearly succeeded.'

'He tried to stab the king at court?'

'At dancing, my lady, aye.'

Cora groaned. She could believe it all too well. Poor Kendrick had felt so abandoned by them that he had decided to eliminate their father's killer alone. Whether he had succeeded or not, he would never have made it out alive. She was robbed of a brother, Macbeth of a friend and poor Aila of a groom. Sadly, she covered Kendrick's swollen face and went back to sit on the slab beneath the Moray Stone, welcoming its cold, dark shadow. Macbeth came with her and Cullen shuffled forward as a guard brought up a small barrel of ale and wooden travelling cups. Cora took her cup, cradling it in her hands and looking out to the far-off sea as the two men waited deferentially.

'My brother was a good man,' she said eventually. 'His blood was too hot perhaps but it had fair cause to be, as I know all too well.'

Cullen looked nervously to his guard but they were being served ale too and were not looking their way. He leaned in towards Cora.

'Lady Duncan begged me to convey to you Lord Kendrick's last words.'

'His last words?'

'He spoke them to her, my lady, and she charged me with passing them on.'

'What said he?'

Cullen took a deep drink of his ale.

'He said, "Tell Cora I'm sorry."'

The tears came then, as fast as if Cullen had pulled a rock away and let loose the water dammed behind. She curled in on herself as Macbeth's arms encircled her and Cullen dipped his head. She noticed neither of them. Kendrick had thought of her at the end; it was both a reproach and a comfort.

'Why didn't I see what he'd do?' she wailed. 'I knew him best of anyone. I knew he wouldn't cool down. I knew our father's death was a wound that festered inside him and I let him go. And now, and now . . .'

She gestured helplessly to the bruised body in the heather behind them.

'Every man chooses his own path, my lady,' Brother Cullen said quietly. 'His actions are between him and God. I saw him before the attack and I do not think anyone could have deflected him from his course.'

Cora looked at him.

'That's kind of you to say. And kind of your lady too.'

'She is not *my* lady.'

'Well, no ... of course not. But you are clearly close in her confidence.'

'I hope so. She is, as you say, a very kind woman. Brave too. She tried to stop Lord Kendrick with her own body but he cast her off.'

'No!'

'Fret not – I caught her.'

'She is lucky in you.'

The monk turned almost as purple as poor Kendrick's bruised neck and suddenly reached out and grabbed Macbeth's arm.

'Her husband is weak.'

Macbeth looked confused.

'Prince Duncan?'

'He is not worthy.'

'Of her?'

Cullen spluttered, drank deep.

'Of Alba. Old King Malcolm holds the country together. His methods are ruthless but effective. Men know this and follow him for it. But Duncan ...'

'King Malcolm bade you tell us this?'

'No! Lord, no.' He leaped up as if startled by his own daring. 'I must be on my way.' He shoved his empty cup at Cora who, surprised, fumbled it. The cup fell to the icy slab and bounced with an audible crack. Cullen took a few steps back and spoke again, his voice unnaturally loud. 'Consider this a warning, Mormaer Macbeth. Hold Moray strong for King Malcolm and for his heirs.'

155

His eyes flashed at them like sparkling jet then he turned and
fled to his guards, who hastily fell in behind. More ale cups hit
the ground, tangible reminder of those moments of strange, awkward goodwill, and then the king's men were gone. Cora looked
to Macbeth.

'What was that about?'

He shook his head.

'The monk seemed with the one hand to be delivering a
brutal warning against treachery and with the other the means
to commit it.'

'He does not like Duncan.'

'No.'

Cora looked up at the stone again, wishing for a crazy moment
that she were in Rome or any other place far away from here. The
monument had at last pierced the clouds and they were thinning
out around it, letting sunlight leak through to sparkle in the half-
snow lacing the heather.

'Is Duncan truly weak, Macbeth?'

His eyes followed her gaze upwards. He placed one hand
upon the stone then the other as if drawing strength from this
symbol of Moray.

'From all I have heard he is not strong,' he said carefully.
'And he will need to be strong, you know, to hold Alba for the
Constantins against the proper order of inheritance.'

'You will challenge him then?'

'It is what Kendrick wanted.'

'But is it what you want?'

'To be King of Alba?' She nodded. Macbeth looked to the
stone, then back to where Cullen and his men were disappearing
over the southern horizon. He watched them in silence for some
time then said, 'It is what my father would have done.'

Cora looked to Kendrick's poor body.

'Retribution,' she said softly.

She owed that to her father and now to her brother too, and

blessed Macbeth for embracing her cause as his own once more. She would bury Kendrick with love and then she would ride forth with hate. King Malcolm was a cruel tyrant and this time she must stay fixed to her purpose of destroying his cruel grip on her life, her family and her country.

Chapter Eighteen

Scone, May 1032

Sibyll looked around the compound at Scone and felt giddy from all the frantic activity. In three days' time King Malcolm would reach his eightieth year and Alba had gone mad with preparations for the great day. Malcolm had ordered a new palace built at Scone to commemorate this landmark and the master carpenters had been shipping in more and more men to complete it on time. There was a vast labourers' camp stretching out across the fields behind the Hill of Belief, but thankfully they were putting the finishing touches to the magnificent great hall.

Made of the finest oak, it glowed like spring honey and the whole of the compound smelled deliciously of fresh-cut wood. Every pillar was carved with an individual design of Malcolm's own choosing and even the brooms with the finest bristles were struggling to clear the endless shavings from their bases. New trestle tables were stacked at one end ready for the birthday feast and the old ones were set in a pyramid in the middle of the compound, ready for the great fire that would start a run of beacons across Alba all the way to the edge of the Mounth.

No one had approached Mormaer Macbeth to join the party

but every other noble in Alba had been invited and there was excitement in the air from St Andrews in the east to Partick in the west. Malcolm was thriving on it but Sibyll was tired of the whole performance and had snatched at the chance it would give her to ride downriver to meet her brother at the port of Perth. Ward was sailing up to join the festivities, bringing Beorn, and Sibyll could not wait to see the six year old who had been but a babe-in-arms when she left York.

She had persuaded Duncan to let her bring Malky with her since he was almost five now and was hoping that Beorn would keep the younger child busy and out of the way of his grandfather. Yesterday Malcolm had brought Malky up to the dais before the whole court and presented him with a miniature crown, 'to stop him stealing mine'. Malky had been delighted and Sibyll had been forced to make a show of pleasure on his behalf when it had been all she could do not to weep with frustration at this deliberate and very public slight to Duncan.

She had tried to persuade her husband to come out to Perth with her but he'd chosen to stay with eighteen-month-old Donald and welcome Maldred into Scone. That had been another good reason for Sibyll to get away. When Maldred was in the west she could just about block him from her mind, but when he was at court she seemed newly on fire and she was forever scared that this time it would consume her. It was with relief, therefore, that she guided her horse out of the thronged royal compound and headed south.

It was only an hour's canter to the river-port but Malky was keen to show her his new galloping skills so they took it at pace and crested the hill above the valley in time to see Ward's ship coming up the Tay.

'Is that it?' Malky asked, standing up in his stirrups to point. 'Is that Uncle Ward's ship? It's so beautiful, Mama.'

Sibyll could only nod for her eyes had misted with foolish tears. It *was* beautiful – long and sleek with a painted prow curving like the neck of a woman. This far upriver, Ward was using his oarsmen and something about the perfect harmony of their movements caught at Sibyll's soul. She had spent much time in ships as a child and had forgotten how they thrilled her.

Sometimes her father had taken them out to sea, usually just when he was checking his shellfish pots but occasionally on a full fishing trip, and as Sibyll watched Ward's boat drawing closer she could almost see the silver flashes of a hundred flapping fish on the middle-deck. She shook the image away. Ward was now an earl and one of England's greatest men. The fisher-life had been burned out from under them and they had forged a new one from its embers – and what a life it was! Suddenly all Sibyll's petty worries seemed as naught. Why was she fretting about her son being given a jewelled crown? How spoiled had she grown that such a trifle was now her sole concern?

'Come, Malky,' she called, 'let's race them to the jetties!'

Her son needed no second urging and together they galloped down the grassy slope to the port. Not that it was truly a port, not like in Denmark or even in England, protected by walls and lined with buildings and bustling with traders. No, Perth was a small line of wooden jetties looked over by two neat cottages in which dwelled the elderly boatman and his family. A cow, two pigs and a handful of sheep were the only other inhabitants and all looked up with faint interest as Sibyll and Malky rode in, halloo-ing to the boat.

Sibyll saw Ward's imposing figure in the prow and waved keenly. He waved back and as the boat drew close he leaped from the deck to land squarely before them. His beard was laced with river-mist, his face ruddy from the winds and his cloak redolent of fish. Sibyll fell into the blissful familiarity of his arms.

'It is so good to see you, Ward.'

He hugged her so tight the breath was squeezed out of her then released her to clasp Malky's hand. Sibyll had to bite back amusement as her son stared up in clear awe at his giant of an uncle.

'Is he truly a man?' he whispered to her when Ward turned back to see his ship safely pulled up on the shore.

'He truly is,' Sibyll assured him. 'He has always been big.'

'Will I be like that?'

'Maybe, if you eat lots of fish.'

'Fish?' Her son considered this carefully but now Ward was holding out his arms and another figure was leaping from the boat. Ward spun the boy round then set him on his feet before Sibyll and Malky.

'Beorn,' he said proudly and Sibyll looked down at a miniature version of her brother.

The boy was far too young for a beard, of course, and was still slender, but the set of his shoulders, the glint in his blue eyes and even the way he put his hands on his hips as he looked around him were identical to his father's.

'He's so like you,' she gasped.

Ward beamed.

'Is he not? And he's as strong and brave and foolhardy as me too. I am forever pulling him out of scrapes.'

It was said gruffly but with clear pride.

'Scrapes?' Malky asked eagerly, sidling closer to his cousin.

'Scrapes?' Sibyll echoed, but Ward just laughed.

'Nothing major, sister, don't you worry. Beorn will be an earl one day and knows how to behave himself. Just tree-climbing and rope-swinging and river-swimming – the usual.'

Malky's eyes shone.

'You can swim?' he asked Beorn in his best English.

'Of course. It is easy. I'll teach you, if you like?'

'Yes, please. Now?'

Both boys looked at the river, glinting invitingly in the sun.

'Oh no ... ' Sibyll started but Ward cut her off.

'Why not? That looks a good spot.' He pointed to a shingle beach a little way upriver. 'And once you've got the hang of it, you can dive off the jetties.'

'Yes!' Malky raced to the water followed by Beorn, shedding clothes as they went.

'Should they . . . ?' Sibyll started to say but Ward silenced her with a powerful clap on the back.

'Of course they should. We can keep an eye on them from here and it will keep them busy. I've fish caught fresh this morning and plenty of ale. Let's sit, relax, talk.'

Put like that, it was impossible to refuse.

'Ah, Ward,' Sibyll said, tugging him down to plant a kiss on his salty cheek, 'it is lovely to see you. Life at court is good but I sometimes forget the simple pleasures.'

'That's me.' Ward grinned. 'A simple pleasure. Now, sit.'

Sibyll looked round to see that his men had somehow unpacked two pretty stools, an ale barrel and an iron fire-pit. Already men were kindling wood and more were sitting on the shoreline gutting salmon. Others were pouring flour into bowls and adding water and dried herbs to make bread and Sibyll's mouth watered at the prospect of this surprise meal.

The boys were in the river, splashing and laughing. Malky's English was good but their accents differed and many gestures accompanied the chatter as they strove to make themselves understood. Beorn had found a buoyant log and was making Malky tuck it under his chest and kick across the surface of the water. Sibyll could hear his cries of delight from here. Simple pleasures.

'Is all well in York?' she asked her brother.

'All is very well,' he agreed, a glint in his eye.

'Ward? What are you plotting?'

'The usual. I have been winning some border skirmishes in North Northumbria and Earl Eldred is weakening. I swear all I need to take Durham is an Alban ally. King Malcolm thrives?'

'He does but I think his troops are more concerned about affairs to the north of them than to the south. Moray is restless.'

'Damn. Their Mormaer is coming to this feast?'

'Lord, no!'

'Ah, well, perhaps I can persuade Malcolm a trip south would be a welcome diversion. Or Duncan maybe for the king is surely old to fight? Eighty years is a mighty long time to tread this earth.'

'Malcolm is a mighty man. I'm not sure death dare approach him.'

'You must hope it will or you shall never be queen.'

'Ward, hush!'

Sibyll looked round nervously. Ever since Lord Kendrick's attack, Malcolm had been on high alert for any hint of treason but his men were oblivious and her own were down at the jetty admiring the boat. Even so, she needed a safer subject.

'I was thinking as we watched you row in of our life back in Denmark,' she said to her brother.

'You were?' He smiled at her. 'It seems a long, long time ago, sister.'

'Where would we have been now, think you, if the Wends had not come?'

Ward looked up the line of the Tay, considering.

'I suppose I would be running Father's fleet and you would be birthing Danish bairns to some farmer or butcher or artisan. Life took us on a very different path but it is a good one, is it not?'

'A very good one. You saved us, Ward, by gaining service with Cnut.'

'You did your share.'

'How? I was nothing but a burden to you.'

'Is that how you remember it?' he asked, looking at her curiously.

'It's how it was. I wasn't much older than that pair in the river and far slighter and weaker than they. You had to see me safe and well. You even had to share your bed with me.'

Ward took her hands.

'I did not *have* to, Sibyll, I chose to. I was weak too, weak with grief and fear. If I had not had you to cling to at night, I might never have found the will to go to Cnut. Strength isn't just physical, you know. You were the one who whispered to me that we could do it. You were the one who scavenged food and patched up our clothes so that we looked presentable and coached me in what to say when we finally found the king. Mine was the sword-arm, yes, but yours was the will behind it. Do you not remember *that*?'

Sibyll nodded slowly.

'I do, I suppose, now that you talk of it but it did not seem like bravery at the time – just what we had to do.'

'And therein lies the strength of it. Did not Crinan see that the moment you talked to him? I think maybe, Sibyll, even if we had stayed in Denmark, you would have become a queen.'

'Nonsense!'

'There I'd have been, a humble fisher-boy selling his wares to the local lord with my sister to help lug the basket.' Ward leaped up, pulling her after him and pretending they were holding an imaginary load between them. '"Buy my fish, Lord," I'd say. "Finest fish, fresh caught today." But he wouldn't be looking at the fish, only at you. "I will buy your fish," he'd say, "if your sister will serve it." Oh, but I'd protest at that. "She is no woman of easy virtue to be paraded before lords like a hoyden," I'd tell him and he'd say, "I know that. This one is a jewel . . . "'

'Ward, please!'

'A *jewel*. So I'd say you could go but only if I could come too and it would turn out that this lord was entertaining the king and with him his son, the prince. And this prince would have been looking all over for a wife but found the noble ladies too whining and spoiled and dull, and the moment he'd see you, Sibyll the fisher-girl, he'd fall in love and . . . '

'Ward, enough! Marriages are not made for love.'

Her brother subsided.

'Some are. I loved Beorn's mother dearly.'

He sank onto his stool, dropping his imaginary basket and Sibyll felt mean.

'I'm sorry. You must miss her.'

'I do.' He wiped a hand roughly over his face then straightened up. 'But I have Beorn and he is a great consolation. Look – I believe your boy is starting to swim!'

He pointed and Sibyll saw Malky pushing the log aside and kicking out unsupported. It was a splashy performance, all hands and feet and flying water, but he did seem to be afloat.

'Bravo!' Ward called, clapping loudly. 'Bravo!'

Sibyll felt a rush of love for her big, exuberant brother. He would have succeeded without her help she was sure, but she was glad he hadn't had to. She thought of Ward's prince stepping up to the fisher-girl then, with a horrified start, realised she was picturing him as Maldred. She shook the thought away. It was just a crazy story, a hearthside fantasy. Duncan was her prince and she was blessed indeed to have him as a husband.

'Wait until you tell Papa you can swim,' she called to Malky.

She was rewarded by a keen wave and then a slightly panicked, 'But not yet, Mama. We don't have to go yet?'

'Not yet,' Sibyll confirmed.

Ward's men were tossing fish onto a skillet over the fire and the smell of the flesh rose on the riverside air. Ale glugged into tankards and Sibyll accepted one and sank contently back onto her stool at her brother's side.

'To us,' he proposed, 'fisher-folk made lords.'

'To us,' she agreed, clinking her tankard against his. 'And to simple pleasures.'

Already she felt buoyed up for the celebration ahead. In three days, she would sit gladly at Duncan's side as King Malcolm celebrated eighty years of life and twenty-seven as king. She would wear all her fine jewels and Malky would wear his little crown and they would toast their country and their line and their future as rulers of Alba and it would be magnificent.

It had to be, for while this happy conversation with Ward had reminded her where the journey to glory had begun, it had also reminded her how easily good fortune could be reversed. As she'd told Ward, the Moray men had not been invited to Malcolm's feast and they would not like that. They would not like that at all.

Chapter Nineteen

Glamis, October 1034

It was a host vaster than any Cora had seen before and she looked proudly down on it from her vantage point above the battlefield. To the south stood King Malcolm's formidable fortress at Glamis and she eyed it keenly. They would take it before the day was out, she was sure of it. This was the attack she had dreamed of for so long; this was the start of her family's restitution and Macbeth's rise and she was glad to be here to bear witness.

In truth it had been a hard journey south for her body was sore from twice conceiving and twice losing a child. Determined not to give into grief she had channelled it into the attack and, when the time had come, had left Lachlan with Aila and ridden over the Mounth with the army.

'You are Aed, I am Constantin,' she'd told Macbeth when he'd objected. 'We must be seen to be united.'

She had dressed herself as a warrior queen in men's trews and tunic with a mail coat over the top. A helmet had topped her red hair and she'd worn sturdy boots on her feet to give an outward show of strength even if inside she had felt as weak as the babies she had lost. Every step of the way had reminded her keenly of her mad dash in the other direction ten years ago with just Kendrick as her protector. She was determined to see Macbeth's men avenge the deaths of both father and brother.

That was why, with the battle finally at hand, she had climbed a crag overlooking the field to bear witness, though it wasn't at all as she'd expected. The date of the battle had been established with much to-ing and fro-ing of messengers, spouting rhetoric alongside practical arrangements, so that eventually the two sides lined up more like partners in a dance than deadly enemies. The whole thing started with much waving of flags – Malcolm beneath the Constantin cross and Macbeth beneath the Aed lion – as the leaders rode out to parley.

Cora was too far away to hear their words but Macbeth had rehearsed his speech often enough for her to know that he would be demanding to be recognised as Tanaise in Duncan's stead. He would be asserting Finlay's Aed blood-right, reminding them of her, his Constantin wife, and calling on King Malcolm to see the level of support ranged at his opponent's back. Her husband would be citing Moray's long allegiance to the crown and promising its continuation throughout Malcolm's lifetime and then he would be challenging Duncan to single combat so as to decide the matter without spilling more than one Albaman's blood, whichever of them that might be.

Cora looked nervously for Duncan but there were several men with the king and none stood out as Macbeth's intended challenger. All, though, looked very big and very well equipped and she dreaded their response. It came from King Malcolm himself, loud and clear even to Cora high up in the rocks, and her whole body shook at the once-familiar sound of the murderer's coarse voice.

'You do not deserve the courtesy of single combat, Mormaer, for in calling us to battle you make yourself a traitor to the crown and should be hung.' Cora remembered Kendrick's poor neck and gripped tight to the rocks to stop herself from charging down and running Malcolm through herself. How could Macbeth stand there and listen to such arrogant treachery? 'I have named my Tanaise and he has been accepted. I do not need a Moray stripling to question my wisdom. Alternate inheritance is dead. The line of Aed is all but dead too and if you cannot accept that I will make sure it is terminated this very day. Withdraw or draw!'

Macbeth's response was to whisk his sword from its scabbard and cut the stave of Malcolm's white and blue banner in two before galloping back to his own line, his men hot on his heels. Barely had they ridden through the parted ranks to take up their place in command at the rear than the king's men were charging.

Cora's heart beat faster but even now this was not the slaughter she had long imagined. Malcolm's forces attacked, withdrew, attacked, withdrew. Then Macbeth's did the same. The two sides jostled for position in the centre ground, stabbing and thrusting from behind their shields, one or other forever pulling back to reset their ranks, like a complicated game.

The morning ground past. Rain began to fall and Cora saw men look to the skies and grumble to each other as if the weather was spoiling a pretty feast and not a fight to the death. A few lay dead, a few more had limped to the rear, nursing severed limbs or gushing wounds, but neither side seemed to have the upper hand.

And then, suddenly, as the rain thickened still further, a Moray arrow went wild and struck the breast of one of Malcolm's horses that had strayed into the lush grass at the edge of the fighting. The animal reared up, shrieking in pain and lashing out with its hooves. The men at that end of the royal ranks pulled away from it, opening a gap into which the poor horse, half-blinded with the hurt of the barb, went charging wildly. Men leaped out of its path and the Moray ranks watched, stunned, as the animal caused more chaos among the enemy than they had all morning.

The creature was deep into Malcolm's soldiery now and heading, it seemed, straight for the king. Perhaps the vivid cross on his banner was all the poor thing could make out in the driving rain. Several big hearth-guards made a brave grab for its bridle but it bucked and shied away.

'Kill it!' someone roared, perhaps the king himself, and as his repaired standard was struck aside by the horse someone thrust at it with a sword. Blood spurted from the poor animal's breast before, in a last flurry of kicks, it fell.

'The king,' someone called from the chaos at the very heart of the royal ranks. 'The king is hurt!'

Cora felt a thrill at the cry – the murderer was finally murdered! She looked excitedly towards Macbeth. *Attack*, she willed him. He was talking urgently with his lead commanders. The rain was heavier now and a mist was rising, shrouding the men's feet so that the paused battle seemed to hover before her. *Attack*, she thought again.

King Malcolm's men were pulling in tight around him, re-setting themselves after the horse's crazy bolt. A thickset, dark-haired man was shouting them into place as a small group carrying a prostrate man hustled out of the rear line and made for the old fortress.

'The king!' Cora shouted down, but no one heard her over the noise of the field and the hiss of the rain and still the dammed mist rose as if God was sending a cover for Malcolm's retreat.

But now, at last, Macbeth was sounding a horn. Cora leaned forward through the near-darkness to watch. This was it. This was the moment when her husband won Alba. Water was running down her hair, turning it rust red. Her feet were cold and her fingers frozen to the rock but she gripped tighter and peered through the gloom, determined to witness this vital point in their family history so as to be able to tell the tale to Lachlan. She spared a glance for the sky, so low now she almost felt she was part of it.

'I hope you're watching, Kendrick.'

Almost she felt him nod, heard an echo of his laughter in the mist, but as she looked back to the field strange things were happening. Both lines were drawing back. Step by slow step they were opening up the gap between them, leaving the two commanders standing at the centre of the field with just a handful of men at their backs. With Malcolm withdrawn, was it to be single combat after all?

Cora looked nervously at the figure who must be Duncan. He was taller than Macbeth and thicker across the chest. He looked slow, perhaps, but powerful and stood resolutely, sword gripped in both hands. Her eyes swung to Macbeth. The mist was so high now that his legs were totally obscured but he too stood solidly, arms folded, sword pointing upwards in readiness. Who would attack first? Both sides seemed to bristle with intent and she felt a fear colder than any rain run down her sodden spine.

What if this Duncan won? What if she witnessed the death of Macbeth? What if this grey, damp half-battle saw her widowed? She could not bear to lose him again. Bracing herself against the crag, she peered down at the men but now both Macbeth and Duncan were bowing. Bowing? And Duncan was laying his sword on the ground, or so she assumed for it disappeared into the mist, and he rose again with both hands bare and held out towards Macbeth. *Charge him*, Cora willed, but no, Macbeth was mirroring his rival and laying down his arms. For a moment longer they stood there, facing each other, then with another damned bow, they were both retrieving their weapons and retiring from the field.

Cora sat there, stunned, as the battleground before her emptied. The wounded and dead were carried or supported away and within a ridiculously short time the soldiers were all gone and there was only mist wisping carelessly across the site of what had not even seemed to be a true fight. No one sang the Shepherd's Psalm to soothe the lost, for few *were* lost – save Cora herself who felt not just lost but utterly adrift. What had happened here?

She thought of Macbeth while they'd been waiting at the Moray Stone for Kendrick's poor body. What had her husband said then? 'I am not yet sure that I could be king'. Did he doubt it still? Was that why, at this critical point, he had pulled away? How could he do that? He had promised her restitution, promised her it at their first betrothal and again at their second, and both times she had believed him, trusted him. And all for this – for retreat?

Cutting through the turmoil of Cora's emotions came the clarity of burning anger. She spun round and marched down the steep track, barely noticing the scree skidding beneath her feet or the rain battering down in her headlong dash for Macbeth's camp. She all but ran down the last of the slope and over to the tents, huddled in the trees like the miserable cowards within. She made straight for the Mormaer's grand pavilion, flinging up the flap and marching inside. Macbeth was there with Davey and his other commanders, all nursing goblets of wine as if this had been a hunting expedition not a fight for Alba itself.

'What the hell happened?' she demanded. They stared at her, apparently confounded by the question. 'Out there, on the field – why did you retreat? Malcolm was injured and their ranks were in disarray. The day was ours to claim and you all stood there watching.'

The men's eyes flickered nervously to one another then to Macbeth. They took a few surreptitious steps back. Cora folded her arms.

'You don't understand, Cora,' Macbeth said.

'Then explain, please, because it looked pretty simple to me. You ducked the fight.'

'We did not. We took a considered tactical decision.'

'To duck the fight.'

'No! Did you see the mist, Cora, the darkness, the rain, the state of the ground? If we'd attacked then, we'd have lost too many men. You could barely tell friend from foe down there and we could have been killing our own and not knowing it. It was an honourable withdrawal by both sides.'

'Honourable? You could have won, Macbeth! You could have

finished off the king and crushed Duncan. They were terrified, panicked – yours for the taking.'

'They regrouped.'

'Because you let them! *I* should have come into battle. I should have led – because I would not have been so lily-livered as to withdraw and by now the throne of Alba would be ours.'

'And there would be no men left to rule.'

'Rubbish! Duncan's forces would have fled.'

'I doubt it. It is harder in conditions like these to flee than it is to stand and fight. I would be king of ghosts, if I were not a ghost myself.'

'Excuses.'

'Tactics, Cora. You don't understand. As commander I cannot waste my men. It would not be fair.'

'So now?' she demanded.

'The king is injured.'

'Aye. And?'

A pause.

'So now we regroup and wait.'

'Here?'

Another pause, a longer one, and then, 'In Moray. We are safer over the Mounth.'

Cora recoiled.

'Safer? Lord, I thought it was meant to be women who begged for safety not Alba's own warriors. No wonder it took you five years to come back for me if this is how you fight. Are you truly telling me that we have marched all this way to trade pleasantries in the mist and scurry back over your precious bloody Mounth? It's pathetic.'

'Cora, silence.' Macbeth's voice was icy now. 'You speak out of turn. It is the only sensible course of action. We're all agreed upon it.' She took a step back but Macbeth grabbed her by the shoulders. 'I am happy for you to ride with me, Lady Macbeth, but I am not happy for you to question me. I am the war leader, not you. I hold the lives of my men in my hands and I will honour their trust in me that with considered wisdom, not foolhardy glory-seeking. We will retreat over the Mounth. We have signalled our opposition, weakened the enemy and wounded the king.'

'A stray horse wounded the king.'

He shrugged.

'Such is the way of battle. I apologise, wife, if it has not been as glorious as you had hoped but war is a messy, dirty, frustrating business. Do not believe all the legends tell you – this is the reality.'

Cora looked him up and down.

'This is the reality you have chosen, certainly. Rest well.'

'Where are you going?'

'To pray. To pray for Kendrick looking down upon this and for Lachlan waiting for the inheritance he was promised – and for King Malcolm's recovery.'

'Why?'

'Because it seems to me that the old murderer, at least, has the guts to be a true king.'

And with that she threw herself out into the louring darkness, turning her face up to welcome the battering rain as just punishment. Her husband had turned out to be no ally at all and, on her knees in the mud, she wept alone for their failure today.

Chapter Twenty

Glamis, November 1034

Sibyll eased back the heavy woollen curtain and looked cautiously into Malcolm's makeshift chamber. His prostrate form had been too heavy to carry upstairs to his usual bed so instead Duncan had ordered a corner of the great hall curtained off. The king had lain there ever since the disastrous battle two weeks ago, casting gloom over all who had stayed on to defend Glamis against any further attacks. Spies had reported that the Moray men had headed up the north road, but they weren't taking any chances with the king so struck down.

'Sibyll?'

Crinan was standing just inside and ushered her forward, holding back the curtain to let Malky follow. Sibyll felt her son's hand squirm into hers and suppressed her surprise. The sight of his indomitable grandfather brought so low must have knocked her proud seven year old back a few years and she tugged him gently forward, glad of his warm fingers in hers as she approached the bed.

The horse had kicked Malcolm in the lower ribs, cracking them open and cutting a half-moon wound deep into his flesh. Doctors had tried to flush it with sour wine and bind it with linens but it was clear the damage had gone deeper than they could reach and the wound was putrefying. The king's groans had punctuated every sombre meal since he'd been brought back and the only thing worse than the terrible noise was its recent lack.

'Is he awake?' Sibyll whispered, looking to Bethan who sat at her father's side holding a bowl of cool water to soothe his fever.

'As much as he ever is,' she said, her voice tight. 'Come close or he won't see you.'

Sibyll crept closer. Malcolm was raised up on several pillows to aid his rattling breathing. His cheeks seemed to have sunk in on themselves and even his arms looked thinner. He wore his golden armlets still but they hung limply, as if relinquishing their hold upon his flesh and though his eyes were open they were fixed on the middle distance as if already searching for heaven's gates.

'Has he long?'

'No. Talk to him, woman, before it's too late.'

She nodded, crossed herself and shuffled forward, Malky dragging reluctantly behind her.

'Sire? My lord king?' Still he stared forward. 'King Malcolm!'

Suddenly his head swivelled and his eyes fixed upon her like an owl's upon a mouse.

'Lady Duncan, thank you for coming.' His voice was as raw as if there were shards of iron in his throat but his meaning was clear. 'I wanted to see you. I *had* to see you. You, my dear, are the key to Alba.'

'I am?'

'You are. I asked Crinan to find me a strong woman and he did.'

'Thank you, Sire. I am proud to be Duncan's wife.'

'Malcolm's mother.'

'That too.'

'That *first*. Protect the boy.'

'Of course.'

'Is he here? Is he with you?'

An eager light came into Malcolm's eyes as he searched for

176

his grandson. Malky shuffled forward reluctantly then visibly squared his shoulders and looked the king in the eye. Malcolm nodded his approval.

'You will be a good king, Malcolm.'

'If I can be half as good as you, Sire, I will be thankful,' Malky said dutifully and Sibyll felt her eyes mist with pride.

Malcolm gave his little namesake a nod of approval and then turned his attention back to Sibyll, groping for her hand.

'You will see him king?'

She hesitated and Crinan stepped in to speak for her.

'Of course she will, Sire. Did she not wrap him in our Constantin colours the very day of his birth?'

'So you tell me, Crinan – but I want to hear it from her, from Sibyll herself.'

She swallowed.

'I will, of course, do everything in my power to see my son to the throne one day, Sire. But Duncan first.'

Malcolm snorted and sank back against his pillows, muttering, 'It looks that way.'

Sibyll glanced to Bethan for support but Duncan's mother refused to meet her eye. Anger prickled at Sibyll's skin.

'Duncan will be a good king,' she said firmly, 'and would be a better one if others would believe in him.'

Bethan fumbled the bowl and a little water spilled onto her gown. The king smiled thinly.

'I hope you are right.'

'Oh, I am. And you should know that if he rules well it will be in spite of, not because of, you.'

Sibyll felt Malky shift uneasily behind her and Crinan take a nervous step forward but Malcolm smiled, more sincerely this time.

'A strong woman,' he repeated. 'You, at least, deserve to be queen. You do wish to be queen, Lady Sibyll?'

'I do, Sire.'

'Why?'

'Why?' Sibyll swallowed nervously. 'To support my husband and honour my family and serve my adopted country.'

'Very dutiful. But why really? What's in it for *you*?'

She glanced around but there was no escape and it was, she supposed, a valid question. Eventually she said just one word: 'Security.'

Malcolm sighed.

'Security? You disappoint me. Is that all you seek?'

'If, like me, you had known its lack, Sire, you might value it more highly.'

He gave a hard laugh that morphed into a bitter cough. Bethan leaned in but he waved her crossly away.

'You may be right,' he rasped, 'but I have found that it is better not simply to cling to what you have but to risk all for more. You should remember that when . . .'

But whatever advice he'd intended to give was lost in a violent cough. Bethan pressed the cloth to his lips and Sibyll, caught still in the king's grasp, watched in horror as she brought it away stained deep red.

'I am choking on my own lifeblood, my lady. It is a poor way to die,' he told her.

'Then it is good, Sire, that you lived so well.'

He nodded and gripped her fingers with surprising strength.

'You may be cautious, Sibyll, but I like the fact that you are not afraid of the truth. Hold Alba for me.'

'I will.'

Finally he released her.

'I am tired. God calls me.'

Moved, Sibyll dropped a kiss on his pain-creased forehead. He looked surprised but pleased and his fingers fluttered in a little wave, more like a child's than a king's. She returned it then turned sorrowfully away, her arm around her son.

'Sibyll.'

It was more breath than word.

'Sire?'

Her hand was on the curtain now and Malky was through and gone but it seemed she could not yet escape the dying king.

'Malcolm III.'

She looked back at him, pale and folded inwards, his flesh eating itself up, and wanted to soothe him but he did not deserve it, not even now.

'Duncan I,' she insisted and then, pulling back the curtain, she fled.

King Malcolm died that night, fighting desperately to the very end.

'He was too fond of Alba to let go of it willingly,' Crinan said piously.

'He was too unwilling to trust her to anyone else to let go,' Sibyll corrected him, but Duncan hushed her.

Crinan proclaimed Duncan king that night but only to the most loyal lords and churchmen. Malcolm was laid out in the church at Glamis with Bethan to keep vigil over him, but the doors were sealed and a guard left on his sickroom as if he were still within. His death would not be announced until tomorrow, to give Duncan time to get safely to Scone. No man was truly King of Alba until he had been anointed on the Stone of Destiny and they all feared Macbeth might be lurking nearby, plotting to get there first.

'And if he did that, what then?' Sibyll asked Duncan as they mounted up at first light.

'Then he would be king – until we killed him.'

It was a dark warning and their travelling party was a nervous one but after a day's hard riding they arrived to find Scone thankfully deserted of all but Malcolm's retainers.

'*Your* retainers now,' Sibyll pointed out to her husband.

'Apparently so.'

He crossed the leaf-strewn grass to the Hill of Belief. It was almost dark but on Crinan's command men were rushing to set up flaming torches to either side of the steps to the stone set on the hill's flat top – an altar to kingship for all to see. The ceremony must take place tonight and Abbot Crinan was already dashing around making arrangements. He called for Duncan but to Sibyll's joy her husband put up one hand and calmly refused.

'I am busy, Father,' he said.

'But your clothes, Duncan. You must . . . '

'First I must spend time with God.'

And with that Duncan turned his back on his father. Sibyll stood and watched as Duncan took the ten steps up the mound, looking almost otherworldly in the torchlight. For some time he stood there, an unmoving silhouette, lost in his own thoughts and Sibyll stood there too, lost in him.

Malcolm had summoned Duncan to his bedside but her husband had refused to tell her what had been said. She hoped that his grandfather had given him his regal blessing as a last act of charity but somehow doubted it and while she stood watching Duncan embrace his kingship in his own quiet, solid way, she prayed he could hold to that steadiness in the years ahead.

Seeing her, he put out a hand and she went to him, picking up her skirts before climbing the steps to his side. A shiver of awe ran through her as she reached the top. This ancient mound had seen the inauguration of many Alban kings and it seemed to hold the memory of every one in its soil. Now Duncan's name would be added to the list for all who followed to remember – and Malcolm's after him, God willing.

She bent and ran a hand over the red stone. It was nothing special to look at. It had no jewels set into it, no carvings even – nothing to mark it out save a simple square marking the spot where the king should take his seat in history, but that alone imbued it with an almost sacred charge. She looked at her husband.

'You are ready?'

'Is a man ever ready for this? It will not be easy, Sibyll. We are turning the old order upside down and that will not be welcomed by many. Macbeth has already shown his intent and it will not have melted away in the mists of Glamis. He will come again.'

'And we will see him off again.'

'We will.' He pulled her against him and crushed a kiss onto her lips, surprising her with his passion. 'Thank you, Sibyll.'

'For what?'

'For believing in me, for helping me, for giving me sons, just for being here. You make me stronger.'

'And you me.'

'Truly?'

'Of course.'

'Because I sometimes wonder if a woman like you would have been better with a man like Maldred.'

'Maldred?' She jumped as if fat had spat at her from a roasting spit. 'Why Maldred?'

'He always seems so sure of himself.'

Relief shuddered through her. Duncan trusted Maldred and he trusted her – as he should. She was his woman and now, it seemed, his queen. She reached up and kissed him.

'The main thing that Maldred is sure of is that he wishes he were you. You are King of Alba, Duncan.'

'Not yet.'

'Very nearly.'

She gestured to the palace where Crinan was mustering men into lines, more torches over their heads so that, despite the darkness, Scone was lit up like midday. Sibyll felt a giddy rush of pride. She must command a messenger south to tell Ward that the lost girl he had pulled out of the ashes many years ago was crowned Queen of Alba. She squeezed Duncan's hand and he squeezed hers firmly back.

'You are ready?' she asked him again and this time he put up his chin and squared his big shoulders.

'I am ready.'

Chapter Twenty-one

Loch Ness, March 1035

Cora kicked Balgedie into a gallop and charged down the side of Loch Ness on the back of a delicious spring breeze. At last the ice had released its grip on Moray and the world was coming tentatively back to life. For the first time since the non-battle at Glamis the sun was offering warmth instead of stark white light and for a moment she closed her eyes to revel in the feel of it on her face.

Opening them again, she glanced over her shoulder and saw Lachlan effortlessly matching her pace. He had turned eight some weeks back and had grown so much this last year that she'd three times had to extend his tunics and set the leather-workers to craft him new boots. She had stored the old ones in a casket in the hope that another child might one day need them, but so far there had been no sign.

Mind you, she and Macbeth hadn't exactly been leaping into bed together. The argument after Glamis still simmered between them, kept alive by the privations of what had been an especially bitter winter. They'd made a truce of sorts but sometimes their usually happy life had felt more like the grind of her marriage to Gillespie. Cora had mainly kept company with Aila who had, poor girl, sworn off men since Kendrick's death. She had told herself she was consoling her friend but consolation was not her strength and in truth she'd missed Macbeth's easy company. Not that she'd tell him that.

'Watch out for the water-dragon,' she called over to Lachlan, who had now come up alongside her. He laughed but cast a quick look at the shimmering waters of the loch all the same. No creature rose from them for him to race and Cora doubted one ever would but the hearthside tales of the great water-dragon were compelling and she kept half an eye on the loch herself just in case.

It was St Columba himself, they said, who had banished the creature in the Lord's name when he had ridden up the Great Glen to bring Christianity to the Picts nearly five hundred years ago. The terrible beast had been terrorising the local population by snatching fishing boats full of men until Columba had come along and showed it the error of its ways. Armed only with a cross and his faith, the saint had commanded the beast to the great depths at the centre of the loch and there it had remained ever since.

It was a good story, made better by occasional 'sightings' of the water-dragon, usually by moonlight and almost certainly after a measure of uiskie. There was clearly no monster in Loch Ness but a part of her wished that there were and that she might be the one to see it. At the very least it would provide some much-needed excitement.

'Can we go to the falls, Mama?' Lachlan called to her as they approached the southern end of the loch.

Cora slowed Balgedie's pace.

'Why not? They should be magnificent with the breakwater flowing over them.'

Lachlan cheered and she had to smile at his easy joy. She should learn from him and stop being a damned grumpling. They hadn't defeated Duncan but the bloody murderer Malcolm was dead and that was some measure of retribution at least. The man who had ordered the deaths of her father and her brother had finally been sent to join them and she hoped they had kept the hell fires hot to torment his vicious spirit.

It was small consolation, though, and Cora sighed unhappily as Lachlan led her eagerly up from the lochside towards the plateau from which they could reach the secret glory of the Falls of Foyers. Macbeth had shown them to her in the early days of their marriage and even talked her into bathing in the jewelled pool at the base of the great cascade, warming her afterwards in ways that made her blush to recall. She loved him so much and that made her disappointment in him all the more acute.

'Come on, Mama,' Lachlan urged impatiently and she cast off her regretful thoughts and concentrated on pleasing her son.

This day was too nice to waste on resentment. If Macbeth truly did not wish to be king she must accept that and concentrate on her son again. He was eight now, after all. In some five or six years he would be man enough to lead an army and it was her job to be sure that he was ready to do so. She offered him a hand and was pleased when he waved it aside and leaped down towards the track to the falls unaided. He had spirit, her son – he would be a good king.

Their two guards came rushing forward but she waved them away.

'You wait here with the horses, please.'

'But, my lady . . . '

'We will be quite safe.' She gestured to the narrow path cutting through the trees. The sun was at its height and penetrating easily between the young leaves of the birches, hazels and alders. 'What harm can come to us here? There is only one way to the falls and if you remain you can guard its entrance for us.'

Grudgingly they conceded the truth of this, though one of them insisted on hacking noisily some way into the trees to satisfy himself no war band had camped out in the vague hope of a noble lady and her son fancying a look at the waterfall. Cora waited for him to finish with as much patience as she could muster, soothing Lachlan with apple pastries from her saddle bag, and at last the guard declared himself content for them to go.

Cora smiled her thanks and stepped in among the trees, clutching Lachlan's hand as much to steady herself as him. They were at the top of a hidden valley and had to work their way down it to reach the cascade that emptied itself into the great green bowl of water on the far side. The path was steep and wound between a tangle of trees, spring-grown saplings nearest the light and then thicker, more resilient pines further down. She kept her eyes firmly on the path, watching out for roots or hollows in the earth that might catch an unwary foot, but Lachlan had no such concerns.

'See the bluebells,' he called, skipping sideways between the trees and sending earth tumbling down the slope.

'Careful, Lachlan.'

'I *am* careful. See the flowers – they seem woven across the whole forest floor.'

Cora looked.

'They do, Lachlan, they look just like that. I didn't know you were such a poet.'

He paused and looked across at her.

'I love the skalds, Mama. They make such patterns with their words.'

Cora blinked at him. Truly he was growing up, becoming his own man with his own ideas, and she could use that to shape him for the kingship. But as soon as she thought this he moved to try and leap a fallen tree trunk, caught his toe and went sprawling across the ground, laughing wildly and looking instantly three years old again. She scrambled across to him.

'Are you hurt?'

'No!' He leaped up, brushing leaves and earth carelessly from his tunic. 'Look – I see the falls!' The land dipped away so fast that they could look down birdlike on the crowns of the lower trees and there beneath, cutting between them in a glorious rush of almost pure white, was the top of the Falls of Foyers. 'Let's go!'

Together they scrambled down the slope. They shuffled some of it on their bottoms, more like peasants than nobles, and Cora felt relieved they'd left the watchful guards at the top. She felt alive, whole, happy.

'Do you like Moray, Lachlan?' she called across to him.

'Like it? Of course I do, Mama.'

'Good. That's good for it is a beautiful place, but there are many other beautiful places in Alba too, you know.'

'Where else is there?'

'Fife, where I grew up, and Perthshire and Lothian and all the lands of the south.'

He considered this, his head on one side.

'I would like to see those places.'

Her heart swelled.

'You will, Lachlan, I swear it. One day you will – one day, indeed, you will rule over them all.'

'As Mormaer?'

'Nay, Lachy, as king. King of Alba.'

He looked bewildered and she feared she had gone too far but then he grinned and said, 'Will I have a crown?'

'Of course.'

'And a painted shield and a patterned sword?'

'If you wish, yes.'

'And a great chair with an Aed lion on its back? Like the one I lost.'

Cora stared at him, taken aback.

'You remember that?'

'I do. It burned.'

'It did.' Cora swallowed. 'What else do you remember, Lachy?'

But the boy was bored now and heading down the slope again.

'I remember the fire,' he cast over his shoulder. 'And the horses whinnying like lost souls.' Cora felt her breath catch at how vividly his words conjured up that dread night. 'And I remember Papa saving me.'

'Papa?' Cora all but whispered. 'You mean Macbeth?'

He tutted crossly at her.

'Of course I mean Macbeth. Who else? Honestly, Mama, you are very odd today. Are you getting old?'

He gave her a cheeky grin, which shocked her out of her sudden melancholy and made her smile back at him. And now they were coming out of the line of trees and found themselves at the edge of a stone-sided pool, alive with froth and roaring with sound. They lifted their heads back as one and looked up into the cascade that seemed to tip out of the very heavens itself. The light was sending a million tiny suns dancing in the mist above the surface and, just over their heads, so close it seemed they might be able to reach out and pluck the strand of their choice from the middle, was a rainbow.

'Look,' Lachlan squealed excitedly, all debate instantly forgotten. 'It's like a multi-coloured hoof print across the sky.'

Cora looked askance at her son. It was. It truly was.

'You make patterns with your words, Lachy,' she said and he flushed.

'Only because I want to catch this sight and keep it so I can remember it still when we are no longer here.'

She hugged him against her.

'I love you, Lachy.'

He looked at her in surprise.

'And I you, Mama. Truly you are being strange today. Are you well?'

'Very well. Why would I not be?'

'You don't usually say such things.'

'I don't? Well, then, I should. Now – do you fancy a swim?'

'A swim?' His green eyes widened until she could see two mini-cascades reflected in the depths of them. 'Here? Now?'

'Aye,' she said decisively, leading him back from the damp edge and removing her clothes. He looked around, giggled, and then, seeing she meant what she said, swiftly shed his own garments until the two of them stood naked and shivering in the sunshine that no longer felt quite so warm.

'You first,' Lachlan said, giving her a nudge.

'Very well. But you have to follow.'

'I will.'

He gave a little jump of encouragement and Cora edged forward. A part of her regretted the mad impulse now but she was not going to stop. She shuffled to the brim of the pool and looked into the water. It was so clear she could see to the rocks at the bottom. She dipped in a toe. Lord, but it was cold!

'Go on, Mama – jump!'

She looked back at Lachlan, feeling the weight of his expectation. Before she could disappoint him, she jumped. She hit the water with a loud splash and a rush of cold so sharp it seemed to force all the breath up and out of her. She gulped at the air until her lungs filled again and her skin tingled as if all the miniature suns were kissing it. Cold and warmth mingled inextricably in her blood and joy crashed across her as if delivered straight from the cascade. She threw open her arms to her son.

'Now you!'

He did not even hesitate but leaped in trustingly, hitting the water just in front of her so it flew up into her face. He kicked wildly and clutched at her shoulders.

'It's so cold!'

'I know. Let's jump again.'

They scrambled out, skin pink, and leaped back into the swirling water together.

'Not too close,' Cora warned as Lachlan drifted towards the falls. 'It could crush you.'

'It's just water, Mama.'

'Water is powerful, Lachy, when driven hard.'

'Like love.'

That sucked the breath from her even more than the first shock of the water had done.

'Like love,' she agreed and hugged her son's lithe, wriggling little body close.

'What's all this?'

The deep voice coming from between the trees seemed to boom out across the valley. Cora's grasp tightened instinctively around Lachlan and she tugged him up against the edge of the rock, ducking round into a shadowed area to try and hide from whoever had found them. The cold bit, suddenly fierce, and she felt Lachlan quiver.

'It must be elves a-diving to welcome the spring.'

'Macbeth!'

He came into sight through the trees and, heart beating with wild relief, Cora scrambled out of the water, pulling Lachlan with her.

'Papa!'

Lachlan bounded across and Macbeth hugged him, sliding his cloak around the boy as he looked over his head to Cora, standing on the rock.

'Now that is a heavenly sight. Finer than all the wonders of Rome.'

'Isn't it, Papa? Do you see the rainbow?'

Lachlan squirmed round in his arms to point upward but Macbeth was looking straight at Cora.

'I see all God's glory,' he said softly, 'and I thank Him for it. Why don't you get dressed, Lachy?'

The boy nodded and scrambled for his clothes, taking Macbeth's cloak with him. Macbeth did not even look back but came slowly towards Cora.

'It has been a dark winter.'

'It has.'

'But you have shown me spring.' He put out his arms and she fell gratefully into them, stepping up onto his boots for the rock felt like ice against her feet. 'I've missed you, Cora MacDuff.'

'And I you,' she admitted. 'I was very angry.'

'I noticed. But you were right to be. I am too cautious.'

'And I too impetuous. There must be a middle way.'

'If there is we will certainly find it, my heart. I won't duck the fight this time.'

'I'm sorry I said that . . . ' she started, but he put a finger to her lips to silence her.

'The past matters little, 'tis the future we must look to. I have been putting out feelers in the south and it seems your uncles are not dead, just hiding.'

'What? Where?'

'That I do not know but I am consulting men who might. Thanks to you, Cora, there are many in Fife who will rise to join us, but we must tread carefully. Duncan is weak, everyone agrees. Let us wait, then, for him to prove it and once the people are disillusioned we can strike.'

She nodded slowly. It meant more delay, more patience, but what he said made perfect sense and the thought that her father's brothers might still breathe filled her with hope. It was a giddy emotion but there was one thing still troubling her.

'You would be king, Macbeth?'

'For you, my heart, yes.'

'Not for me, Macbeth – for yourself. Would you be king for yourself?'

But at that he shrugged.

'I know not, for you are part of that self now. Your fight is my fight and what matters to you matters to me too.'

'But . . . '

'Hush, Cora – do not resist all the time, my sweet.'

His arms closed around her and at last she reached up and clasped her own around his neck, holding on as if he might otherwise slip through and leave her. She might have spent her winter railing against men with Aila but in truth she loved them – well, one of them. Macbeth's hands ran down over her waist, found her bare bottom and squeezed.

'Goodness, but I'm a lucky man.'

'You are,' she agreed huskily, warmth spreading rapidly through her.

'Remember last time?'

'Of course.' She felt his arousal against her and knew he remembered too. She gave him a little push. 'Lachlan!'

'Oh, don't worry,' he said. 'I can wait – just. But I think it best I get you home and into bed as soon as possible, in case you catch a chill.'

He ran a hand between her breasts, bringing the scarred skin alive and making her shiver indeed, though not with chill.

'That would definitely be best, my lord,' she agreed archly, gazing up at him.

His eyes darkened but now a little voice called out, 'Papa, my trews keep sticking to my legs,' and with a laugh he let her go.

'Let me help you, Lachlan. Let's get you warmed up, shall we, though your mother, I think, should ride home exactly as she is.'

Then, grabbing her clothes, he ran off, pulling a delighted Lachlan with the other hand as Cora chased, naked and squealing with indignant laughter, in their giddy wake. It seemed she had underestimated Macbeth and his plans. Yes, they would take time but for once she was happy to let them do so. Malcolm was dead and they could let Duncan have Alba a little while yet for here in Moray God's horses were carving rainbows in the air and they must make the most of His blessings.

Chapter Twenty-two

Forteviot, May 1039

'Durham?' Sibyll demanded. 'Why Durham?'

She had just clambered thankfully into bed at Duncan's side but his casual announcement that he was planning war had chased any sleepiness from her.

'Because your brother wants Durham, does he not?'

'Ward? Of course he does. It's the key to Northumbria, but what has that to do with us?'

'Everything. If Ward holds Durham we will have an ally just over the border. Lothian will be secure and we will not have to worry about attacks from the south.'

'Only from the north?'

'Aye. Macbeth has been very quiet but it won't last. He's waiting for something, though I know not what.'

'Maybe for you to get yourself killed attacking Durham?' Sibyll suggested darkly. 'Have you been there, Duncan?'

'You know I have not.'

'Well, I have. It is a formidable city, fortified first by the natural rock on which it stands and second by thick, high walls. It is almost impossible to attack.'

'My grandfather did it in 1018.'

'Your grandfather won a battle *outside* Durham – he never took the city itself.'

'Then if I do it, I will better him.'

'But you will not do it. No one . . . '

Duncan leaped out of bed.

'Enough, wife. What do you know of war?'

'I know that too few come back from it. Duncan, please . . . ' She too rose and went to him. There was high colour in his pale cheeks and his eyes flickered restlessly around the chamber. 'Why must you attack anyone?'

He avoided her gaze. Reaching out, he took a candle from the sconce on the wall and held it up before him, shining it on his other palm, seemingly intent on studying the lines criss-crossing his own skin. He had been like this too often recently, especially when they were away from Dunkeld as they must often be these days for a king had to tour his residences to see all his people. She missed the pretty abbey she'd been so happy to call home but Duncan missed it more and she feared for his state of mind. She put a hand on his arm and he jumped.

'Sibyll?' he said, as if he had forgotten she was even there.

'Come to bed, husband.'

'Bed? Aye. Aye, very well.' He let her lead him over but then stopped. 'I must attack, Sibyll, to prove I am a worthy king. It is tradition.'

'Surely your worth is better proved by wise, stable rule, such as you have provided for the last five years?'

He laughed.

'If only it were so. A king must be seen to be strong.'

'But there are more ways to show strength than with a sword.'

'Maybe.'

'Who has been talking to you, Duncan?'

He fixed her suddenly with a sharp stare.

'King Malcolm, my grandfather.'

'Duncan, Malcolm is dead.'

He tutted.

'I know that, Sibyll. I am not going mad. I meant before he died. He called me to see him and told me that a good king must risk all for more.'

Sibyll sighed.

'He told me the same but I disagree, Duncan. A good king should hold what he has secure and not chance it on foolish risks for unnecessary gain.'

Something like hope flared briefly in her husband's blue eyes but almost immediately it was extinguished.

'Attack is the best form of defence.'

This was not him talking and it scared her.

'But why now, Duncan? Is someone threatening you?'

'No more than usual but they will. I saw it in council today. Earl Eldred holds lands in Lothian for Durham Abbey and our churchmen want it back in our own hands. I have offered to exchange it for some of our own Northumbrian holdings but Eldred's men have returned only insulting replies. I have to do something or they and others after them will believe they can walk all over me.'

'I see.' Sibyll climbed into bed and tugged him in with her. Duncan acquiesced but sat rigid as if his spine was spiked in place by the sharpness of his thoughts. 'But why Durham?' she persisted. 'It is such a hard city to win, my love.'

'And *that* is exactly why. I am sick of men calling me weak. I hear them, Sibyll. They think that they whisper but I hear them as I heard my grandfather and my father besides, although he, at least, is more subtle. Durham is my chance. If I fail, I will only confirm what they believe, but if I win . . . If I win, Sibyll, I will no longer be viewed as weak. I will be strong and those around me will truly accept me as their king.'

Sibyll knew not what to say. He was right, she supposed, but she feared for him. Crinan and Bethan had brought up their son as the linchpin in their own rampant ambition. They had trained him in statecraft and warcraft and all the practical essentials of kingship but had never thought to offer him the true key to successful rule – self-belief. Every day she tried to repair the damage done to him but she feared there were not enough days for her to do so. If he led this foolish attack without truly believing himself capable, his chances were slim. And yet, if she doubted him too, they would be non-existent.

'Perhaps you could bring them to battle outside Durham?' she said. 'Then you could truly exhibit your skills as a commander instead of being subject to the whims of a siege.'

'Perhaps,' he agreed, but she knew he had his sights set on the city and her heart quailed for him.

As his army grew so did her fears and then, thankfully, Ward sent word that he would meet Duncan and fight with him. Sibyll had to work hard to hide her relief at this welcome news. Ward breathed battle and would surely never be fool enough to try and storm Durham. What's more Beorn, now a youth of thirteen, would be riding with him and Sibyll knew her brother would never risk his precious son's life on a fool's fight. As she waved Duncan's forces off, roaring with that strange battle-lust that seemed regularly to infect men, she could only trust to her brother's war-wisdom and to God's grace.

Duncan was a good king. Not a noisily assertive one like Malcolm but diligent, conscientious and hard-working. Many was the night they retired from dinner with the court and he took a candle to the table in the corner of their chamber instead of coming to bed. It was, perhaps, why Sibyll had not yet conceived a third child for Alba, but both Malky and Donald were thriving and Duncan delighted in them.

Malky was almost twelve so was starting to train with the men and proving a natural with a sword. He had grown considerably, thanks perhaps to the copious amounts of fish Sibyll had been amused to see him eat whenever he could, and he was strong and tall. Duncan talked often to him about the responsibilities of leadership and Malcolm listened well enough but was always off to join the other boys the moment he could. It was Donald who sought his father out. His younger son was very like Duncan in both looks and thoughtful temperament and Duncan spent as much time with him as possible. He would be sorry to leave both his boys.

'Take care,' she begged her husband the night before he rode out. 'Alba needs you home alive or Macbeth will come and we will not be able to resist him without you.'

That gave him pause but not for long.

'If I do not return you must have Malky declared King Malcolm III and you must stand as his regent. That is, after all, why my father brought you to Alba.'

'That's not true.' She caught him in her arms. 'Your father brought me to Alba to be your wife and your queen and I am honoured to be both. Come back, Duncan, not for Alba, nor for your bloody grandfather, but for *me*.'

She kissed him before he could object further and pulled him to her and prayed he'd left her another babe in her womb. But in the end there was neither babe nor victory. Within the month Duncan crept back a broken man, his army trailing miserably in his wake and the whispers about him now openly voiced.

'It was impossible,' he told her as she tended to the myriad cuts slashed across his poor skin like a penitent's scourging.

'What happened?'

But he did not wish to say and the men spoke only in hyperbole, their accounts skewed by their own heroism or lack of it. Crinan cloistered himself in his rooms, suddenly more monk than prince, and in the end there was only one person left to ask.

'What happened, Maldred?'

She caught him in the abbey church at dusk as the sparsely attended court was about its separate preparations for dinner.

'Truly?'

'Please. I hear only evasions and exaggerations from everyone else. Where was my brother?'

'Earl Ward was gathering additional troops and came later than expected.'

'You did not wait for him?'

'Duncan thought it best to proceed.'

'Proceed with what? Please, Maldred, surely you, at least, can do me the honour of telling the truth?'

He ran a hand down the line of her cheek and smiled sadly.

'There is much I would like to offer you in honour, Sibyll, but if this is all it can be, I will do my best.'

He drew her into the shadow of a pillar and fetched two of the stools kept for those too infirm or elderly to stand throughout a service. Then, with a guilty glance around, he also fetched the jug of Communion wine.

'Maldred!'

'It is not yet consecrated and I will see it replaced myself, I promise, but I need a wee drink if I am to re-tell Durham and you, perhaps, to hear it.'

His voice was so sombre that she resisted no further and took a deep draught of the wine straight from the jug when he passed it to her. If nothing else, she needed the false courage it brought her just to sit this close to Maldred without touching him.

'Tell me,' she urged.

'It was wrong,' he said eventually. 'It was all wrong from the start, Sibyll. Not the tactics but the feel of the campaign. It was a desperate attack and they are the worst sort. Sometimes, just occasionally, such an undertaking yields results by the sheer manic passion of the men who make it, but for that they need something to believe in. *Someone* to believe in.' He grabbed her hand. 'You know that I love my brother, Sibyll?'

'I know it. As do I.'

'I have been jealous of him, I admit, and ten times more so since you came to Alba ... '

'Maldred . . .'

'Let me speak, please. Whatever my personal feelings, always I have wanted him to succeed. How can I not? He's a good man – too good maybe. He should have been an abbot like Father. Indeed, he would have been a better abbot than Father. He has shouldered the wrong destiny, Sibyll, and that lies heavy on a man.'

He had put his finger on it exactly. Sibyll felt Maldred's hand warm around her own and the church walls wrap comfortingly around them as darkness descended. She leaned closer to him.

'What happened, Maldred?'

He sighed.

'We charged uphill at Durham's great gates. We charged again and again with arrows flying at us and tar falling on us and spears spiking through us. We charged until our own dead blocked the way to the gates and we had to trample them for the privilege of joining them until, eventually, the men refused to carry on.'

'Refused their commander?'

'I'm sorry, Sibyll.'

'What will happen now?'

He shrugged.

'I am told Earl Eldred was injured so maybe your brother will yet have the victory.'

'That is good, I suppose, but I meant here in Alba.'

'I know not but you should, perhaps, keep your jewels close.' Sibyll swallowed and his eyes met hers, brimming with sorrow. 'I'm afraid I will have to return to Strathclyde soon and see to my own borders for we have all been tainted by this.'

'Are you happy there, Maldred?'

'Happy enough.'

'How happy is enough?'

'It depends what you look for. I have rich lands, a dutiful wife and three fine children – it *should* be enough.' He leaped up. 'Look after Duncan for me, Sibyll.'

'I cannot. I have tried but I cannot. I warned him not to attack Durham but he didn't listen. He wanted glory.'

'And it might have worked if he'd truly believed it was possible. Will you then, my lady, at least look after yourself?'

'For Malky I will.'

'No, for me.'

And then he pulled her against him and planted a slow, deliberate kiss upon her lips and the world seemed to swirl and then somehow settle around her. Never had she felt more acutely in danger and yet never, either, so utterly safe. She clung desperately to him until, with a sigh of sorrow, he pulled away and was gone. She sank to the ground, listening as his boots rapped across the floor slabs, then the door creaked open and slid shut with a small click of the latch. Even then she sat on, a finger to her lips as night-time gathered like a pack of wolves around her.

'Should you have done that?'

The muffled voice, coming suddenly out of the heart of the darkness, made her scream. She spun round, desperately striving to make out who stood there, but whoever it was gave her no clue.

'Done what?' she demanded, feeling round the pillar and edging towards the door.

'I saw you.'

'I did nothing.'

'You kissed him.' The voice, even muffled, was not so much threatening as petulant.

'That's not true.' Sibyll drew herself up straight. 'He kissed *me*.'

Her heart beat wildly as she heard feet shuffle backward over the stones, a stark, ominous contrast to Maldred's purposeful stride. What had she done? She'd thought Duncan's crazy attack on Durham a threat to them all but maybe her own foolish feelings were every bit as dangerous.

'Who is this?' she demanded, trying to stay strong.

'A well-wisher,' the voice said, more muffled than ever.

'Then why not wish me well?' she threw after it.

'Oh, I do,' came the floating reply, 'just not with him. With either of them. Ah well – dark times are coming, my lady, but fret not, I will look over you. I will keep you safe. Good night.'

And then he, too, was gone and Sibyll fumbled for the door, desperate to escape. It was not just wolves, it seemed, who prowled in the darkness, but foxes too. She dreaded them all.

Chapter Twenty-three

Dunsinane, November 1039

Cora looked out across the troops arrayed upon the plain at Dunsinane and felt proud to be a part of their undertaking. This second battle would be theirs, she was sure of it, for the country was behind them. As they'd marched south more and more men had joined them, calling 'Macbeth for King' as if it had been their battle-cry for years. It seemed that Duncan's day was done and Alba was theirs for the taking.

It had been Brother Cullen who'd first brought word that the time was ripe. He'd come north under the guise of trading uiskie but later, in the hall over dinner, he'd spoken of more weighty matters.

'After his disastrous attack on Durham, Duncan has lost the confidence of Alba. Any man challenging him now would find great support in the south.'

He'd said it quietly, slipping them the information between mouthfuls of game pudding as if he were merely commenting on the state of the weather rather than the nation.

'Why would you tell us this?' Cora had asked him.

'Because it is the truth. And because it favours no one.

201

Duncan's sortie south may have been a disaster for Alba but it weakened Durham enough for Earl Ward to capture the city later. He killed Earl Eldred personally, I am told, and has taken his enemy's daughter Elsa as wife. He is now undisputed ruler of all Northumbria and will have set his eyes on Lothian for his damned son Beorn. Duncan cannot keep us safe.'

'But is Duncan not married to Earl Ward's sister? Surely he will not attack his own kin?'

'Or perhaps she will help him to do so?'

'Turn on her husband? Why would she do that?'

Cullen had looked strangely sad when he replied.

'Maybe she is not as loyal as we'd thought. Maybe she is as weak as her husband, swayed by petty human concerns and not, therefore, as capable of fulfilling the office of queen as Alba deserves.' He'd coughed then and added 'delicious game' and Macbeth dutifully changed the subject but had been eager to return to it with his wife once they had escaped to their chamber.

'Now is the time, Cora. Duncan has exposed himself and we must strike. I will send out the muster tomorrow. The men are ready, I know they are. They are keen to prove that Moray can rule. You must send to your people in Fife and pray to God that if the monk is right they will rise too.'

Cora's hopes had swelled, though with them her fear. She grew old and, to her shame, anger seemed a less powerful force than in her youth when she had felt wrongs as raw and dark and almost blissfully painful.

'But *is* the monk right?' she'd fretted. 'He's from Dunkeld, Macbeth, Duncan's father's abbey. Why would he want his own men unseated?'

Macbeth had pulled her into his arms.

'It sounded to me, my little grumpling, that for all his pro-testations of loyalty to Alba, his feelings are very much for Alba's queen.'

'Macbeth, nonsense! He is a monk.'

'And a man besides. Ah, but what does it matter? I will send spies to verify what he says is true and then – then we will strike.'

And now here they were, ranged once more upon the battle-field, and it seemed that Cullen had, indeed, spoken true for the two forces were visibly unequal. Cora's uncles, Mormaers Fergus and Sean, had come out of hiding and brought mighty forces to join their own swollen ranks and though she had not yet seen them herself she felt their support and was glad that she was here on what must surely be a glorious day for her family.

'Are you certain you want me to come this time?' she'd asked Macbeth as the troops had gathered up in Moray.

'I am certain. This is *our* journey, Cora, ours and Lachlan's, and it's important you're fully a part of it.'

She'd nearly cried then. She was forever crying at the moment. She'd lost another babe in the winter, feeling it quicken one day before the terrible cramps of expulsion the next, as if God had been tormenting her with its all-too-transient existence. That was when the crying had started and it had been a long battle ever since to dry her foolish eyes. Macbeth had been so kind, so loving. He'd taken her out every day, walking along the shores of the firth and telling her how blessed she was, how beautiful, how strong.

'But I don't want to be strong,' she'd wailed. 'Or, at least, I don't want to *have* to be strong. I want to be with child.'

'We have Lachlan,' he'd told her and she'd cried again at that easy 'we' and at his selfless adoption of her son and her cause.

Now the crown was within their grasp. She could sense Kendrick and her father on high ready to witness their family's restitution and fought to enjoy the moment but it didn't seem as easy as it once had. Lachlan, now a hardy twelve year old, was to fight too. He would only be in the rear lines and Macbeth had assured her he would be well guarded but Cora could not bear the thought of losing him. Furious with her own weak heart, she had decided to keep back with the other women in the medical tent, but as the trumpets sounded out the start of the strange parade of battle it suddenly felt worse to have to witness it by sound alone and she could only pray Duncan would surrender before too much Alban blood was spilled.

But God, it seemed, heard her prayers for the battle did not take long. Barely had the first men come staggering into their tent before the roars rose to a triumphant volume on their side and then drifted away again as the victors chased the losers into the hills.

'That's it!' the man Cora was treating said, beaming delightedly despite a gash across his collarbone so deep that she feared his arm might drop out its socket. 'That's victory.'

He leaped up, his pain banished by the magical word, but all Cora could do was stare into the red flesh of his wound and see 'victory' in its raw, ugly lines. She shook herself furiously. Was she grown so weak that now, at the moment she had so long awaited, she thought more of loss than gain? And then suddenly Lachlan was rushing in like a spring gale, beaming and jumping and filling the tent with all the triumph and joy she craved.

'It was amazing, Mama,' he gushed. '*We* were amazing. The men were so fierce and so determined and they cried out over and over again for Moray and for Macbeth and for Alba. They never wavered once and Duncan's forces crumbled beneath our onslaught.'

Cora felt her heart lift.

'And Duncan himself?'

'Dead. I saw it, Mama. He was alone and our men surrounded him. There had been men with him, that tall abbot for one with a cross on his mail, but Duncan stepped away from them, actually sort of shouldered them out of the way and came on. Our men closed in then and he seemed almost to walk onto their swords. The rest fled when they saw it and we let them go. Papa said we must show mercy, which was a shame really because I didn't get a chance to kill anyone.'

'There will be time enough for that, Lachlan, and it is good that we have won without too many lives lost. Those are Albamen, remember; they are all your father's subjects now and he *should* show mercy.'

Lachlan shifted awkwardly but Cora scarce noticed for the import of her own words had just struck her. 'Your father's subjects'. Macbeth was king. They had done it! They had won. Her line was restored and her father and brother avenged. The wonder of it began to swell inside her, but now Lachlan was tugging at her arm and she had to focus on him once more.

'Oh, but they are not his subjects yet, you know, and that's why I'm here. Papa says you must come. Now! Your uncles are here to greet you and we must ride to Scone before the abbot can sneak his grandson onto the Stone of Destiny.'

Cora nodded keenly. That could not be allowed to happen. There must not be another Malcolm on the throne of Alba; it was theirs now and they must claim it before all men. Heart beating wildly, she ran out of the tent, Lachlan on her heels, and there, striding towards her, was Macbeth.

'You won,' she said, almost shy before him, for he seemed somehow to have acquired new stature with his victory. 'You are king.'

'And you queen.'

The titles shimmered in the air as if conjured up by wishing-pool faeries and Cora wanted to cry for the joy of it. Macbeth pulled her into his arms, crushing a kiss onto her lips, and she twisted her hands into his tunic to keep him against her. But they had a duty to more than each other now and with reluctance she had to let him go.

'There are men here who wish to greet you,' he told her with an encouraging smile.

'My uncles?'

'The very same,' said a deep voice and there was Mormaer Fergus and, at his shoulder, Mormaer Sean, and then they were on their knees in the battle-mud before her, ageing heads bowed low.

Cora rushed forward.

'Rise, please.'

She touched Fergus' shoulders to lift him and he looked up at her with such reverence she almost toppled back under the weight of it.

'God bless you, Cora – *Queen* Cora. You have fought for our family and we are so very, very grateful.'

She blinked madly as more crazy tears threatened to spill down her flushed cheeks. She tugged more tightly at her uncle's shoulders to get him to stand and at last he did so, Sean with him.

'We are glad to see you again,' Sean told her, kissing her hand. 'For too long we feared you and Kendrick were dead.'

'Kendrick *is* dead.'

Both men bowed their heads again.

'We know and we're sorry. He was a brave young man and it was his death that alerted us to the fact that you were still alive. We should have supported you when your father died but you never gave up and at last your time has come. You are Queen, Cora – Queen of Alba. Your father would have been proud of you.'

Cora flung herself at both uncles, hugging them tight, and they embraced her gladly but already Macbeth was tugging her away.

'There will be time to get to know each other again later, Cora, I promise, but you are not actually queen until you are crowned at Scone. You can ride?'

She looked from her newfound family to her husband, squared her slim shoulders and nodded for suddenly it felt as if she could do anything.

The inauguration was a glorious day. The men of Moray had all marched on from the battlefield, many still in the same clothes they had worn to win the throne for Macbeth. Indeed many were still in their mail coats and were forever glancing suspiciously around the strange south, expecting ambush at any moment. But their fears were ungrounded for Macbeth was being welcomed not just by Moray men but by those from Perth, Fife, Lothian, Argyll and all the areas of Alba. The Aed lion was flying high and all, it seemed, welcomed it.

Even Crinan, Duncan's father, was there. Macbeth had pardoned the abbot for his part in stealing his throne for his son and allowed him to stay on in office. Cora doubted the wisdom of that decision but Macbeth had insisted that Crinan was God's officer and without Duncan the abbot was little threat.

'And the boy, Malcolm – what of him?' she had demanded.

'He is gone. He and his brother are fled with their mother but we will find them.'

'And then?'

'You know this, my heart.'

'They are children, Macbeth, innocents. How can we slaughter them?'

'It is hard, I know, but if we do not they may one day slaughter us.'

She'd seen the truth of it but thought of Lachlan if it had gone the other way and hated that it must be so.

'You will be gentle?'

'We will be swift.'

It had been the best she could hope for but a part of her pitied the woman who must be trembling somewhere in the stark heather of Alba with her two doomed princes. Duncan's body had been dispatched to Iona for royal burial with his grandfather and all those who had gone before them. Cora had been nervous about allowing this too but Macbeth had insisted that it was just. When his time came, he said, he wished to take his place in an unbroken line of honoured kings and now she could see that he had been right to do so for when he stood on the Hill of Belief, arms open wide to his people, they shouted an unreserved welcome. He beckoned her forward, seizing her hand and holding it aloft so the people could see their interlaced fingers.

'Today,' he called, 'we unite the great lines of Constantin and Aed. Today we end division in Alba and in so doing stand stronger against her enemies. Together we can create a new line – a line that runs through every one of us so that, whatever our personal origins, we are above all else Albamen!'

More cheers and now the Abbot of St Andrews was coming forward to anoint Macbeth. Cora tried to step back but his grip on her hand tightened and he pulled her to her knees at his side as the abbot took out the holy oil.

'Macbeth,' she whispered, 'I must go back. The oil is for the reigning monarch only.'

'I know,' he said calmly. 'Lift your chin, Cora, let the people see their queen.'

'No, Macbeth, I . . . '

But now the abbot was raising his hand before her and leaning in to press a holy cross upon her forehead and she could do nothing but hold her head high as he declaimed aloud: 'May God bless and protect Cora MacDuff, anointed Queen of Alba.' And now the people were cheering wildly, the noise so great that it almost drowned out Macbeth's own blessing, and he was pulling her to her feet as their own Abbot of Rosemarkie stepped up to place Alba's crowns upon their heads.

'They made me queen regnant,' Cora stuttered.

'I know,' Macbeth agreed calmly. 'I insisted upon it. This is as much your crown as mine, Cora MacDuff, more even, for it was you, not I, who held fast to our vow to secure it.'

'Nay, Macbeth, it has been more you in recent times.'

He laughed softly.

'It matters little for we are one. Alba is ours, my queen, and I have what I asked for – a wife to stand not at my back but at my side.'

And with that he lifted her hand aloft and the crowd below cheered louder than ever and Cora felt joy rise within her and finally let it fill her up. She was in the sun at last and as she turned her eyes to the sky, she thought she saw in the shapes of the few lazy clouds above them the faces of Kendrick and her father – and they were smiling.

Chapter Twenty-four

The Borders, May 1041

'I don't like it. You know I don't like it. I'm fed up of living like this.'

Ten-year-old Donald threw his bowl of pottage against the rough wall of the dark cave as if he were a toddler again. It splattered across the stone, seeping downwards in a trail of phlegmy fluid dotted with barley and slimy wild mushrooms. Sibyll, sitting side by side with her elder son, now almost fourteen, watched it all slide to the dirt and hadn't the heart to shout. Not that they were allowed to shout or talk or even to go out in daylight. She and the boys lived like voles these days, scurrying from one hidey-hole to another with nothing more to do than survive. No wonder Donald was angry.

She tugged him towards her. He resisted at first then flung himself into her lap, sobs wracking his strong young body, and Malcolm, who had been stoically supping at his own pottage, put it gladly down and threw fierce arms around them both. Sibyll's eyes met Cullen's as he hovered nervously to one side.

'We cannot do this much longer, Cullen.'

He nodded helplessly but what alternative was there? For

months she and the boys had dodged around southern Alba, hiding in remote churches and shepherds' huts. Occasionally they were offered shelter in the cellars of families sympathetic to their plight and keen to curry favour with Malcolm in case Alba's tide turned back in his direction – though Sibyll could not see how that would ever be. She was tormented by the older Malcolm's deathbed demand that she should see his namesake onto the throne and knew that the weight of that behest fell on her son too. They must both honour the promise, for their own sakes and for Duncan's. Poor Duncan.

Bethan, in an all-too-late rush of posthumous motherly care, had ridden out to escort Duncan across Alba to his final rest in the royal burial grounds on Iona. Sibyll had longed to go too but it was the first route Macbeth's murderous troops would have chosen to hunt her down so even that last tenderness had been denied her. She missed Duncan. She missed his steadiness, his kindness, his gentleness. And she ached for the man he could have been without the yoke of kingship.

He has shouldered the wrong destiny, Maldred had said and that destiny, in the end, had taken him from her. But what of Malcolm? What was his destiny? And Donald? To find out she had to keep them alive.

'It will get better,' she promised. 'I'll make it better.'

'How?' Malcolm demanded, his voice already a man's low growl, and she had to admit that she had no answer.

They were stuck in a cave somewhere in Atholl, one in a desperate run of dank homes, and Sibyll hated that it had come to this. She had made one vow in her life, to keep her sons from the fearful uncertainty of her own childhood, and she had failed in it. But she could not let it drag her into oblivion.

'Hush,' she soothed her youngest, as if he were still small. 'Hush now.' It was growing dark and they would soon have to extinguish their tiny fire for Macbeth's men could be anywhere. 'All will be well. We have each other and that is what counts.'

'We don't have Papa,' Donald pointed out.

'No.'

'Nor Grandpapa,' Malcolm added dryly. 'And we don't have palaces or crowns or grapes or even beds.'

'We have each other,' Sibyll repeated. 'I fled once before when I was about your age, Donald, and I survived, did I not?'

He looked up, his bad mood momentarily lifted by curiosity.

'Where did you flee from, Mother?'

'From my village in Denmark. Rebels called Wends rode in and burned it. Both my parents perished and I had to hide beneath a pile of smouldering timbers until Ward rescued me.'

Donald looked at her with new respect.

'What did you do then?'

'We ran. All our boats had been burned so we ran across country for three long days and threw ourselves on the mercy of King Cnut. Ward was taken on as a soldier and, God bless him, he excelled. When Cnut conquered England my brother was one of the men invited over to join his guard as a housecarl – an elite warrior. I went with him and that journey, too, was very hard. We slept in caves and at roadsides as we three do now but at the end of it we found service and reward. We moved into the earl's hall at York and eight years later my brother had risen to be the earl himself.'

Donald stared at her, mouth wide open, and she smiled. Revisiting the memory had not been as painful as she'd feared. She hated the situation they were in but she had climbed out of a hole once before and she would do it again.

'Fortunes change,' she concluded more confidently. 'The important thing is to keep going and that is what we are doing, is it not?'

'It is, Mother.'

'And we still have some friends, you know.'

'Our Uncle Ward for one. Why can we not go to him if he is such an excellent warrior?'

Sibyll sighed. She had considered that option, but after his victory at Durham Ward was busy subduing both Northern Northumbria and his reluctant new wife and did not need Sibyll's concerns on top of his own. Besides, there was ever talk of rebellion against the usurper Macbeth and Crinan wanted them close for when the men were ready to rally. It was looking increasingly unlikely, however, that they would ever be so. She looked helplessly at Cullen who shuffled over and gave Donald an awkward pat.

He had saved them, she knew. He had stayed in Dunkeld with Crinan and bowed the knee to the new king and queen, but whenever he could he rode out to find them and keep them in food and clothes and news. She was very grateful but he was not, God bless him, inspiring company and she missed her true friends.

'How is Morag?' she asked him now, desperate for talk of something other than their own desolation.

'Morag?' He looked surprised. 'She is the same as ever.'

'The new king has not bothered her?'

'Oh no. Nobody bothers Morag. Why should they? She barely leaves her crannog and has no interest in politics or in the wider world of Alba. Morag is happiest in her own company and always has been.'

'Always?' Sibyll queried. 'I hear she was quite a lively young woman. Perhaps it was losing Crinan that drove her to isolation?'

'Losing Crinan?' Cullen frowned and she realised guiltily that Morag's confession had been for her ears alone.

'Not losing. That is . . . They seemed fond of each other.'

'What do you mean?' he snapped. 'Abbot Crinan is a married man.'

'Of course, of course. I meant nothing. It is sad that she has no friends to watch over her, that's all.'

'I will keep an eye on her,' he said tightly and she knew the topic to be over.

'Does Crinan have a plan for us?' she asked instead.

'He has a plan,' Cullen said, 'but not the means to put it into action. As you know, he has been trying to raise a rebellion now most of the Moray men have gone back over the Mounth but it is hard. Macbeth's queen is from Fife and her one-time family have been quick to come out of the woodwork and seize what control they can.'

'Who can blame them?'

'That's very gracious.'

'Very realistic. If ever my chance to climb out of this peril and return to power comes, I will seize it with both hands.'

'Of course. And it *will* come. As you so wisely said, my lady, fortunes change. But in the meantime we need to get you to safety.'

'Where? Northumbria?'

'No. Not there. You must be seen to stay true to Alba.'

'But we have been all over Alba, Cullen, and nowhere is safe.'

'Nowhere in the east.' He swallowed and looked away as if pained. 'As you have got this far west, Lady Duncan, Crinan thinks it best you go still further – that you move on to Strathclyde.'

'Strathclyde? To Maldred?'

'To the safekeeping of his household, yes. As you know he has powerful allies in Rheged and the Western Isles and that, more than the Mormaer himself, will keep you secure.'

His tone was sharp and suddenly Sibyll recalled the shadow-voice on the night Maldred had kissed her in the church at Forteviot.

'It was you,' she said slowly.

'What was me?'

'It was you who told me off when Maldred kissed me – kissed me as a brother,' she added hastily as Malcolm looked up curiously.

'I did not tell you off, my lady. I would never do such a thing. I warned you, that is all. And I was right. I was right that dark times were coming and I was right too that I would keep you safe – *will* keep you safe. Your life is in my hands.'

He sounded almost gleeful about this and Sibyll shivered and for once was glad of the onset of night.

'We should put the fire out,' she said

'Of course. I'll do it.'

'And is there any pottage left? Donald spilled his, did you not?'

The boy looked up at her, considered for a moment and then gave in.

'I did, Mama.'

'He will need his strength if we are to travel all the way to Strathclyde. Crinan will send a guard?' she asked Cullen.

'Of course. And I will travel with you.'

'No,' she said. 'No. I think, Brother Cullen, it is best you do not.'

'But . . .'

'It will only raise Macbeth's suspicions if you are gone too long. This time, it seems, you will keep us safe best by keeping away.'

He looked mutinous and, strangely scared, she disentangled herself from Donald and rose to go to Cullen. She was tied to no man now and, for the first time in her life, must act in her own interests and on her own initiative. Moving close to the monk, she placed a hand on his chest in appeal.

'You know how grateful I am, Cullen, how much your care of us means to me.' He had frozen where he stood, breath held in his thin chest and, steeling herself, she reached up and placed a kiss upon his forehead. Even in the gathering dark she saw him flush. 'You will come and visit once we are safe?'

'Of . . . of course,' he choked out. 'Of course I will, my lady.'

'Sibyll,' she said. 'Call me Sibyll, Cullen, for we are surely friends – good friends.' He nodded dumbly and, satisfied, she stepped back. 'The fire?' she suggested and he scuttled gratefully off to take care of it.

Watching him stamp with unusual energy on the embers, Sibyll felt a little guilty but she had precious few advantages at the moment and must make the most of those that remained. And, besides, she was getting away, getting away to Maldred, and for the first time in too many terrifying months her heart felt light.

214

Chapter Twenty-five

St Andrews, September 1043

Sometimes, usually when she woke in the darkest part of the night and sleep danced away from her on the moonbeams, Cora thought about the other one – Lady Duncan. At first it was a curiosity to imagine her out in the wilds with her boys but as the months went past without them being tracked down it became more of a concern. Then they heard that Lady Duncan had somehow escaped to the west and concern turned to a sense of threat.

Mormaer Maldred of Strathclyde had sworn nominal allegiance to the crown but his seat of power was at Partick, close to the ancient kingdom of Dal Riata, and he was backed by the large Brittonic and Norse kingdoms in the west. They were allies powerful enough to make it madness to consider attacking Maldred so the Lady Duncan was safe in his stronghold with her growing sons and the thought haunted Cora in the empty midnight hours. What she needed was more sons of her own to keep the balance of power on their side but no further sons had come, nor looked likely to do so.

She was only thirty-five but already her courses came irregularly. Macbeth never complained nor never, as far as she knew, took a more fertile woman to his kingly bed, but that almost hurt her more. Last night had been one of the worst, for her bleed had come yet again, waking her with an ache in her belly and a far greater one in her soul. She'd fled outside at dawn, seeking solace from the sea air.

They were staying at the pretty coastal abbey of St Andrews to oversee the building of a grand new church there to house the blessed remains of the sacred apostle. For now St Andrew's sarcophagus was standing under God's skies and Cora threw herself down before it, pressing her forehead against the stone and beseeching the saint for the strength to bear her seeming barrenness.

'Cora? Cora, my sweet, are you well?'

She scrabbled to her feet.

'Quite well, thank you.' Her husband looked at her suspiciously and she hastily bowed her head over the sarcophagus. 'Just, er, praying to St Andrew – promising him he will not be left out in the open for too long.'

Macbeth reached out and patted the tomb with something like fondness.

'It will be worth the wait. This will be a glorious church, fit for our blessed saint. It may not quite match his brother's basilica in Rome but we will do our best for him.'

Cora looked sideways at her husband.

'You still hanker for Rome, Macbeth?'

'Not hanker, Cora, but it would be good to see it one day. It would be an . . . an affirmation.'

'Of your kingship?'

'Only a strong ruler could make such a journey.'

'And you *are* a strong ruler, Macbeth. We will plan it. Soon.'

'But, Cora, what if you are . . . '

'I am not.' It came out like a wolf's bark and she turned away before the damned tears fell but he was too quick and caught her back.

'You have bled?'

She nodded dumbly.

'I'm sorry.' He kissed her until she felt a little of the hard hurt inside melt away. 'Truly, my heart, I am sorry, but you must remember that you are so much more than simply a womb. You are queen regnant, Cora. *That* is your duty, not mere whelping. Why not pass on such mundane tasks to others?'

She was too busy spluttering at the idea of 'whelping' to pick up on his suggestion immediately but as she recovered she noticed the glint in his eyes.

'Others, Macbeth? What others?'

Maybe he did have a mistress after all. His answer, however, was far more of a surprise than a simple infidelity: 'Lachlan.'

'Lachlan! In case you hadn't noticed, Macbeth, Lachlan is a boy.'

'A man more like.'

'But not one with a womb.'

Her husband gave an exaggerated sigh and took both her hands in his. The sun was rising over the sea and cast his handsome face in a soft pink light that made him almost glow.

'For an intelligent woman, Cora MacDuff, you can be very stupid. Lachlan wishes to marry.'

'Marry?'

The word came out half stutter, half screech. Cora looked around the empty abbey as if others might be hiding behind the pillars, waiting to laugh at this foolish trick. How could Lachlan marry? He was her baby, her boy. He wasn't old enough for a wife. What did he even know of wives? And why hadn't he spoken to her about it first?

'How do you know?' she gasped.

Macbeth pulled her over to sit on a pile of stones.

'He came to me last night at the end of battle practice. Said he had something to ask me. He looked pretty shifty . . . '

'As you do now.'

He gave her an apologetic grin.

'Most likely. I thought he was going to ask for a hawk or even a new horse but what he was after was a wife. A good wife. I mean, he's chosen well.'

'He has a specific lady in mind?'

'Very much so. Lachlan, I would say, is in love.'

Cora blinked hard. The salt air seemed to be stinging her eyes. How could her son be in love? She'd surely have noticed. But, then, she hadn't known to look. As she considered it more, however, she could picture him in the hall of an evening, his clothes remarkably clean, chatting away in corners and dancing. Always dancing. And always with the same dark beauty . . .

'Lady Fiona!'

Macbeth clapped. She glared at him and he leaned over and kissed her instead.

'You *did* know.'

'Way down inside. But I'm still not sure I can believe it. He's only sixteen, Macbeth.'

'So? Do you not remember us at his age?'

She pictured a sunlit pool, herself and Macbeth tangled in each other's arms within the sheltering bulrushes. But swift on the heels of this tender memory came a recollection of the blood-drenched wedding-eve attack and she shuddered to think of it.

'Sorry,' Macbeth said, seeing it in her eyes. 'I'm sorry. That was foolish of me. But, Cora, at least with Lachlan we can see him safe to his marriage bed. He will not suffer what we suffered – I will see to that.'

He was so fierce in his love for the boy he had taken unwaveringly as his own that she could not let her bitterness bite. She hated the thought of losing Lachlan to a wife but it was only natural and clearly she had lost him already so she would be a fool not to embrace her son's desires. Plus, as Macbeth had said, Lachlan had chosen well. No doubt his enthusiasm was for Fiona's silken black hair, ice-water eyes and luscious curves, but her political standing was an incentive too. Her father was the formidable Mormaer Artair of Dunedin and an alliance with Lothian would cement their strength in the south.

Cora stood and looked slowly around the building works. The stark pillars and half-built walls seemed suddenly like their own rule here in Alba – strong, yes, but in need of further strengthening. And now Lachlan could be a part of that. He was already named as Tanaise but if he married he could cement further alliances and they could increase his role in government. She drew in a deep breath.

'He can marry here next spring when the church is complete. We can consecrate it to our holy St Andrew and celebrate our son's union at the same time. We will invite all Alba. It will be a show of power to let the Strathclyde rebels know that we are not to be trifled with.'

'You are sure, Cora? This must be a shock to you.'

She smiled at him.

'It *is* a shock but a good one.'

Still he was staring at her and she forced a smile. In truth it hurt badly that she might now stand more chance of becoming a grandmother than a mother, but the best way to cure hurt was with action and at least if she was busy she would be less likely to wake in the night. The moonbeams would have to dance without her.

Lachlan and Fiona married on the abbey steps the following spring with the sea hurling itself against the cliffs, the gulls screeching their joy overhead and all of Alba's finest lords and ladies staring in wonder at the new Church of St Andrew as its bells sang out the young couple's union. Beyond them, gathered in their hundreds on the meadowlands, the common folk were noisy in their glee and it seemed nothing would quieten them until Macbeth stepped forward, one hand raised authoritatively. He stood there a moment longer, letting the crowd settle, then he spoke.

'Before we go inside to ask God's blessing on this young couple, I wish to confer one more honour upon them.' He looked at Lachlan and Fiona. 'It is enough, I know, on this happy day to stand together as bride and groom, but I hope that, with my own blessing, you will go to the altar also as Mormaer and Lady of Moray.'

'No!' The word escaped Cora's lips before she could think to stop it. Macbeth looked at her, amused. 'That is,' she amended hastily, 'are *you* not Mormaer of Moray, Mac . . . Sire?'

'I am, but willingly I hand the title and the lands – most precious as they are to me – to my son and his new wife, for I know they will care for them as I have done. I have all Alba in my charge now and can think of no one more worthy of holding Moray than Prince Lachlan. You agree, my queen?'

Cora fought to find her voice but could only nod fiercely. She looked at Lachlan and saw that he, too, was stunned. Macbeth was beaming at the effect of his surprise and Cora made a fierce note to flay him alive later for springing this upon her in front of all Alba, but for now they must celebrate.

'Lead the way, Mormaer Lachlan,' she said and, shoulders back and fingers laced tightly through his bride's, Lachlan did so.

All through the service Cora longed to be able to speak to her son and cursed herself for the grand psalms and prayers she had spent so long arranging with the abbot. The effect was impressive but the ceremony seemed to go on forever and she was grateful when the clerics said the last Amens and they could process to the hall for the feast. When they finally stepped out of public view, she ran to Lachlan.

'Congratulations, Mormaer.'

'Thank you, Mama. Though, truth be told, I'm shocked.'

'As am I, but your damned father does like to surprise me from time to time.'

She turned to Macbeth, recalling him arranging to have her anointed Queen Regnant, and felt anew the blessing of his generosity towards her. So many men would prefer to keep their wives in the shadows but hers had ever welcomed her by his side. She smiled up at him and he tugged a little sheepishly on one of her curls that had, as usual, escaped her elaborate headdress.

'You don't mind Fiona taking your title?'

'It's a little late to ask that, isn't it?' He grimaced but their new daughter-by-marriage was at Lachlan's side and Cora turned hastily to her. 'Of course I don't mind. You are welcome to it, my dear, and Moray will be happy to have rulers in residence once more.'

Pretty Fiona was looking more startled than anyone.

'We will live in Moray then? Over the Mounth?'

Cora smiled at her.

'It is not as fearsome as it sounds, I promise you. Moray is beautiful. The firth is gentle and warm. It has dancing dolphins and pretty waterfalls and a monster.'

'A monster?'

'Not truly,' Lachlan assured her, pulling Fiona close against him. ''Tis but a legend. I will show you the loch and the waterfall besides. There is a crystal pool beneath that is a lovely place for a private swim.'

His green eyes darkened at the prospect and as his bride returned the look with a cheeky one of her own Cora realised that this pair, unlike Macbeth and herself, had not waited for their wedding night. Well, good. Life was short and you never knew what was around the corner. Happiness should be seized and her heart swelled with joy that Lachlan understood that.

She pictured him standing at the falls as a skinny boy, his mother the only woman in his life then, and felt a twinge of loss but brushed it aside. Lachlan was a man and must make his own way; she was glad that for now at least it was a happy one. Let him enjoy life as Mormaer and groom while he had the chance to do so for one day, providing they kept Lady Duncan and her sons shuttered up in the west, he would be king.

Chapter Twenty-six

Partick, October 1044

'Beware – evil is everywhere!'

The voice boomed along the frozen Clyde and bounced off the line of islands along its centre. The speaker followed his dramatic pronouncement with a cackling laugh then swept across the ice and into a breathtaking spin so fast his red robes rose up around him like living flames. The crowd on the riverbank gasped delightedly.

It was All Hallows' Eve and with the cold come early this winter Maldred's court was celebrating the feast on ice. Sibyll, who'd learned to skate in Denmark almost as soon as she could walk, was loving the release the sport offered from the grind of day-to-day life. Maldred had welcomed them to Strathclyde three winters back but it had taken them time to adjust to his rugged westerly lands and even now she felt awkward about her place in his eclectic court of Albans, Britons and Norse.

The boys, at least, were content. Maldred had given first Malcolm and now Donald posts in his guard and life with the soldiery suited them both. Last Christ's Mass he'd also made them a gift of two beautiful bay foals, which they were training up together. Sibyll's heart nearly broke with emotion whenever she saw them ride side by side. Duncan would have been very proud, but Duncan was gone and they had to move on without him.

Sibyll had tried to make herself useful wherever she could but had found her true satisfaction lay in working with the monks at Govan to set up a distillery. She had traded her Celtic cross for a copper still and been pleased to find that she had learned enough from Cullen to create an enjoyable spirit. Not that the knowledge had been all her own for Maldred had a keen interest in distilling and his involvement in the project was every bit as enticing as the final product.

Her heart still pulsed like a giddy gull whenever he was near and she was forever striving to avoid touching him in the cramped confines of their little distillery. She sensed from the looks he sometimes sent her way that he felt the same but his wife Edyth was a sweet woman, currently in confinement with their fifth child, and Sibyll would do nothing to hurt her.

'Race you!' Startled, Sibyll looked over as a figure shot past her with a mischievous glance back – Maldred. 'Race you,' he called again, circling round to her side. 'First one to the end of the island. Go on – I'll give you a head start.'

Sibyll was pretty sure she didn't need it but she took it anyway, crouching low and pushing off hard, praying the straps on her skates held firm as she made for the far end of the long mass of Whyte Inch Island. She heard the soft hiss of the ice as Maldred came up behind her and drove forward harder.

'Lord, you're fast,' she heard him gasp and it made her laugh out loud.

She shot past the far tip of the island, curved round to the shingle beach at its head and ground to a halt, sending up tiny shards of ice from each blade like spume on the night air.

'Whoa!'

Maldred came careering in less gracefully. He tried to stop but failed to dig his blade in hard enough and tumbled head-over-heels onto the pebbly bank. Sibyll scrabbled after him.

'Are you well?'

It was dark round the curve of the island but the moonlight shone on his body. He was lying very still and, heart thudding, she crept up and put a tentative hand to his chest. He couldn't be dead. It would be too cruel. It . . .

'Oh!'

Suddenly he grabbed her and pulled her down. She fell on top of him and his arms went right around her.

'Fooled you!'

She tried to batter herself free but he held her too tight.

'I thought you were dead.'

'No. Very much alive.'

His eyes met hers and they both stilled. She was suddenly hotly aware of her body against his, of her weight pinning him down and his arm holding her there.

'Sibyll.'

His voice cracked on her name as if it were breaking in his throat and it seemed the most natural thing in the world to cover his lips with her own to soothe it. His response was instant and like nothing she'd known before. Duncan's kisses had been soft, sweet, even polite, but Maldred's were raw and fierce as if he wanted to draw everything from her and, in its place, to give everything of himself back.

She surrendered to it, lost in him. His fingers dug into her spine, tangled in her hair, grasped at her shoulders, and then he was turning them so she was below him and running his hands over her bodice and she scrabbled to lift her own skirts like a fisher-girl, desperate for more of him. Their breath came hard and fast, mingling in a frosty cloud around them.

'Maldred, we shouldn't,' she gasped, not meaning it.

'Once,' he said into her neck. 'Just once, my dear, sweet Sibyll. My love.'

It was too much. She grasped at him, willingly lifting her hips, and felt him enter her and the sheer, shuddering release of his touch exploded inside her like a pine cone in the flames. She could hear the squeals of the boys on the bank, the hiss of skates, the pop of the flames, but from miles away. She was outside the circle of the court, outside the eyes that had been watching her ever since she came to Alba and outside her own, dutiful self. And it was glorious.

Slowly they came to. Slowly they disentangled themselves, smoothed skirts and breeches, plucked twigs from hair. Slowly the cold of the frozen bank seeped into their limbs and they stood up, separated. But it was not awkward. Their eyes barely left each other, their lips never ceased smiling.

'I didn't realise,' Sibyll said. 'I didn't realise it could be that way.'

He seized her, kissed her.

'Nor I.'

They looked at each other in the ice-bright night. Maldred's words hung between them: *Once. Just once.* Sibyll swallowed.

'We should go back.'

'Aye. You first.'

'No, you. I . . . I want time to compose myself.' Still he stood there and she gave him a gentle shove. 'Go, Maldred. They will be missing you.'

'But I am missing *you*.'

'You are Mormaer here – it isn't about what you want.'

'I know it.'

He kissed her again, softly this time, then with a sigh he turned and launched himself unsteadily onto the ice.

'I won the race,' she reminded him lightly, fighting for normality.

'And my heart,' he said with a rueful wink and then was gone.

Sibyll stood on the bank for a while, fiddling with her dishevelled hair and hoping no one had noted her absence. The party seemed to have grown quieter. The court must be withdrawing to the hall before the spirits came out. She had to go back. She pushed off, following Maldred's tracks. The torches were guttering and the pool of light spilled only a little way across the ice so she was nearly to shore before anyone saw her.

'Mother!' Donald came running, Malcolm in his wake. Both boys looked pale.

'All is well,' she assured them. 'I am hale. I just went a little too far and . . . '

'All is not well,' Malcolm interrupted her gravely.

'Why?'

She knew she was flushed and kept her face turned from the light. Had someone seen? Was she disgraced? And was it her poor sons who had to tell her? She looked furtively for Maldred but could not see him. Those of the court left on the riverside were huddled together like sheep without a shepherd. Her heart plunged.

'What is it?' she demanded. 'What's happened?'

'It is Lady Maldred,' Malcolm said. 'I'm afraid, Mother, that she has lost her baby and . . . and her life.'

'Edyth is dead?' Flames seemed to dance all along the line of her vision. 'When?'

'Not long since. The midwife came running to fetch Lord Maldred but he was on the ice and did not reach her in time.'

Sibyll turned to the river. She looked along the great darkness of it and felt shame grip her. Maldred had not been there for Edyth because he had been with her, *in* her. A tear fell onto Sibyll's cheek and froze there.

'I am very sorry.'

'Come inside, Mother. You are shivering. Come inside and warm up. Please.'

Sibyll let them lead her up to the great hall but only because they were shivering too. For herself she could have stayed out in the cold forever – one with the other evil beings walking the dark earth that night.

*

226

'I want to marry you, Sibyll.'

'No. It's not right.'

'It *is* right and you know it is. Why punish yourself so? Why punish me?'

'Because we deserve it.'

'We do not!' Maldred's eyes flashed fury. 'The timing was unfortunate but ... '

'Unfortunate? It had a direct result. We sinned and God took Edyth to himself.'

'Where she is probably happier.'

'Maldred!'

He turned from her and slumped suddenly into his chair. He looked exhausted and Sibyll longed to go to him but dared not, for the moment she touched him her resolve would crumble. It had been a hard, sorrowful winter. Many had spoken of Maldred's clear grief but none had known it was less for Edyth than for Sibyll, who had refused to let him near her again. Today though, with spring finally coming, he had persuaded her to ride out into the woods south of the pretty church at Govan, and having 'lost' his young steward, they were alone in his hunting lodge. Without the wall of the court to keep her from him, she was having to fall back on force of will and it was not easy.

'It is true, Sibyll,' Maldred said, as much to the rough earth floor as to her. 'Edyth was a sweet girl and a dutiful wife but she was happiest at prayer. She was delicate, tired easily. It's God's miracle that she survived four births and perhaps this time He decided to spare her further torment.'

'It just sounds better that way.'

'Maybe but it's true too. And as for me, she merely tolerated me – in bed, I mean.'

'Maldred, please ... '

'What? We should speak honestly, should we not? We *must* speak honestly. Edyth and I were friends, Sibyll, partners in the rule of our lands and our family, but we were not lovers. She must, poor woman, have been very fertile to have conceived so often.'

'Maldred ... ' Sibyll objected again, but with less certainty this time.

He leaped to his feet and came over to her. She backed up a few steps, looking at her horse grazing on the fresh green shoots pushing through the last of the snow, but she didn't run. Not this time. Maldred was right – they had to talk honestly. She steeled herself to look him in the eye.

'I've loved you, Maldred, from the first time I saw you when I arrived in Dunkeld as a green girl. I thought you were Duncan, my future husband, and my heart leaped for joy.'

'See,' he said, 'what can be wrong about that? I *was* your future husband – just further ahead than either of us knew.'

'But can't you see, Maldred – what if God saw that? What if God knew the sin in my heart? What if he took Duncan because of it? Edyth too?'

Maldred gave a gentle smile.

'That makes no sense, Sibyll. You did not know who I was when you loved me so how could it be sin? Did God not give you the very heart that beat that way? Maybe he took Duncan and Edyth because our duty to them was done. Maybe we are now a gift to each other. Would you refuse God's own gift?'

'You twist His workings to suit you.'

'As do you.'

'This does *not* suit me.'

'I think it does. I think you find shame easier to bear than happiness.'

She gasped.

'How dare you?'

'Is it not true?'

'No. That is ... No. Shame is the right emotion to feel. We did wrong.'

He took her hands.

'Very well, we did wrong. We are sorry for it. We have asked

228

His forgiveness and I think we have it. Now we must consider the future. My children need a mother, Sibyll, and your boys a father.' His grip tightened. 'You are sworn to help Malcolm to the throne and can you not do that so much better with me at your side?'

She looked into his eyes. They were burning with intent but this was her fight, not his.

'I cannot ask that of you.'

'You do not ask. I give it freely. I have been talking to Malcolm. He is a strong and intelligent young man now, my love, and eager to challenge Macbeth. Crinan is raising troops to back him and I would like to do so too but I need your blessing for that.' She bit her lip and he gave her a gentle shake. 'Think, Sibyll – if you and I marry we unite Strathclyde and Northumbria. Our power will extend around Lothian and Perth, creating a rich bed in which to grow the seeds of Malcolm's power. Would that not be good?'

Sibyll looked into his eyes. She so wanted to believe him, so wanted him to be the prince to her fisher-girl, but that was a story, a fantasy.

'Is Malcolm not just a convenient excuse for us to be together?' she stuttered.

'Convenient?' He laughed and moved closer. She felt the warmth of him and had to dig her toes into her boots to stop herself from leaping into his arms. 'You think raising an army and invading the heart of Alba to remove a well-established king "convenient"?'

'No. No, I . . .'

'I love you, Sibyll.' He released one of her hands so that he could cup her chin. 'You are as much a part of me as the hills are a part of Alba and you are ten times dearer. I would lay down my title, my lands, my life for you. How can that be wrong?'

She put a tentative hand to his chest and felt his heart beating beneath her fingers.

'I so want it to be right, Maldred.'

'Then let it. Please. I am asking you to marry me, Sibyll, before the court and in God's sight. I wish to honour you as my wife, rule with you as my lady and take you as my lover every single day left to us.'

Desire shuddered through her and with it a little of the self she'd revelled in on the ice back before all had turned to sorrow. Maldred was right. Surely he was right? This match would be so good for Malcolm and if it was also good for her then was that such a sin? She took the last step towards him and looked up through her lashes.

'Every single day, Maldred?'

'Aye. Starting now.'

And then his lips were on hers and his hands all over her and she could only pray that God truly blessed this match for she could not stop now.

Chapter Twenty-seven

Scone, August 1045

Cora stared down at the babe in her arms, gathering in the soft scent of him, the wisps of his hair, the trust in his blue eyes.

'He's beautiful.'

Lady Fiona flushed and Cora saw her fingers twitch to take her baby back and, remembering how she had been with Lachlan in the early days, hastily handed him over. Murray – named for his Moray homeland – had been born to Fiona and Lachlan two months ago and was here in Scone to be presented to the court as the next in their royal line. Cora had a grand celebration planned to celebrate this triumph and solidify their five-year rule and if in a little part of her it still hurt that the child was not her own, she was trying hard to suppress it.

'Congratulations, Lachy,' she said, turning to kiss her son before he was swamped in well-wishers.

He laughed.

'Lachy, Mother?'

'Yes, Lachy,' she said defiantly. 'You may be a father now, but you're still my little boy.'

Lachlan rolled his eyes at his wife, who smiled indulgently.

Cora felt a little blinded by the glow of their joy and was relieved when someone called her name across the grand palace yard.

'Excuse me,' she said and spun gratefully away but as she turned she collided with a horse, newly arrived in the compound.

She shied back, as did the beast and its poor rider lost hold of the reins and fell in a heap at Cora's feet.

'I'm so sorry.' Cora bent to help the man, a monk judging by his robes. 'Oh! Brother Cullen!'

He scrambled up and bowed before her, batting dust from his robes.

'My Lady Queen.'

'I'm so sorry, Brother. I didn't see you.'

'Or my horse?'

He looked towards the big creature, now being calmed by a groom. Cora grimaced.

'No. Sorry.'

'No matter. I am glad to see you well and the king too.'

He bowed again to Macbeth, who had come up at her side.

'And we you,' Macbeth agreed easily, sliding an arm around Cora's waist to steady her. 'What brings you to court? Have you uiskie?'

Cullen frowned.

'That is not all I do, you know.'

'Of course not. Sorry.'

'I am here today on God's work.'

'Excellent, excellent. What does the Lord want of us?'

Cullen looked around with exaggerated furtiveness.

'He wants you to talk with me in private.'

'I see. Come then, to my chamber.'

Macbeth led the way, Brother Cullen on his heels and Cora reluctantly following. Cullen had aged, she noticed. The hair around his tonsure was thinning to nothing and was more grey than brown. His skin had lost its greasiness and seemed grey and flaky. He looked weary but, more than that, he looked sad.

'Something troubles you?' she asked once they were seated and mead served.

'Aye, my lady. My duty troubles me – my duty to you and the king.'

'In what way?'

He sipped at his mead and fiddled with the cup, turning it round and round in his thin fingers.

'As you know, I am a monk at Dunkeld.'

'Aye.'

'And should be loyal to my holy father, Abbot Crinan.' Cora realised she was holding her breath, as was Macbeth. 'But is not my loyalty to the crown of Alba greater?'

'It is!' they agreed vehemently.

'I feel so too and that is why I am here to inform you . . . ' Again he supped at the mead. Cora could not tell if he were nervous, indecisive or just making the most of his moment. She knotted her hands together and prayed for patience. 'I am here to tell you that Crinan plans an attack.'

'An attack?' Macbeth demanded. 'But how? We have kept a close eye on him and he has no forces.'

'Not in Dunkeld but he has Strathclyde ones from his son Maldred, who has, has . . . ' Cullen finished his mead in one draught. 'Who has married Duncan's widow.'

'Ah! And he means to put his new stepson on my throne? Well, not if I have anything to do with it.' Macbeth grabbed both of Cullen's hands. 'Thank you, Brother. Alba is in your debt today and she will remember it. You shall have money for whatever cause you wish and when Crinan is defeated in this treasonous enterprise, I will make you Abbot of Dunkeld.'

'Oh no, Sire, I don't ask for that.'

'I know it but today you have proved yourself fit.'

'No, truly, I am not the right man to be an abbot. It would tie me too closely to one house and take me from my distilling.'

He seemed very distressed by the prospect and Macbeth swiftly changed tack.

'Well, we couldn't have that, could we? Fret not, you shall have a fine new distillery wherever you want it. Would that please you more?'

'No! I mean, it would be too ... obvious.'

So that was it. Cullen did not want his spying known, though there would surely be precious few to notice if Crinan were defeated. Cora shuddered. War. Lachlan would be glad of it for he was yearning to lead an army.

'When will they strike?' she asked Cullen.

'Soon. Crinan went to Strathclyde for the ... the wedding, though he was too late as they had married with unseemly haste. They must have decided on war then for he came back only long enough to send out messages to all his secret allies. He has gone again now, making for Stirling to meet Maldred's troops. I came as soon as I could but it may only be a matter of days before they attack.'

'Then we have no time to lose.' Macbeth leaped to his feet. 'Cora, take good care of our honoured guest. I must to my men. Time is short but would be shorter yet without this warning. God bless you, Brother Cullen.'

He patted Cullen heartily on the back and was gone, leaving the monk with his head down

'You did right,' Cora said gently.

'For you,' came the dark reply.

'For Alba. Can I fetch you food?'

Cullen shook his head.

'I would rather pray.'

'Very well.'

She showed him to the chapel and he stayed there on his knees for a full day then rode off to find Crinan before his absence was noted. Already troops were riding into Scone. The men of Perth and Fife came first, summoned in vast numbers by Fergus, Sean and their sons. Atholl was next and then Lothian, Angus, Mearns and Mar, and within days the peace of the palace was shattered by the clank of war-steel. Cora's celebrations for baby Murray's blessed birth were on hold and instead the valley rang with the sound of swords being sharpened and shields beaten smooth.

'God bless that monk,' Macbeth said to her when he crawled under the covers on the fifth night, finally satisfied that he had a full army in place. 'Lord knows why he came to us but I thank him over and over that he did for we'd have been caught like rats in a trap without his warning.'

'He cares for Alba,' Cora said.

'He cares for the new Lady Maldred,' Macbeth replied. 'But so what? The end result is the same. They must have heard by now that we are mustering. It may even be why they have hesitated, but if they still plan to attack we are ready. Let them come!'

But they did not come and when the Moray men arrived to join them two days later Macbeth marched his vast army out towards Stirling to seize the initiative, leaving Cora at Scone to guard the Stone of Destiny. Macbeth said she was queen anointed and could rule alone if she had to, but she had no desire to attempt it and once the men had ridden out she and Aila were on their knees almost as long as Cullen had been, praying for victory. It took her some time, therefore, to recognise the great banner that came rolling over the hill, lit by the low evening sun.

''Tis ours!' Fiona squealed at her side. ''Tis our victory. See, my lady, 'tis the red lion rampant and there's Macbeth beneath it and Lachlan at his side . . . and, listen – they are singing!'

Cora strained to hear and, sure enough, on the soft evening air came the lilt of a thousand Alban voices singing the Shepherd's Psalm. The sound seemed to roll off the hills and curl towards them like a lover's finger and, despite herself, Cora felt a surge of joy so sharp she physically staggered beneath it. Aila was at her side in an instant.

'My lady? You are well?'

'Quite, quite well. Come, let us go and greet our troops. No one will dare to challenge Macbeth after this. No one.'

And so it seemed. The men were afire with their cunning victory. Macbeth had positioned himself in the Auchterarder valley, his central force on show but both left and right flanks hidden behind the curves of the hills. The enemy had whooped and descended on them and only once they'd been truly committed to battle had Macbeth unleashed Lachlan on the left and Davey on the right. It had been a rout.

'They fled like cats from a flood,' Lachlan told Cora gleefully, pulling his wife onto his lap and taking his baby son in his arms, oblivious to the dried blood caked beneath his fingernails. 'We killed a fair few until Father stopped us. I wasn't happy about it, was I, Father? I told him we'd shown mercy last time and look how they'd repaid us, but he was adamant and might have been right. Row after row of them fell to their knees and swore eternal allegiance to us. They saw, I think, that in Macbeth they have a mighty leader and will not want to attack him again.'

'That's good. That's very good. And Abbot Crinan?'

'Dead. We found his body when they'd fled the field.'

'It is laid in state in the chapel,' Macbeth confirmed. 'We will send word to Brother Cullen to come and fetch it home with honour. And we can offer him proper thanks too, for without him we would never have secured the victory today.'

Cora bowed her head.

'He will be much saddened by the loss of the abbot.'

'He will. It was not Crinan he wished dead and to compound his grief I believe Mormaer Maldred survived the battle with only minor injury.'

'And young Malcolm?'

'Fled, I'm afraid, his brother too. They will be lurking in Strathclyde, licking their wounds. Let's pray those are deep enough to make them think twice about attacking us again.'

'Amen.'

Cora moved closer to Macbeth. For a brief, private moment she thought of the woman on the other side of this feud and her heart went out to her for taking the grief of this day, but that made it all the more important to make the most of her own good fortune.

'You aren't bad at being king, are you?' she said, smiling cheekily up at Macbeth.

He gasped in mock-affront.

'You're too fulsome in your praise, my lady.'

'Well, I am quite impressed. I might even consider letting you take me to Rome.'

He pulled back, properly surprised this time.

'Truly?'

'It would be an affirmation, would it not?' she said, recalling his own wistful words back at St Andrew's tomb. 'Only strong rulers can travel so far.'

'Perhaps,' he agreed cautiously. 'But we must settle Alba first, my heart. Only then could we even think of leaving her.'

'For Rome?'

'Perhaps,' he said again, but his eyes were shining at the thought and she prayed that she could one day reward him in this way for his unending hard work for herself and for their blessed country.

Chapter Twenty-eight

Partick, September 1045

''Tis just a bruise, Sibyll. It will heal.'

'But it looks bigger than it did yesterday.'

'As it should. Such wounds get worse before they get better. I have seen it many times.'

Sibyll looked unhappily at the mark on Maldred's side. The bruise had been made by a sword, swung with such force that it had severed the iron rings of his mail coat and dug into the thick leather jerkin beneath. She was grateful for the craftsmanship that had saved him but still did not like the look of the dark mark on his flesh. Yesterday she had been able to cover it with her palm but she swore that today she could see the edges of it seeping out around her hand.

'Please let me call the physicians in,' she said for probably the twentieth time, but he shook his head.

'They will suggest bed-rest as they always do and I have no time for lying around. I must talk with my cousins on the western shores and we must strengthen our borders in case Macbeth decides to come after us.'

'After Malcolm, you mean.'

He inclined his head.

'I'm sorry, Sibyll.'

'Don't be. You are home and Malcolm with you. For a time we must live quietly and be content with what we have.'

'Malcolm will not be content.'

'He will have no choice. If he is restless I could perhaps send him to my brother to train with his household.'

Maldred considered this.

'That might work well. Macbeth wouldn't dare attack over the border and Malcolm might make useful friends in England – friends who could one day support a successful bid for the throne.'

She heard bitterness in the word 'successful' and flung her arms around her husband. He flinched and she wanted to look again at the wound but he'd pulled his tunic down over it.

'Such are the fortunes of war,' she consoled him. 'Macbeth's spies were better than we knew.'

'Indeed. It is always the risk with a civil challenge, I suppose, but we were too impetuous.'

'And we have learned from it for next time.'

'Some of us have. For Father there will be no next time.'

Sibyll ran her fingers gently through her husband's hair, pushing it back off his face. Through the curtain she could hear the court gathering for dinner but Maldred did not look well enough to face them. He was as pale as if his blood was draining away but grief could do that to a man.

'Crinan chose to attack, Maldred, and he chose to ride in the front rank as he always had before.'

''Tis true. He was not a man to hide away. He will be a great loss to Alba.' Maldred looked down but beyond the curtain a horn sounded the arrival of a visitor and he was instantly alert. 'Come, the court waits.'

'Let them wait. I'll say you are ill.'

'I am not ill!' His words came out as fierce as dragon's breath and Sibyll leaped back to avoid the heat of them. He looked to the ceiling for a moment then back to her. 'I'm sorry, my love. I'm all out of sorts. I will be better in a day or two, I promise, and for now, we have a visitor. It may be important. We must go.'

He pushed himself out of his chair and she looked away to avoid fussing him over the pain it clearly caused him. He offered her his arm and she took it gently and felt him interlace his fingers in hers, the grip far stronger than any words. Together they moved to the curtain and swung it aside just as the new arrival was being ushered to the dais.

'Brother Cullen, welcome.'

Sibyll flushed. She had not seen the monk for three years and had not felt the lack. She'd heard he'd been most condemnatory of her marriage and was discomforted to see him here now, but he was, thankfully, focused on Maldred.

'I bring news, my lord, news from Dunkeld.'

'What is it?' Maldred stuttered. 'What's happened?'

'It's Abbot Crinan.'

'My father? He lives?'

Cullen looked aghast.

'No. Oh, beg pardon, my lord, but no. 'Tis not that. But his body has, at least, been brought home to lie at rest within the grounds of his own dear abbey.'

'Brought home by whom?'

'By myself, Lord. I rode to Macbeth at Scone and begged.'

'You did? You surely put yourself in great danger, Cullen.'

'Even Macbeth would not hurt a man of the cloth. And, besides, I had to – for the abbot.'

Cullen's eyes flickered nervously around the hall as if he feared enemies were lurking behind every beautifully carved pillar. He seemed lost and, remembering that he had been with Crinan ever since he was a boy, Sibyll guessed he was grieving every bit as much as Maldred was.

'That was very good of you, Cullen,' she said. 'And Macbeth granted you the favour?'

His eyes swung in her direction and seemed to lock onto her with sudden intent.

'He did, my lady. He was reluctant but I pleaded.'

'You are too good, Brother, and we are very grateful. You have lived your life in service to Abbot Crinan and it is fitting you have brought him to his rest.'

To Sibyll's shock, tears brimmed in Cullen's eyes. She looked to Maldred for help but her husband had fallen back against a pillar, his fingers clutching at it and his eyes filmed. All her worry over Cullen fled and she ran to her husband, pushing back those already gathering around him.

'Maldred? Maldred, what is it? What's wrong?'

'Pain,' he croaked and nodded to his side.

'Can you lie down, my love?'

Sibyll took his elbows and at her touch he let go of the beam and his knees crumpled. Men eased him onto hastily laid out cloaks where he curled in on himself, panting like a dog. Sibyll knelt at his side.

'Let me see.' She tugged away his tunic to expose the bruise and stared at it in horror. It was raised as if something was pushing to get out and when she hovered her palm over it the blackness beneath stretched farther around as if her hand were an island in a hellish ocean.

'It's spreading,' she said. 'Where's the healer?'

There were murmurs around the hall but no one came forward and in the end it was Cullen who spoke.

'He is bleeding inside, my lady. I have seen it before. Something is ruptured.'

She looked up at him.

'What can we do?'

'I know not. I'm no physician.'

'What did they do when you saw it before?'

He drew in a deep breath.

'They cut his skin to let the blood out so it could not swamp him.'

'Did it work?'

'It did not but the physician said it could have done and it did ease the man's pain.'

'Cut his skin?'

Sibyll took out her knife and held it to the pulsing black bruise. She held the tip poised over the skin but her hand was trembling. She looked into Maldred's face. His skin was grey and sweat was forming on his brow. His eyes were half open but only the whites showed as if he was lost inside his own head.

'Maldred?' she said, her voice coming out as a ridiculous yelp. 'Maldred, shall I release the pressure?'

He nodded frantically. Again she lifted the knife to his skin but still her hand shook. Then suddenly someone was at her side, taking it from her.

'I will do it, Mother.' Malcolm's voice was low and commanding. He looked up at the spectators. 'I'll need cloths, clean ones.'

Someone ran to the bower and a bunch of linen squares was passed forward. The court held its breath. Malcolm pressed the knife to the blackness and in a small, precise movement, cut a finger-nail's length line into Maldred's flesh. Blood spurted out as if fired from a catapult. Sibyll felt it splatter across her, warm and sticky, but forced herself to concentrate on padding the hole with the cloths. She dared not press too hard but already blood was soaking through, turning the creamy linen a garish scarlet.

'More!' Malcolm bellowed and somehow more squares were found and the sodden ones tossed aside but those too filled quickly and Sibyll forced herself to press down harder. Maldred grunted but the flow of blood, it seemed, slowed slightly.

'It's working,' she gasped. 'Maldred, it's working. We will mend you, I swear it.'

He blinked and opened his eyes. To her delight he smiled.

'It doesn't hurt.'

'Good. That's good.'

'I feel a bit giddy though.'

'Lie still.'

The second set of cloths was soaked, more slowly perhaps but soaked all the same. Sibyll lifted them off and looked hopefully at the wound but still the blood was coming. Maldred laughed, an alien sound in the hushed silence around his makeshift bed.

'Why are the spiders dancing?'

'Spiders? What spiders, my love?'

He lifted a hand.

'There, in the rafters. They are dancing a jig. A spider jig.'

Sibyll did not need to look up to know there were no spiders or to tell what this meant.

'He is hallucinating, Malcolm.'

'Aye. It is, at least, making him happy.'

'It is,' she agreed. She lifted the cloths but the cut had lengthened and still the blood was oozing out. She shoved them back. 'How much blood can a man lose?'

'Lots,' Malcolm said. 'I've seen it. And he can make more.'

'How quickly?'

'I'm not sure.'

They looked at each other but neither of them spoke what they both feared – that it would not be quickly enough. Sibyll draw in a long, jagged breath.

'Can you hold this in place?' she asked Malcolm.

'Of course.'

Once he had the cloths tight, she rose and went round to the other side of her husband. Kneeling, she bent low so her face was next to Maldred's. His wide eyes locked onto hers.

'I'm dying, aren't I?'

'Maybe. I don't know. We're doing all we can. We . . .'

'Hush. It's not your fault. It's mine. I led the attack. I fell into Macbeth's trap. I lost. All my fault.'

'No, Maldred, Please . . .'

He grabbed for her hand.

'All I've wanted for too many years was to be with you and

when at last I had that in my grasp, I rode away to war. I was a fool. I have lost Crinan and I have lost Alba and above all else I have lost *us*. I'm sorry.'

'No,' she said again and then more forcefully. 'No, Maldred. I will not have that. It is not how it is. You have not lost me anything. You have given me such love as I did not know possible and even if I only had that simple pleasure for a few weeks it has still made my life worth so much more.'

She bent over and kissed him. He kissed her back, though he had to battle for breath afterwards, then looked to Malcolm, still trying to hold onto his dwindling life.

'Take care of your mother, Malcolm. She is a very special woman.'

'I will.'

'You must keep each other safe now and my wee ones too.' Sibyll nodded fiercely, blinking back tears. 'Go to England, my love, to Ward. It is your only chance. Talk to King Edward. Get support. You can do it, Sibyll, I know you can. And when Malcolm is king, raise a cup to me – and to your father. We will be watching you together.'

Maldred tried to reach for her face but his strength failed him. She took his hand and guided it. His skin was warm, so very warm. He felt so alive and his eyes burned with all the passion she now knew so well. Perhaps they had got this wrong. Perhaps the bleeding had stopped. She glanced over to Malcolm but saw red seeping up between his fingers and knew then that this was Maldred's last spark.

'I love you,' she whispered. 'I always will.'

'And I you. I wish it had been more, Sibyll. I wish . . . '

His voice cracked as it had on the ice back at the start of last winter. As she had then, she covered his lips with her own. She felt the faintest pressure in response and then he sucked in a last breath straight out of her and was gone.

Sibyll stayed where she was, frozen in Maldred's last moments, and then realisation hit and, behind it, battering grief. She stumbled up and away from Maldred's broken form, his unbearable stillness. She felt her arms flailing, her fingers clawing at the air as if she might get purchase on the chaos of her life. She felt her hair in her mouth and tears on her cheeks and blood running down her arms and knew herself to be nothing more than a spiral of emotion.

She wanted to stop. She had to stop. The court was watching, horrified. She should not fall apart in front of them but there seemed nothing left to hold her together. And then arms went around her, holding her lightly but firmly, and she smelled incense and wool and uiskie and a man's soft voice said, 'I've got you. I've got you now,' and, helpless, she surrendered herself into Brother Cullen's care.

'It is so good to see you, sister.'

Ward did not say she looked well and for that Sibyll was grateful. She was a wreck and she knew it. All she had been able to hold to in these dark weeks of grief had been Maldred's last instruction to her to head to England. Now, at last, she was here, but at what cost? She looked up at the oh-so-familiar walls of York and felt ashamed to present herself to those within. She was as skinny as a litter-runt and her hair was lank and lifeless and falling out in clumps as if it disdained to be part of her; she didn't blame it. It was only thanks to Brother Cullen's devoted care that she had made it to Northumbria at all.

He had hovered so close that sometimes she felt he'd been stitched onto her clothing like her dwindling supply of jewels. He'd made sure she had a bed at night even if she barely slept in it. He'd seen food put in front of her even if she'd barely eaten it and had brought her warm, clean clothes even when she had barely cared what she looked like.

Malcolm and Donald had gratefully left the care of their grieving mother to the monk and Cullen had ridden close to her all the way south, urging her gently on as the mountains around Partick had given way to the lakes of lower Strathclyde and then the moorlands of her brother's earldom. Now, somehow, she was back before the gates of York, the very city in which Crinan had first materialised to ask her to come to Alba and, save for the lines on her face and the scars on her heart, it was as if none of it had ever been.

She was back at the beginning.

'It is good to see you too, Ward,' she managed eventually, looking up at him. She'd forgotten how very large he was and how very kind his smile.

'Life has been hard on you, Sibyll. It cannot have been easy to escape.'

'Not this time nor the last, though I was stronger after Duncan died than after Maldred. Perhaps because the boys were younger and needed me to be so.'

'Or perhaps because you loved Maldred more?'

She bowed her head.

'That too.'

'There is no shame in loving, sister. It is a blessing to feel so.'

'It has not felt so these last months but I'm sure you are right.'

She looked over to Gytha and Margaret, Maldred's daughters and all she now had left of him. They had left his sons, twelve-year-old Patrick and ten-year-old Mal, as heirs to Strathclyde in the charge of his most trusted lieutenant, but the girls had fled with her to their mother's land. They would all have to put themselves into the care of their Northumbrian relatives now and Sibyll, emptied of emotion, was glad of it.

'And you, brother,' she managed. 'How is your new wife?'

He grimaced.

'Wild. She did not come willingly to the altar.'

'Perhaps because you killed her father?'

'It cannot have endeared me to her,' he agreed wryly, 'but things have grown better over time. Elsa and I rub along well enough and ... who knows? She may even bring me more children one day.'

'Beorn is well?'

He beamed.

'Very well. You will meet him inside. He is a fine man. Not quite as big as his father, though sadly stronger.' He did not look sad at all. 'But come, let us go within. Elsa has a feast prepared and we will all feel better with full bellies, I promise you.'

He was right, Sibyll supposed, as she sat back later in the warmth and noise of the hall that had been her home in her childhood. Elsa had offered a warm, if guarded welcome, but the place itself seemed willingly to encompass Sibyll. It almost felt as if York had been expecting her back and she didn't know if that was a comfort or a concern.

'You look melancholy, sister.'

She looked up as Ward sank down beside her on the bench.

'I do? I'm sorry. I am not ungrateful, truly.'

'I did not think it.'

'I seem always to be running from someone and it is wearing me down. I swear I only made it here because of Cullen's care.'

'Brother Cullen – ah, yes.'

Sibyll looked curiously at her brother.

'You do not like him?'

'It is not that. He seems a good enough fellow for a monk – if he truly is a monk.'

'What do you mean?'

'He does not seem to me like a man driven by his service to God.'

She considered this.

'He came to Dunkeld as an orphan. Crinan rescued him and brought him up at the abbey. It was natural for him to join the order but I think he cares more for the distillery than for the church. Is that so wrong?'

'Not at all. And yet he is happy to leave his beloved uiskie to bring you all the way here.'

'He has been very kind.'

'Sibyll.' Ward placed his huge hands on her shoulders and she looked up at him. 'I swear you used to be more astute. Is it grief that has clouded your eyes so?'

She wanted to ask him what he meant but intimations were already creeping in. She remembered Cullen in the church back in Forteviot when Maldred had first kissed her; the confrontation in the cave; his words after Maldred's death – 'I've got you now.'

'I have been watching Brother Cullen all evening,' Ward told her, 'and I would say that he knows what it is to love.'

Sibyll felt colour rising in her cheeks.

'He is a monk. Even if he has … feelings, he knows nothing can come of them. He has been my friend, that is all, and you dishonour him by suggesting otherwise.'

'Maybe. I hope so. Shall we see?'

'How?'

But already Ward was summoning one of the door-guards and asking for Cullen to be fetched to his ante-chamber. He drew Sibyll after him and within moments the monk came panting eagerly towards them.

'You called for me, my lord?'

His eyes darted to Sibyll and she saw the raw hope in them and felt her spirits drop. She stepped awkwardly forward.

'I was telling my brother, Cullen, what a very great friend you have been to me on this sad journey.'

He beamed.

'It has been my pleasure, my lady.'

'I will not forget it and would like to see you rewarded for that friendship.'

Sibyll felt Ward casting amused looks at her emphasis of 'friendship' but refused to meet his eye.

'Rewarded?' Cullen asked. 'Oh, I have no need of reward, my lady, save the chance to serve you.'

'Serve her how?' Ward asked, deceptively casual.

Cullen looked uncertainly at him.

'However is required.'

'You would serve her as her friend?'

Cullen looked from one to the other, swallowed visibly, and then gathered himself.

'As her husband.' Sibyll gasped. He did not look her way but addressed a point on a beam somewhere above her head. 'It is permitted in Alba. Was not Abbot Crinan himself married? Twice. I would take very great care of her, very great. And I can give more besides. Not just uiskie. I am more than uiskie. Macbeth has offered me an abbacy so . . . '

'Macbeth? King Macbeth? Why would he do that?'

Cullen froze. He rolled his head uncomfortably on his thin neck.

'Because I am a senior monk, I suppose.'

'At Dunkeld? He has offered you Dunkeld?'

'Well, yes, but I . . . '

'When?'

'After the dear abbot died. But . . . '

'Why you?'

'I . . . I told you. I am a senior monk. It was I who went to fetch Crinan's body back. I who knew him well.'

'Knew Crinan, who was a traitor to Macbeth? I cannot see that being much of a recommendation.'

Cullen visibly bristled.

'Aye, well, Macbeth's queen knew me from when I took my uiskie recipes to Rosemarkie. We talked. She knew I was – I *am* – a good man.'

'I see.' Ward leaned back, steepling his fingers before him. 'So you are to be Abbot of Dunkeld?'

'No. That is what I have been trying to say. I turned it down. It would be too painful for me to step into Crinan's shoes.'

'So you are not to be an abbot?'

'I am, if I wish it. Macbeth is building a monastery on an island in Loch Leven that has excellent conditions for uiskie.'

'A monastery on an island?'

'Aye.'

'For better contemplation?'

'Exactly.'

'For prayer and reflection and the service of God?'

'Aye.'

Cullen looked puzzled and Ward stepped a little closer to him.

'Do you think then, Brother – or should I say Father? – that a woman would be welcome in such an environment?'

'*My* woman would be.' He looked with sudden ferocity at Sibyll then, to her great surprise, flung himself on his knees before her. 'My lady, I offer myself to you as husband. I will cherish you as no man has ever cherished a wife. I will love you and honour you and care for you as I have cared for you always.'

'And especially since Maldred died?'

'You have no one else.'

'That's not true.' Sibyll tried to pull her skirt out of Cullen's clawing grasp but he held it too tight. 'I have my sons and my brother. I have friends and allies. I am sorry, Brother Cullen, but I do not want another husband.'

He frowned.

'You must do. You were quick enough to leap after Duncan died.'

'How dare you!'

Sibyll sprang back, sending him sprawling before her. He scrambled to his feet.

'I am sorry but it is true and I thought, I thought . . . '

'That I would "leap" again? I loved Maldred.'

His face fell.

'And you do not love me?'

'Not in that way.' He stared at her uncomprehendingly. 'I am sorry if I have in some way misled you,' she told him, trying to soften the blow. 'I was weak, grieving. You helped me and I am grateful but that is all. We can be friends, I hope?'

250

'I do not wish us to be "friends". I am sick of being "friends".'

'I'm sorry but it can be no more and you could not, honestly, take me into Alba. Macbeth would not allow it.'

'Why not?'

'Because of Malcolm, of course.'

'Malcolm is a man full-grown; he need not come.'

Cullen gave a careless little wave and Sibyll felt anger bubble up through her pity. She drew herself straight and faced him down.

'If you cannot see what is wrong with that answer, Brother Cullen, then it is clearer to me than ever why I cannot marry you. I am sworn to see my son to the throne – sworn to his father and his grandfather and great-grandfather. Maldred understood that.'

'But was not strong enough to do anything about it.'

'That's not true. He was betrayed. Someone informed on him.'

'Someone stronger.'

Sibyll stared. Cullen's hand went to his lips as if he might push the words back inside and it was that, more than the words themselves, that alerted her. God's teeth but she had been even blinder than she knew!

'You,' she cried. 'You told Macbeth of the planned attack.'

'No, I . . .'

'You sent Crinan, the man who had loved you like a father, to his death.'

'I didn't mean for that . . .'

He stuttered to a halt. Sibyll faced him. She could feel Ward at her shoulder but he hung back, letting her fight this one for herself.

'You betrayed us all.'

'Not you. I didn't betray you. I did it *for* you. Sibyll, please . . .'

'Don't dare call me that. Get out of my sight! Go back to your precious Macbeth and don't ever, ever try to "help" me again. You are no friend of mine.' Cullen looked stricken but she cared not. 'You are a traitor.'

'I am not! Macbeth is king. It is in helping *you* that I committed treason. I sacrificed myself for you.'

'And sacrificed Crinan and Maldred too. You are every bit as bad as young Lord Kendrick, who tried to kill King Malcolm. No, worse, for he at least had the guts to do it in the open. They hung him, did they not, there and then in the rafters?'

She let her eyes rise to the ceiling above.

'You would not . . . '

'I suggest you do not wait to find out.'

'You are casting me off? You cannot. You must not. I love you.'

Sibyll looked at him. Revulsion shivered across her skin.

'That is not love, Brother. Now, get out!'

He went, head down, feet shuffling, hands waving in indignation and fury and despair. When he had gone Sibyll sank down onto a bench, burying her head in her hands, and Ward patted her shoulder.

'Do not blame yourself, sister.'

But how could she not? She felt a tight, harsh weight developing in her chest, as if her heart was physically hardening. Lifting her head, she looked around the hall she had not stood in for over twenty years and nodded slowly. Despite all the memories of living here with Ward one important thing had changed. She was here with her brother again, yes, but here too with her sons and her stepdaughters. She was an Albawoman now and though she might be back where she had started, she was *not* back at the beginning.

'Oh, I do blame myself, Ward, and rightly so. I have lived too much for myself and am done with that. I have but one purpose now – to put Malcolm on the throne of Alba where he belongs. It will take time but I *have* time.' She rose, feeling purpose seep through her grief-wracked body at last, and with it strength. 'Let Macbeth enjoy his kingship while it lasts, for I swear that will not be long.'

Chapter Twenty-nine

Rome, April 1050

'St Peter's basilica!'

Macbeth stared in awe at the huge church rising up on the curve of the Vatican hill and Cora looked at him, her heart bursting with love at his delight. They were truly here, truly in Rome at last and it was an affirmation indeed. After ten years of peace Macbeth had finally felt confident enough to leave his beloved land in Lachlan's eager care and she was delighted that for a brief period of time he could take something for himself from his unlooked for kingship.

'Let's go in,' she said to him, eager as a child.

Macbeth needed no urging and together they went up the steps and into the spacious atrium then paused, stunned by the gigantic span of the marble arches all around them.

'Look!'

Macbeth pointed to the centre where, beneath a domed canopy, sat a bronze pine cone as tall as a man with water rippling out of the top and down the sides into a basin below. It was guarded by two giant peacocks and Cora ran forward to inspect them.

'Is it not amazing what man can achieve?' she said, stroking the bronze feathers. 'We can take this idea back to Alba, Macbeth.'

'You want peacocks for St Andrews?'

'Maybe not peacocks but we must be more ambitious – we must learn from all we've seen.'

'We must,' he agreed earnestly. 'Nay, we *will*.'

This had been a constant theme throughout their travels. For two months they had ridden across Europe as King and Queen of Alba, making valuable alliances with foreign princes and learning different ways of governance, which they could use to make improvements in their country on their return. They had talked of establishing a coinage, starting towns and developing the royal council and now, staring up at the stately grandeur of St Peter's, Cora's resolve hardened.

Prince Malcolm still lurked in England but so far he had not found the troops to help him invade and Macbeth had refused to launch an attack for he was a man more intent on increasing his country's wealth than its borders. His steady approach had frustrated Cora but now she could see its value. For a country to prosper you needed peace and stability and she vowed to support Macbeth in maintaining that. For the moment, though, they were here at St Peter's blessed tomb and it was time simply to look around and thank God for all they already had.

They had found themselves a very willing guide in a lively young Norman they had met at dinner in their hostel, the Schola Anglorum, the night before.

'Count Osbern,' he'd introduced himself in fluent English. 'I am a Norman, come to Rome for the good of my battered warrior's soul.'

Osbern's easy grin had suggested his soul was not battered at all but he was certainly much taken with Rome and over some local firewater had offered to show them around. The *grappa* had seemed to Cora every bit as lethal as uiskie only without the taste of peat and heather to remind a man how much of it he was drinking and she had refused a second glass. Macbeth, however, had not and he'd squinted unhappily into sunlight this morning, much to the amusement of both Cora and the apparently granite-headed Osbern. The glories of St Peter's, however, seemed to have breathed new life into him and he was keen to see more.

And there was so much more to see for when they turned back over the Tiber into the centre of Rome they found a crazy jumble of beautiful buildings. Ancient temples and bath houses hunched on every corner, their mosaics splitting apart so that lost gods leered out through single eyes above broken noses like so many battlefield casualties. And between them, jostling for space, were new buildings of shiny stone with porticos and towers and gilded statues of saints. As they took in sight after sight, Cora wondered how anyone found enough air here to breathe.

'Could we see Trajan's Column?' Macbeth asked Osbern as the hot sun began, thankfully, to tip towards the west.

'Of course, of course. Excellent choice. This way.'

And off he went, dodging down tiny side streets before suddenly bringing them out in an open square at the centre of which stood a gigantic obelisk. Macbeth stopped dead and threw his arms wide.

'It is just like the Moray Stone!'

Cora looked at him askance, remembering the bleak sandstone pillar beneath which they had received poor Kendrick's body. She would excuse her husband a little partiality but this monument was ten times grander than its Alban counterpart. It was made of marble in eight huge panels and every surface was covered with the lone craftsman's frieze detailing the Emperor Trajan's apparently boundless victories in Dacia.

The obelisk was some ten paces wide and it was possible, on payment of the right coins, to climb up a stone staircase inside it to the very top. Osbern, who had made the giddy climb several times before, said he would wait below so Cora and Macbeth mounted alone. The staircase was tight and spiralled round so that Cora felt as if she had truly turned in on herself in the near-dark before, suddenly, she stepped out onto a dizzying parapet at the top and all Rome was before her. She clutched gratefully at the iron rail and feasted her eyes on the amazing expanse of the city.

'Imagine ruling all this,' she said to Macbeth.

'I scarcely can. It feels so alien.'

He looked around in contemplative silence and in the end Cora asked, 'You are glad we came?'

'Of course. I am so thankful to be here, Cora, and Rome is very impressive but it is not, I think, as lovely as Alba.'

'You mean that?'

He turned to her.

'I do, Cora, truly. No walls, however vast or well constructed, can bound a land as well as the Mounth. No river, however sweeping, can match the peace of the Moray Firth, and no fancy city, however long it has been inhabited, can make a man as proud as setting his own hall on the natural curve of the Black Isle.'

Cora looked curiously at him.

'You talk of Alba?'

'Of course. Where else?'

'It sounds to me as if you are describing not the country as a whole, but Moray.'

He looked away.

'They were just the examples that came first to mind.'

'I see.'

He shifted and let go of the rail long enough to wipe sweat from his brow.

'Is it wrong, Cora, to love your homeland?'

'Of course not, but you have been king ten years, Macbeth – surely *all* Alba is homeland to you now?'

'And I thank God for it daily and for Lachlan to hold Her in his care.'

'He will do a good job.'

'He will for he was born to be a king.'

'And has learned from the best.'

'Maybe.' Macbeth wiped his brow and edged past her towards the door. 'It's hot, isn't it? We are very close to the sun up here. I think perhaps we should go down before our fine Alban skin blisters.'

'Macbeth ...' Cora protested, for there seemed more yet to say, but he was gone and she turned hastily to follow him back down the endless steps.

Osbern was waiting, keen to know how they had found the 'best view of Rome' and when they assured him it had been wonderful, he clapped his hands.

'Onwards then – to the Colosseum, to see the wonderful people who live there. Follow me!'

He was off already and they had little choice but to scurry in his wake. Within just a few turns they came out into an open space to find a huge oval building, four storeys high and guarded by a vast Colossus of Nero. It was made of endless decorated panels, each with an arch soaring to the region of the long-disproved gods, and Cora stared in disbelief. Did men really live in there? Even in the topmost storeys? It surely wasn't natural? Osbern grinned at her.

'Come – everyone will be keen to meet the King and Queen of Alba.'

He held out his arm but Cora shook her head.

'Don't tell them, please, Osbern. I would rather go just as myself, as Cora MacDuff.'

'Very well. And Macbeth? Ah, there are not many named Macbeth. You will be known instantly, Sire.'

'Then I shall be Andrew – Andrew of Cromarty.'

Macbeth's voice was soft and sure and he rolled the name around his mouth as if he liked the taste of it. Cora tried to catch his eye but they had moved inside the Colosseum and there was no time to look anywhere but at their astonishing surroundings.

It was the most exotic residence Cora had ever seen. The amphitheatre was a crazy mass of people, most of them artists, sculptors and architects, seemingly drawn to the mathematical symmetry of the great limestone oval. There was a church at its centre and a rough-and-ready market selling inks and textiles mixed in with spicy sausages, sharp lemons and funny smooth bread shapes the locals called *macaroni*. There was even a cemetery beneath what had once been the Roman stage and the whole place was like a topsy-turvy city frenetically inhabited on several levels.

Many were selling food. With the sun dropping, Cora felt hunger bite and gratefully accepted Osbern's suggestion of thick slices of meat cooked on a griddle and served on soft bread. There were pots of the green nuts they called olives and oil favoured with garlic in which to dip the excess bread, plus a large jug of deep red wine.

'*Saluti!*' Osbern cried and they all set to with relish.

Day somehow merged into night. Macbeth, keen to repay Osbern's hospitality, ordered more wine and then more. The light faded over the Colosseum and gradually the stalls were cleared away and musicians gathered. Cora had never seen such a mix of people, nor such a colourful array of clothing. Fabrics were lighter here because of the heat but worn, it seemed, in layers with bands around waists or criss-crossed over chests or even tied around bare ankles. Head coverings were tied in jaunty knots and most had shoes crafted of a simple sole tied with leather thongs, to let air to their feet.

And how those feet danced! The music was all fiddles and pipes, fast and abandoned. Macbeth took Cora in his arms and they danced with the Italians as if they were the only people in the world. When at last, with the moon high over the Vatican Hill, they set their steps home for the Schola, her feet ached but her heart felt deliciously light.

'It has been wonderful evening, thank you, Osbern,' she said, linking her arm with his.

'It's not over yet, my lady. I have *grappa* at the hostel.'

'Oh no. No, thank you. I have had enough.'

'Macbeth?'

'Why not! Oh, come, Cora, we are away, free. Let us not waste time in sleeping.'

It was good to see him content and so Cora agreed to stay up with them around the last of the fire in the great hall, though not to drink Osbern's *grappa*. She was, therefore, still sharp of mind when, much later, after Macbeth had been describing his beloved Moray to Osbern in lyrical if slightly slurred detail, he asked the Norman, 'And you? Where is your homeland?'

'Mine? It was Bayeux in Lower Normandy.'

'Was?' Cora probed.

He raised his glass to her.

'These days I live in England. Nearly in Wales in truth.'

'England?'

'Nearly Wales,' he repeated. 'I went over with King Edward in '42 from the Norman court. He grew up there, you know, after his father was kicked out by Cnut.'

Macbeth sat up a little, set his *grappa* down. He looked around the hall but they were the last ones still up and no one was there to listen.

'You are part of King Edward's court then?'

'Sometimes.' Osbern sipped his drink. 'Mainly I'm on my own lands. They're nearly in Wales, you know.'

'You said.'

'Very pretty. Hills. Not like your Alban ones, I'm sure, but a fine enough view. I am building a castle. Only a small one but it is an excellent design – stone, as here on the continent.'

'Has the king visited it?'

'Not yet but he will. And he will commission more, I warrant. In Northumbria, for example.'

'Northumbria?' Macbeth leaned forward, all the wine-ease gone from his limbs.

'Borderlands,' Osbern said sagely, staring into his *grappa*. 'Tricky places.'

'Aye. But is Earl Ward not in firm control of his earldom?'

'Earl Ward? Big man? Hairy? Yes, yes, he's in full control. His son Beorn is a man now and a worthy heir and I hear he has another by his second wife so he is settled. But he has the boy with him, does he not?'

'What boy?'

'Well, he's not a boy, not at all. That's just what King Edward styles him – "the Scots boy". That's what they're calling it, you know – Scotia. Sounds grander than than Alba.'

Osbern ground to a halt and looked from Macbeth to Cora as if suddenly realising to whom he spoke.

'The "Scots boy" is Malcolm?' Macbeth asked quietly.

Osbern nodded.

'I meant no offence.'

He looked worried and Macbeth leaped up and went to him, clapping him on the back.

'None taken. We're all friends here.'

'We are? Oh, good. Very good. I like you Macbeth, King of the Scots.'

'King of the *Albans*.'

'Albans, yes, sorry.'

'Don't apologise. I like you too. But tell me – King Edward takes an interest in this Malcolm?'

Osbern's shoulders tightened and Cora could see that he too had sobered but he nodded reluctantly.

'I am told he sees in the Scots boy's situation a little of his own as a youth for Edward was an exile too until God saw fit to restore him to his birthright.'

'And he thinks Alba is Malcolm's birthright?'

'Is he wrong?'

Macbeth sucked in a sharp breath and looked at Cora.

'Our son is next in line to rule,' she told Osbern firmly.

'Of course, and having met you, I pray he succeeds. Not for a long time, of course, God have mercy, but . . . '

He was getting himself tangled up again. Cora leaned over and patted his knee.

'We know what you mean, Osbern.'

'Do you? I'm glad because I am beginning to lose the thread of it myself. I think I should retire.'

'In a moment.' Macbeth's voice was steady; Andrew of Cromarty was long gone and he was king again. 'Do you consider Alba to be Malcolm's birthright?'

Osbern sighed.

'May I speak honestly?'

'Please do.

'Then you must see, my lord king, that Malcolm has a claim. He is son of a king who was grandson of a king. Alba has long, I'm told, passed the crown from line to line and Malcolm believes it should be his turn next. I ask you again, for I know little of it, is he wrong?'

Macbeth sighed.

'From his viewpoint, I suppose he is not. The important question is, will King Edward back him?'

Osbern shrank from answering this.

'I know not, truly, my lord. I am not important enough to be in the king's confidence and I am often in my own lands, nearly in Wales, far from the seat of power. For now, though, I think the king is more concerned with domestic matters. He looks to make an alliance with Duke William of Normandy and his eyes are turned south.'

'For now?'

'That is all I know.'

'It is enough. Thank you. Come, let us not spoil our night with talk of politics. One last drink, hey?' Macbeth grabbed his cup and held it high. 'To Rome!'

'To Rome,' Cora echoed and Osbern gladly took up the cry, though he drank his remaining *grappa* in one and made his excuses straight after.

Cora and Macbeth stood together watching him scuttle away to his chamber.

'Let us pray Normandy holds King Edward's attention as Osbern suggests,' Macbeth said, his voice low. 'It has, perhaps, taken this distance from it to show us the value of home, my heart, and we should not linger here too long for Alba may have need of us.'

Cora nodded slowly. They had worried about Prince Malcolm ever since he had evaded them as a youth and now their worries might prove to be well founded with the might of the English at his back. In the face of such news the exoticism of Rome seemed a little hard to bear Although her bed was soft and welcoming, thoughts of home ran round and round in Cora's head so that she was still awake when St Peter's bells heralded another warm dawn over Rome.

Chapter Thirty

Gloucester, Christ's Mass 1052

'This is the Lady Maldred my sister, Sire.'

Sibyll curtseyed as low before King Edward of England as she could without her joints creaking. Ever since her year spent living in caves her bones ached in the wet or cold and here, in a place called Gloucester, it was both wet *and* cold. Sharp winds seemed to whip off the mountains to the west day and night, lifting stinging half-snow into the faces of the court who were gathered to celebrate Christ's Mass here as they apparently did every year.

Why they chose this miserable place Sibyll had no idea. No doubt it was very pretty on a sunny day but there had been precious few of those since her party had arrived a week back. Still, she was before the English king at last and, as Maldred had urged her, she must fight to secure his help.

'And this is my son,' she said the moment she was raised, 'Prince Malcolm.'

She noted interest quicken in King Edward's knowing grey eyes and moved back to make space for Malcolm. There was not a trace of the boy left in him nowadays. He was a head taller than her and had an athletic strength and poise that drew eyes to him whenever he entered a room. She had sold one of her last jewels to buy him fine clothing and was relieved when King Edward's eyes travelled the length of him, from his highly polished boots to the modest diadem on his dark brow, and he nodded approval.

'You are a man in exile, Prince Malcolm?'

'For now,' Malcolm replied, head held high.

Edward smiled.

'You intend to retake the throne of Alba for your family?'

'I do, Sire, if God sees fit to bless me with the forces to do so.'

'Oh, I'm sure he will. He has, after all, sent you to me. Sit.'

Edward patted the stool to his left and Malcolm glanced at Sibyll, who eagerly nodded him forward. She looked back to see many eyes noting the favour the king was doing her son and smiled to herself. The English court was at least three times the size of the Alban one but it was no less jealous of attention and she stepped quietly in front of her son to offer him a little privacy in his audience with the king.

'You were an exile yourself once, I believe, Sire,' she said, keeping her voice low.

'I was indeed, so I understand your plight very well, my lady.'

'Why did you have to flee, Sire?' Malcolm asked.

Sibyll flinched at the directness of the question but Edward seemed to enjoy the open interest.

'My father was driven out by King Cnut,' he told Malcolm. Sibyll flinched again for had not she and Ward come to England on the back of Cnut's invasion but Edward, noticing, looked up at her. 'Fret not, my lady. I know you were once a Dane but I do not hold it against you.' He laughed thinly. 'Fortunes change like the tides and those caught on them must do what they can to stay afloat.'

'I was just a child, Sire, when Ward and I came to England.'

'As was I when I fled to Normandy – and look, my lady, we have survived. Even, I flatter myself, done rather well.'

'You have excelled, Sire.'

He laughed again.

'I would not go that far. Rather, I held on by my bleeding fingertips until I could grasp power once more.'

'I'll drink to that,' Malcolm said, drawing a flask from his belt. 'May I offer you a little usquebauch, Sire?'

'Usquebauch?' Edward repeated, faltering on the Gaelic word.

'The water of life. It is what fuels an Albaman's soul.'

Malcolm unscrewed the flask, took a small leather cup from his pocket and poured out a little uiskie. Sibyll instantly caught the scent of it, like a moorland evening, and remembered her own first taste.

'Take care, Sire,' she said as King Edward accepted the cup. 'The drink is very fiery. You need only a small sip to enjoy it.'

'Thank you for the warning, Lady Maldred.'

Edward lifted the cup and sipped. The fumes rose on the warm air of the hall and Sibyll recognised a Dunkeld spirit and felt a sharp pang of longing for her one-time home, but she could only return there with this man's help and she willed him to like their offering.

'Heavens!' The English king looked into the cup as if checking nothing breathed inside it, then took a second sip. 'That is a mighty drink, Prince Malcolm.'

'And the Albans are a mighty people, Sire.'

'They must be,' Edward said dryly and handed the cup back. 'And you, Prince Malcolm, when did you have to flee?'

'When my father King Duncan was defeated by Macbeth.'

Malcolm's voice was raw and Sibyll caught shades of both shame and defiance in it. Edward clearly did too. He gave a funny snort and said: 'It happens. My father, too, was defeated. They all said that he was weak. They called him "unready" and made jests at his expense, but he was fighting horde after horde of fearsome Vikings with no moral code and no fear of death. Their pagan priests told them that warriors earned a place in the feasting hall of the gods. I'll bet they're feeling bitter now they've found out the truth, hey? I hope the hellfires are keeping them warm while they rue their mistakes.'

'I don't doubt they are, Sire. And your father did his best, I'm sure.'

'He did, Malcolm, he did. The odds were stacked against him and we will never know if another man would have done better or even worse. No one favours the vanquished, but the vanquished do not have to stay that way. I came back from Normandy to reclaim my throne and no one jests about me now. It will be the same for you. You will restore both yourself and your father's memory.'

Sibyll saw Malcolm's eyes shine and blessed this strange, imperiously benevolent king for his surprisingly tender words. She had not realised how much Malcolm had been labouring under the yoke of shame about his father's defeats and cursed herself for not seeing it before. But no matter. King Edward was right – winning would be the best salve of all, if they could achieve it.

'God be praised that you returned, Sire,' she said.

He gave a nonchalant little wave.

'How long were you in exile?' Malcolm asked.

'Twenty-eight years, all told.'

'Twenty-eight!'

Edward leaned over and patted the younger man's knee.

'It will not be so long for you, Prince, with the Good Lord's blessing.'

Sibyll eased herself forward. The rest of the court were pressing in around them and there was little time left.

'And with a bold king's help,' she suggested.

Edward turned sharp eyes upon her and gave a small smile. He looked back at Malcolm.

'Your mother is a great support to you?'

'She is, Sire. I am blessed in her.'

'You are.'

Edward got to his feet and moved towards Sibyll. His fingers clamped over hers but he said nothing, just stared deep into her eyes. Sensing a test, she willed herself not to flinch and after almost more time than she could bear he suddenly laughed and said, 'I am glad, Lady Maldred, that you are supporting your son. My mother was not so gracious and it greatly hindered my cause. You will be more powerful if you stand together.'

'And if, Sire, we can find others who will stand with us.'

'Indeed.' He looked to the rafters, considering. 'Why do you wish Malcolm to be king, my lady?'

The question was sharp; the answer had to match. But she was ready.

'Because he was born to it, Sire. He was born to a king, grandson of a king, and he must be a king in his turn. It is God's will, I am certain, but God will not hand the crown of Alba to us unless we prove ourselves worthy of it by fighting in his name.'

Edward looked at her again and then at Malcolm.

'You are blessed indeed, not only to have a mother who supports you but one whose support is well worth the having. You are widowed, Lady Maldred?'

'Twice over, Sire, and both times at the hands of Macbeth.'

'Ah! Then you wish for your own vengeance.'

Sibyll considered this.

'No, Sire, not that. I do not believe Macbeth fights to spite me, any more than I fight to spite him. There is no malice in this contest, but it is a contest all the same and one I want to win.'

She heard her voice harden and saw Malcolm look at her with something like shock but it was the truth and must be spoken. Edward gave a bark of a laugh.

'I like your fire, Lady Maldred. I have known your brother for years as a tough and able man but it seems his sister is equally so. Your parents must have been formidable indeed.'

Sibyll felt sorrow sear her like a scab ripped off and looked for Ward. He stepped up behind her, close enough for her to feel his strength, but she had got this far alone and would not falter now.

'I hope to do them honour, Sire, by raising their grandson to his rightful throne.'

'A noble aim. So, tell me, what do you need to take this Alba of yours?'

Sibyll looked to Malcolm who stepped forward.

'We need permission, Sire, to lead the trained men of Northumbria into battle over the border.'

'And in return?'

'In return, once I am King of Alba, I will swear fealty to you as my overlord.'

'I see.'

Edward sat down again, seemingly deep in thought, and Malcolm glanced anxiously at Sibyll. They had talked long and hard about what incentive to offer the English king as the hearth-fire guttered and the ale soured. None of them had wanted to make Alba subservient to the English crown but they could think of no other suitable enticement to offer Edward. And, after all, such oaths were just words – empty packaging on a gift that would mean much to Edward and cost them little. Malcolm had railed against it the most but in the end had conceded the point and she was impressed to hear him deliver it so smartly now.

'Overlord of Alba,' Edward said, clearly relishing the prospect. He clapped his hands and they all jumped. 'Very well. For you, Prince Malcolm, as a fellow exile, and for you, Earl Ward, as my loyal servant, and for you Lady Maldred, as a model mother, I grant you permission to take the men of Northumbria against King Macbeth when you see fit.' He smiled benignly on them and then suddenly added, 'And one hundred of my finest house-carls besides.'

Ward fell to his knees, Malcolm and Sibyll just a heart-beat behind.

'You are too good, Sire, truly. We are honoured.'

Edward smiled and patted their heads as if they were children.

'A bit of fighting will do them all good for England has been at peace many years and it makes men lazy. Send word when you are ready and they will ride out. Now, where are the minstrels?'

And just like that Malcolm found himself in possession of a battle-force. He looked incredulously at his mother while they stepped deferentially aside.

'Is a housecarl what Uncle Ward was when you first came to England, Mother?'

'That's right. They are the king's personal troop of highly trained, professional soldiers – the best fighting men in the country.'

'Having one hundred of them on our side will make all the difference, Malcolm,' Ward said keenly. 'You did well there, lad, and your mother was peerless. She had the king eating out of her hand.'

He winked at Sibyll, who flushed with the warmth of his praise. She had done as Maldred asked and had, praise God, succeeded.

'As soon as we return to York we must start making plans,' Ward went on, but Sibyll put out a hand to stop him.

'You have been very good to us, brother, but this is Malcolm's fight. You do not have to ride with him.'

He looked scornfully at her.

'I know I do not have to, Sibyll, but I want to. Indeed, I am desperate to! As the king said, there has been endless damned peace and I feel younger already just thinking about drawing my sword. Besides, it will do Beorn good to get off his backside and lead an army. The youngsters today have it too easy. By his age I'd killed a hundred men at least and he's barely shot a rock-dove from the sky. No, I will welcome war, sister, and life will be richer for us all once Malcolm is ruling Alba.'

'Beneath Edward as overlord?'

'Of course,' Ward agreed with a wicked wink. 'I am sure Edward, who has never, note you, been further north than here in Gloucester, will take a great interest in his new kingdom – from afar. Fret not – Malcolm will rule and rule alone. Watch out, Macbeth, for we are sharpening our swords and your time is done!'

And with that, Ward flung himself into the dance, knocking people flying with his clumsy-footed exuberance and Sibyll could only stand with Malcolm, watch and laugh and pray that Alba could be won as easily as the dance floor.

Chapter Thirty-one

Scone, March 1053

The smell was intense – acrid smoke, heat you could taste on the tip of your tongue and a strange timber sweetness, as if some sort of metal beast was being gently spit-roasted. Cora stood in the lee of Macbeth's big body and watched in fascination as the smith's boy pumped the leather bellows that sent air into the earthen kiln his master had installed with much solemnity at the edge of the Tay.

They had returned from Rome to find a country thankfully at peace and thriving under Lachlan's government and had spent long nights sharing their new learning with him. In the last two years they had brought in coinage experts from Francia to set up a mint and commissioned masons to build workshops and stalls around the palaces here at Scone and at Forteviot, to sow the seeds of what might, eventually, become towns or even cities. It was an exciting time but a fraught one too for Macbeth's spies reported movement in Northumbria and they were ever on the alert for an attack.

Now they were in a peated-up side-channel of the pretty Tay because Macbeth had decided he needed a new sword and the smith had invited them to see the weapon literally drawn out of the ground. The day was frost-bright but made warm by the intense fire needed to 'bloom' the iron. Cora stood as close to it as she dared.

'Hover your hand over it, my lady queen,' the smith invited her. 'Hover, no more. I would not want your delicate royal hands scorched.'

She did as bid and even from several hands' span away it felt as if her skin might peel off. The smith beamed broadly and showed her his own palms, as leathery as a newly tanned cow's hide and scored with deep scars.

'See that, my lady queen – done as a green youth when my wits were as soft as my skin. I learned the hard way. Wouldn't want you to do the same.'

Cora agreed she would not want that either and stepped back to let him take centre-stage in this mystical 'blooming'. He showed them the bog iron, trapped in reddish patches within stones flushed from the silted river, and explained how it was placed above red-hot charcoal in his precious kiln to crack open the stone and release the 'bloom'. Cora imagined it as a beautiful mineral flower and watched eagerly as, at last, the smith plunged long tongs theatrically into the kiln to fish out the raw iron. He lifted it high and placed it triumphantly on the ground before them. Cora stared.

'Is that it?' she whispered to Macbeth.

'I think so,' he whispered back.

They both looked at the bloom – less a flower and more a jagged lump, grey and swollen, like the end of a rotting limb.

'Goodness,' Cora said eventually, 'how on earth did you manage that?'

The smith gave a funny little bow.

'Years of learning, my lady queen – years! But the process is not done yet.'

'Really?' Cora managed. She could feel Macbeth trying not to laugh beside her and did not blame him for she had rarely seen anything look less like a lethal weapon than the stubby lump before her. 'I can't wait.'

The smith, thankfully, was intent on settling himself before the burning fire revealed by the lifting of the kiln. In the centre was a low, flat stone onto which he lifted the bloom before, in a sudden rush, he hit down on it with a large hammer. Cora flinched and he glanced up.

''Tis a violent business, my lady. You do not have to watch if it disturbs you.'

Macbeth raised an eyebrow at her but she did not rise.

'I am a queen, smith, and must inure myself to violence. Besides, your artistry is most impressive.'

He smirked at this confirmation of his own opinion and turned back to his hammering. The bloom softened and flattened, glowing as orange as the sun as black specks flaked from it.

'Slag,' the smith told them between blows. 'What we will have left, my lord king, my lady queen, will be purest iron from which to forge a majestic sword.'

'Fit to cut up the English?' Macbeth asked.

'Fifty thousand of them,' came the instant reply.

Macbeth nodded approval but Cora shivered and peered more closely at the glowing, shifting lump as if she were watching the very birth of battle. The orange substance seemed to flicker like hell itself and she turned away, looking to the skies for relief. Instead, she saw further cause for alarm.

'Men!'

'Where?'

Macbeth spun round, his hand going straight to his sword. His guard leaped to attention and even the smith stood, the bloom held before him as if it were already deadly. They all looked to the hilltop where several men crested the rise and began to descend towards the palace.

'At ease,' Macbeth said to his guard when it became apparent

273

that no great host followed. He put up a hand to shield his eyes against the low sun. 'I don't recognise them. Do you?'

'No, my lord,' Davey said, stepping forward, 'but to my eyes they're on the run. Their horses are dragging their fine feet and the men are bowed in the saddle and have their fancy cloaks clutched tight around them.'

Cora looked more closely and could see the truth of Davey's observations.

'Whoever it is,' she said, 'they seek sanctuary and believe they will find it in our court. We must go back to the palace.'

'Back?' the smith squeaked in childish disappointment.

Macbeth grimaced.

'I am afraid, smith, that my wife is right as usual. Duty must come before pleasure but this has been most enlightening and I hope we can see more of your work before it is done?'

'This part is almost finished anyway,' the smith grudgingly admitted, kicking at the ashy edges of his fire. 'I will fashion the sword in my forge with all my tools.'

'Excellent. Then I will visit you there. But for now we must return to the palace – and quickly if we are to beat our unknown guests.'

He turned and strode towards the compound but already the new arrivals were pounding over the open ground before it. They spotted the king's group and their skittish response confirmed Davey's assertion that they were on the run. Macbeth was quick to cry welcome and one detached himself from the group and trotted forward, removing his helmet to reveal sweat-soaked hair and tired but very familiar eyes.

'Osbern?' Cora said, stunned. 'Lord Osbern, is that you?'

He leaped from his horse and bowed low.

'At your service, my lady queen.'

'Nay, 'tis plain Cora MacDuff to you,' she joked, but he did not return her smile and she hastened forward. 'What's wrong, Osbern? What's happened to bring you so far north?'

274

'All Normans are cast from the English court.'

'All? Why?'

'Duke William is out of favour and his countrymen with him. 'Tis the Godwinsons, you see – a noble family who were in exile and now are back, trumpeting "England for the English" and poisoning everyone against honest incomers like myself. We had to flee before we fell prey to the king's housecarls.'

'Housecarls?'

'His best fighting troops,' Davey said. 'Well equipped and trained. Dangerous men.'

'Yes,' Osbern agreed, 'very dangerous – as you may, Lord King, find out for yourself.'

'Why?'

'I have ridden to you for two reasons, Macbeth. The first is to seek sanctuary in our troubles and the second is to bring you warning.'

'Sanctuary you are welcome to, friend, and your men besides.' The soldiers gave audible sighs of relief, almost sobs. 'But warning of what?'

'Of invasion, my lord. Last Yule the king welcomed the young Scots boy to court and his mother with him. She is sister to Earl Ward of Northumbria and seems a determined lady. The king, I am told, was much taken with both her and the young man and has granted his permission for Malcolm to lead the men of Northumbria against you.'

Macbeth sighed and looked over to the stark mound of the Hill of Belief beside the palace.

'I see,' he said eventually. 'Ah, well, 'twas to be expected, I suppose. And, after all, it is nothing we have not faced before.'

He gestured Osbern towards the compound but still the Norman stood his ground.

'King Edward has granted him the men of Northumbria, Macbeth, and one hundred of his own housecarls besides.'

Macbeth stopped dead. He stared at the Norman.

'King Edward will commit his elite against us?'

'So I have heard. I'm sorry.'

Macbeth could only stare, the implications of this ghosting across his face like a frost, but then he recalled himself and clapped his troubled guest on the back once more.

'Nay, Osbern, 'tis not your fault. Come – you deserve Alba's finest hospitality for these tidings, however bitter. The English will not ride on us tonight so let us relax and enjoy God's bounty together while we can.'

And with that he led their friend towards the gates, talking of Rome as if this were nothing more than a social call. Cora blessed her husband for his kindness but as they reached the palace she saw him hesitate, look up again at the Hill of Belief and then over at her, raw fear in the back of his brown eyes and her heart ached to see it. It seemed the peaceful years of their reign over Alba might be coming to an end just as they begun to truly grow her.

Chapter Thirty-two

York, May 1054

Sibyll sat on her horse a little way back from her two sons on their matching bays and watched with pride as they commanded a mass of excitable men with apparent ease. She had promised King Malcolm on his putrid death-bed that she would one day see his namesake to the throne and at last that day might be close. It had taken a frustratingly long time to plan the attack and raise the men but finally the formidable English housecarls were here and foot soldiers had been arriving in the camp at York all week. The thought of war churned like an endless pain in her gut but it had to be this way. As she had once told Morag there was no use in hiding and it was time for her to go home, whatever the cost.

She looked to the backs of her boys – men now. Their beautiful bays marked them out wherever they went on horseback but even on foot their noble birth was clear in their bearing. They were as tall and broad as each other but Donald always stood two steps back from Malcolm, tensed and ready to defend his elder brother. She realised now that this was how Duncan should have been supported and suddenly she could see two other brothers laid over these ones.

If only Maldred had been Bethan's son too he could have carried his grandfather's hopes for the throne and Duncan could have stood at his shoulder as Donald was doing for Malcolm. Together they would have been unstoppable. She would have married Maldred, as she had thought she was to do the very first time she'd ridden into Dunkeld, and even now both men might still be alive and well, Maldred as her husband and Duncan as her brother-in-law.

But then, she reminded herself sternly, she would not have had Malcolm and Donald, nor Gytha and Margaret, Maldred's two daughters, who had in these dark days of exile become almost her own. Gytha was recently married into Northumbria. Margaret was also attracting a great deal of interest but she was a sparky young woman and Sibyll was determined to find her a man strong enough to appreciate her. Marrying off daughters was a joy she had not thought to have and she was making the most of it.

And now, in a final flourish, Malcolm was declaring that they would march on Alba tomorrow and his troops were cheering as hard as if he'd proposed a three-day feast. With much waving and head-bowing, he turned his horse and guided it to Sibyll's side, to escort her back to the ancient great hall of York.

'You look thoughtful, Mother,' he said as they traced their way carefully through the crowd.

'There is much, is there not, to consider?'

'And much to do.'

'That too. Do you remember Crinan's grapes, Malcolm?'

'Grapes? Are you quite well, Mother?'

'Of course. Crinan planted vines at Dunkeld. They may still be there for all I know. We thought he was mad but he persisted and made wine. Good wine. I hope someone has kept the rootstock going. Morag, perhaps, if she is still hale.'

'Mmm.' Malcolm looked impatiently across his troops. 'And your point is?'

'Do you remember when all the court gathered to see them planted?'

'I'm not sure.' Still he was not really listening.

'Do you not remember standing in one of the holes so that you could grow as fast as the vines?'

'Me? No!'

'Or taking your great-grandfather's crown from his head to place on your own?'

Malcolm froze. He dragged his eyes from his troops and looked straight at her.

'Oh, aye, Mother, I remember that. Was that at the vine-planting? I'd never have known but I do remember the crown. I remember how it shone, how its edges were sharper than a haw-thorn and how very heavy it felt upon my head.'

She sucked in her breath.

'The crown felt heavy, Malky?'

He gave a soft laugh at the childish name but then sobered.

'Heavy, yes, but right too. It felt like mine.'

Sibyll released her pent-up breath in a relieved smile.

'That's good because you will have to wear it a long time.'

'I pray so. I would like to be a good king.'

'Then you will be. And you are lucky in having your broth-er's support.'

'I am.' He looked across at Donald, riding on Sibyll's other side, then frowned. 'Is that . . . ? No. Surely not. Not here. Why would *he* be here?'

'Who?' Sibyll asked, straining to see anyone who might stand out amongst the myriad men ranged around the meadowlands.

'No one,' Malcolm said hastily – too hastily. 'I was wrong. Come, Mother, let's get you inside. It is very warm out here and your delicate skin will burn.'

He dismounted and held out his hand to Sibyll, who laughed at him as she leaped down.

'Delicate! Malcolm, my sweet, my skin has not been delicate

for many a year, if ever. Too many Alban winters have seen to that. Malcolm, what's wrong? I . . . oh!'

She started as a ragged bundle of a man flung himself at her feet, wrapping his arms around her legs so she was caught in the grovelling tangle of him. He was babbling at the earth: 'I'm sorry. I'm sorry, I'm sorry. I beg forgiveness. Plead for it. Have mercy, please.'

She put her hands up and tried to back away but he was holding on too tight. Panic gripped her and she looked desperately at Malcolm.

'Get off her!'

Malcolm's hand clamped around one thin arm and he lifted the man bodily aside. He scrambled up and looked set to fling himself before Sibyll again until Donald seized and restrained him. Sibyll's heart wrenched as if a blacksmith were twisting it in his tongs but she had to stay calm.

'Brother Cullen,' she said coldly.

Malcolm stepped between them.

'How dare you assault the Lady Maldred?'

'Assault?' Cullen's voice squeaked with indignation. His pale face was blotched with spots of colour and his eyes were red-rimmed. 'I did not assault her. I would never assault her. I ask only for mercy, for forgiveness. Please, my lady, for the friendship we . . .'

'Hush!' Malcolm commanded and, shocked, the monk did so. But not for long.

'I have travelled far, Prince,' he said, adding with a sly wink, 'I have travelled from King Macbeth's court.'

'Why?'

'I told you – to beg for mercy, to plead for forgiveness, to . . .'

'All right. Mother, do you forgive Brother Cullen?'

'No.'

Sibyll saw Cullen crumple in Donald's grasp but she could not lie.

'Christ Himself preaches forgiveness,' Cullen whined.

The sound of his voice grated on Sibyll. Had he always been this pitiful or had she, God forbid, worked this sad transformation in him? She wavered and, seeing it, he wrestled himself free from Donald and threw himself flat on the ground before her.

'I repent. Truly. I come to you on my knees. Surely you cannot turn me away?'

Sibyll looked down at the monk. He was right that Christ had preached forgiveness but all she could see was Maldred curled up on himself as his poor, dear body still bled from the impact of a sword wielded because of this man's treacherous information.

'He comes from Macbeth's court, Mother,' Malcolm whispered in her ear and she understood the implications instantly.

As she had learned a long time back in a cold dark cave she had to use all the advantages at her disposal. She sighed.

'I forgive you, Cullen,' she said stiffly.

'You do?' He looked up from the dirt, light flooding his eyes. 'Oh, my lady. Oh, my Lady Sibyll, I . . . '

He was getting up. She raised both her hands and stepped hastily back.

'I forgive you, Brother, but I do not wish to see you.'

'But . . . '

'No, Cullen.'

She was going to cry. She was trying to be strong but she could feel long-suppressed misery uncurl within her. Cullen was looking up at her as if he could somehow pull her back into the past and she couldn't bear that.

She turned and fled. Hearing footsteps behind, her heart battered against her ribcage and her fingers clawed at the air and when he grabbed her, she screamed.

'Shhh, Mother, shhh! All is well. It's me. It's Donald. I have you safe.'

'Donald!' She collapsed against her younger son, quivering with relief. 'Where is he? Where's . . . ' She could not say his name.

'Malcolm has him. Don't worry, Mother, Malcolm has him and will see him gone from here. You need not fret.'

He sounded so calm, so assured, so very, very kind, and she gave in gratefully.

'I want to go forward, Donald, not back.'

'We will. We will return to Alba but it will be a new Alba, one of our own making, and you will be a part of that. Indeed, you are at the very heart of it. Now come, rest.'

And she went, though rest, she suspected, was a long way off yet. On the morrow they would march forth and this encounter with Cullen had reminded her how very vulnerable they were. She could only pray that King Edward's housecarls were as powerful as all had promised for now the sword must lead them and only God could know which way it would swing.

Chapter Thirty-three

Forteviot, July 1054

'Retreat!'

Cora bolted awake to find Macbeth sitting upright, his naked chest silhouetted against the pale dawn light creeping round the leather curtain of the royal chamber. His blond hair was in wild tangles and his hands were held aloft to men only he could see.

'Retreat!' he called again, his lips barely moving so the sound seemed to rise up out of the very centre of him.

Cora shook him.

'Macbeth . . . Macbeth, wake up! All is well. You are safe.' Still he sat there, eyes staring through their bedchamber and straight into the dread battlefield, though the terrible reality of it was ten days back. 'Macbeth, dearest, please.' He blinked suddenly and turned his head to her. 'Macbeth it's me, Cora. We're in bed.'

'We are?' He looked almost comically startled. 'Of course. The battle is over.'

'Aye,' she confirmed.

'We lost to Malcolm.'

'You retreated from him.'

He looked at his still-raised hands as if they were no part of him, then slowly lowered them.

'I retreated from him, aye.'

Although he was awake now, he still seemed to stare. Malcolm and his English troops had hit them just outside Falkirk on the Feast of the Seven Sleepers and had come with such force that Macbeth had seemed stunned ever since. His fresh new sword had cut hard but the Albamen had been helpless before the might of the English professionals at the invaders' core and had been forced to flee.

'I have never retreated before, Cora,' he whispered, his voice hoarse with shame.

'I know.'

'I have made terms.'

'I remember.'

'But I have never turned the Aed-lion's head from battle, never sounded the three blasts to tell my men to flee, to give up.'

'Not to give up, Macbeth, to retreat. It was a tactical decision and a wise one. Malcolm's forces outnumbered yours and the English housecarls were too much to withstand. You chose to withdraw to spare your men and that was right. Now Lachlan is coming with the Moray men and you can fight again, knowing you did not waste lives needlessly on the wrong battlefield.'

'Ah, yes, Lachlan,' he said heavily.

Cora frowned.

'You do not want him to come?'

'Oh no, I want him very much for he is younger and stronger and fitter than I.'

'Nonsense.'

'He *is*, wife, and you know it.'

Cora shrank away from his searching look for he was right and she had been praying keenly for her son's arrival. Macbeth drew men to him at court with his calm, thoughtful ideas, but in wartime Lachlan's vigour and enthusiasm fired the soldiers more.

'It will be good to have the Moray men at our backs,' she said diplomatically.

'Aye,' Macbeth agreed. 'Aye, Cora, you are right. Lord, but I am blessed in you.'

He grabbed her chin and placed a fierce kiss on her lips, lifting her up so that she sat astride him.

'If it is anyone's fault, Macbeth, it is mine. Do you remember when Duncan's widow fled with her boys and I did not want them killed?'

'I remember. You couldn't bear the thought of slaughtering innocents and rightly so.'

'Save that now those innocents are trying to slaughter *us*.'

He nodded and grasped at her waist in a sudden, welcome show of purpose.

'They will not succeed, Cora. Lachlan is coming and together we will see Malcolm and his bastard Englishmen out of Alba.'

'You will,' she agreed, arching her back invitingly and feeling him stir beneath her.

The scarring on her chest had, in a kind twist of fate, kept her breasts high and Macbeth ran an eager finger up towards them, then paused once more.

'This Malcolm is of an age with Lachlan, you know. They were born in the same year.'

He was looking up at her with strange light in his eyes and she sat back a little.

'Is that important?'

'It might be.'

'In what way? Macbeth – in what way?'

But his fingers were moving upwards again, caressing her nipples.

'Hush, wife,' he whispered against her skin. 'I've had enough of politics. Let's for a brief moment forget it all and just be us.'

Her skin was coming alive at his touch and she, too, was sick of all the recriminations and fears.

'Not too brief,' she murmured and, with a low laugh, he pulled her beneath the covers.

Lachlan rode into Forteviot later that day on a triumphant fanfare that set alight the vast war camp. Cora was helping Aila and the cooks make great cauldrons of vegetable pottage but when she saw her son she dropped her ladle and went running like a hoyden between the tents.

'Mother!'

He stood up in his stirrups and leaped from the horse like a feast-day performer before sweeping her into his arms and spinning her around.

'Lachy, don't!'

'Lachy?' He laughed. 'I haven't heard you call me that for ages.'

'You haven't been this giddy for ages. You are like a wee boy again. What's happened?'

'Victory.'

'Victory?'

Cora's heart pounded with joy. She'd known Lachlan would bring them the vigour they needed and looked keenly round as Macbeth came sprinting from the stables.

'Victory?' he echoed, pushing everyone out of his way as they started to press towards the dynamic new arrival.

Lachlan let Cora go and as he faced Macbeth, commander to commander, she saw her son grow in stature.

'Not total victory,' he said hastily, glancing around at the hordes crowding eagerly in. 'But we routed a big group of them – maybe a thousand men. They were Strathclyders on the way to join Malcolm at Dunkeld, but they will not join him now.'

The men cheered and the noise rippled across the camp. Lachlan leaped up onto the plinth of the great cross at the centre of the royal compound, clutching one arm around its broad upright and waving his vivid lion standard in the other.

'I am sorry, Albamen, that we were too late for your first battle and so very glad you had the sense to retreat so that we could join you for the second – and decisive – one. The blame is mine, the wisdom yours, and the next victory we will share.'

His voice rose and even those men too far away to hear the exact words made out their cadence and cheered.

'We are strong,' Lachlan went on. 'Alba is ours and we will not let Englishmen take it from us. Let them sit in Lothian for a few days more for they will not know what has hit them when we next attack. My wife is of Dunedin, which has held strong against the invaders. I have people everywhere in the south and I know what they are up to. They are moving north, looking to take Fife from my mother's dear kin, but they will not have it!'

The camp roared its approval. Retreat at the Battle of the Seven Sleepers had sucked the fighting spirit out of them, making them listless and low-spirited. Now they welcomed Lachlan's enthusiasm like the first warm breeze of spring. Macbeth looked at Cora.

'He brings new heart to our troops. You should be very proud of him.'

'*We* should be very proud of him. I consider him your son too, Macbeth.'

'And I am honoured to call him so. Come, we must find out more of what's happened and plan for what comes next.' Already he looked more purposeful, more alive. 'The English border has merely shifted north a little as it has many times before but we will shift it back – and further besides if we can. We might even take Durham.'

'Durham?' Cora remembered tales of Duncan's humiliation there in '39 – a humiliation that had opened their own way to the throne. 'Not Durham, Macbeth. Alba is just right as she stands.'

'She will be once she is ours again.'

'Of course.'

They talked long into the night and dawn saw both Macbeth and Lachlan up early, rousing the men. Lachlan's spies had seen enemy troops heading along the Firth of Tay towards sacred Scone. They had to move fast.

'If he thinks he's getting his arse on the Stone of Destiny he's got another think coming,' Macbeth fumed. 'I have a better use for it.'

'You do?' Cora asked, but he was too busy mustering the men to reply.

It was only later, as they mounted their horses to ride out at the head of nearly six thousand men, that he had time to explain himself.

'I am old, Cora.'

She reined Balgedie back and stared at Macbeth in surprise. Her dear pony was slowing up but they, surely, were not.

'Forty-five is not old.'

'It is and you know it.'

'Am I too, then, old?'

'You are, my grumpling. We are old together as we were once young together.'

'I preferred that bit.'

'Truly?'

Cora considered. She had been wild and angry those first months in Moray, but looking back now it was the sweetness of their courtship that stuck fast in her mind. Time, it seemed, was kind.

'It was easier,' she said. 'All I really wanted was you.'

'And now?'

He nudged his horse closer to hers, urging them both on so they gained a few paces on the procession. She glanced back.

'Now I suppose I have all of Alba to care for.'

'You do. But, Cora, what do you *want*?'

'Are you looking for compliments, Macbeth? Do you seek to know that you are still all that matters to me?'

He smiled at her.

'Not *all*, no, but I would like to know if I am still enough.'

'Enough for what?' she demanded, impatient with his riddles. He cleared his throat.

'Lachlan was born to be a king, Cora.'

'What do you mean?'

'It was always the intention. Do you remember us talking of the ultimate heir?'

'Of course I do. 'Twas the day we were betrothed.'

'And here he is, all things to all men. You've seen how they rouse themselves for him and that is right for he was intended to be the king who united Alba.'

'So? Things don't always work out as anticipated. You have been a good king, Macbeth.'

'Thank you, my heart. It has been a great honour to rule.'

'*Has* been? Macbeth, what are you planning?'

He looked up into the skies. They were bright overhead but in the east dark clouds were rolling in off the sea, making the still sunny land look sharply vibrant against their gloom.

'I wish, Cora, to demit my kingship to Lachlan.'

'Demit? Give it up? No, Macbeth. You can't . . . '

'It is his time. You saw him yesterday. Men look to him, follow him.'

'As *your* son. You . . . '

'Will still be there, will still be his greatest supporter, but as Mormaer of Moray only.'

'Of course.'

Suddenly it seemed so clear. She remembered Macbeth stepping forward at Lachlan's wedding to hand him the Mormaership while he himself ruled as king and saw now that he had always intended this reversal. She remembered him telling Osbern all about Moray while they were in Rome, eyes shining with love for the land of his birth, and she remembered him praising their son's regency on their return. She'd thought him relieved because Alba was safe but in truth it had been because he had found someone to relieve him of the burden of the throne.

'Have you hated being king?'

'No! Lord, Cora, no, of course I have not. It has been an honour to rule and a joy too, for I have ruled with you. And that is why I ask what you want, my heart. You are Queen of Alba – queen as my wife, aye, but anointed queen in your own right too, through your father's blood. Even if I demit, you can continue to rule.'

'I hardly think Lachlan would want his mother hovering over him. And besides, if he is king, Fiona should be queen.'

'Which is why, wife, I ask if having me might be enough for you?'

He held out a hand, palm upwards. It was worn and sword-callused, marked with the years of their life together as Alba's rulers, but his brown eyes were still those of the boy who'd been snatched from her on their wedding eve and they were filled with uncertainty. In truth her princely blood itched painfully at his suggestion but she saw wisdom in it too and how, after so many years of service, could she deny him the peace he so clearly sought? She drew in a deep breath.

'Having you, Macbeth, is more than enough.'

'Truly?'

His eyes sparked with hope.

'Truly,' she insisted, 'though I wish you would not keep springing such surprises on me.'

He laughed and gathered the reins tighter in his worn hands, setting his eyes on the horizon with new intent.

'To Scone,' he cried almost gleefully. 'We have a ceremony to prepare.'

They pushed on and reached the royal palace late that afternoon. As the sun dropped towards the Hill of Belief, Macbeth led a stunned Lachlan up to the Stone of Destiny and outlined his plan.

'I cannot, Father,' he insisted. 'You are king.'

'I demit.'

'You cannot.'

'I can. Constantin II did so before me to become a monk.'

'You wish to become a monk?'

'No! I wish to become what I am in my heart – Mormaer of Moray.'

Lachlan looked over at Cora, who could not meet his eye.

'What's so marvellous about Moray, Father?'

Macbeth shrugged.

'For me, everything. And that very question tells me why you are the best man for the kingship. Alba will thrive beneath your rule.'

'Because of the reforms *you* have brought about, you and Mother.'

'No one denies it,' Macbeth agreed, 'but we must look to the future and that future is you.'

Again Lachlan looked to Cora and this time she met his gaze. Her dear son had been born in fire and pain and darkness but now Macbeth was offering both of them light and they must snatch at it with gratitude.

'We will still be here, Lachy,' she said firmly. 'Now come, you can hardly be crowned King of Alba in a muddy cloak.'

She rushed him away to dress in the finest clothes she could find and within the turn of an hourglass returned him to the Hill of Destiny, clad in best wool. The Abbot of St Andrews stood before him, arms raised. He had ridden with them at Macbeth's suggestion, ostensibly to bless the battlefield but also, Cora could see now, to perform Lachlan's inauguration. Macbeth, it seemed, had been planning this for some time.

The abbot's white robes glowed in the dying light as he anointed the new king. Cora watched, thoughts of their own reign threatening to stifle her with bittersweet sobs as Macbeth stepped up, removed the crown from his head and placed it reverently upon Lachlan's. Fiona was at home in Inverness carrying their third child so for the moment Cora would remain queen but she removed her diadem all the same. It seemed fitting.

'Hail, Lachlan, King of Alba!' Macbeth roared and six thousand men roared it back.

They roared louder still when he ordered Scone's cellars raided to provide ale for all to drink the new king's health. Barrels were rolled out and fires lit. Bands of youngsters had been sent into the forest to hunt and had come back with three deer, a boar and any number of pheasants. The meat would not be ready until well into the night but the ale was deemed food enough to be going on with and the army celebrated their new ruler in giddy triumph. Cora stood against a tree watching and jumped when a voice spoke suddenly at her side.

'So, your husband is truly Andrew of Cromarty now.'

'Osbern!' She embraced their friend, now one of their key commanders. 'It seems so.'

'It suits him.'

Together they watched Macbeth dance a jig to cheers from the men, then Osbern added, 'But you, I fear, were not made to be plain Cora MacDuff.'

Cora swallowed.

'I can be anything I want to be.'

The Norman smiled.

'That, I am sure, is true.'

'And Lachlan is my son. I am proud he is king.'

'That is good then. And it suits him too.'

It did. Lachlan was going from man to man, shaking hands and offering drinks and assuring everyone that the next time they danced it would be on Englishmen's corpses. Watching him, Cora could see that he brought life and hope to the camp and Macbeth had had the wisdom and humility to know it. She looked down at the diadem still clutched in her hand. She had not, she knew, taken it off because it felt right to do so but in case she were too tempted to hold fast to it. Now, she looked up into the tree at her back and, seeing a small branch jutting out too high up to reach, she set her teeth, took aim and threw.

The diadem caught, sparkled briefly in the dying rays of the sun and then seemed to nestle in against the bark. Good. It was done and Cora stepped out determinedly to join the celebrations. Alba must be kept safe and Macbeth was right – the young could do that best. She must embrace her new role as queen mother gladly and look forward to a new dawn for her country.

Chapter Thirty-four

Berwick, July 1054

Sibyll waited at Berwick, a funny little border town with more walls than houses and no clear idea whether it was Alban or English, which felt frighteningly apt as the days ground away without any news from the battlefields. She was alone save for her stepdaughter Margaret and a rough-edged guard of old men and cripples and every day they went up onto the walls to look for any signs of soldiers on the flat horizon to the north. Messengers had brought welcome reports of an initial victory for Malcolm somewhere outside Dunedin over a month ago but since then there had been nothing.

'Why is it taking so long?' Sibyll wailed as July gave way to August with still no news.

'Maybe they are pursuing the enemy north?' Margaret suggested.

'North? Into Moray?'

'Maybe. Or maybe they have taken Scone and Malcolm is even now being crowned king.'

'Or lying dead on a battlefield.'

'Ah, Mother – do not think that.'

'It could be true.'

'And if it is then we will be sad soon enough.'

The logic was impossible to fault so Sibyll tried hard to imagine her sons happy and victorious – tried so hard that when a lad finally skidded into the rough ladies' bower one day to say he could see dust on the Alban road, she ran for the walls looking eagerly for blue flags flying over the approaching soldiers.

They were not blue flags.

Then again, they were not red either but darkest black, snapping in the first of the autumn winds like ravens over the heads of the trudging men. They came slowly on and as they neared the walls Sibyll could see a large figure leading them that was surely her brother. Ward's head was bare of a helmet and his mop of hair looked greyer than she remembered but the great bulk of him could belong to no other. Behind him were four guards and behind them a wagon or, rather, a bier. Sibyll's heart stopped.

'Malcolm,' she gasped and now she ran for the gates, bellowing at the wizened guards to open them wide and tumbling up the road towards the men.

Ward called his troops to a halt and suddenly Sibyll felt foolish to be standing in the middle of the road with hundreds of men straining to see what was keeping them from camp, but she had to know.

'What news, brother?' Ward swung himself out of the saddle, landing with a wince of pain though he was as tall as she remembered when he walked towards her. 'You have ... have lost?'

Ward gave a small, sad smile.

'No.'

She waited for more but it did not come.

'You have then ... won?'

'We have driven Macbeth from Fife, yes.'

'You've taken Scone?'

'We have.'

'So Malcolm is crowned king?'

'No.'

Her eyes darted to the bier and now Ward crossed the last steps to pull her into his arms, clutching her so close she could scarce breathe.

'Malcolm is safe, sister, Donald too, but he has refused to be inaugurated until the existing king is dead.'

'Macbeth?'

'Nay, not him for he had his son Lachlan declared king in his stead before the battle. It was a bitter fight, sister, but in the end the housecarls helped us carry the day. The Moray men have fled back over their damned Mounth, taking their royal title with them. The fight goes on.'

'I see.' Sibyll battled to draw air into her lungs. 'So who, brother, do you bring so sadly south?' Still he held her and suddenly she realised it was not to comfort her but to draw comfort for himself and, with sickening clarity, she knew. 'Beorn?' He nodded against her and she felt moisture on her hair and prayed it might soak up his grief for him. 'I'm sorry, Ward. I'm so, so sorry.'

But already he was pulling back, batting tears from his eyes and forcing his shoulders straight.

'He died in honour, Sibyll. Men will sing of him for he did not sell his life cheaply. He took many of them with him to tip the balance of his account.'

'Is that how it works?'

Ward stared fiercely at her.

'Of course. Beorn is in Valhalla now.'

'Ward, no! Valhalla is for pagans.'

'Valhalla is for *warriors*. Oh, fret not, sister. I pray Christ has Beorn in his safekeeping but somehow I prefer to think of him feasting with other warriors than cushioned on clouds. He would prefer it too for he was turning into a man who, who . . . ' Ward's voice cracked and he screwed up his dear face, fighting tears. Sibyll looked down to spare him her pity and in a moment he had control again. 'Will you ride in with me, sister? We must see Beorn laid out in state.'

'Of course.'

He leaped into his saddle before reaching down to swing her up behind him as if she were eight years old again. She wrapped her arms around his waist and felt the passing of so many years in its thickness and in the grey of his long hair against her cheek as he signalled his troops to march his poor lost son home beneath the raven-black banners of grief. They had the victory, it seemed, but little joy.

'You must ride north,' Ward said into her sadness. 'Malcolm wants you at his side and has sent a guard to see you safe to him.'

She straightened her back.

'Where?'

'Dunkeld.'

Dunkeld! So, she was to return at last.

'Who is there?'

'Who? Malcolm, of course, and Donald and Patrick and Mal. Margaret is to go with you to return to Strathclyde with her brothers.'

'She will be pleased.'

'As will the men of Partick's court, I am sure.'

It was a flash of the dry-witted brother she knew of old and she snatched at it.

'We have been so grateful to you, Ward, for harbouring us all this time.'

'Nonsense, sister. What else would I do?'

'We have cost you dear.'

'No!' He twisted in the saddle to stare into her eyes. 'You must not think that. I fought this battle for my own purpose as did Beorn. If God were to turn back the handle of time we would ride out again.'

'Even knowing what awaited you?'

'Especially then, for I could see the bastard Albaman who crept up on my boy while he dispatched two others and send him, not Beorn, to his maker. But there now, there is no such handle and we must ever go forward. You must see Malcolm to his throne, Sibyll. You must see him there for Duncan and for Alba and for me. It has been a long road thus far and a good one, whatever the losses, but we must not stop now. Not when we are so close. You should leave tomorrow.'

'So soon?'

'I'm afraid so. I need to take Beorn back to York and in this heat . . . '

'Yes. Oh, yes, of course. I'll come with you and see him committed to God's care.'

'No. I mean, that's kind but not necessary. Beorn died to win Alba for his cousin Malcolm and he would want you to go to him in Dunkeld.'

Dunkeld! Again that word, as if it was calling to her.

'You will be sad, brother.'

'Yes, but sadder still with you mooching after me.'

'Ward!'

''Tis true. I have known sadness before, Sibyll, and can fight it without my little sister's help, kind as it is of her to care. You must return to Alba and I shall look forward to joining you for Malcolm's inauguration once Lachlan and Macbeth are both dead. Let them lurk in Moray all they wish – it will simply give your son time to consolidate his power in the south. Lachlan is king in name but not in deed; Malcolm in deed if not yet in name. All must be resolved and you, my dear, must be there when it is.'

Sibyll rode into Dunkeld almost a week later, exhausted after skirting nervously around Dunedin, held by King Lachlan's forces in the name of his Lothian wife. It was like going back thirty-three long years to be finally dipping down off the bleak moorlands of Perthshire and into the pretty green birches and alders that lined the road to Dunkeld Abbey. This place more than any other was Alba for her and, oh, how she'd missed it.

As the track curved and the trees gave way to rolling meadowlands she saw the abbey, its setting proud and open, with animals grazing contentedly in front and the river running silver behind. So many times she'd been forced to leave places behind that to come back to one she loved was a fierce, joyous thrill.

And now here was Malcolm coming out of the abbey, as Crinan had once done before, and Donald behind him as always, looking so like Duncan it was momentarily as if God had, indeed, turned back the handle of time. Sibyll looked giddily around and there too was Maldred – her own, dear Maldred. Her head spun and her insides swirled and she clutched desperately at her horse's reins but her grip was weak and could not seem to connect and then everything went black.

She woke in the dust with faces crowded around her.

'Mother? Mother, are you well?'

Sibyll blinked furiously but Maldred was still there. She sucked in air, gulping for sense with it. He looked so young, so perfect, as if the hard years had barely touched him. He must be a ghost. A ghost or . . .

'Patrick!'

Maldred, or rather his son, darted forward.

'Aye, Mother?'

She smiled ruefully and put out a hand to him.

'I thought you were your father.'

'Ah, sorry. I do bear a passing resemblance.'

'Passing?' Sibyll choked. 'You are nigh-on identical.'

'I'm sorry,' he repeated.

'Do not be, please. It was just a shock. I felt seventeen again. It was most disorientating.'

'It would be.'

Patrick looked at Malcolm and Sibyll saw them exchange

amused looks. They thought her old, and no wonder. She picked herself up hastily and did her best to brush off the dirt.

'Uiskie!' she commanded. 'And a warm bench. I must know all that has happened.'

'Of course.'

Malcolm offered her his arm and she took it, making sure not to lean upon him but to walk tall as a monk was sent scurrying off to the distillery. Her throat cramped.

'Is Brother Cullen here?'

'No, Mother, of course not. He has scuttled over the Mounth with Macbeth.'

'He no longer wishes for our forgiveness?'

'I know not. Maybe he has found it in God. Ah, look, here is your uiskie. 'Tis a new blend, heavier on the peat. It is too much for some but not, I'll wager, for you. Try it.'

Sibyll took the cup and went to sip it but at the last moment something inside her – a stubborn resistance to her own ageing perhaps, or a tribute to a past only she was now here to recall – spurred her on to toss back a large measure. A fire raged inside her mouth, filling it with a sensation balanced precariously between joy and pain so that Alba herself seemed to explode inside her head. She tasted heather and spring water, crofters' fires, cattle's breath and capercaillie flesh . . . and it was glorious. She swallowed.

'Beautiful. More, please.' She held out her cup to the monk. 'Or better still, leave the flask.'

The monk looked uncertainly to Malcolm who, with a broad grin, nodded for him to comply. Sibyll sent a silent toast up to Abbot Crinan who had first introduced her to this wonderful Alban lifewater and settled herself as Donald and Malcolm took seats opposite.

'You are happy to be back in usquebauch country then, Mother?' Malcolm asked.

'More than that, my son, my king-elect – I am happy, at last, to be *home*. Now come, tell me all.'

They talked long into the night. They told her of the battle at Falkirk and she shuddered to hear of it. There had been nearly five thousand dead and even if her sons could be gleeful that it had been three thousand of 'theirs' to two thousand of 'ours' it was still five thousand souls fled this earth. And one of them, at least, very dear to them.

'He fought so hard,' Malcolm said of Beorn. 'So hard and so well. He was on the left flank with Ward while Patrick took the right and Donald and I the centre. We had the English house-carls with us and we hit them like a spearhead. They fight like the furies, those men.'

'Nay, not like the furies,' Donald interrupted him, 'for they have such control. They have no passion, Mother, for there is nothing personal in the fight for them but instead they have precision and calm and deathly, calculated skill. And such equipment! I swear that for the cost of one of their mail shirts we could have kitted out half our army.'

'Donald, you exaggerate!'

'Very well, a quarter, but it is still a great deal. I tell you now, Mother, I am unendingly glad they were fighting on our side for we would not have succeeded without them.'

'*Were?*' she asked sharply.

'They are returned to England.'

'All of them? They don't want land for their service?'

'No, just coin. I told you, fighting is all they do and they are paid well for it.'

'We don't have coin.'

'No, but Ward did.'

'My brother paid to lose his son?'

'No! Mother, do not be so emotional about it. He paid to ride out in glory at the head of a victorious army and he did that. He understood the dangers; we all do. You cannot have a battlefield contest without deaths.'

That much seemed true.

'I'm sorry,' she said. 'I know too little of battlefields to say.'

Malcolm put an arm around her.

'Which is as it should be. More people, men and women, should grow up without knowing a battlefield and when I am king I intend to make that possible.'

'Good.' Sibyll felt weary now in this heated male company. 'Tell me, Malcolm, is Morag still here?'

'Morag? The funny old girl in the crannog?'

'Funny old . . . ' Sibyll spluttered but caught herself. 'Yes, her – is she still here?'

'She is. Shall I take you there tomorrow?'

'No need. I remember the way.'

Sibyll rang the tree-bells herself. Morag came cautiously out on to the balcony of her loch-steeped house and peered across the water. Her eyes lit up.

'Sibyll? Sibyll, is that really you?'

'It is.'

'Lord be praised!'

Morag might be old but she let down her funny drawbridge with such enthusiasm and strength that it clattered to the lochside. Sibyll leaped onto it and ran and the two women met midway, clutching at each other and laughing and crying and nigh-on spilling themselves into the loch in their tumbled joy. Sibyll glanced to her guard but the men were all backing up into the trees to avoid accompanying her onto the crannog and that suited her very well.

'Come in,' Morag was saying. 'I have wine. Plum, I think, and blackberry – and grape besides.'

'The vines still live?'

'They do. I have seen to it myself. Oh, it is so good to see you, Sibyll. I have heard so much of you. You married him then?'

'Maldred, aye.'

'I'm so glad. It was good?'

'It was perfect, Morag. But short, far too short. And what of you – you have survived under Macbeth's rule?'

'Of course. He is no tyrant, Sibyll. That is . . . Well, he barely came to Dunkeld.'

'I'm sorry Crinan was lost.'

'Not lost. He is here, buried in the abbey as is right. But come, let us not dwell on the dead. Take your cup for I raise a toast to the boy who was born here in my own crannog and who is now rightfully returned. To Malcolm!'

'To Malcolm.'

'And now . . . ' Morag pulled two stools up to her funny fire-box hearth and patted one for Sibyll. 'Tell me everything.'

It took a long time and much wine so that soon it became hard to know if plum was blackberry or blackberry grape and harder to care. Sibyll spilled out every last detail of her flight across Alba, her time in Strathclyde, her all-too-brief marriage to Maldred and her flight, again, to Northumbria before the road brought her finally back to Dunkeld. Her life, it seemed, was destined to be led in circles.

'I heard Cullen came to you in York,' Morag said as dusk licked at the sky and the poor guards nervously called Sibyll's name.

'He did, snivelling and grovelling.'

'He was in a terrible state about what he'd done.'

'As he should have been. He betrayed us, Morag.'

'I know. He told me.'

'Told *you*?'

Morag shifted.

'Everyone needs confessors, Sibyll. And Cullen especially. I encouraged him to visit me often before he disappeared into Moray.'

'Really? He told me you only like your own company.'

'He did?' She looked stricken for a moment, then said, 'He loves you very much, you know.'

'Then he has a twisted way of showing it.'

'Aye. He never learned how to be with women. His feelings, I think, overwhelmed him. Blame his mother.'

'His mother? It can hardly be her fault, poor woman. She wasn't even in his life.'

'I know.'

Morag looked so down-heartened that Sibyll grabbed her hand.

'Morag, Cullen's mother died. It's tragic but it's no one's fault.'

But at that Morag shook her head and poured more wine with a suddenly unsteady hand.

'She didn't die,' she said into her cup. 'That is, she only died to him.'

'What?'

Sibyll looked at her friend and saw, to her horror, a single tear run down her still beautiful cheek and hiss against the fire-box.

'Crinan thought it best,' Morag said in a tiny voice. 'For the boy, I mean. For Cullen. I agreed. I don't know why now but I was scared. And I thought he'd be better off. Better a wonderful education in a rich abbey than a battle for survival in a silly little crannog, right?'

Sibyll stared at her old friend, stunned beyond belief.

'You? You are Cullen's mother?' Morag nodded silently. 'And Crinan – Crinan truly was his father?'

Another nod. Sibyll's wine-fuddled mind flew. She remembered Morag telling her of her golden summer with Crinan. 'It was a long time ago,' she'd said. 'He will soon be twenty-five.' She'd brushed her slip aside by claiming she was talking of Maldred, and Sibyll, ever thrown by his dear name, had not pushed her further.

'Does Cullen know?' she asked now.

'No.' It was a whisper on the evening breeze.

'You must tell him, Morag.'

'I cannot, Sibyll, not after all this time. He will hate me.'

'Maybe but you will, at least, be able to love him and that is perhaps what he needs most of all. As do you.'

'I know it.' Morag took a shaky breath. 'And seeing you here, after all these years, has only made that clearer. I am getting old, Sibyll – I should make my peace with those on earth before it is too late. But he isn't here to tell.'

'And might never come back if you do not find him.'

'Find him? You mean, I should seek him out? Leave Dunkeld and follow him over the Mounth?'

Sibyll looked at her friend. She was shaking and looking around her pretty little crannog as if it held the only air she could breathe.

'Why not, Morag? I will gladly provide a guard and you are a capable woman, a brave one too.'

Morag grabbed at her arm.

'Oh no, I am not. I am not brave at all. I'm a coward – a selfish, useless coward. I have never left the loch since my mother died. I gave birth here alone and I let Crinan take my boy away and did not dare to follow in case, in case ... ' She gulped at her wine. 'The world is a scary place, Sibyll.'

'I know it,' Sibyll said gently. 'I have seen much of it and too often in flight, but you would be going towards something not running away.' Morag looked down and Sibyll reached for her thin hands, pressing them tightly between her own. 'You cannot hide, Morag, for in the end, without the sustenance of others, you will wither up and die. You must step out into the open and face the world.'

'I must?'

'We all must. I have had to learn to fight, not just to keep what I have, however meagre, but to stand up and risk that to win more. It is the same for you. You must risk the rejection of your own tight-held love for Cullen on the chance that it may be returned and increased tenfold.'

Morag lifted her wine cup to her mouth with a shaking hand but then, without drinking, set it decisively down.

'You are right, Sibyll. I have hidden away too long, trapped by my own fears. You have not let yours trap you. You have gone out and fought them and look what it has won you.'

'It has won me the chance to come peacefully back here to my home. And it will do the same for you.'

'I pray so. You will keep an eye on my house?'

'Of course.'

'Then I shall go. Soon. Tomorrow. I shall see this great Mounth all seem to talk of in whispers and I shall cross it and I shall find my son. Wish me Godspeed, my dear friend.'

And Sibyll did, with all her heart. She would never agree to be Cullen's wife but maybe, just maybe, finding his mother would bring him a little peace.

Chapter Thirty-five

Cromarty, June 1056

'Up here! We must have men up here now!'

Macbeth's voice carried on the damp morning air. Cora heard a note of desperation in it and picked up her skirts to run.

'Bring fire!' was his next command.

She paused for breath. Macbeth was over the rise of the hill and it was steeper than it had looked. She could no longer run for as long as she used to and bent over, gasping for breath.

'That's it,' she heard her husband's resonant voice say. 'Fire is good. We can win with fire. And juniper. We need more juniper.'

Cora finally made it to the top and took in the scene. She saw Macbeth first, clad in a plain tunic and with a long staff in his hand. He had taken to dressing this way since they had limped back to Moray after their battering by the English housecarls two years ago. Lachlan chafed both at the defeat and the restrictions it had placed on them and she understood his frustration, but Macbeth, it seemed, was content to farm.

Right now he was doing nothing more fearsome than commanding the lighting of herb-scented fires around a large cattle-pen full of frightened beasts. His men were ringed around the cows, fanning the smoke towards them, while three milk-maids carried a fiery branch solemnly around the circle, softly chanting 'deas soil, deas soil'.

Tutting quietly, Cora stepped up next to her husband to watch the girls complete their ritual. The ancient practice had long been a part of any ceremony of thanks, protection or blessing in these parts but Cora had not seen it in action for many years. Three times they walked the circle, their steps quickening on the third as the great branch burned close to their pretty hands. Then, with a flourish, they plunged it into one of the fires and the men cheered. The cattle looked on, bemused.

'Will that work?' Cora asked Macbeth.

He shrugged.

'The deas-soil? Not on the cattle, no, but it makes those who tend them feel they are doing something.'

'Something that will fail?'

'Not necessarily. The juniper in the smoke is known to help contagion so we must pray that God sees our efforts and rewards them with His grace.'

'Unless he is offended by us parading around like druids?'

Macbeth smiled.

'Oh, Cora, I do not think God is that petty. And men need their rituals.'

'Especially in Moray.'

He looked at her sharply.

'Why do you say that?'

'Because it's true. It is, I suppose, inevitable that remoter communities cling to old beliefs longer.'

'Moray is not remote. Have you not seen the ships in our waters? There are ever men landing from Norway or Denmark and there is no track in Alba more regularly trodden than the ancient one up the Great Glen. We are the heart of trade in the northern seas and you know it.'

'In the northern seas, aye, but they are dark, cold seas, are they not? Remember the beautiful waters around Italy? That is where men look now.'

Macbeth sighed and turned back to his cattle, part-obscured by the cleansing juniper smoke.

'You despise me.' She barely heard what he'd said and had to ask him to repeat it, which he did, his voice suddenly loud and sharp as a dagger tip. 'You despise me.'

'I do not!'

'You do. You despise me for retreating over the Mounth after the defeat at Falkirk. You despise me for giving up the kingship and you despise me for finding satisfaction in mere farming when once I controlled all Alba.'

'That's not true.'

'Are you sure?' She hesitated a moment too long. 'Think on it, Cora. I must check the beasts.'

He strode forward, his back rigid as he disappeared into the smoke with his precious cattle. Cora stood watching. Think on it, he'd said and she supposed she owed him as much, though she usually fought to avoid any introspection for it inevitably led her mind back to the horror of the battlefield.

She had not known such slaughter possible. She'd heard tales, of course, but tales of sword wounds could never truly pierce the skin when you were sitting around a comfortable hearth-fire with a full stomach and an ale-spun head. Now she had seen the full horror of one hundred professional killers ripping up ranks of men and knew that next time a skald rose to conjure war on his harp, she would weep for the pity and the horror and the ugly misery of it.

Three thousand men they had lost. It sounded simple – a neat, round number, big enough to shock but incapable of capturing the screams of men crawling from the fighting with a leg half-severed and jarring against every bump and stone and corpse; incapable of showing the tremors that wrack the body of someone with half his face cut back to the bone as he clutches your hand to lend him the strength to step over into the release of death; incapable of conjuring the taste of blood and mud and urine that creeps down every throat, or the wild-eyed weariness of men who can fight no more but somehow do.

Three thousand men. Three thousand wives widowed, three thousand farms struggling, many thousands of children fatherless. And them too, the 'enemy', the men on the other side of the field. Two thousand they lost – another round number, spoken of, no doubt, as a victory, but two thousand dead all the same and who, really, could tell one side from the other when the ravens came picking the next day?

No, Cora did not despise Macbeth for calling the retreat. Lord, someone had had to or the rest of the men would have died too. Fergus had been speared in the first charge, one of his sons with him. Sean had escaped and fled at Cora's side but the bitter battle had weakened his old bones and he rarely left his bed now. Still, at least he was safe in Moray with the three thousand others who had not died. Surely any one of those was worth more than their son's petty right to sit on a damned throne? And yet, her blood itched to rule as she knew Lachlan's did and she could not see how Macbeth did not feel it too.

Cora looked out across the hillside. The smoke was starting to clear from the ground upwards so that all she could see were feet – some cloven, some in sturdy boots, all planted firmly on Alban soil and one indistinguishable from the rest – Macbeth. Did she despise him for giving up the kingship? She thought back to that heated night at Scone when he'd handed his crown so gladly to Lachlan and she had acquiesced because it was how they'd always intended it to be. Had she not taken off her own diadem and hung it on a tree in support of the decision? And yet ... She had not simply hung it there but flung it high enough to stop her itchy blood from sending her climbing up the trunk to grab it back.

She had come to Moray thirty-two long years ago burning

with anger and fierce fury, determined to take the throne from Malcolm and avenge her father's murder. Winning it had been such a glorious restitution that giving it up, even to her own son, had not come easily and she could not truly understand how Macbeth had been able do it. Cora squinted over the Moray Firth as if she could look into the south – her homeland and seat of all Alban power – but Macbeth's smoke was still drifting across her vision and she could not see further than the edge of the water. She felt trapped here as she had back at the beginning.

Restlessly, she twisted to look down the length of the Black Isle. Here, at least, the air was clearer and she could see all the way to their hall at Inverness and, somewhere just above it, the wishing pool where she had railed at Macbeth back when they were still new to each other. She could almost see the blue sky framed by bulrushes and the fanciful heart-shaped cloud above and fought to remember how it had been back then. The memory came hazily at first but then with greater clarity and, though her mind fought to resist, one moment forced its way to the fore:

'I have a claim, Cora.'

He'd offered it himself, quietly perhaps but of his own volition. He'd wanted to be king then, hadn't he, so how could he give it up? And yet she knew already why he had said it. For her. He had said it to please her, to satisfy her, to win her. He'd offered his claim to the throne of Alba as a token of his love and she'd snatched at it and held him to it all his life. When Kendrick had died her husband had offered it again to assuage her grief and after she had berated him for withdrawing in the mist at Glamis he had offered it once more. And he had succeeded, not through might with the sword, though he was a skilled warrior, but because so many had flocked to his banner and to him as a man they could respect.

Macbeth had ruled for fifteen years because the people of Alba loved him. He had carved his governance in thought and gentleness and care – the same care he had ever shown for her.

And what had she given him in return? Tears and tantrums and demands. And even now, when he had handed the throne to Lachlan – her son, not his, though he had never once made issue of that – she asked more of him. She asked him, she saw now, to be something he was not. She asked him to be her, with all her burden of itchy resentment, instead of himself, his glorious, kind, utterly selfless self.

'Macbeth!' Suddenly she was running across the hillside, limbs all anyhow and skirts high around her ankles like a peasant girl. 'Macbeth, you fool, how could I ever despise you?'

The men turned, smiled, nudged each other. They looked to Macbeth, who rolled his eyes but stepped out of the mass and held his arms wide. Cora flung herself into them and felt him lift her off the ground and whirl her round like juniper smoke.

'How could I ever despise you?' she said again, pulling back so they were nose to nose.

'How could you not,' he replied, 'for I despise myself.'

'Macbeth, no! I'm sorry. I am the one who deserves to be despised for I am ever asking for more. You were king for me, just for me.'

He shrugged.

'And you were worth it – *are* worth it.'

The tears came but he just held her tight and let his strength seep into her, as he had always done, and she knew for certain that he was no coward but rather the bravest man she had ever had the good fortune to know. She swiped furiously at her eyes.

'Lachlan is king, Macbeth, and I bless you for that.'

He grunted.

'I'm not sure that he does, for he is king in name only.'

'For now. The Englishmen have gone?'

'They have. They are back with their king and I heard tell Earl Ward was sick with grief at the loss of his son. They'll not be back without his lead.'

'So Malcolm will have to fight fair.'

'Employing foreign troops is not necessarily unfair, Cora.'

'Perhaps not, but it weights the scales. Why should Englishmen decide Alba's fate?'

'*That* is not right,' he agreed. 'Alba is her own land and must stay so. I may have given over the kingship, Cora, but I will stand as Lachlan's right-hand man when the time comes. I will raise troops for him and I will fight for him and I will see him back into the south where you soft pair belong.'

'Soft!' she gasped. 'Moray is the softest bit of Alba. At least in Fife we stand proud against the northern seas and don't cower in a pretty wee firth.'

'Cower!'

He looked at her open-mouthed and she grinned and kissed him.

'Don't call me soft then.'

He kissed her back.

'You win.'

'Always. And now, Macbeth, while there is time still left to us there is somewhere I wish you to take me.'

'Where?'

She cast her eyes down the Black Isle once more.

'A wishing pool I know, high in the hills above Inverness. I missed an opportunity there a long time back and I'd like the chance to put that right.'

'A wishing pool?' He looked up to the rapidly clearing skies. 'Well, no time like the present. Saddle the horses, Cora MacDuff, and let's ride!'

Later, as they lay amongst the tall rushes by the pool with their feet in the cool water and their clothes more than a little askew, Cora laid her cheek on Macbeth's bare chest and listened to his heart slowing after their exertions.

'Why not?' she could almost hear him calling all those years earlier. 'We'll be married this time tomorrow so what difference does it make?'

In the end, it had made all the difference – or maybe none at all.

'If only ...' she started to say but he levered himself up and stoppered her mouth with a kiss.

'We cannot change the past, my grumpling.'

'No, but ...'

'Do you see the dolphins wasting time on recriminations?'

'Dolphins?'

In reply he pointed out into the firth, now sparkling in the low sun. She followed his lead and caught the flash of a sleek back before suddenly a large female leaped upwards, blasting out of the water and turning a joyous somersault. Dolphin after dolphin followed, twisting and leaping as if their very souls were reaching for God.

'They are alive with the simple joy of being alive,' she said.

'As we should be – while we still can.'

It was true and she leaned back into his warm, welcoming arms to watch the beautiful creatures play. This was an uneasy peace but it was peace all the same and should be cherished. Soon they must muster men and court influence and support Lachlan, their son and their king, ready for the time when Albaman faced Albaman once more. The final battle þeckoned and they must rise to meet it but at last Cora knew that they could do so together, secure in their own joy in each other. It was enough.

Chapter Thirty-six

Dunkeld, March 1058

'Over the Mounth?' Sibyll stared at her son in horror. 'You are going over the Mounth, Malcolm?'

'Aye, Mother. It's not a mystical barrier, you know, just a run of hills.'

'*Big* hills.'

'I am an Albaman – I think I can tackle a few hills, however big. Morag managed it, did she not?'

'She did but she went alone, not with an army waving flags and inviting attack.'

'That is not what an army does, Mother.'

'No, of course not. Sorry.'

Sibyll looked around for support but the only other person in the antechamber was Donald and he would always back his brother. It was true that Morag had made it into Moray and finally found Cullen at a place called Rosemarkie. She had spoken with him and had, so she'd assured Sibyll, secured his forgiveness.

'Did you see Macbeth?' Malcolm had demanded to know but she'd refused to be drawn. Now it seemed he was heading out to see for himself.

He was right, of course, to want to win Alba for good but Sibyll had grown strangely used to this half-kingship. Only Dunedin, home of Lachlan's wife, and St Andrews, his mother's heartland, held out against Malcolm so he was largely able to operate as king. He was not, however, anointed and she knew that ate away at him. Now approaching his thirtieth year, he should be settling to raise a family but he'd refused to take a wife until he had the throne and refused to take the throne until Lachlan was dead so all was on hold. Or had been.

'Why now?' she asked.

'Why not? We are as ready as we will ever be and we cannot let Alba linger undecided in this way. Your brother would not have approved.'

Sibyll sucked in her breath. Ward had died not long after Beorn, ostensibly from a crippling gut disease but perhaps in truth from grief.

'That's so,' she conceded, 'but my brother was ever cautious in his choice of battleground. It is not the hills themselves that are the problem but the men who inhabit them. You will be going into enemy territory.'

'Which is why I have been planning this attack for the last three years.'

She was annoying him.

'Right. Good. Excellent.' She rose and headed towards the door but as she looked back at her sons her heart turned over with unbearable love for them both. 'But still, Malcolm ... over the Mounth?'

'Mother!'

'I'm going.'

She put a hand to the latch but Donald stopped her with a gentle hand.

'It is *for* Alba, Mother, you must see that. She needs stability to move forward. We have such plans. We want to create monasteries, build up towns, secure the new coinage. Macbeth has started much here and we owe it to Alba to build on it.'

'On Macbeth's legacy?'

'Of course,' Malcolm agreed. 'Why not? Then it will become *our* legacy. But we cannot do that until Moray submits.'

Both men's eyes were shining with ideas for the future and Sibyll felt foolish for wanting things to stay as they were. Donald was right; it was no way to live. His father would have been proud of them both. She remembered the stiff way Duncan had told her he 'had' to be king, the very first time she met him. The weight of that responsibility had been too great for him but it was not so for Malcolm. Having to fight for his throne was shaping him into a man with a will to rule and to advance his country and with loyal Donald at his back surely he could not fail?

'And to make Macbeth submit you must go over the Mounth?'

'We must, Mother.'

'So be it.'

She rode out with them two weeks later, tucking in behind their beautiful bay horses so she could watch their backs all the way without them noticing. Morag came as guide and Sibyll was glad of her calm, easy companionship on the long road north to a place called Lumphanan on the western edge of the dreaded Mounth. It sounded drear and Sibyll rode towards it with a heavy heart but it turned out, to her astonishment, to be a very pretty place. The meadowlands were rich with flowers, barley waved from fields already near golden and all felt sheltered and peaceful – until, that is, they came up over a rise and saw the first peaks ahead of them.

Sibyll reined in her horse to face the great barrier. The Mounth was not, as she'd fearfully imagined it, a craggy wall of granite but rather a gradual accumulation of hills. Nearest to them the slopes were rounded and gentle, dotted with hardy sheep and patches of crumbling, pale rock, but beyond these darker peaks reached high into the sky as if daring her to come near. Cora could see why men living past this God-made divide might feel themselves to be set apart.

All the more reason they should not look to rule the rest, she told herself stoutly and diverted her gaze down to the plains instead. There, in the very centre of the wide landscape, she saw an ancient fortress. Three vast rings of earthworks rose up to a top level run round with sharp-pointed palisade fencing, enclosing what must surely be an ancient dwelling.

'It will surprise you,' Morag assured her and reluctantly Sibyll let her lead the way up to the gates and into a surprisingly spacious, curved courtyard running around the fortress. Neat stable buildings were shaped to fit against the hillside and when Morag leaped from her horse, Sibyll was left with little choice but to follow.

'Trust me,' her friend said with a wink, heading for the next, smaller gate.

Beyond it lay another curved yard, this one full of craftsmen, each with their own open-fronted shelter. Sibyll saw woodcutters and potters and even jewellery makers, but there was no time to linger for Morag was ushering them up steep wooden stairs to the third, thinner courtyard, which was filled with pavilions of all colours.

'For your commanders tonight,' she told Malcolm. 'See – you can keep a close eye on the camp from here.'

He nodded approval and followed her to the first of several towers set into this rampart. Sibyll watched, fascinated, as Morag, like an experienced commander, showed him around. What a change there was in her! Was it finding the courage to step out of the enclosed world of her crannog that had allowed her to grow like this, or was it the result of finally claiming her son as her own? Sibyll stepped up into the tower after them and looked out across the plains they had crossed. Close to the fortress Malcolm's vast army was busily pitching tents and lighting fires.

'There are a lot of men,' she observed.

'A lot of loyal men,' Malcolm agreed, surveying them with her. 'They want me as king, Mother.'

'And will have you. You will win, son.'

'Even over the Mounth?'

For the first time the hesitation was his.

'Even over the Mounth,' she said firmly. 'Now, come, shall we climb to the top?'

He smiled and held out an arm to escort her up the last run of steps to the big open area at the top of the ancient fortress. Sibyll looked around her, stunned.

'How old is this place, Morag?'

'Hundreds of years at least. But the best bit of it all is that this . . . ' she gestured to the clutch of oak buildings in the very centre ' . . .was only built a few years ago so is one of the most comfortable residences in Alba. Come and meet our friends and allies, Mormaer and Lady Stewart.'

Sibyll went forward as their hosts came to greet them and lead them into a pretty hall for a fine meal and entertainment by exceptional musicians. Sibyll had to keep biting back her surprise that all was so elegant up here in the wild north. These were not savages but sophisticated people and she wasn't sure if that made her more or less nervous about her sons facing them in battle. But face them they would and as the meal drew to a close she rose to propose a toast.

'Thirty years ago,' she told the rapidly hushing crowd, 'I gave birth to Malcolm under the guidance of this good lady here,' she gestured to Morag, 'while men of Moray attacked my home. I did not know if my baby, his father's heir to the throne of Alba, would survive that very first dread night but we drove the Moray men out then and we will do so again now.'

The men cheered wildly. Malcolm stared at her.

'Macbeth attacked Dunkeld?'

'Not Macbeth, his predecessors, but Moray men all the same. They were not made to rule, Malcolm.'

'And we will prove that.'

The faltering confidence of earlier was gone. He was ready. Sibyll looked at his broad shoulders, his cheering lords and vast army beyond and tried not to think of the dark mountains to which they currently had their backs but which, tomorrow, her sons must scale. If they won the battle on the far side of those, it would be a victory indeed.

Chapter Thirty-seven

Essie, April 1058

'Never!' Lachlan roared. 'You will never take Moray!'

The cry was picked up by his troops and bounced around the moors as if the Aed lion itself was roaring. Cora, watching from a crag above the field, saw every last Moray man eyeball the southern invaders with vicious intent. They were incensed that Malcolm had dared to breach the Mounth and were baying for his blood.

'He's a fool,' Lachlan had said gleefully when a messenger had tumbled into court with the first reports of a great army coming over the mountains. 'And we will make him pay for it. The kingship will truly be mine now.'

And so it seemed. Cora should be in the medical tent with Aila and Brother Cullen but she'd had to see this so had climbed a cray above it. Now she watched intently as Malcolm's soldiers eyed the heather with clear trepidation. Lachlan had chosen his spot perfectly, so as to lure the unknowing invaders into patches of deep, sucking bog, and was keeping his own men under strict instruction to hold their line on the firm rising ground.

'Come on then,' Lachlan taunted. He lifted the crown of Alba from his head and held it high. 'Come and seize it, Malcolm, if you wish to be king.'

'What sort of king hides behind mountains instead of ruling his people?' Malcolm called back, his voice clear and certain.

Lachlan laughed.

'I am not hiding. Look, here I am. Come, kill me and it is yours. See how pretty it is, Malcolm. See how the jewels glow as if God has placed his own light within them.'

Cora felt a sharp burst of pride at his eloquence. She remembered him pointing out the multi-coloured hoof print across the sky at the Falls of Foyers and wished momentarily that he could be using his poetry like that again rather than on a battlefield foe, but that way weakness lay and today she had to be strong. They all did.

'God puts his light in men, not objects,' came the reply and Malcolm's supporters bellowed their approval.

Cora glanced to the sky. The sun was already past its height and still they were trading insults. Why did Malcolm delay? Was it fear, or something more? She squinted into his ranks. There was activity in the small copse at their rear and when she listened closely she caught the sound of sawing. Clever. She jumped down from the crag and ran, pushing between the startled soldiers.

'Macbeth, Macbeth, they are cutting planks.'

He turned, astonished.

'Cora, what are you doing here? It's not safe. It . . . '

'Please, Macbeth. They are cutting planks to ford the bog. I've seen it.'

'Ah. That's why he delays.'

'It is. You must stop trading insults and get them to attack.'

'I agree, but how?'

She shrugged.

'How do you get cattle to move?'

Macbeth looked at her then smiled.

'We herd them.'

'Exactly.'

'Good. Lachlan, hold the line here. Weave all the pretty words you wish for your princely guest.'

'And you, Father?'

'I must take your rebellious mother out of the frontline – and perhaps take a foray around the back of that copse.'

Lachlan looked across the battlefield, nodded and smiled a near identical smile to Macbeth's as if it were upbringing not blood that bound a man to his father.

'Look, Malcolm,' he called across the divide. 'The Queen of Alba is here with us. Would you like her crown too?'

'You fight alongside women, Lachlan?'

'Our women are worth ten of your men.'

And so it went on. Macbeth made a show of escorting Cora off the field but the moment the front lines closed around them he was all action, summoning men with curt, efficient orders. They took Cora to the camp tents and then, instead of returning to the ranks, performed a wide flanking movement through the low boggy ground so as to creep up behind Malcolm's army.

'Take care,' Cora called.

Macbeth looked back, blew her a kiss and was gone. Cora glanced around the tent and then, with an apologetic wave to a worried Aila, shot back up the crag.

Her timing was perfect. Men were coming to the front of Malcolm's lines with rough-hewn planks to throw across the marsh. Malcolm looked smug until Lachlan performed a nice show of horror, then he frowned but before he could do anything a bloodthirsty yell rang out from the trees behind and Macbeth's troop charged his reargaurd, cutting through it like butter.

Malcolm had no choice but to order the charge, though barely a third of their planks were in place. It was carnage. The Moray men had stone-slingers in their front rows with great barrels full of painstakingly chosen stones that could knock a hole in a man's skull or, at the least, deaden his sword arm. Many fell in the first rush but their bodies provided a footing for the next wave and suddenly the two lines were clashing and there was nothing of herding or insulting or game-playing about the ferocious fighting that rent the day apart. Cora crept down from her crag and made for the tents.

'My lady, thank heavens,' Brother Cullen cried. 'We need your help, for already the wounded are coming in.'

She nodded and moved towards the makeshift pallet beds. Cullen had the tent well organised. He'd seemed happier recently. The gossips told her he'd finally found the mother he had never known and though he'd kept the mysterious woman to himself she could believe it from his new air of peace. Of purpose too. She feared their work here would be as useless as it had been at the Seven Sleepers but any life saved was a minor victory and she threw herself into administering bandages and salves and prayers.

It went on and on. The shouts became less roars of fury and more grunts of effort. Every so often Cora heard Macbeth or Lachlan yelling commands and sent up a thank you that they were still there to give them, but she could tell little more of the progress of the battle save that many were suffering because of it.

Then a man limped in, one of his eyes held in his hand like a sweetmeat, and announced, 'We are winning.' Cora ran to him. Blood was dripping from the empty eye socket but he was grinning through its scarlet trail. 'We are winning,' he repeated.

'How do you know?'

'We are driving them back. Their losses are far greater than ours and there is desperation in their eyes. Their prince is looking more over his shoulder than to his attack. He awaits only darkness to flee, I swear it.'

'Is darkness close?'

'Very close, my lady,' said Cullen, coming up at her side.

Cora looked around her and suddenly realised how gloomy it had become in the tent.

'And the king knows it,' the warrior added. 'He seeks to kill Malcolm before he can scurry away.'

'Lachlan does? Himself?'

'He is our finest swordsman, my lady.'

Cora felt pride and then, hard on its tail, fear.

'Malcolm fights well too, I'll warrant.'

'Not as well as the king. Lachlan will take him and take Alba too.'

Cora could only pray this loyal young warrior was right but now the darkening air was cut through with the sound of three horn blasts.

'The retreat!'

'Ours or theirs?'

He licked his lips.

'Theirs, my lady. That reedy horn is theirs. We have seen them off.'

She would have run on to the field but Cullen held her back.

'Not yet! It's too dangerous. Those who are still in combat will fight like cats to get free. You must wait, my lady, please.' There was sense in that, though the need to see Lachlan and Macbeth itched at her like a thousand nettle stings. 'There are men to tend,' Cullen reminded her gently and as the latest arrival held out his lost eye she swallowed and nodded.

'Come, I will bandage you.'

She put the eye back in the socket before she bound it. She doubted it would help but God might see fit to knit it back and at least it saved her disposing of the strange, seeing part. Beyond the doors of the tent the sound of steel clashing on steel lessened and finally died away. Someone lit braziers, which cast as much shadow over the wounded as they did light but at least offered warmth and some comfort.

The men of Moray began to sing the Shepherd's Psalm in their soft lilting voices and the field took on a strangely festive mood. And then, at last, her family were there, Macbeth with his arm around his stepson's waist as he hobbled forward.

'Lachlan!' she cried. 'Lachlan, you are hurt?'

'A wee bit. 'Tis nothing, Mama, truly. A scratch.'

'Made by Malcolm?'

'No. Sadly I didn't get close enough to him to see more than a flash of his tail as he fled.'

The men on the pallets and benches all around gave a thin but heartfelt cheer. Cora ignored them.

'Let me see.'

'I told you, 'tis nothing.'

'I'll be the judge of that.'

Lachlan rolled his eyes at Macbeth who gave Cora a swift kiss before saying, 'Do as your mother tells you, lad. You may be King of Alba but she still has command of you.'

Lachlan sank onto a bench with a dramatic groan and let Cora kneel to examine the cut in his trews. He wore leather protectors but the left one had been slashed through and his leg was bleeding from a deep cut. It was not, thank the Lord, likely to be fatal but it must be cleaned carefully for by such doors infection could soon invade a man's body and claim it. Cora called for water and Cullen came scurrying up with the pail. She peered into it and saw a scum of other men's blood floating on top.

'Is there no clean water for the king?'

'None. I'm sorry. I've sent a lad to the brook but in the dark it will take him some time.'

'Hhhmm. Have you uiskie, Cullen?'

'Uiskie, my lady? Erm, I do, but only a weak, inferior blend I keep for those men who have to go under the knife. It is not fit for a king's lips.'

'Good, because that is not where I intend it to go.'

'You mean to put it on the wound?'

'I do.'

'It will sting like hellfire.'

'And cleanse like it too.'

'Hellfire?' Lachlan echoed unhappily as Cora clamped his leg in place and held out an imperious hand to Cullen, who scuttled off to fetch the flask. 'Mama, I'm not sure . . . '

'Do you want to be fit to chase Malcolm down? You will, I assume, chase him down?'

'Oh aye,' Lachlan said, 'at first light.'

'Not with a dirty wound.'

'Very well then. Get on with it.'

He was in too good a mood to argue. Victory shored a man up against many a hurt, though his yell when she poured the uiskie onto the exposed cut was loud enough to wake the battle-field dead.

'Hellfire,' Brother Cullen mumbled piously as Lachlan pounded at the bench and the men gathered curiously to watch their king tortured by his own mother.

Cora felt as lightheaded as if she had poured the spirit down her own throat. When Lachlan's paroxysms subsided she finally began to absorb the import of the day. They'd won. Malcolm had retreated, leaving half his troops in the Essie bogs, and tomorrow they could chase him down and reclaim Alba in deed as well as in name.

Men would desert Malcolm now for he had only really made it this far because of his English troops. True Albamen had been content beneath Macbeth's rule for many years and would as easily accept Lachlan. They were like sheep following the most determined shepherd, the one with the fiercest dogs.

'You've done it,' she said to Macbeth.

'We've started it. That'll teach him to march on Moray.'

'You will pursue him over the Mounth?'

'Over and beyond. You will soon be back in Fife, my southern softie.' She kissed him quiet, but his eyes glowed with renewed fire. 'We will see Lachlan back to Scone and this time he will be inaugurated, not in darkness but in the full glow of God's sun and all of Alba's acclaim. Aye, Cora, we have started it. Lachlan will be king again and I . . . '

'You will be Mormaer of Moray.'

''Tis a glorious province.'

And for once, with the singing still ringing out across the heather, her men safe at her side and Malcolm scuttling away into the darkness of the Mounth, she had to agree.

The next morning Cora was shaken awake by Brother Cullen.

'My lady. Beg pardon, but you should come to the king.'

She leaped up instantly and then, seeing Cullen flush wildberry red, realised she was naked and grabbed the covers after her. Macbeth stirred and sat bolt upright.

'What is it?'

'It's Lachlan.'

'Is he ill?'

'The wound does not look good,' Cullen told him.

They ran from their own pavilion to the hospital tent where Cullen and his fellow monks had been tending the sick through the all-too-short night. Lachlan was sitting up on a bench and looking grumpy enough to allay the worst of Cora's fears.

'Brother Cullen says I can't ride but that's nonsense, isn't it, Father?'

'I'm not sure. Let's see the wound.'

Cullen peeled back the bandages like a man unveiling a work of art. The wound looked discomfortingly yellow and swollen.

'It doesn't hurt,' Lachlan insisted.

'But it will if you ride with it, Sire,' Cullen told him. 'It is just below the knee and the motion of the horse will worry endlessly at it.'

'He's right,' Macbeth said.

'I can bear it.'

'I am sure you can,' Cullen agreed, 'but you will weaken and be of no use to your men.'

'I am no use to them sitting here.'

'But in a few short days you will be. Three, maybe four days' rest here will make all the difference. I have herbs that can ease the swelling and you are young, you will heal fast. But not in the saddle.'

'He's right,' Macbeth said again. 'A few days, Lachy.'

'Lachy!'

Macbeth flushed and took Cora's hand.

'You're still our son.'

'A son is a precious thing,' Cullen said piously.

Cora remembered the tales of his own newly discovered mother and smiled.

'It is, Cullen. A mother too.'

She thought she saw a tear glitter in the monk's faded eyes but he turned away and before she could follow Macbeth was stepping forward to grab Lachlan's hands.

'Let me ride for you, son, please. Let me command your troops for just a few days. We will hunt Malcolm down so that we have him trapped when you arrive.'

Lachlan frowned but nodded slowly.

'I suppose it makes some sense.'

'I'll stay with you,' Cora offered.

'No.' It was Cullen who spoke and she turned on him indignantly.

'No?'

He bowed low.

'I mean simply, my lady, that the people of Fife love you and Macbeth may need that.'

'But Lachy . . .'

'Has Fiona,' Lachlan said gently. 'I will go back to her, Mother. 'Tis only an hour's ride to Inverness. I can surely manage that much?'

'You can if you will permit me to go with you, Sire,' Cullen told him.

Lachlan laughed.

'Done! You and your herbs. But I will be hot on your heels, Father.'

'I know it. I will see you on the far side.'

'You will. Now go – the men are stirring and there is no time to be lost. If you're quick, you'll hunt down our prey in the mountains before ever they squirm out of Moray for no one knows this land like you.'

Macbeth smiled, bowed to him.

'Nor wishes more to see it free. You are coming, Cora?'

'Aye,' she agreed, but her eyes lingered on Lachlan, nursing his knee like the toddler he'd once been. 'Could the king not ride in a wagon?' she asked desperately.

'Over the mountains?' said Cullen.

He had a point but she did not like the way he stood so close over her son.

'You are sure of your herbs, Cullen?'

'Very sure. I will do all I can for him.'

Still Cora was uneasy. Lachlan rose, wincing, and placed his hands on her shoulders.

'I am a grown man, Mother.'

'I know it.'

'You can leave me and I will join you on the road to Scone, I swear. Now please, go.'

There was nothing left to say. Cora flung her arms around his neck and pulled him close. His hands patted her back consolingly but already he was pulling away. She felt a desperate urge to cling to him but knew it was just the weakness of her mother's heart and she must resist.

'Take care of him,' she said to Cullen.

'Oh, I will. I know how precious the King of Alba is to his mother.'

It sounded tender, even if it did not feel it.

'To all of Alba,' she said.

'That too. All will be well. The rightful king will rule – I will see to it.'

'Thank you.'

Macbeth was disentangling her hands from her son's neck and she had no choice but to walk away and trust to God and, it seemed, to Brother Cullen, to see him safe.

Chapter Thirty-eight

Lumphanan, June 1058

'You are worse than me, Morag.' Sibyll tugged at her friend's sleeve. 'Come inside. It grows chill.'

'Just a wee bit longer. He said he'd come. Cullen said he'd come to me.'

'And he will. There's a war out there. He cannot just trot across the Mounth as he wishes. He will come with Malcolm once Lachlan and Macbeth are defeated.'

'I thought he meant sooner.'

'A man is not always free to do as he chooses – nor a woman neither. You surely know that?'

Morag turned to look at her.

'I should have told him years ago.'

Sibyll sighed.

'You said all was well between you.'

'It is. Cullen understands. He has forgiven me fully and once Malcolm has secured Alba he will come home to be with me. You do not mind that?'

'You know I do not. I have forgiven him, truly. We are too old for grievances. You did tell him so?'

'I did and he was glad of it but he said it needed more to settle matters between you. He said he had a gift in mind for you, to make restitution.'

'What sort of a gift?

'I know not. He said he hadn't yet crafted it but as soon as he did he would be sure to bring it.'

Sibyll considered, pleased by this distraction from the interminable waiting.

'Is it a new uiskie, do you think? You said he was very pleased with the water at Rosemarkie. Maybe with more time there he has been able to do something really special?'

'Maybe but I do not think it was that. This was something more personal.'

'My own blend, perhaps, named after me? That would be a fine gift.'

'It wasn't uiskie,' Morag snapped, then clapped a hand over her mouth. 'I'm sorry. I'm unbearable at the moment, I know I am. It's just . . . he said he'd come.'

Sibyll linked arms with her friend.

'And he will. Let's go inside. There's a weave needs finishing and then perhaps you can make the cloth into a winter cloak for him?'

Morag nodded and let Sibyll lead her towards the ladies' bower but a shout from the far side of the fortress-top halted them both. A young lad was standing, his pail of milk spilled at his feet and his finger pointing up into the peaks of the Mounth.

'Men!' he called. 'I see men.'

Sibyll and Morag spun back but their ageing eyes were not as keen as the lad's.

'Where?' Sibyll demanded.

'There, coming down over the rise of the Hill of Balnagowan. Can you not see? There are hundreds of them.'

He waggled his finger in frustration and at last Sibyll did make out shapes moving across the grass.

'Can you see their faces?'

'No, my lady, but their horses look to be fine creatures so I think they must be important men.'

'Horses?'

'Of course horses. Men do not have four legs, do they?'

'You are blessed in your eyesight,' was all the answer she could find.

The lad smirked and clearly decided to make the most of this rare superiority.

'The front horse is a bay, the second too. They look to be almost a matching pair.'

Sibyll gasped. Her sons, it had to be.

'Do they ride high?' she asked, straining to see. 'Do they look victorious?'

'They look tired. They are moving fast, though perhaps they are just keen to bring you good news?'

There was little conviction in his voice but the shapes were indeed moving fast. The front ones were almost at the bottom of the slope now and riding out onto the plain.

'Well,' Sibyll said, 'we won't have long to find out.' She turned to Lady Stewart. 'We should warn the kitchens. The men will be hungry.'

'Of course, my lady,' she agreed. 'But . . . '

She pointed. The men were close enough now for even Sibyll to make out both Malcolm and Donald but they were reining in, turning around so their backs were to the fortress. Other men were falling into formation behind them and flags were being raised.

'It's a battleline,' the lad squeaked excitedly.

'It is,' Sibyll agreed grimly, placing a hand on his shoulder to stop him leaping up and down. 'And we are but fifty paces behind it. You know what that means?'

'I might get to fight.'

'You might get to die.' He shrivelled beneath her grip and she felt cruel but there was no hiding from the truth. She turned to him and said more gently, 'Will you ride out, lad?'

'Me?'

'Yes. If you're so keen for glory, will you ride out and get the news from the rearguard?'

He looked to the army, still streaming down the hill and into position behind their leader, then up the rise in search of pursuers. Clearly he saw none.

'I will do it. Trust me, my lady.'

And with that he was gone. They all stood, frozen to the palisade fence watching him ride out of the gates, tight with excitement and fear. He exchanged hurried sentences with a group of men then came cantering back.

'They were routed in Moray,' he said, stumbling over the words. 'King Lachlan led them into a bog and ambushed them from behind and though they fought valiantly for some hours Prince Malcolm thought it prudent to withdraw when night fell. It is a tactic, the men say. He is drawing the Moray men out of their homeland. Here at Lumphanan he can defeat them.'

'The men of Moray are close on their heels?' Sibyll asked.

The lad's face fell.

'I didn't ask that.'

'You didn't need to,' Morag said. 'It is surely clear that Malcolm expects them at any minute.'

It was. He could hardly be planning to stand in battlelines for days on end just in case the Moray men came.

'It is to be today then,' Sibyll choked out. 'Here. In front of us.'

She wasn't ready for this, hadn't prepared. She'd been waiting for news of battle but not to see it played out bloodily before her.

'Shall we go inside?' Morag suggested but Sibyll shook her head.

'We cannot. If they can stand and fight, we owe it to them at least to stand behind and bear witness.'

'It will make no difference, Sibyll.'

'It might. Men fight better with something to fight for. Seeing

335

us here will remind them of their wives, their mothers and their daughters, and that might help stiffen their spines when they need it most.'

Morag nodded, Lady Stewart too. Almost Sibyll hated them for giving in so easily for she longed to be dragged from this scene, but there was no virtue in hiding. The lad was shouting 'Men!' again and pointing to the hilltop where the enemy were showing themselves. Now, when it counted most, she must stand in the open with her sons.

'We should help,' she said. 'We should muster all the servants to carry water to our men. Bread too. They are defending us so it is the least we can offer.'

It was a relief actually to do something. They busied themselves organising a line of servants to pass supplies up to the back lines for the commanders to distribute. It was a small gesture, perhaps, but better than none at all and returning to her post, Sibyll saw Malcolm look up and raise his hand to her in thanks. She raised hers in return but there was no time for more because the Moray men were reaching the plain and lining up in their turn. They looked frisky, somehow. Excitable. Confident.

'He is drawing them out,' the lad had reported, but this looked very much like a force content to be drawn. They bristled with purpose and the red lions over their heads seemed to claw the air eagerly as if keen to grab the Constantin crosses and fling them into the mud.

'What do we do if our men lose?' Lady Stewart whispered.

'They won't lose,' Morag snapped and Sibyll hung desperately onto these words.

There was nothing in the way of parley for both sides believed they had the rightful ruler of Alba, though however hard she looked Sibyll could see no crown glinting in either rank.

'Can you see the king?' she asked the others.

'Which king?'

'Any king.'

'No. There's no one.'

'That's Macbeth.' Morag pointed to a big man with blond hair at the head of the opposing line. 'But I cannot see his son.'

'Stepson,' Sibyll corrected. 'He is not even of his direct line, unlike Malcolm.'

But it mattered little now who was son of whom for the horns were sounding and the lines were advancing towards each other and only the sword would speak from here. Sibyll watched with sickness in her stomach as the two sides clashed and clashed again. Every Albaman that went down, on either side, was like losing a friend and she prayed each time for it not to be Donald or Malcolm, then felt evil for ill-wishing someone else's son.

'How do they do it?' she asked Morag as the battleline became scrambled with corpses. 'How do men ever ride into a second battle?'

'How do women birth a second child?'

'Because they have little choice.'

'True. But perhaps men feel that way about battle too.' Morag studied the field. 'I think maybe it is easier to be a part of it for then you must think only of your own survival, not the impact of the whole confrontation.'

'Unless you are in command.'

'I still believe we have the harder task. We can only stand and watch.'

'We could go inside,' Lady Stewart said hopefully but none of them moved.

Sibyll could swear their own men were being pushed back. The rearguard looked closer to the fortress than it had been and those at the back were glancing over their shoulders as if seeking retreat. They would find none. The walls that were keeping Sibyll and her women safe would trap their side before their enemy – if it came to that.

She searched for Malcolm and Donald, willing them on. They were impossible to distinguish from the mass of soldiery tangled below her but their standards still waved valiantly from near the frontlines and she knew not whether to curse her princes for drawing attention to themselves or to be thankful she could track their progress. If progress it was.

'We are losing more than them,' she heard Morag gasp out and feared it was true.

The wild Moray men were shouting louder and louder, sensing their advantage, and the battle was turning into a massacre.

'We should lock ourselves away,' Lady Stewart wept.

'You do so,' Sibyll said. 'I shall stay. Whatever happens, I shall stay. I am done running.'

She fixed on her sons' standards, close to each other and but a few paces from the Aed lion of Macbeth. Where was his son, Lachlan, the supposed king? There was a man moving towards the Mormaer but he was no king, nor even a soldier. He wore a rough mail coat but his head was bare and she swore she saw a pink monk's tonsure where there should surely be a helmet.

'Who on earth is that?' she asked.

Morag leaned forward. Sibyll heard her breath catch in her throat but could not tear her eyes from the field for the monk, surely at great danger to himself, was placing a hand on Macbeth's broad shoulder and the Mormaer of Moray was turning to look. Macbeth's sword arm seemed to shake and for a moment he let his great weapon drop as if it were suddenly too heavy for him.

Sibyll felt herself point, heard a hoarse cry spring up out of her throat, too thick with fear to form into a word though her heart cried: 'Malcolm.' And he heard. Or, more likely, saw for himself. He sprang forward, his men tight behind him, and Macbeth had time only to half turn before Malcolm's sword was high and arching round into the ex-king's neck and he was falling.

Sibyll gripped the ancient wall before her as Macbeth's hands went up to the sky in entreaty. The battlefield froze momentarily then their long-time foe hit the earth with a thud that seemed, impossibly, to judder all the way up through the fortress as if Alba itself had been shaken.

Morag clutched at her friend. Chaos had broken out below. The monk was cut down by many. His hands, too, went to the sky but more in a curious show of joy than sorrow before he fell across Macbeth. He was tossed aside as the Moray men struggled to pull their leader from the front line. Swords were clashing again and Sibyll knew she should look for her sons but her eyes were fixed on Macbeth.

'Is he dead? Morag, is he dead, do you think?'

'He's dead.'

'How do you know?'

'I can feel him in my heart.'

'Macbeth?'

'No. Cullen. That was Cullen, I am sure of it, and that ...' she pointed to Macbeth's limp form ' ... is his parting gift to you. Macbeth's life for Maldred's – his final retribution.'

Chapter Thirty-nine

White-hot horror seared across Cora's skin as a name hissed along the lips of the Moray warriors: 'Macbeth. Macbeth is down.'

'He can't be!' she cried. 'Not now. Not after all this.'

She looked out across the field but could see little beyond the jostling backs of the rearguard.

'What does "down" mean?' she asked Aila. 'Injured? Do you think it means injured? Or . . .'

She didn't say 'dead' – wouldn't say it. Macbeth had been so strong in the chase over the Mounth, so intent on victory. Men had leaped eagerly to his command and scrapped to sit near him at the hearth-fire and though Lachlan had not yet caught them up his adoptive father had been keen to bring the invaders to battle. It had taken longer than they'd expected as Malcolm's troops had scattered far and wide but Macbeth had greeted every day with a smile at God's skies as if he'd been born to live free in the Mounth – as maybe he had.

He could not be dead. He'd been so determined to chase the southerners away, so certain of success. As predicted, much of Malcolm's support had leaked away during his retreat and several lords had come over to Macbeth, which had seemed a good sign. But the whispers were growing louder amongst the men and, pushing past a gaggle of wounded soldiers resting on the rocks, she began to run.

'Cora, no!'

Aila's voice echoed after her but Cora wasn't listening as she thrust her way through the ranks. Men were beginning to look at each other with an unease that Cora's frantic push did nothing to allay, but she didn't care. She had to get to him.

As she reached the front, the lines opened up where the hand-to-hand fighting began and suddenly Cora found herself within touching distance of a swinging sword. She cowered back as a man fell in front of her, his head part-severed at the neck and blood pumping almost joyously forth, and suddenly she was face to face with a soldier. His hair was slicked back, eyes wild, his sword already swinging, though he stayed his hand when he saw her and put the other to his slick forehead as if fearing for his wits. Cora seized on his hesitation to duck aside.

'Hold!' she heard someone bellowing and felt the earth shift as a thousand men planted their feet more firmly around her. But Malcolm's commands were shouted louder and with the note of triumph in them and again the Moray men faltered. And then, over the shouts and the screams and the clashes of the field, Cora heard three long, resonant notes ripple over her ranks and the word 'Macbeth' twisted and morphed into the word 'retreat'.

'No!' she cried, but already men were melting away around her and the field was opening and suddenly there was Macbeth, laid on the ground with Davey crouched over him. She ran again, ducking past men who cursed her as they tried to flee the other way, and at last she reached her husband. 'Is he dead?' Davey blinked up at her then shook his head. She fell to her knees at her husband's side and saw the blood oozing from a wound in his neck. 'Macbeth?'

'Cora?'

'Aye, Cora, your wife.'

'My heart.'

She grasped his hand.

'We have been blessed in each other.'

He summoned up a smile.

'We have, though you must insist on charging around like a hoyden in places not fit for women.'

'Are you not glad of it?'

'Very.' He tightened his grip on her. 'I am dying, Cora. I do not want to die. I do not want to leave you.'

'You will not, for I am coming too.'

'No! Please, Cora, you must take me to Iona to sleep with the other Kings of Alba. Will you take me? And ... and Lachlan?'

'Lachlan?'

Macbeth closed his eyes in pain and she looked desperately to Davey. Behind them the field was emptying. Malcolm had called his men into line and they stood, heads bare and bowed, as the Moray men made for the Mounth like ants scurrying for the nest. There was time. Indeed, it felt as if there was nothing but time for all else seemed empty of significance.

'Lachlan is dead,' Davey said. 'I'm sorry, my lady. So very sorry.'

'How?' For answer, he gestured to the ground nearby where a monk lay sprawled on his back, his chest pierced with myriad wounds, his eyes set on the heavens and an eerie smile on his face. 'Cullen!'

'He must have poisoned the wound, my lady.'

'We left Lachlan in his care and he betrayed us to them?'

'As he betrayed Maldred to us. He embraced his death crying "Retribution".'

'But we did not ask him to betray Maldred. We did not invite his treachery. It was freely given.'

'And freely regretted, it seems. I know no more, my lady, save that he fought his way to the front of the line to deliver the news personally. It shook Macbeth momentarily, as well it might, so that when Malcolm pounced he was helpless before him. Trickery,

Cora. Macbeth fell to trickery. And Lachlan besides. I'll kill him for this – I'll kill Malcolm.'

Davey lifted his sword and made to rise but Cora felt Macbeth's fingers convulse and saw his head shake.

'You must not,' she said firmly. 'Alba needs a king and if it cannot be ours it must be theirs. Fortunes change. One day Malcolm too will lie in Iona with Duncan and Macbeth and Lachlan and all this will be for naught.'

'Not for naught.' It was Macbeth who spoke. His voice was low but sure and she bent close to catch it as Davey backed away. 'Not for naught,' he said again. 'The years we ruled, Cora, the fifteen glorious years we shared as king and queen together, were the best of my life and we must treasure them all the more for being done. You will, Cora – you will treasure them?'

'I will.'

'I was only ever happier as one thing than as king.'

'Mormaer of Moray,' she said on a sigh but he shook his head vehemently.

'Nay, not that, but as your husband and father to Lachlan.'

'You ever loved him as your own.'

'Because he was yours.' His breath caught and for a moment she thought it was his last but he gasped in one more. 'Heaven, Cora,' he said, 'will be a sunlit pool with you.' And then, on a shadow of a smile, he was gone.

She fell across him and prayed someone would run her through, to skewer her to her husband and to the Alban soil where she belonged. Instead, a soft voice said, 'Lady Macbeth? Queen?' and she had to look up through her tears into the eyes of the innocent she hadn't wanted slaughtered as a child.

'Prince Malcolm.'

'*King* Malcolm,' he corrected gently. 'Come, please, you are safe and we must see your husband laid in state.'

And just like that, fortune's tide turned and she was washed up on Her shore.

Chapter Forty

Sibyll stared at the woman who had been ushered into her chamber, head bowed. She was small and slight but she walked proudly and her very hair, near white but still streaked with the red of a fiery youth, seemed to bristle with resentment.

'Lady Macbeth, welcome.'

'Lady Maldred, you are very kind.'

'I can afford to be.' The newcomer looked up, surprised, and Sibyll held out a hand to her. 'Rise, please. We have both been Queen of Alba, have we not? Surely we can meet as equals.'

'You are the victor.'

'My son is the victor.'

'And mine is dead. Dead at the hand of your double-dealing monk.'

Sibyll inclined her head but could not bring herself to answer for she was still trying to work out what Cullen had truly done. Yesterday had been a giddy round of celebrations and men had crammed onto the top of Lord and Lady Stewart's grand fortress to hear Malcolm proclaimed King of Alba.

Her son had accepted their acclaim with tears in his eyes and when the cheers had finally died down, had turned to Sibyll and proposed a private toast of their own: 'To Father and to my Uncle Maldred. They will be drinking to us together tonight, remember?'

How could she forget Maldred's last words?

'You truly think they will?'

'Truly. We were blessed in them both.'

It had been a balm to Sibyll's soul to hear him say so and she had thrown herself giddily into the happiness of the night. Today, though, with bodies still littering the ground and this woman before her, wife to one dead king and mother to another, it seemed harder.

'Have a seat, my lady,' she offered hastily. 'Please. You must be weary.'

'Not weary, sad.'

'I know the feeling well. Uiskie?'

Lady Macbeth looked up sharply.

'Brother Cullen's uiskie?'

Sibyll shrugged.

'Of course. He made the best. He brought it to Moray, I hear?'

'He did – and treachery with it.'

Lady Macbeth's eyes, a captivating green, glowed with dark fire but she accepted a tumbler of uiskie. Sibyll raised hers in silent respect but her adversary looked at the cup warily and drank without acknowledging the toast – a small sip at first, then another and another.

'A Dunkeld recipe?' she asked eventually. 'I have never been there.'

'Nor I to Rosemarkie.'

Lady Macbeth sniffed.

'It is a beautiful place. There are dolphins . . . '

Her voice cracked and she gulped at her uiskie, spluttering a little, though whether from the lifewater or from grief Sibyll could not tell.

'I have wine if you would prefer? It is from Dunkeld too.'

'Alban wine?' Her voice was controlled again now, dry. 'How the country has progressed.'

'Much of it thanks to you and your husband.'

'Until your son hunted him down.'

Sibyll sucked in a breath and took a sip of her own drink.

'Until then, yes.'

A servant came up to add logs to the brazier. They were in Sibyll's own chamber for privacy and with the day closing out beyond the window the flames shone forgiving light onto the women's faces and drew them together in seeming intimacy.

'What happened to your son?' Sibyll dared to ask when the fire was stoked and the servant gone.

Lady Macbeth looked at her.

'Do you really want to know?'

'I do.'

'King Lachlan took a wound at Essie but it was nothing serious. I bathed it myself. I *saw* it myself. It needed a few days' rest so I left my son in Brother Cullen's care. Care, ha! He was working for you, was he not?'

'No! At least, not to my knowledge.'

'How do you mean?'

'It's complicated.'

'When isn't it? Tell me, please, for Brother Cullen poisoned my son's wound, Lady Maldred – poisoned it until it rotted his leg and he caught a fever and died. And then the monk strode onto the battlefield to tell my husband and so blindsided him with his loss that he did not see your son's sword stroke in time to defend himself.'

'I'm sorry.'

'You're not.'

Sibyll put up her hands. It was like having a wildcat in her chamber. The other woman's eyes glowed and her hair seemed to flare like the hackles of a beast on guard. Sibyll stroked her own faded blonde plaits and felt for her diadem.

'You are right, in a way – I am not sorry that Malcolm won the battle for had he not, it would be I, not you, sunk in sadness. But I am sorry all the same that you must be.'

Lady Macbeth let out a sigh so deep it set the flames flaring.

'Thank you,' she said in a small voice. 'But it seems you had a secret weapon in your little uiskie-monk.'

'No.' Sibyll edged closer to her. 'That is, we were not working with him. We had not heard from him in years, save via his mother.'

'She was one of yours, this mysteriously found mother?'

'A friend, yes, but not a soldier. Morag had no interest in wars, only in being reconciled with her son before it was too late.'

'Then she was just in time. But why, if Cullen was not working under orders, would he do this to us? We were kind to him, treated him well – or so we thought.'

Sibyll sighed.

'Brother Cullen unfortunately seemed to ... to care for me a little.'

She felt her colour rise and saw the other woman's intelligent eyes notice that too.

'He was in love with you?'

'Perhaps.'

Lady Macbeth laughed suddenly, a brittle, fragile sound.

'Macbeth always said as much. Lord, he saw the heart clearly for a man.'

'He said that? When?'

'When Cullen came to Rosemarkie after Duncan had become king. He loved you all that time?'

Sibyll grimaced.

'He looked after me when I was fleeing from your husband after Duncan's death. I thought he was merely doing his Christian duty but it seems it was more than that. When I remarried he was not content.'

'And that's when he came to us to say Mormaer Maldred was about to attack. He was ... was jealous?'

Sibyll spread her hands wide.

'It seems so. It cost me the man I loved.'

'I know the feeling well.'

Sibyll heard her own words and looked up sharply but saw only bittersweet amusement in the other woman. She raised her uiskie tumbler to her again.

'You and Macbeth had been wed a long time?'

'Twenty-seven years, though it should have been five more. I was stolen on my wedding-eve and dragged to the altar by the wrong man. It took Macbeth all that time to raise the forces to reclaim me. I was not happy.' A smile ghosted across her face, then suddenly she grabbed for Sibyll's hand. 'You tried to stop my brother, did you not? Kendrick. He tried to kill King Malcolm.'

'King Malcolm *II*,' Sibyll corrected her, then hated herself for how pious that sounded. 'And, yes, I did try to stop him. He looked wild, unhappy. His eyes ... He had eyes just like yours.' She looked directly at the other woman, who nodded sadly. 'I could see he wasn't thinking clearly but I ... I was too slow.'

She stared into the flames, seeing the body of this woman's brother dangling over old King Malcolm's feast. She shivered. Malcolm had been a brutal king and she hoped his namesake could afford a more considered style of rule.

'"Tell Cora I'm sorry,"' she said, as much to herself as to her guest. She could see Lord Kendrick so vividly as he choked out those words just before the noose cut off his voice. 'You received the message?'

'I did and I was grateful for it. Our paths have crossed a great many times, Lady Maldred.'

'Alba has woven them that way.'

'Was it worth it?'

Now it was Sibyll who sucked in her breath. The battle to be queen had lost her both Duncan and Maldred – a bitter price. But as her lungs filled, her sight cleared.

'Of course it was. To be a queen is a privilege few are granted. I loved it.'

'As did I.'

Sibyll raised her cup again and, after just a moment's hesitation, Lady Macbeth – Cora – raised hers in return. No words were spoken for none were needed. They simply touched edges and drank to times past, to men lost and to years not-quite-shared.

Chapter Forty-one

Loch Ness, September 1058

Cora stepped into the low barge and moved purposefully to the front, setting her face away from Inverness and the curve of the Moray Firth that had made her welcome for so many years. She looked, instead, down the long line of Loch Ness, gateway to the Great Glen leading to Iona – the burial place of Alba's kings.

At the rear of the barge six burly oarsmen were taking their places and in its oak centre, laid out side by side beneath a single piece of golden fabric, were Macbeth and Lachlan. Cora did not look at them. She had looked enough, wept enough. Her grief was parcelled up deep inside her, to take out and cherish later as proof of a life lived in love. For now she must see them honoured as kings – not as part of the pattern of her own life, but of Alba's.

The boat was pushed away from the jetty and now she did look back, not for Moray but for the people waving her off on this sorrowful journey. There was Fiona, Lachlan's poor widow, holding the hand of their second child and too heavy with the third to make her husband's final journey with her mother-by-marriage. Twelve-year-old Murray stood dark-eyed and solemn at her side. He was Mormaer of Moray now aided by the ever-faithful stewardship of Davey and it soothed Cora to know that Macbeth's dear homeland was, at least, still in their family's charge.

On the end of the line stood Prince Donald, the new king's brother, who had escorted her and Macbeth's body home in quiet honour. He was to marry into Moray to bind them more closely to the throne and perhaps in so doing to lower the peaks of the Mounth a little, as Cora had first done when she'd fled Malcolm II and started the whole strange cycle of her life in motion.

Aila, dear faithful Aila who had been robbed of a husband when Kendrick had gone to his misplaced vengeance and never looked at another, stood to one side, her hand on Balgedie's neck. The ancient pony was staring solemnly at her with his faded eyes, his half-ear twitching, and Cora put a hand to the near-faded scarring on her neck then forced herself to take it away and give the pony a little nod. They had both taken wounds in life and both survived. She would be back one day but not yet for she had a sacred duty to fulfil.

The watchers waved in silence until her little namesake cried out a lusty farewell. Everyone laughed and Cora was glad of it. This was not to be a journey of sadness but of celebration. The monks of Iona were waiting and Malcolm had ordered tombs built for both her men as they had ordered one for Duncan. Macbeth would lie at his side now, united in death as they had never been in life. It was fitting.

The barge moved into the middle of the great loch and Cora felt the breeze lift her near-white curls. Already, thanks to the power of the oarsmen, the watchers on the bank were fading into the distance and for the first time since planning this trip her heart quailed. She had wanted to do this alone, just her, Macbeth and Lachlan once more, but now the moment had come she doubted her own strength. Almost she called to the oarsmen to turn, almost she asked Davey to come with her, but then, just ahead, a cloud crossed the sun, casting a dark, sinuous patch across the lively blue waters, and she fancied it was the monster come at last to see her down Loch Ness and stood firm once more.

The sky was a fierce blue with a scud of rain-thick clouds dancing across it as they only seemed to do in Alba, daring you to be too content. The loch was darker, as if it had all the sky squashed into its great depths, and dotted with mischievous white spray where the wind funnelled up from the west. The monster curled before her bows and then, as the sun broke free once more, it dived and was gone. Cora lifted her head and listened to the sound made by six oars leaving the water in perfect time as it echoed up the hills to either side like Alba's very own heartbeat.

She glanced to her left. They were passing the curved pathway up to the Falls of Foyers. Somewhere behind the trees water cascaded over the rocks and cast itself recklessly into a deep pool below, sending rainbows across the mist. And maybe, somewhere beneath it, a woman and her son dived and laughed and dived again as a man came to claim them into his arms forever more. With a soft smile, Cora set her face forward, gripped at the bulwark and looked down the Great Glen.

Her heart had not been forged simply but it had been forged strong and had beaten out a rhythm she could never regret. She had not asked to be queen but neither had she refused. She had made her destiny and followed it all the way across Alba to its throne and, now, its tomb. She had been Lady Macbeth and she had been Queen and she could only hope that, in some small way, Alba was richer for it.

Historical notes

Writing this novel has been an especial joy for me as I am of Scottish Heritage, was born in St Andrew's, and consider myself very much a Scot (especially where rugby is concerned!). Discovering the history of my country of birth has been a fertile and fascinating journey and I hope that through these notes the reader can enjoy a few more of the facts that I unearthed in my research but cannot, by the constraints of the narrative, include as fully in the novel itself as I would sometimes like.

Real names

Although I am in many ways reluctant to change names from what we believe they were at the time, some can fall heavy on a modern ear so in the interest of narrative fluidity I altered those to sound more natural to us.

Finlay	Findláech
Macbeth	Macbethad (son of light)
Cora	Gruoch
Kendrick	Invention. Records suggest Gruoch's brother

	may have been called Maelbaethe or Boite but both are flimsy so I chose something more distinctive.
Lachlan	Lulach (Gruoch's father may well have been Boite but, as with her brother, records are flimsy. Names usually had family connections so I decided it was possible that she named her son after her father.)
Muir	Mael Coluim (Malcolm as below – changed to avoid confusion)
Gillespie	Gilla Comaign
Ward	Siward
Sibyll	Suthen
Duncan	Donnchadh
Crinan	Crinan
Bethan	Bethóc
Malcolm II	Mael Coluim
Crinan	Crinan
Malcolm III	As with Malcolm II above
Donald	Domhnall

Scotland

The country we know today as 'Scotland' does not seem to have been referred to by that name until the eleventh century and then only by English chroniclers writing in Latin. The natives knew it as Alba and so that is the name I have used in this novel.

The terms 'Scots' and 'Scotia' are found in many early Latin sources but exclusively to refer to a tribal people originally from Ireland, some of whom came to the mainland and formed the kingdom of Dal Riata in modern-day Argyll on the west coast. Brian Boru, High King of Ireland 1002–1014 referred to himself in an inscription as Imperator Scottorum but this, again, referred to the people, not the land. If the term was ever was used to reference a country, that country was Ireland.

The earliest known reference to 'Scotland' is in the Anglo-Saxon Chronicle for 1066 when the chronicler states that Earl Tostig sought refuge 'in Scotland under the protection of Malcolm III, King of Scots'. For a long time 'Scotland' was employed alongside 'Alba' and the use of the latinate word only became common in the Late Middle Ages. Even today many natives of the country prefer to call it Alba.

The Mounth

It is hard to pinpoint exactly what people in the eleventh century meant by 'The Mounth' but in essence it referred to the mountain range that became known (in the early 1500s) as the Grampians – a huge belt of hills running across central Scotland below the Great Glen and including the Cairngorms range. The term appears to have come from the Pictish Gaelic, Monadh, meaning simply mountain, and the use of the definite article 'The' implies the significance this range held.

The Mounth was considered a wall – a natural fortress separating those dwelling above it from those below. Despite ancient drovers' passes, the mountains were formidable to climb and few men ever bothered. The climate in Moray, above The Mounth, is surprisingly mild and those that lived there seem largely to have been content to stay behind their 'wall' and enjoy life free of the political machinations of those in what became the seat of Alban power around Scone. Certainly Macbeth is the only king to have come from that area, making his reign even more remarkable.

Alternate succession/ Cora's claim

Prior to Malcolm III, The Kingdom of Alba followed the practice of alternate succession, much as their Irish cousins did for the High Kingship of Tara. The first King of Alba was Kenneth MacAlpin, a Dal Riatan king who seized the opportunity afforded by the Viking raids in the early 800s to overcome the Picts and unite east and west Alba. Kenneth had two sons – Constantine and Aed and the throne seems largely to have passed from the lines of one to the other throughout the ninth and tenth centuries.

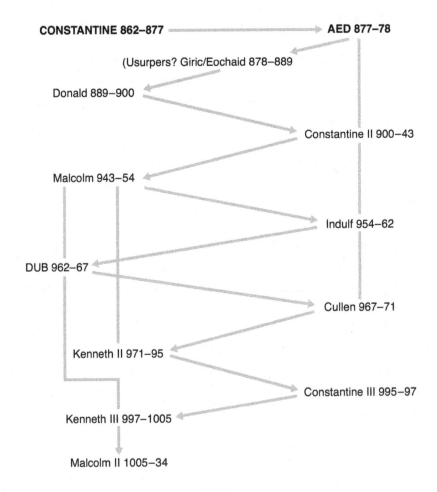

Inevitably, family lines weren't this simple with many branches developing that had to be kept loyal to the central ones. It would appear that there was a branch of the Aed line that, at some point, travelled beyond The Mounth to Moray and, liking what they found there, stayed put. They rarely strayed south but still carried royal blood and it is this that gave Macbeth his claim.

Similarly, as noted above, Cora was part of a secondary branch of the Constantine line based in Fife, although it is hard to establish exactly where she fits in the royal family tree. Her father, possibly called Boite (I have used Lachlan), could have been the son of Kenneth II or Kenneth III or even of Dub (and therefore brother of Kenneth III). Dub is thought to be a possibly origin of Duff, so Cora was quite probably of the MacDuff line, a resonant name for any fan of Shakespeare and I chose to go with the idea of her being his granddaughter. Malcolm II – who had only daughters of his own blood – killed Lachlan (his own cousin) to eliminate his claim and would doubtless have killed Cora and Kendrick too had they not escaped to Moray and the shelter of Finlay and his son Macbeth.

It is unlikely that the Moray branch of the line of Aed would ever have become involved in the scrap for the throne had the more southerly branch not died out and had Malcolm II not decided to challenge the established order of alternate succession by naming his direct grandson as his heir. To be fair to Malcolm, alternate succession was rare by this period. The more accepted model – for example in England and on the continent – was for a direct line of rule so he was perhaps trying to modernise. And, indeed, after Macbeth, his grandson Malcolm III succeeded in doing so as his line, with his English wife Margaret, led directly down to James VI of Scotland and I of England.

Some historians believe that Macbeth was the son of one of Malcolm II's other daughters and, indeed, that Thorfinn, Earl of Orkney was the son of the third. It's a romantic idea and there is some evidence for it but in the end it was scarce and I found it hard to see why Malcolm would not have been more welcoming to another grandson so I decided to instead pursue the more historically fruitful idea that they were of alternate lines.

Uiskie and Brother Cullen

When conceiving the story of this novel, I was looking for a vehicle to connect the two stories of Cora and Sibyll. A travelling monk seemed the perfect solution but why would this monk travel? Looking into the practices of monasteries in Scotland at the time I came upon one of those magical discoveries that make writing historical fiction such a joy: that whisky, as far as it is possible to tell from the sparse records, was first seriously produced in the eleventh century. From this Cullen was born and he rapidly grew into the story as a whisky expert and, eventually, the linchpin of Macbeth's downfall.

Linguistically, I love the fact that our 'whisky' comes from the shortening of the Gaelic usquebauch, as described in the novel, but archaeological evidence suggests that the grain-based spirit itself was probably originally made in Babylon and Mesopotamia thousands of years ago. It may have been brought to Scotland and Ireland with the waves of missionary monks after the birth of Christ but it is also quite possible that locals had long since worked out how to distil their surplus barley themselves. The comparative lack of grapes in these northerly lands made both whisky and beer popular and men – and quite possibly women – must soon have mastered their production.

Cullen poisoning Lachlan's wound is, I confess, a product of my own imagination. The Annals of Ulster do, however, report that he was killed 'by treachery' so it seemed a possibility. Cullen's motivation – that of love – is perhaps unlikely but other moments of history have turned on less and the story is rooted firmly in the facts as we know them so I hope the reader will enjoy my flight of fancy.

The flags of Scotland

There has long been speculation about why Scotland has two flags – the blue and white Saltire (or St Andrew's cross), and the red and yellow lion rampant.

The Saltire has been the official flag of Scotland since the four-teenth century. Saint Andrew was named as the patron saint after Robert Bruce's victory at the Battle of Bannockburn in 1314 and the Parliament of Scotland agreed in 1385 that Scottish soldiers should wear the white cross as a distinguishing mark.

But how did St Andrew – one of Christ's apostles – get to Scotland? There are two stories: one that Saint Regulus brought his remains over in the fourth century; and the other that Saint Wilfrid did so in the seventh. He apparently became immortal-ised in the flag in 832 after the Pictish king Angus II, dreamed of St Andrew assuring him of victory against the Northumbrians under King Athelstan. The next morning he saw clouds forming a white St Andrew's cross against the blue sky and, after victory was duly delivered, he adopted this as his flag.

The lion rampant is harder to pin down, not apparently having so much as a legend to establish its origins. It is first officially recorded as an emblem of Alexander II in 1222 and may have links to Richard I 'Lionheart' of England who brought 'rampant' animals into fashion and whose banner is very similar to the Scots one. However, it is often the case in history that first records are merely a reflection of something that has been practised for a long time and it seemed to me interesting that in the roots of the Alban kingship there are two core lines that could well match up to the two different flags. I then applied artistic licence for the sake of the story.

Crinan's vineyard

There is much evidence that the climate in the eleventh century was several degrees warmer than it is now, even in the more northerly Alba. There is evidence of a vineyard in Dumfriesshire until 1507 and of vines in Renfrewshire in 1483 so it is entirely possible that grapes were grown in the fertile valley around Dunkeld.

Towns/Cities/Ports

I was astonished when first researching Scotland in this period to discover that there were no cities, towns or even really villages as we know them (and as their English neighbours knew them) anywhere in the country.

What would eventually become the key cities *were* in existence but only as royal residences. Rulers back in the early half of the first century had lived in huge stone fortresses such as the one at Dunedin, or Edinburgh (built on the rock on which the castle still stands today). By the time of this novel, however, many had moved to large, low-lying farms, often associated with growing bishoprics and monasteries. These would house quite a large community, including craftspeople, and with scope for an irregular market, but they were all within the king's personal ownership and were not, therefore, towns as we know them in England.

The situation was similar in Norway, a country with many parallels to Scotland and in constant contact with them via a strong Norse community ruling in Orkney and Shetland. The market towns of Kaupang and then Oslo were only really forming in the late eleventh century and markets were often held on beaches where trading ships pulled up and set up shop – as shown in Dunkeld in this novel.

Edinburgh was probably the first town to truly begin to develop, most probably under Malcolm III and his wife Margaret (later St Margaret). Margaret had grown up in England and Malcolm had spent time in Northumbria in exile so both had experience of town/city living to bring to Scotland. I also like to think, however, that Macbeth's trip to Rome inspired him and that he and Cora were already encouraging such development before their reign was brought to an end.

Crannogs

I first saw a crannog when travelling to the Moray Firth on a research trip and knew immediately that I had to have one in my novel. As a girl I loved all secret hideouts, so the idea of a little house stuck in the middle of a loch was wonderful to me and I was delighted to be able to create Morag to live in one.

Crannogs were houses on stilts, connected to the mainland by timber walkways (though not, as far as we know, ones like Morag's with a wind-down handle). They were probably an Irish design, brought to Scotland with the 'Scots' of Dal Riata. Today we know of around 1200 crannog sites in Ireland with 347 official sites listed in Scotland, mainly across the central belt.

According to archaeological evidence the first crannogs date back to 3000 BC but some were lived in well into the seventeenth century. More than twenty sunk crannogs have been identified in Loch Tay and for those who wish to know more there is a wonderful centre there where visitors can experience Iron Age crannog living for themselves: www.crannog.co.uk

King Duncan and the attack on Durham

Shakespeare took huge liberties with the portrayal of King Duncan as a worthy old king, much venerated by his people. The real Duncan was of a similar age to Macbeth and was thrust onto the throne by his fiercely ambitious grandfather in an attempt to perpetuate his own line (see notes on alternate inheritance). He ruled for only five years and any security seems to have been as much from his grandfather's legacy as his own power. Macbeth's forces killed him in open battle (and very much not in a dark coup in his bedroom) and Macbeth was freely acclaimed king. It does not seem that Duncan was a man suited to the kingship and I have chosen to explore the tragedy of that in this novel.

It was an unfortunate custom of new Alban kings to deliberately pick a fight with someone shortly after accession to prove one's worth as a ruler. This was known as a 'crech rig', or king's raid and, like much in Alba in this period, seems to have originally been an Irish custom. Once Alba was a united (or semi-united) nation the only real target available was England and rulers were not slow to attack. (And, to be fair, their southerly neighbours were just as quick to head north.)

Malcolm II's 'crech rig' was in 1006 when he took a large army and besieged Durham. However, Uhtred of Northumbria led out their army and routed the invaders. Malcolm was one of the few to escape with his life as the rest had their heads placed on spikes all around the city where they apparently stayed for many a year. It must be testimony to Malcolm's hardiness that he was not deposed in its wake (or perhaps just to the fact that any challengers had died in the raid) and he eventually attacked again in 1018, winning a huge victory at the Battle of Carham and securing Lothian for Alba for good.

The one thing Malcolm did not achieve, however, was taking Durham. This was no big surprise as the city, built on a huge rock and surrounded on three sides by the River Wear, was as close to a natural fortress as it is possible to be. Taking it was nigh-on impossible and we have to wonder why Duncan chose to do so in 1039. It can only have been in a desperate attempt to get one up on his dead grandfather and to truly prove his worth, perhaps because it was already in serious question. His power, such as it ever was, seems to have been waning from this point and it is likely that many men came over to Macbeth's side when he attacked the following year, making his victory almost inevitable.

Stone of Scone

The Stone of Scone, otherwise known as the Stone of Destiny, seems to have been a vital part of Alban royal inaugurations from early times. Legend has it that it was brought to Scotland by Fergus, MacErc, the first King of the Scots on mainland Dal Riata, who transported it from Tara in Ireland so he could be crowned in the established, sanctified manner. Others say the original remains at Tara, so it is possible that Fergus' was actually a copy. Either way, it became a centrepiece of royal power and no man could truly call himself king until he had sat upon the stone. As a result, mad dashes to Scone after victory in battle were an important part of claiming the country.

The Stone (if it is the original that we still have today as rumours of replicas abound at all points in its history) is a very simple piece of red sandstone and can be seen in the crown room at Edinburgh Castle, though there is also a replica at Scone. In 1296 it was captured by Edward I and taken to Westminster Abbey where it was fitted into a wooden chair, known as King Edward's Chair, on which most subsequent sovereigns were crowned. In 1328 England agreed to return it to Scotland but riotous crowds prevented it from being removed from Westminster Abbey and it remained in England for another six centuries, even after James VI of Scotland assumed the throne in 1603.

On Christmas Day 1950, a group of four Scottish students stole the stone from Westminster Abbey for return to Scotland and after various adventures (during which the stone was broken in two and then repaired) they left it on the altar of Arbroath Abbey in the safekeeping of the Church of Scotland. The London police, sadly, insisted on its return to Westminster but it was eventually restored to Scotland in 1996 by the English government. The last monarch to be crowned on it was our current Queen Elizabeth II.

The Moray Stone

The large column described in the novel as the 'Moray Stone' is a real Pictish monument which stands on the north-easterly edge of Forres. These days it is known as Sueno's Stone, though this seems to be a nineteenth century name based on a spurious story that it commemorated a victory over the Danes in 1008 under a warleader called Sueno. Nineteenth-century historians tended to attribute all stones to victories over the Vikings and in fact the carvings are far more suggestive of an internal fight.

Most historians now agree that it depicts Kenneth MacAlpin's victory over the Picts. There is a particularly gruesome carving of multiple decapitations and this was very much a Scots practice rather than a Viking one. There is also a scene showing a leader executing seven figures which may well be a symbol of the victor cutting off the power of the original seven kingdoms of the Picts, and another scene showing figures surrounding a man on a throne that is almost certainly an inauguration. Considering all this, I believe it does commemorate MacAlpin's victory and am certain that would have been important to Macbeth.

St Columba and the Loch Ness Monster

The Loch Ness Monster remains an enduringly popular myth even today. A huge industry has grown up around Nessie's supposed existence and when I discovered that the story came all the way from the late 500s I loved the idea that Cora could have been monster-spotting in the same way as people still do now.

The myth is first found in Adomnan's famous Life of St Columba, written in about AD 700. It is associated with a trip St Columba, then the abbot of his own foundation on Iona, made to King Bridei of the Picts in the early 580s. The Picts were still pagan at this point and it is quite possible that Columba was leading a mission to try and convert the king. If so, it doesn't seem to have succeeded, but what he did achieve was safe passage for other monks in the Pictish lands and, of course, the banishment of the monster.

The story, as reported by Adomnan, tells us that a giant reptile had been attacking locals in the Ness river, dragging them underwater to their death. Columba sent a follower to swim across the river and when the beast approached the poor, doubtless terrified, man Columba made the sign of the cross and banished it to the depths of the river/loch forever. Now, miracle stories were stock-in-trade for religious biographers in this period so clearly this cannot be taken as 'true', but I do believe that it can be taken as a story that was, at that time (and since) *believed to be true* and I could not resist including it in my novel.

Visit to Rome

Marianus Scotus (an Irish monk and chronicler, living about 1028–82) tells us that King Macbeth made a pilgrimage to Rome in 1050 and 'gave money to the poor as if it were seed'. Such trips were very much the in thing for progressive northern monarchs. We know that King Dyfnwal of Cumbria travelled to Rome in the tenth century, then King Sihtric of Dublin and King Flanncan of Brega in 1028, King Flaithbertach Ua Neill of Ailech in 1030, King Cnut in 1031, and the King of Gailenga and his wife in 1050.

The detail that King Gailenga took his wife is important as it shows that high-born women made the pilgrimage and Judith of Flanders, wife of Tostig Godwinson, is also recorded as doing so in the early 1060s. We do not know for a fact if Cora travelled with her husband but it is perfectly likely that she did so, especially as they had Lachlan to stand as regent, so I felt justified in sending her along.

The fact that Macbeth went to Rome is, however, not just interesting in itself, but also a vital snippet of history as it tells us several important things:

That Macbeth was sufficiently secure in his reign to make the pilgrimage all the way to Rome – a round trip of about half a year.

That Macbeth was sufficiently interested in continental affairs to wish to do so. It is very possible that Macbeth's trip to Rome started with him attending the reforming Synod of Rheims, held on 3rd–5th of October 1049. This was the first church synod held this far north in four hundred years and, interestingly, was where William the Conqueror (as he would become) was forbidden to marry Mathilda of Flanders, a prohibition he flouted. I chose not to explore the synod as there was no room for it in my narrative but attendance at such a key gathering certainly indicates a man keen to meet other northerly rulers and to be a part of the development of both church and state.

That Macbeth was rich enough to throw money around. There was no coinage in Scotland at the time so he must have bought coins on his way through Europe and, having done so, was surely keen to bring them to his home country.

I am firmly convinced that Macbeth's pilgrimage reveals him to us as a forward-thinking, energetic and highly engaged political ruler and the things he saw on his travels must have helped him decide on the way he wanted to take Alba once back home. He travelled at the height of his rule and it must only have been the attack from England by Earl Ward and Malcolm that stopped him from implementing many of his ideas. Thankfully for Scotland, many were introduced by Malcolm III and I like to think that he was building not just on his and his wife's knowledge of English customs, but also on Macbeth's earlier vision.

Chronology of Malcolm's invasion and Lachlan and Macbeth's deaths

Records of the progress of Malcolm III's invasion of Scotland and of the deaths of Macbeth and his stepson Lachlan (Lulach) are both sparse and contradictory.

We are on firmest ground with the 'Battle of the Seven Sleepers' (so called because it happened on the feast of the Seven Sleepers – June 27th) in 1054. The Anglo-Saxon chronicle reports that: 'This year went Earl Siward with a large army against Scotland . . . and put to flight the King Macbeth.' The Annals of Ulster also record the battle, though not the outcome, suggesting it was indecisive and certainly the next three to four years seem to have seen Malcolm building a power base in the south and Macbeth shoring up his defences in the north. The throne was still very much up for grabs.

But what happened next? The Anglo-Saxon chronicle does not report Macbeth's death but Marianus Scotus says that he was killed in 1057 on the Feast of St Mary (September 8th) – the exact anniversary of Duncan's reported death. This is less contrived than it might sound as many battles were arranged in advance and it would have been a good date for Malcolm to pick to avenge his father.

As Malcolm was not made king until spring 1058, this would suggest that Lulach succeeded his stepfather for the intervening period. However, Lulach features very clearly in Alban kinglists, suggesting that he was inaugurated at Scone – a condition of kingship. It seems highly unlikely that with Macbeth dead up in the north, his stepson was able to ride to Scone, in the heartland of Malcolm's power, and be peacefully and successfully inaugurated before riding north again to be there for his own death a year later. Historians have therefore suggested that Macbeth may have demitted his kingship to his stepson after the defeat in 1054 and I chose to embrace that version of history for this novel.

What's more, there is dispute over the order in which Macbeth and Lulach died. Two versions of the Annals of Ulster report that both Macbeth and Lulach died in 1058 and that Lulach was first to be killed in either January or February, with Macbeth dying in June. If this is true, then the only way Lulach could make it onto the official kinglists is if he'd been king whilst Macbeth was still alive. Macbeth would then have had to resume the kingship on his stepson's death to continue the fight against the invaders.

The order of these deaths is important as it says much about the way the power-struggle was going. Sources seem clear on the geography of the deaths: Lulach died at Essie, above the Mounth, and Macbeth at Lumphanan just below it. If Macbeth was first, then Malcolm must have pressed north to kill Lulach and claim the throne. If Lulach was first, Malcolm must have struck in the north, over the Mounth (possibly in alliance with the Norse in the Orkneys, though I sadly had no room to explore these links in this novel). He would then have surely had to be in retreat to be driven back to the southerly Lumphanan before Macbeth died.

It is this latter version that I chose to follow, partly because I enjoyed having my hero in the ascendancy before his death, but also because it seems the more likely turn of events. Lulach's wounding by Cullen and Cullen's appearance on the battlefield are, I admit, a conceit of my making but it is my job to entertain as well as to inform and with the historical mists surrounding the deaths I felt I had licence to offer my own interpretation.

Differences to Shakespeare

Macbeth's 'story' (as opposed to his history) is absolutely fascinating to trace as it has a clear line through various literary versions over the centuries, each with their own additions and all feeding into Shakespeare's eventual, massively corrupted, masterpiece.

The earliest stories would have been oral and were quite

probably performed in Macbeth's lifetime and, indeed, before him. The first written record is in the *Prophecy of Berchan*, probably written by a collection of people in the eleventh century. Macbeth features in here as 'the red, tall, golden-haired one' whose reign brought prosperity to Alba.

The next written reference is found in a thirteenth century kinglist, *The Chronicles of Melrose*, which refers to Macbeth as bringing 'fruitful seasons' to Alba – with harvest analogy often meaning general good rule. So far, so good.

The changes start to come in with the *Chronicle of the Scottish People* written by John of Fordun some time before his death in 1370. Fordun's account of Macbeth suddenly portrays him as a usurper, a murderer and a tyrant – the start of the character Shakespeare developed so memorably. Fordun's motive seems to have been to emphasise the rightful line of kingship coming from Malcolm III which would be why he chose to make Macbeth into a 'bad guy' but it caught on fast. (Note – Another Fordun addition is that of MacDuff, the thane of Fife, quite possibly derived from King Dub, Cora's probably grandfather.)

The real roots of Shakespeare's play, however, are to be found in the next incarnation of the story: the *Original Chronicle of Scotland* by Andrew of Wyntoun, written at the start of the fifteenth century. In this lively text (which includes a very early mention of Robin Hood as a forest outlaw somewhere near Carlisle) we first hear of the murderous Macbeth as the 'thane of Cromarty' and, indeed, the 'son of the devil' – this apparently meaning that he could only be killed by someone of unnatural birth, a feature of the play. Wyntoun is also the first to introduce the 'weird sisters' speaking to Macbeth in a dream in which he is told he will be king and that he will not be defeated 'until Birnham Wood comes to Dunsinane', another key feature of the play. Three prophetic witches or 'norns' were a very common feature of Celtic mythology and have clearly been blithely shoehorned into history here, perhaps because Wyntoun was writing at a time of multiple witchcraft trials so they were going to capture the public imagination – as they did!

The next Macbeth tale comes in the 1527 *History of the Scottish people* by Hector Boece, the first principal of King's College in Aberdeen. His notable refinements were the addition of the totally fictional Banquo and, crucially for my novel, the portrayal of the Eve-like Lady Macbeth as a power-hungry queen and the one who pushes her husband to murder Duncan in his bed.

The final pre-Shakespeare version was *The Chronicles of England, Scotland and Ireland* by Ralph Holinshead in 1577. This is a similar tale to that told by Boece and was largely important because it brought the Macbeth story to an English audience for the first time and, therefore, to the attention of the budding playwright, William Shakespeare. It also listed Banquo as a distant relative of King James VI of Scotland who would become James I of England in 1603 just as Shakespeare was looking for a suitably Gaelic story with which to entertain the court . . .

All Shakespeare had to do was to drastically shorten the time-frame from Macbeth's true reign of somewhere between fifteen and seventeen years to a handful of weeks and the perfect drama was born. It has been hugely popular ever since and with good reason as it is a fantastic play, but it was my mission in this novel to strip away the glorious layers of fiction and let the true Macbeth and Lady Macbeth out once again.

Acknowledgements

My first thanks have to go to my mum and dad for both being Scottish so that I got to spend many a wonderful childhood holiday with grandparents on both the east coast at Gullane and the west coast at Barrassie. I was born in St Andrews and early on developed a great fondness for Scotland which has stuck with me through a life led largely (and treacherously!) south of the border. I still support Scotland in the rugby and the Calcutta Cup is one of the only points of tension in my marriage to a devoted Englishman, especially if (and it's a very rare if) Scotland actually win.

I am lucky to also be blessed with several wonderful Scottish friends. An especial mention has to go to Maggie and Jacky. I will never forget us heading off to our University Burns Night as freshers, so pleased with ourselves in our elegant long kilts. As I recall I had to do the 'reply from the lassies' that night, though having, like Sibyll, an unfortunate fondness for 'uiskie' I couldn't say how coherent it was! Then of course I must mention 'Nana Brenda' – the woman who regularly walks 500 miles with me (there may be 'uiskie' involved on those occasions too) and is my oasis of Scottishness in our Derbyshire village.

Despite knowing much of Scotland well, I'd never been over

'the Mounth' (the Grampians – see historical notes) before last summer and I must thank my trusty research assistant Johanna who came all the way to Moray with me. She ably tended our children whilst I had far more fun tramping the Black Isle, drinking Cromarty ale and watching the dolphins in the firth. Thanks also to Adam, Isabel and Alec for expert fire-tending way into the glorious Moray nights. It's a truly beautiful part of the world and it was lovely to share it with you all.

When it comes to the writing of this book there are, as always, so many people who have helped and supported me. Thanks go, as always, to my mum, Jenny, for always being there to talk to and for always backing me 100%. Her own mum, Sandie Shaw, was president of the Scottish Writers' Association for years and I like to think she'd have been proud of this novel.

I'm not sure how I'd write at all without my family at my back so I thank Hannah for keeping me humble and for (once) making me a cup of tea; Alec for agreeing with me that fictional worlds are so much more involving than real ones (albeit via Fortnite); Rory for making a highly sustaining martini; Emily for her genuine love of historical fiction; and George, my nearly-son-in-law, for his genuine love of Emily. And then, of course – and indeed, above all – Stuart for . . . well for being Stuart. My rock.

I am forever grateful to my wonderful agent, Kate Shaw, who was so supportive about me exploring Lady Macbeth's story and who pushed me into developing the novel into the trilogy it now opens. I cannot wait to write the next two and bless her for her insight and vision.

I must say thank you, too, to my lovely editor, Anna Boatman, who has been so fantastically enthusiastic about this novel – and those to come – and whose astute editorial notes have massively helped to fashion this final tale. It's a privilege and a joy to work with someone who cares so much about my characters and I'm lucky to have found her, as well as Ellie and Sophia and the rest of the fabulous team at Piatkus.

Finally a massive thank you to my readers. A good review is one of the most wonderful things a writer can receive and I so love hearing from people who have enjoyed my books. Please do get in touch any time on Facebook: @joannacourtneyauthor, twitter: @joannacourtney1 or via my website: joannacourtney. com. Thank you all.